The Time Travelling Tourist

By

Nick James

D1529098

For permission requests, please contact:
[nickjames@thebooksofnickjames.com]

Find out more about the author and upcoming books online at [thebooksofnickjames.com] or [@NickJam50890645] for Twitter & Facebook @thebooksofnickjames.

Produced in United Kingdom.

Also by author

Time travel used to be thought of as just science fiction, but Einstein's general theory of relativity allows for the possibility that we could warp space-time so much that you could go off in a rocket and return before you set out.

Stephen Hawking

Chapter One

It was midday on 4th July 2020. A man and a woman stood in front of a weather-beaten New England farmhouse that the man had grown up in with his family. His name was Adam Partridge. He was just under six feet, broad thanks to his occupation, and in his early thirties, though the grey flecks that patterned his once jet-black hair belied the fact that he was older than his years. He had admitted to himself that his body was still in good shape, though it fought the early onset of the dreaded middle-aged spread. He now lived opposite a fried chicken takeaway establishment, which he was convinced had not helped in the battle.

Standing hand in hand with him was a tall, lithe woman, his wife of ten years – though, if you asked her that question, she would say that Adam was her husband, and not the other way around. They were both clothed in jeans and flannel shirts, which came with the Zip code. Tabatha loved her husband to distraction, and he held the same level of emotion for her. They had coped well with the devastating realisation that she could not give him the child that they both hoped for. It was not some heart-rending accident; just mere genetics that had destroyed that dream. An important life-giving switch in her had never been created, so any egg that she produced could never grow into a new life. She literally thought of her body as a machine – that is because, as an engineer by profession, that was how her brain worked.

Tabby, as she is known to her husband, played with her long, auburn ponytail, using her spare hand as she gazed at the farmhouse.

'What are we doing here?' she asked and realised, by the look on Adam's face, that there was not an answer forming in his head quite yet. 'What does your dad want us to do here? Burn it down at last?' She winked playfully and let slip a chuckle.

Her husband's face still held firm, as if he were in a trance. A sigh of frustration escaped from her mouth and then she smirked to herself.

'We have to hurry, Adam,' she said mischievously. 'Jenny is coming over for a threesome and she's wearing a maid's outfit, which in this hot weather can't be comfortable.' Tabby smiled as Adam's face twitched.

Adam turned to his wife. 'What...? Who...?' he stammered. 'You're right... we should go,' he said, though he wasn't quite sure what he was agreeing to.

All he had heard was the name Jenny, Tabby's friend who, at only five feet, had an incredible figure. They had agreed one drunken night that, if his wife ever died before him, Jenny would be his replacement wife. Jenny enjoyed being single but would give it up to care for her friend's husband. Tabatha had chosen Brad Pitt as Adam's replacement. *Good luck there, wife*, he thought and shook his head. And, as that last thought faded, he found his wife giving him a playful nudge waking him from his revelry.

'Dreamer,' she joked and with a chuckle she pulled him closer to her and looked back to the old farmhouse, casting an eye over the white paint that had flaked off the walls of the building. 'So, dear husband of mine, what are we doing here on this, our country's finest national holiday? When we could be eating our fill until we have to wear stretch pants?'

Adam rested a hand on his wife's shoulder as he regained his thought process. She'd always had a good sense of humour.

'Well,' he explained, 'Dad is worried about Doc as he hasn't answered any of his calls or letters.' He looked at the shuttered windows. 'We are here to search for proof of life,' he added and gave Tabby his biggest smile.

The farm hadn't been worked by the family for over a decade, as Adam and his brother had no interest in the farm. They had watched their father work for so many years after their grandfather had retired, and for so little gain. Eventually, their father rented the land to a fellow farmer and moved into a large cabin twenty miles away.

'Doc' was their nickname for Brian Partridge, Adam's uncle and younger brother to Adam's father, Jacob Partridge. They called him Doc due to his infatuation with science fiction, though mainly he sought out time-travel based books and movies.

Doc was born eight years after his brother, Jacob, so there was always an age divide. As a teenager, while Jacob would be working hard on the farm for their father, Brian would be playing and enjoying the love and attention that his mother gave them both. However, in Jacob's mind he thought that he was missing out, and the relationship between the siblings soured. The day it all changed was when Brian had been pestering Jacob to let him ride along in the tractor cab with him. All Jacob had wanted to do that day was go to his friend's house, but instead he had to work as usual. In anger, Jacob pushed his brother from the moving tractor. Brian fell, slamming his head into the sun-hardened, New England mud.

The doctors had declared Brian fit and well except for a small concussion, but after that day he never played around the farm or in the fields again. Instead, his passion for literature grew, and he immersed himself in books, from science fiction to the classics. One thing was certain after that day – the brothers' relationship was broken and would never mend.

As the years went by, the family pulled away from each other. Instead of remaining close-knit, they became nothing more than passing acquaintances, from going on the occasional holiday together, to dinners and, finally, the odd phone call.

More noticeably, however, was that Brian became a ghost to them. He left the family home for years on end and only came back after hearing that their parents had died in a plane crash. He returned for good and came to live in the family home, as Jacob and his family had already moved away.

Adam and Tabatha looked at the door of the cabin and walked up the three wooden steps, which creaked with annoyance at being awoken from their slumber. Unlike houses in town, there was not a single piece of artwork hanging from the doorknob, the advertising flyers claiming it to be the best Chinese takeaway joint in town. Clearly, it was even too far for those delivery drivers to reach.

The once shiny bronze doorknob was now dulled following years of abuse from rough-skinned land workers. Adam tried the handle, and with a slight push, the door creaked noisily open. Adam and Tabatha look at each other with concern.

'It's like a horror movie, isn't it?' joked Adam, though a rivulet of sweat ran down the nape of his neck, showing his hesitancy.

His wife barked out a laugh. 'Well, I could always dust off my cheerleader's outfit, dye my hair blonde and call myself Trixie?' she chuckled. 'I just have to remember to turn my ankle as I run away.' She looked at her hubby, who was gazing at her wistfully. She watched him licking his lips as he processed her suggestion. 'Oi, mind out of the gutter, you know I was never a cheerleader!'

He awoke from his penthouse moment as a short, but sharp, fingernail was drilled into his chest.

'Quite right, honey… ermm… BRIAN? YOU HOME?' he called out into the darkness. The windows still had the shutters on, so not even a slither of sunlight made it through the curtains. Adam leant in and searched for the hallway light switch. With a flick, the bulb illuminated the place until, with a pop, the bulb was extinguished for good as the element destroyed itself. Once again, they shared a look.

'Get running, Trixie,' Adam whispered and, with a gentle pat from Tabby to his butt, he walked forward. He pulled his phone out from his pocket and switched on the torch feature, which lit their way inside.

'BRIAN!! YOU HOME?' Tabatha called out as she started to open the curtains to allow the sun to do its job. 'Yuck!' She coughed as she got a face full of dust from the ill-used curtains. Dust danced in the air, only visible from the light from Adam's phone.

Tabatha turned to her husband, who had decided to just look around, all slack jawed. Without orders, he always seemed go into standby mode, like all men.

'Adam, make yourself useful and go outside and open up all the shutters!' she instructed and ignored the groan of displeasure in his put-upon tones. As he stomped out, creating more dust from the threadbare rug, Tabby took out her own phone and, like her husband, used the torch to scan the room before heading to the archway, which led to the living room from the reception hall.

Adam grumbled as he walked around the large, single-storey ranch-style house. The shutters were closed by a simple but sturdy hook and eye system, though the hinges did groan as he pushed the wooden-framed shutters flush against the side of the house. Then he used the same system to lock them in so that they didn't flap in the high winds. He worked his way around the house. He glanced through the window at Tabby standing in the living room and chuckled at the thought of the cheerleader outfit. Even if she did have one, it would be covered by all the men's blood who had tried to grab her. To this day, he never doubted how lucky he was to have her in his life. Children or not, they were happy.

As they made eye contact through the window, Tabby could see from the look on his face what he was thinking.

'Pervert!' she shouted. Then, with a wink, she disappeared once again into the gloom.

Adam chuckled, then frowned. He'd started to worry about his uncle Doc. He had always been fun, especially as Doc was only ten years or so older than him.

Adam knew his father felt regret over the way he had treated his brother for all those years; but, being a rough and tough farmer, those emotions were deeply hidden. It was only the rarest of times that they had an airing. His father was pissed about him, Adam, and his brother John choosing different careers, though they were still in the farming community.

John worked as a contract harvester and travelled throughout the country cutting corn or anything for a price, but it allowed him to roam and be happy. Adam, however, ran a business selling everything from tractors to seeds.

The last shutter was opened and locked, then he went back to go inside. The farmer, who rented the land from his father, kept the grounds around the house tidied and well-tended, which had made the task of opening the shutters much easier for him. Once again, the steps creaked as Adam re-entered the home. With the room now full of sunlight, his eyes took in several photos that had been framed. One was of him and his uncle sitting reading comic books together. That's how they had bonded when he was a young boy until his early teen years – but, as girls gradually came on the scene, Brian never grew up with him, and that bond they'd once had faded.

'ANY SIGN, TABBY?' he called out as his toes poked at some dust-covered running shoes. Running had been another one of Doc's passions.

Tabatha strolled out from the swing door at the back, which led to the kitchen. She shook her head while brushing her hands, trying to rid them of the dust and grime.

'Not a thing. The kitchen is clean. Refrigerator is off and cleaned,' she explained and looked over her shoulder, indicating to the kitchen. 'No fresh food rotting. It looks like a dammed show home in there.'

She stood by Adam's side and linked her arm with his. She always loved to touch him, or to be touched by him. It made her feel wanted. Slowly, they checked the whole house and, like she had said, despite the dust, it was clean and looked like it had been devoid of occupants for months.

Adam rubbed his face with his hand. 'Why would he just leave?' he asked his wife as they looked around the lounge and at the empty shelves. They had once been home to many comics and science fiction novels. Then he looked towards a heavy wooden door in the hallway, which looked newer than the other doors in the house. 'Let's check out the basement. He liked to use it as an office…' Adam shrugged. 'Well, that's what he said, anyway.'

It took both of their strength to pull the door open. Clearly, it had missed its calling as the door in King Arthur's castle of Camelot. Once again, stale, uncirculated air hit them in the face; no wonder the hinges had a fine covering of rust on them. Tabby flicked on the light switch and, like any good horror film, the bare wooden steps were illuminated by a single light bulb that swung from an overly long cord. They swapped looks.

'Better get my pom-poms ready, Hun,' Tabatha giggled as they walked together into the gloom.

The steps squealed blue murder under their weight, which hurt their feelings deep down. However, the old wooden steps held true as Adam and Tabatha both descended until there, in front of them, stood a formidable-looking metal door. Luckily, it was made from lightweight aluminium and was unlocked. Together, they pushed it open. It didn't make a sound.

They held each other's hands as they took in Uncle Brian's office/laboratory. The walls were covered in framed photos, some black and white and others colour, though the latter were outnumbered by the former.

'Holy shit,' Adam muttered, staring at two tubes which looked like isolation tanks. 'What are these, Tabby? Bathtubs?' He pointed to them, making Tabatha briefly look over, pausing from her own investigation.

The redhead turned away. 'They are meditation tanks. The type of things you see in ladies' spas,' she explained. She had always thought they were a stupid idea, but it takes different folk to make the world turn.

The tanks were hooked up to a computer by countless cables. There were also larger power cables that ran out of the basement, and Adam guessed they fed directly to the mains.

'What was he up to down here?' he said softly.

Tabatha started to walk around, pausing to study some of the photos. There were lots of the missing man smiling in a way that his family, or even Tabatha, had not seen in a long while. He truly did look happy. She looked around and watched her husband examining the dust-covered pods. Well, that is what she called them for the lack of a better word or understanding of their function, though somehow, they looked familiar.

With a shake of her head, which made her ponytail dance down her back, she headed to the wooden desk in the corner. It was bare, all bar a leather-bound book which was held closed by a leather strap. Upon it sat a yellow post-it note with her husband's name written on it.

'Adam, there's a book here for you,' she called, picking it up and turning towards her husband, whose head was stuck inside one of the pods.

'This is bizarre,' he called out to his engineer wife. 'They are coated with gel. And that one has copper wire and what look like diodes submerged into the gel.' Adam smiled at Tabatha's look of excitement as she skipped over, stuffing the leather-bound book into his outstretched hand, before sticking her head into the same pod.

'Wicked,' she muttered and ran her fingers over the gel. 'Hmm, what was he up to?' She looked up and pointed to the book she had just given him. 'Read it!'

Standing upright, Adam began flicking through the pages. He instantly recognised his uncle's script.

'You okay,' Tabatha asked, pulling herself away from the new toys.

Adam and Tabby pulled up a pair of office chairs to the desk and untied the strap that had bound the diary. Then, with a hesitant look at each other, they opened the diary to the first page and began to read.

'*31st December 2019, Building of the Time Machine.*'

They looked at each other in shock. They then instinctively turned towards the pods that stood there, daring them to continue reading. So, as one, Adam and Tabatha turned and continued to read...

***

Diary of Brian Arthur Partridge

Well, hello to anyone who is reading my diary... no, journal. Or could this be a nonfiction story with a dash of science fiction thrown in? But, if you want to break it down, this is a true-life story of science, nonfiction. I hope you know who I am, but if you don't here goes. My family like to call me Doc Brown, but in truth my name is Mr Brian Arthur Partridge, Time Traveller. Nope, that's too overused, how about The Time Tourist?

Anyway, enough of all that nonsense. Hopefully, my nephew and his better half will be the first people to read the tale I am about to tell. Adam and Tabby, you are amongst the finest and friendliest people I know, and please stay the course when I start to ramble, or if it becomes too extraordinary to believe. In the end, your dedication will pay dividends. Oh, and if you think you can just skip to the end, well you can, but that will spoil the surprise.

Firstly, Adam, please tell your dad that I forgive him. I know he has been beating himself up about the past, but the accident truly wasn't his fault. So, when you go and see him, give the old geezer a big hug from me. He will really hate that (ha-ha). Just tell him I love him, and that I have found happiness. As you know, I had a love for all things science fiction and especially time travel.

Don't get me wrong. Whilst I believe there to be life in the deepest recesses of space, and at a push that they have visited, I never believed that my beloved time travel literature and movies would be anything but a flight of fancy.

That was until I saw a notification of an estate sale. I have always been frugal with my money, and thanks to your father's generosity in paying for the house utilities, I managed to accrue a good amount of wealth. Not enough to buy Arizona, but I was comfy. So, when the estate sale for my favourite self-published time travel author turned up, I leapt at it like a toddler trying his first taste of soda. George Lancaster Jnr had always managed to write so perfectly about when the characters in his books managed to jump from century to century via his invention. His novels had hooked me from the first page and, before I knew it, the whole collection was in my hands. The price of the house was totally out of my league, but the contents were to be sold as a job lot, especially as the author turned out to be a recluse as well as a hoarder. A bidding war ensued, but I was victorious – much to the chagrin of my competitors.

I paid a local haulage firm to do the house clearance, with a large bonus to make sure that neither of the disgruntled losing bidders helped themselves to anything while they were busy collecting my purchases. When the van arrived, I was excited, but rapidly began to panic when I saw the next van, and then another. I kid you not, they filled the whole house, plus other outbuildings. My hope was to find some notebooks or unfinished manuscripts, as George was famed for being very anti-computer. And yes, I found notebooks upon notebooks full of stories, good and bad.

Over the next few weeks, I had the vans coming back to take the unwanted items to either the rubbish tip or to charity shops. One van had a glorious fine selection of boxes which were filled to the brim with children's toys which I had sent to the local orphanage. I might even get a wing named after me, especially as I told them about several old toys that could bring in some much-needed funds.

After clearing all the unwanted items, I finally made it to all the big containers that were stored in the cellar. I had asked the delivery men to place them down there so that they didn't put any more stress on this poor home's wooden floors and joists. I explained that, if they left them in the sitting room, they would still end up in the cellar by nightfall due to gravity alone. Thank goodness the guys agreed, though they cursed me heavily that day and late into the night. Even to this day, they used some swear words that I have never heard or would ever hear again – and of that I am pleased.

That is when I came across the oddest of finds. It was well publicised that George Lancaster Jnr was a technophobe, to the point that he even stated the fact on his author bio in his books. So, what did this man, the spinner of webs and the writer of dreams, have? A top-of-the-range personal computer. This truly did baffle me, yet it intrigued me at the same time. So, using a photograph of his once work room, or possible laboratory, I aimed to set all the items up as they once were in the great author's home, and I can tell you that was a hard couple of weeks. I must admit I loathe physical work. A book or comic held more appeal than any task that would make me produce sweat, unless it was for my much-loved early morning jog. I never knew why, but that small bout of activity allowed me to centre myself, gather all my thoughts and, finally, to keep my aging body trim.

I spent some time connecting the numerous cables, which came in a multitude of colours. Thankfully, the cable connectors were coloured with matching coloured docking ports, which made assembly idiot proof.

Resorting to the child in me, I would straight away turn the start switch on and wait to see if it would result in either a life-ending shock, or a huge explosion, as happened once on the farm with a gas cylinder and blow torch. That incident allowed me the brief feeling of flight, just as Superman did on a daily basis, though the man of steel could go through a roof without harming himself, where I merely rebounded off the tin roof. Luckily, my father and your dad never found out that gem.

Anyway, I digress. The handwritten manual for this amalgamation of parts was the last item in the very last box I had deemed to go through, the title of which amused me so – 'THE TEMPERAMENTAL PORTAL OF TIME!' What was hidden in the subtle undertones of said title made me loudly declare that I would never turn the accursed mess of wires on.

However, you can imagine that, as I read the manual and journal late into the night, my decision changed, for the better and worse.

As you know, throughout history, with great power comes even greater responsibility. And, as I read through the author's trials and tribulations, I knew that, if I – or, more likely, *when* I – chose to follow in the great man's footsteps, I would try to change things for the betterment of the human race.

Somehow, the man had made a time machine. How, I hear you ask? Basically, the same way that I have. While in his twenties, George found a scientist's laboratory one day and bought the lot with the aid of an inheritance from the death of an uncle. That alone sparked his fascination with time travel; and, given how accurately he wrote about it, the fact was he had been there, in the future and past. Don't get me wrong, I couldn't help but be suspicious about his claims, so I carried on with his instructions. There was a two-page rant about the power fluctuation on the power grid near him. It is said that even a small dip or spike can cause major problems. So, he went to the trouble of buying a large generator which brought in complaints from unhappy neighbours, then even unhappier police. In the end, he moved to the country to a small farm in the wilds of Pennsylvania.

That is why I have paid for all this to be professionally wired into the mains, along with a clever little gizmo that keeps the voltage without any variants, either plus or minus. It cost a lot of dollars to get it fitted, but when you're talking about possible life and death circumstances, why skimp?

The next thing I chose to modify was the actual pods themselves. I didn't know exactly how they worked, but I thought that standing in an upright galvanised bath, with electrodes wired into the side with electricity coursing through them, wasn't the best idea.

After weeks of working through different ideas, I stumbled across the perfect solution. During a late-night study session, or reading comics – because, once again, sleep eluded me – a late-night infomercial came on the TV. It promoted a new health spa and they had a special deal on sessions providing something called a sensory deprivation tank. It sounded horrific to me, but the tanks themselves looked ideal. They were made of some kind of plastic material, and they looked like they had a void between the inner and outer layers – perfect to hide all the wires.

Let's just say the pretty girls at the spa weren't impressed when I arrived for a tour around their wonderfully hygienic facility. I was still wearing my work clothes, as I had been messing around in the cellar before I left that morning.

They did ask me to leave when I started to bang the sides of the pods with my mud-encrusted boots, but they were still polite as they did it. Better than the hauliers, anyway.

The price alone for those tanks shocked me, so why did I get two? That will be for the ending of this story. It is my heart's desire that this will be a happy ending. And please, Adam, take your mind from the gutter. I imagine currently your wonderful wife is hitting you, and quite rightly so.

For the specialised wiring on the pods, I brought in a contractor who bombarded me with questions. In the end, I came up with 'it was just for a cosplay exhibition in the coming year'. The big man looked around and did agree that it had all the hallmarks of an insane scientist's laboratory.

During the local man's time in my home, I had hidden all my paperwork relevant to the machine – and, if I was honest, I hid myself as well. The man himself was nice enough, but just never – and I mean, never – closed his mouth.

Soon enough, he was done. He had truly embraced the crazy scientist thing to the point where my invoice was addressed to Doc Brown, Insanity Toy. The downside of that was the strange looks that were coming my way when I went into town on my weekly shop. I guess his mouth did run away with him, but at least he is now gone and the machine is ready. Dare I start it?

With a deep inward breath, I walked over to the main power switch on the wall. I pushed the metal handle into the 'on' position, making the box itself hum into life. It reminded me of the noise the proton packs on the backs of the Ghostbusters sounded when they were turned on. The lights on a small control board below it showed all green. The electrician explained that it meant power was running at the voltage I needed, and it flowed without any spikes or dips in the supply.

Next came the computer. Even though it ran on the house's power, I didn't want to start one without the other. This, after all, was an all-or-nothing adventure. Either soon I would find myself in the past, or I would be seeing my parents very soon, which made me smile as I miss them dearly every day.

Soon, the screen showed the manufacturer's logo as it went through its regular start-up routine. Now I dared to sit in front of the screen and let out my breath – firstly, because I was still alive, and, secondly, as the computer didn't require a password to access all of Lancaster's files. There were copies of his books, lots of written accounts of his journeys through time. Those I just skimmed, as I didn't want to lose myself in another man's adventure. I wanted my own so that, one day, I could tell you both, Adam and Tabby.

The late author had files and files of historical data, but not any on the future, so it looked like he had concentrated on the past. I wanted to journey both ways, as the past has been written, whereas the future is unknown. Plus, the thought of seeing it does excite me.

I clicked on the file named 'The idiot's guide to time travel'. That did make me smirk! It showed a diagram of the steps to travel. It was quite simple, really. You just put in the date and place you wish to visit. Then it changes screen to a coloured map of the place you wish to visit – if maps existed at the time, that is. The computer program made sure you were always placed away from people, as appearing inside another person would become painful and messy. His words, not mine.

It wasn't the word painful that concerned me. It was messy. That alone painted way too many images for my liking. Nevertheless, I carried on my research. Yes, I knew where I was heading to, and what year. My first trip would not be too drastic – somewhere in the USA that would be memorable. According to Lancaster's journal, you can have three different types of trip. Firstly, on a timer that will pull your body back to the pod after a set time. Secondly, you carry a temporal remote, the design of which is skirted over briefly in his books. It can be used as an emergency escape button on the timer feature, so that will be tested vigorously. The final one is the one-way trip. That one will shut down the machinery until a code is entered by a trusted person or persons who you wish to be able to use said machine.

Adam, Tabatha, you are the trusted people and I will leave the code at the end of this book.

The adventures I have experienced have been fun, amazing and, at times, truly horrifying. Words on a page cannot and will not do it justice. So, I'm going to come and visit you at your home as soon as I can, though I hope you can keep this a secret for now. I'm sure my brother would have me committed if he heard such tales about me becoming a Time Adventurer, but again I prefer the name Time Tourist.

Anyway, take your time and enjoy the photographs on the wall. They are copies, but also real at the same time, taken by myself or my partner in time (get it?). Keep a bottle of wine handy along with an open mind. Yours, Doc... Uncle Brian.

**

Tabby and Adam gazed around the room at the assorted photos. It was all too much to take in.

'What do you think, Tabby?' said Adam.

She shook her head. 'I really don't know. He might have finally cracked, but with these photos...' She indicated with her hand at the photos surrounding them. 'It all seems too real, but it can't be true.'

They sat quietly, hand in hand, just staring at the pictures. Adam was the first to break the silence.

'Let's take the book and head home,' he said. Tabatha nodded. 'Then we can eat, drink, be merry, and wait for Uncle Brian to turn up. Or, as he said, his partner in time.'

'Great plan,' said Tabatha, smiling happily, shutting down all thoughts of time travel. 'But who's this other person he speaks of?'

Adam shrugged. 'Dr Who?' he said, receiving a condescending eye roll from his wife.

They headed out of the farmhouse, turning off lights as they went and stepped out into the fresh New England air. With book in hand, they climbed into their car and drove away, never noticing that the author of the diary was watching them from a distance. He knew his brother would feel guilty on this day – after all, Independence Day was a day for families.

Brian Partridge pressed his 'return home' button and disappeared in a flash of white light. He was excited by the thought of being able to tell his tale to his family, at last.

Chapter Two

When I started this adventure, it gave me a new lease of life, for which I am forever grateful. The only trouble was that, as time passed and I moved closer to the test day, the nitty gritty of the final checks had started to weigh me down. Lancaster had used a dog to test his newly found toy. That was something I could never do as, having been brought up as a farm boy, I knew the devotion that a canine vowed to its master and friend and I could never abuse that trust.

The first test was done, and I made it as simple as I could get it. Ever heard of a time travelling joint of pork? Yes, indeed, it was only sent one day into the past. The first attempt was done on the timer setting, which pulled the joint back dirty and a few minutes later than the specified time, but it was in one piece and looked the same in every way. My main concern was whether it would be torn apart or cooked as a result of the trip – because, if that is how I returned, it would be a bad way to die.

Looking at the now totally soiled and ruined joint of pork, I realised what the next inevitable step would be. As frightening as it was to get into the machine and test it myself, I knew I had no other option. I could not use another life, be it human or animal as a test subject. This was especially true, as it was not a matter of life or death, just me following my dreams and those of others like me.

So, it was not even a choice in the end. I decided I would be the crash test dummy, even though my nerves and bowels were doing their best to talk me out of it. I sat at my desk and composed a short letter to my brother and nephew each, outlining briefly what the equipment did and also the act I was about to perform. That way, they would understand if I ever disappeared from this world, or if they found my body parts adorning the cellar walls.

With the letters written and left sealed on the desk, I started up the apparatus. All lights were showing green and the computer was awaiting my instructions. I decided just to go a week into the past, at midday on my family's farm, as I knew the farmer hadn't been there for the last fortnight. As the computer program worked through its calculations, I ran off to change, because I didn't think a bathrobe and slippers would portray the best image for a time traveller. I did have an urge to dress like Indiana Jones, but I ignored it and headed back down to the basement in my typical work attire – moleskin trousers, a red and blue plaid shirt, with some heavy-duty work boots.

When I entered the laboratory again, everything was still. The program had finished and the screen prompt was asking what feature I wanted to use. I set the timer for ten minutes, and I also attached the remote to my belt with the hope of testing it instead of using the timer. I pressed 'enter' with an audible click to start the countdown to temporal travel. I walked towards the pod as it counted down from twenty seconds and smiled as the gel that I had coated the pods with almost gripped me in a loving embrace. I watched the counter click down: 5…4…3…2…1…zero.

A bright white flash blinded me for a second, then I had the weirdest feeling of being stretched out. It didn't hurt, it just felt strange – a bit like a slinky as all of a sudden I sprang back together again. My eyes had dots in front of them as I struggled to focus. I decided that perhaps some sunglasses would help with the vision next time – and there *would* be a next time, as I could smell the aroma of home, a very strong aroma. When I did manage to focus, I understood the attack on my sense of smell. I was standing in a cow pat. I had totally forgotten that there had been a herd of cattle on this field a couple of weeks ago.

'Shit!' I said to myself. But I was smiling, as it had worked.

My next test was the remote. Lancaster's writings on its creation were vague at best; he said that a micro wormhole stays open in time, allowing the remote to be linked to the computer. With another deep breath, I pressed the red button which acted as the emergency 'take me home now' function. Then, with another bright light, I landed in the pod. My knees gave out slightly and, unfortunately, the smell and waste from the cows in said field came home with me, but at least it worked.

After a good shower to wash the odour of dung from me, I stood looking at my reflection in the bathroom mirror. I was calm, though my stomach toiled about my upcoming trip into the past. Before I took my next trip back in time, I had to do some more checks and gather some supplies; internet here we come. Within ten minutes, my laptop was working away, and I was reassured that my normal bland clothing would pass muster as they weren't branded, just your typical cheap and rugged clothes from my nephew's store. Thinking of him and his wonderful wife made me smile; they were so kind and there was always an invitation to dinner whenever I was passing, though I never took them up on it. Another one of my major faults.

For dinner, I made a healthy pizza to snack on. I mused how much a pie cost from Gino's Pizza joint and the difference in making one yourself. My face dropped as a realisation came tumbling down upon me – I had no money suitable for different time periods, so what would I use for currency in the past? It would certainly cause problems if I tried to use a new bill in the past before it was even made. So, I headed back on my search. Like I said, the nitty gritty may be boring, but it's just as important as building the machine itself. There is a fine line between success or failure.

It still amazes me to this day that, on the worldwide web, you can find and buy anything from a toothpick to yellow cake uranium, though the latter would most probably bring some member of a three-letter agency coming your way, and the likelihood of you seeing the sun again would be slim to none. In under two hours, I had bought a driving licence, good enough to pass inspection, and three hundred dollars in old currency which was printed for the right time frame for my first trip. All I had to do now was wait.

I didn't sit idle as I waited for my purchases to arrive, as plans for my next few jaunts into the past were made. Something in my heart dared me to jump forward in time, though my head overrode it because I would be appearing into the unknown. I would have no idea about monies used or clothing. What if I appeared in a nuclear wasteland? Or at a time when climate change and nature had wiped humans from the planet? I would die instantly.

Given these worries, I planned for the past only, searching for monetary denominations for the right era and clothing to match the country and time to allow me to blend in. Unfortunately, due to my inability to speak other languages I was limited to certain countries, or else becoming a man of shadow and stealth. But, being 6 feet 2, stick thin and with size 13 feet, that I am not.

Finally, the time had come. It was midday and my new leather wallet was full of the appropriate currency, along with the correct ID card. I was dressed in my normal clothes, as the style hadn't changed in the rural US for years. This time, however, I donned my father's old sunglasses that I had seen him wear for many years whilst ploughing and working other farm duties. Also, I hoped this would help me land with my eyesight intact.

The power hummed away nicely, while the green lights bathed the cellar in an ethereal glow. My stomach gurgled with either excitement or nervousness, not sure which, as I watched the clock count down on the computer screen past five. I sucked in a breath and, in a flash, I was gone.

'Jesus,' I grumbled as my knees bent with the force of the landing. I did a quick survey of the area. I hoped this wasn't a sign, but I had landed in a graveyard, on some poor old dear's grave from the 1900s. 'Sorry, Mrs Gladstone,' I whispered and moved away, while slipping off my shades to take in my new surroundings. I smiled as I looked upon the city of Boston. So this was the correct destination, it all depended on whether it was the right year. I headed towards the nearest graveyard exit and, as I did, I saw my goal in the distance.

The Colonial Theatre sat proudly on Boylston Street, so I knew that I had reached a point in the past, though I couldn't confirm the exact year. I watched with a smile as cars of yesteryear drove past, blowing out noxious fumes. Even though the pollution caused by motorcars still happened back in my early years, it just seemed to look worse seeing it now. There was a gap in the traffic, allowing me to run across the road, though my knees wanted nothing to do with it after my run that morning and the rough landing in the graveyard. I made it across safely and walked up to the cinema. A young girl was sitting at the ticket counter.

I smiled as I approached her, and the blonde, curly-haired girl grinned as she looked at me. She had a kind, round face. She seemed to enjoy her Saturday job.

'Hello, sir, how may I help you today?' she asked.

Her name tag allowed me to add a bit of friendliness to the conversation. 'Good day, Kimberley. May I have one ticket for your next showing please? Somewhere near the back, if possible.' She smiled again

'I'm afraid it's free seating, so first come first served,' the girl replied. 'Would you still like to purchase the ticket?' Her green eyes were sparkling in the Boston sunlight. I nodded in agreement and I nervously slid over the recently purchased five dollars.

'Thank you, sir,' she said. 'That will be $3.50 for the two o'clock showing of *Back to the Future*. Enjoy!' She slid the ticket and change over to me.

'Thank you, I certainly will,' I replied and checked my watch with the clock that hung on the wall behind her head. It matched. 'I'll see you in two hours. Bye for now and thank you.' The girl smiled again and bid me farewell.

With time to spare, I headed off into the city for lunch. Thankfully, I didn't see a Starbucks around, as they would be a plague of the future, but there was a friendly looking Mom & Pop little café. It was near a park where young parents were playing with their children and old men played chess together, while bickering about how things were better in their day.

I bought a coffee and a tasty-looking pastry to help sate my still rolling stomach. The travel back in time had caused hunger pangs, and this delicacy would do the trick. And so I sat and watched the world go past. The changes were only superficial, really; clothes were brighter and gaudier, cars sounded like tractors, sending plumes of fumes into the atmosphere. The main difference, which I applauded, was the lack of cell phones. Yes, there were some about, but only with those who had the money – businessmen, or sometimes law enforcement.

I watched people walking past and listened as they openly chatted to each other, and not on a phone to those miles apart from them. It surely was a nice change. With a faint smile on my face, I soaked up the sun and ate the crispy delicacy. The last few weeks played on my mind, as did the power that I now held, even though there was no desire to wield it. However, I thought of the lives that I could save. Lancaster's writings did stipulate one thing: if you try to alter a major history event to save people, the Grim Reaper will never go without.

The sci-fi author had discovered this, as he had lost a relative in a train collision in Texas, so he went back in time and averted the tragedy. But, when he arrived back in his own time, he went straight to his aunt's house and found that she had still passed. She had died the week after in a car crash on the freeway, and the body count was the same number as the train accident. So, it was true, and that meant all those gory horror films were correct. You cannot cheat death.

For the rest of my time in Boston, I walked around going from thrift shops to antique shops, looking for some budget items I could purchase to assist me in my upcoming trips. This gave me lots of ideas for places and times to visit; but, due to the lack of usable funds, I purchased only a canvas bag and several books to help with my planning.

I looked at my watch. Now for the main reason I was here. *Back to the Future* here I come. I couldn't help but smile to myself as the auditorium started to fill up. With my soda and popcorn in hand, I waited for the show to start.

After the movie, I literally skipped from the theatre. Yes, the sound and picture quality was nothing like the cinemas of today. My heart was singing, as I had never seen the film during its first release in my own timeline, due to reasons I could not quite remember. So, I bow down to the men who created time travel, as they had now made my day. Anything after this would be good, it just would never quite reach that pinnacle.

As my funds totalled about fifty dollars, I went to a small but busy restaurant a couple of blocks away, where I had a lovely steak dinner and a beer, with the hope that they travelled as well as they went down. Soon, the light had started to fade and, after leaving a generous tip for the very helpful and smiley waitress, I headed out into the Boston air and back towards the graveyard – which, luckily for me, was still open. Whilst I believed the time machine was linked to me and the remote, and not the landing site, the remote area would be more discreet given the huge flash of light which resulted in the process.

The safest place I found before initiating my return home was between two big mausoleums. Remaining unseen and, therefore, successful all depended on whether the flash of light could be passed off as a car headlight or if it looked suspicious. Only time would tell. Plus, I could check on the internet to see if there were any strange sightings reported following my trip. The timer had been set for midnight, just in case anything had hindered me, so I did my last scan around. It was as silent as a graveyard.

I pressed the emergency depart button and waited. It took a few minutes before anything happened. Then I was instantly blinded. Damn and blast, I had forgotten to put my father's sunglasses on. The other downside was that the rucksack which was on my back was forcing me forwards when I appeared in the pod. Luckily, I managed to put my hands out as I hit the concrete floor, blinded and with a heavy weight of books on my back pressing me to the ground...

'Ouch!' I cried out. Maybe a rug or carpeting would be wise in the future.

The concrete was cold to the touch as I lay there, waiting for my wrists to stop hurting and my eyesight to return. As the dots in my eyes started to fade, I made a mental list of important things to buy. Firstly, a nice plush rug, just in case I decided to fall on my face again.

It took five minutes to feel like myself again and then I could stand up, albeit shakily. I turned on the main light before closing down all the equipment, starting with the computer. As it went through the shutdown cycle, I decided I should buy a separate standalone hard drive so that I could download all the information from the computer and keep it safe, just in case it decided to destroy itself, as computers are sometimes prone to do.

I moved slowly up to my cold but welcoming bed with the thoughts of having walked through the streets of yesteryear running through my mind. With my bedtime regime completed, I curled up in my bed, smiling about the trials of Marty McFly. I decided not to use the machine to go back and watch the sequels, although I was tempted for the shortest of moments before sleep took me.

***

The next day, the sun was harsh and almost blinded me when I threw back the drapes. I'm so pleased I'm not much of a drinker, otherwise the dinner from the previous night might have taken longer and caused a bigger headache, as the food and beer were cheaper than today's prices. Saying that, I knew my funds would be taking a hit as I had to buy specialised items for my next big jump back.

After having a quick run, followed by a small breakfast of pancakes and strawberries, I readied myself for the day ahead and opened the laptop ready for a day of planning and ordering. A very compact digital camera was purchased so that I could catalogue some memories along the way with proof, if it was ever needed.

With reams of data at my fingertips, the day went quickly, fading into night-time. Then, before I knew it, the sun was coming back up. It was during my brief foray into the past when I realised cash would always be a problem. Yes, I had been well off, but I needed more to be able to travel with the right props and money.

Over the next week, I traded a lot of my cash into gold coins and, with a historical list of good investments, jumped back into the early 1990s, buying up stocks and shares of companies that weathered any financial storms that the 90s and the 2000s could throw at it. I spent three days in the past, sleeping in a motel and meeting a well-established investment trader, who I knew to be financially safe and was still in business in the current time.

When I landed home, I instantly logged into my accounts that I had set up on said trip. It took a while to access them via the internet, but when I finally did my face muscles hurt from the smile on my face and I started to add up my ill-gotten gains. In total, I had amassed over 600,000 dollars. Yes, I could have earned into the millions, but that would increase the risk and the possibility of someone noticing, though that still might change in the future.

So, with my newfound wealth, I spent a small fortune on anything and everything I would need for my next few jumps into the past – from books on the areas and the time periods I wished to explore, to money and clothes relevant to the period. To say I was excited was an understatement.

I found some crucial items that would allow me to witness what was to be a very important, yet tragic, event. I managed to buy them in the past, mainly because their value now was in the millions. Back in the 70s, it was a fraction of that, and the seller was happy to be paid in gold coins, too.

It would be another six weeks before I was ready for my next jump into the past, and not for the lack of preparation, either. I discovered that it was fashionable for most men in the time period I had chosen to wear some kind of beard or moustache, which was something I had never bothered to nurture on my smooth face. It took a while, but finally the strip of hair on my upper lip looked passable.

In preparation, I laid out my clothes and a passport, a copy of which I had made of the original with the owner's name preserved and my black-and-white photo added. I also made sure I had plenty of money so that I could purchase some clothes for the trip.

It was time. I stood in front of the computer and checked that everything was correctly set. Date, time and, finally, the place – Southampton, England in the 1900s. I donned some old-fashioned shades, stood in the pod and, once again, watched the machine count down. With a spike of panic, I searched my pockets and found the emergency return remote. As the counter hit five, I patted myself down to make sure I had the fully charged camera and, more importantly, my wallet. Everything was there, so my body relaxed as light eclipsed me.

Once again, I landed with a thump in a graveyard. *Some deity is trying to tell me something*, I thought as I prised my foot from the freshly filled-in grave of a certain Nicholas Plumridge, the newly placed stone stating he had hoped for a pyramid. With a slight chuckle, I headed out. After a few steps, I put the shades into my inside suit pocket.

As I walked down a cobbled street, I took in the sights. I know everyone back home says the English weather is always miserable and raining constantly. Well, I wish I could say they were wrong, though right now it wasn't raining. It had the look that it should be raining, and everything looked grey.

The streets of Southampton had gotten busier the closer I got to the city centre. You could smell the salty aroma of the sea, which seemed to compete with the other odours, good and bad. As I walked along, I saw a nice hotel. It wasn't top end, alike to which my persona would rather be seen in, but I knew the longer I stayed out of the limelight the better.

I headed inside the quaint building and approached the gentleman behind the front desk. He had a thin, pencil moustache.

'Good morning, sir, welcome to the Dolphin Hotel,' said the man in a very polite and British manner. 'How may I help you?'

'Good morning. Would you have any rooms available for a few days?' I asked, trying to be as polite as he was. It felt like a competition.

The concierge gave me a gracious smile and looked down into his ledger. 'How many is in your party, sir? We are fairly busy now.'

'Just myself, for three days,' I stated and watched the man nod and then reach around behind him and lift a key off a hook.

He handed it to me. 'That will be room six on the first floor. Do you need a hand with your luggage, sir?' He pushed some paperwork my way. 'If you could just fill that out, sir,' he added, pointing to a pen in a small brass pot.

I filled the form out with my false details. 'No luggage,' I replied, 'but I do need to buy some clothes before I leave here. Is there a place to do that nearby?' I pushed the paperwork back to him.

The concierge took a brief look at my details. He frowned slightly. I guessed that he hadn't seen an American address before. The man put the paperwork away in a drawer and gave me a thoughtful look.

'There is a gentlemen's outfitters, just down the road on the right,' he stated knowingly and pointed in the direction of said shop. 'I'm sure they can help you out with everything you need, sir.'

He then mentioned the dining, breakfast and checkout times, and assured me that he would book me a taxi on my day of departure. I bid farewell to the man, whose name badge declared him to be John Adams, and then made my way up to my room.

The accommodation was nice enough for a single room; the bathroom was down the hall, but what else did I expect? The main point was I was here and sitting on a comfy bed, watching people outside my window making their way in life. What the world does miss these days is people wearing hats. All throughout history, men and women alike wore hats for work and social, and I think it brings a certain class to it.

I had a spot of lunch in the dining room, which was decorated in the art deco style of the period. It was a nice, warming stew and a bread roll, and boy was it warming and heavy on the stomach! Though, judging by the lack of central heating anywhere, I would need it. The journey after lunch to the outfitters was a brief one. It wasn't a high-end shop, but it would be sufficient as I was planning to keep out of the public eye as much as possible.

The outfitters' shop was a glass-fronted building and resembled everything I had seen in my research of this time period. So, like the bold adventurer I was, I stepped into what was possibly my doom. There were several men helping other gentlemen choose their items of clothing, so I was able to walk around for a time unhindered.

Finally, an older gentleman came to help me. He was pleasant enough, though he wasn't happy with the clothing I was wearing. It was at that moment that I was glad I had decided to wear plain underwear, and not my Spiderman ones that my nephew's wife had bought me one Christmas. God knows how I would have explained that away.

It took a few hours of being belittled by the man, though he always did it respectfully. I could take everything but the suits with me, as the legs had to be let down slightly. They would be ready in a couple of days. Most importantly, though, I purchased a couple of hats and, though I did look the part, I felt like an idiot.

The day of my departure was coming up fast. I had enjoyed myself in the city, just spending time walking around and stopping in pubs. The English local beer was a bit warm for my liking, but when in Rome... By that, I don't mean go on a worldwide campaign and kill lots of people.

It was my last night at the Dolphin Hotel, and I was having a very nice meal of lamb chops. Sitting across from me was a young couple, who introduced themselves as John and Sarah Milton. They had just married a few days ago and were booked to leave on the *Titanic*, though in second class.

'My uncle has been out in California for a while now, he started a business out there,' John said, turning his innocent blue eyes to his wife. 'He wants us to join him out there, so he paid for our ticket.' They both beamed at me.

My heart shattered. 'What about your parents? Don't they want you here?' I asked. Perhaps I was trying to tug at heartstrings?

'Sarah's parents don't care for me, and my parents passed away years ago,' John said sadly, and found his hand to be taken up and kissed by his quiet wife.

'Do you have family here, Mr Vanderbilt?' Sarah asked, trying to change the subject away from her husband.

I shook my head. 'No, I am here just on business, but I hear reports of icebergs being a danger on the voyage. I'm not sure if I'm going to risk it.' I noticed the look of worry flicker on both their faces.

John sighed. 'Trouble is, we have to go now. We are nearly out of money, and I don't want to let my uncle down.' He looked at his wife, rubbing her hand with his thumb.

'I could pay for another ticket for later. I don't mind helping, if it kept you safe,' I said. They both looked at me in surprise.

'Why would you do that, sir?' Sarah asked sharply. It was then that I knew I had pushed too hard. 'You hardly know us, Mr Vanderbilt!'

I held my hands up to try to stop her tirade, but it was her husband that came to my rescue.

'Now, Sarah, it's very kind of him to offer,' he chided and gave his wife a curt nod, but the look he gave me was one of suspicion. They stood up, with the husband leading the way. 'Thank you for the warning and the offer, sir. I hope you make it safely to your destination.'

'You too,' I replied with a smile and shook John's proffered hand, though Sarah just walked off, making me feel like a heel. If only they knew.

I tossed and turned all night, not being able to stop thinking about the impending event. But, what I had to understand was that the event had already happened. And, like Lancaster had said, the Grim Reaper will always get his numbers, whether we like it or not.

Just as Mr Adams at the hotel had promised, the taxi arrived and placed my newly bought and filled suitcase into the luggage space at the front, next to the driver's seat. I didn't see the Miltons to ask if they wanted a lift. When I asked at the desk, I was told that they had left earlier that morning. That was a shame. I bid farewell to the hotel staff and settled into the taxi.

'Where to, sir?' the driver asked.

The words I had never dreamt I would ever say in my lifetime came out. 'Take me to the docks, please.'

'What ship?' asked the driver. Clearly, he had been living under a rock.

'*Titanic*, please,' I replied. The man nodded before pulling away quickly, startling a pony and trap, whose driver shouted some unrecognisable swear words towards us as he fought for control of the scared animal.

The trip didn't take too long. However, once we were at the docks the foot traffic outweighed cars and horses, blocking all the roads and making the traffic slow to a crawl.

'Just drop me here, driver,' I said. 'I'll walk the rest of the way.' I opened the door and got out. The driver grumbled a little as his car was stuck and there was nowhere he could turn around, plus there was little likelihood that there would be any fares going back the other way.

Taking hold of my suitcase, I followed the mass of people. Thankfully, the cool weather helped, especially with all the walking in these nice new and, rather warm, clothes. My pace slowed as my goal came into sight.

'Holy shit…' I muttered. 'Take that, James Cameron!'

Chapter Three

Okay, so I may have ballsed up royal style here. I had chosen my cover carefully – at least, that's what I thought. Alfred Gwynne Vanderbilt never made it onto the *Titanic* as his family were on holiday in Europe at the time.

This was because a member of the family wasn't happy about sailing on a maiden voyage, as things can go wrong on a new ship. As a result, they didn't sail on the doomed ship.

Despite this, the man was still destined to lose his life at sea, just three years later when RMS *Lusitania* was sunk after being torpedoed by a German U-boat as it travelled to Liverpool from America.

As I waited in line to board the ship, I had a deep feeling of foreboding about choosing Alfred as my identity. It could cause my trip to end quickly – after all, he was a popular man in these circles, and it wouldn't take long before the odd suspicious glances thrown my way became uncomfortable with questions being asked. But, then again, there wasn't much of a choice. Not many people missed the doomed voyage, and even less were male and of my age group.

Alfred was quite well known among the rich families of America, a few of which were on board the ship. The Vanderbilts had a servant who was in the second class section, along with the main part of their luggage, and I prayed I would be able to dodge the man.

I continued with this cover as it gave me access to the first class deck. I had been able to buy Alfred's old ticket and a copy of his passport. All I had to do was smile and walk around, acting aloof. If this went badly, I could leave at the press of a button, though I wanted to spend as much time as I could on this iconic ship. I hoped the young couple from the Dolphin would survive this.

So, as I walked up the gangplank to the first class deck, I saw a few well-groomed people casting curious looks my way. An officer who took my ticket kindly offered to let my servant, Frederick Wheeler, know that I had changed my mind and made the trip; I made a joke of wanting to go incognito and have a break from the man for a time. Luckily, some other passengers thought it was a hoot.

One of the stewards led me to my suite. I was amazed beyond belief, not just because of where I was, but also because of what I knew I would witness. I gasped as I took in the finery of everything – the delicate wood carvings, the gold leaf everywhere. It truly was a sight to behold, though I knew the time I could spend on deck would have to be limited.

The steward unpacked my clothes and headed off to bring me some tea before the ship set off for France, before docking at Ireland and then onto its doom. At dead on twelve noon, I headed out onto the deck, bidding people good day. I made my way to a secluded area of the ship so that I could take a few pictures of the departure.

The gangplanks were hoisted away, causing ripples of applause and cheers from the mass of well-wishers and relations. My emotions were in turmoil as I joined the other passengers in first class, all waving down from the deck, though they did it with much more grace than the rest of the ship.

Creeping away, I headed towards the bow of the ship. As I did so, I took out my small digital camera and switched it on. With a slight noise, the lens moved out and the viewing screen came alive. I was pretty sure that, were I discovered, I would be thrown off the ship as a heretic for having such a thing in my possession.

Hiding among the lifeboats, I aimed and took pictures of the crowds down in the dock and guests who were bidding each other farewell. I tried to capture the joy in their faces… if only they knew the tragedy that would befall them on this journey.

I turned the camera off, slipping it back into my jacket pocket, and moved back to the railings. My senses were in overdrive – the lovely salt air that came from the sea, the hint of fresh paint and French polish wafting around us. I felt sad at the thought that all this would be rotting away at the bottom of the Atlantic for decades to come.

The walk took me the length of the ship and, though enjoying the chilly sea breeze, I could see passengers giving me suspicious looks. I figured it must have been due to the fact that the upper classes would mostly know of each other, and that's why some of the older passengers looked at me closely.

Many of the passengers were still waving at the people on land, who were disappearing slowly as the ship sailed away.

I did notice that we nearly collided with another vessel and, as I had read about this on my many planning sessions, with a wry grin I watched for the said event and hoped that fate would not throw in a surprise. Not this time, though.

Ghosting the ship with my small camera hidden in hand, I recorded as much as I could, letting the video recorder function just run, knowing I had brought several high memory SD cards to swap when full. It truly was like walking through a dream, getting fleeting glances of some of the more notable passengers.

As I passed the dining hall, I managed to grab the attention of one of the waiters and asked for some tea and sandwiches to be brought to my suite, which he was only too happy to do. However, the waiter did mention that all main meals had to be taken in the dining halls. That would be a test of my cover story.

My room had a small window which allowed a nice view of the sea. However, it wasn't at sitting level, so I had to stand to look out, which lessened the impact somewhat. After thirty minutes, my food and hot beverages were brought by a well-mannered waiter in a white jacket. I now took the opportunity to scan through the videos and pictures I had taken while we travelled to Cherbourg in France, to pick up and drop off some passengers. The latter were the lucky ones.

On the evening of 10th April 1912, the ship set sail towards Ireland for its final port of call. With that in mind, I went to bed, not wanting to socialise with the diners at that moment in time. It would be a sour point if I had to leave so early because of my lack of a cover story and acting skills.

The next morning, I awoke excitedly and took an early walk around the ship. At sea, it is seldom warm, so I wrapped up in a hat and coat as I joined the early morning walkers. I managed to get into the dining room first thing to have a light breakfast of poached eggs and fresh fruit with a pot of tea. Luckily, it was only the older patrons who seemed to be dining this early, which allowed me to dine without hindrance.

That was one of the things that was well documented in high society – you dined to be seen in all your finery and only ever ate the best. In the evening, the men would retreat to a separate room to smoke and drink while putting the world to rights.

After we had docked in Ireland, I managed, for the first time, to catch sight of the one and only Captain Edward Smith. His crisp white uniform and matching hair colour and beard glinted in the light of day. Some of the photos I'd managed to take that day were the best ever, and, after a bit of photo degrading thanks to software on my laptop back home, they would eventually be published onto the web.

After we left Ireland, I had tea and scones along with selected fruits to keep me fed overnight. I had planned only to dine on the last evening of my stay, before hell visited these poor souls on board.

My routine continued during the days of 11th and 12th April, but things changed on the 13th. I was walking around the deck after lunch, not something I usually did, but I was starting to get a bit stir crazy. So I sat on a wooden deckchair, watching the foreboding waves flow by. It was then that a stocky woman in a thick fur coat took the seat next to me, wrapped a blanket around her stockinged legs and peered at me from under her large-brimmed hat.

'You, sir, have many people talking,' she announced with a ghost of a smile on her face, which I sensed had seen many things in her time.

I looked at her and my breath caught in my throat. I recognised this woman. 'And what are they saying, madam?' I replied, raising a quizzical eyebrow towards her.

'Please, call me Margaret,' she said and held out her hand, which I shook. She had a grip on her. 'Margaret Brown,' she added. She had an accent of a person from my country, but I knew that anyway as she was the well-documented and no-nonsense woman called the 'unsinkable Molly Brown'.

This is when I knew that my hopeful cover would never hold up. 'Partridge, Brian Partridge, at your service, Margaret,' I said and gave her a faint smile.

'Hmm, that answers one question,' she replied. 'The rumour circle said you were calling yourself Alfred Vanderbilt. You are in his cabin and his name has been on the table plan for dinner since we left England.' She looked at me for a moment. 'So, before I call the master at arms, will you tell me the truth… Brian?'

I called a steward over, asking him to bring us some coffee to warm us up. We made small talk about the voyage while we waited. Once the coffee arrived, Molly waited for me to begin my story.

'A member of Alfred's family did not want to travel on such a new ship as this,' I explained, 'as he believed they always experienced teething problems. So, he decided to take another ship later on, and he gracefully allowed me to take his place.' I took a sip of the hot and harsh beverage. 'I knew I had to hide myself away, as Alfred is so well known, especially as he has a servant on board.'

Molly nodded. I read later she hated to be called that. 'Sounds plausible,' she said. 'And I will not spill your secret. But you should really eat, as the food is rather good here.'

'I'll be having dinner in the dining hall tomorrow night,' I replied. 'But I am not one for such high society events.' I watched her eyes narrow.

'Neither am I, as I am what they class as new money,' Molly admitted, though she seemed quite proud of it. 'However, Brian, I feel there is more of a story here. So, tonight, we shall have dinner in my cabin, and you can tell me all. Or you tell me nothing and we just eat food in silence until you leave, and the whole ship talks about our sordid affair!' She laughed at her joke – which, knowing what people were like, was quite close to the truth.

I stared down into the black waves and thought about what I would tell her. *What harm could it do?* I wondered.

'Then, Margaret,' I said, 'We shall have a nice, long conversation – which, I believe, will leave you wishing that we *were* having said affair, rather than having to listen to my tale.'

'Oh, really?' Molly's eyes sparkled. 'Well, that does sound fun. Life on board can be quite dreary at times, especially as we must always keep up such standards,' she added, with mirth dripping from every word. 'However, tomorrow evening you will have dinner at my table in the dining room. I shall lay the groundwork while I play bridge with the gossip club.' Our eyes locked and I nodded. 'Then I shall see you about seven, Mr Partridge. Enjoy your day.'

'You too, Mrs Brown,' I replied and watched her throw off the blanket and continue her walk. I realised she was a quick-minded woman.

Later that evening, I dressed in one of the suits I'd had made specially; a nice, three-piece pinstriped number, together with black dress shoes polished to a high shine. I stepped out and headed towards Mrs Brown's suite – which, as it happened, wasn't too far away. Clearly, the gossip circle had done its job as, instead of the usual suspicious looks, they just totally blanked me, as if I was as an unknown entity in their world of wealth and breeding.

I knocked at the door to Molly's suite and a man in a white jacket let me in. It was a larger suite than mine and included a view of the pitch-dark ocean. Not even stars could be seen tonight. Margaret Brown walked in, wearing a long white dress with pearls sewn into its bodice. I kissed her proffered hand, as I had seen people do on TV many times before.

'Good evening, Mrs Brown,' I said with a slight tilt of my head.

'Good evening to you, Mr Partridge,' she said. 'And please, call me Margaret.' She directed me to the heavily laden table. 'Please take a seat. We won't stand on ceremony tonight, though tomorrow you will have to play the part,' she added as the steward pulled out the chair for her. I dealt with my own.

The first course comprised a nice and warming soup, and we ate in silence, not a single slurp between us. It was everything I had ever dreamt of at the start of this adventure. The grace of the woman opposite me was amazing, especially when compared to modern times. No burgers and ribs for this gal.

We then had a roast duckling with assorted fresh vegetables. I gave Margaret free rein to chat away about her life and home and the trouble she'd had to be included in high society. She also spoke about her plans to get involved in women's rights.

After dessert, the steward cleared the cutlery away and departed with a hefty tip, as they didn't normally supply room service for main meals. But money talks.

'So, Brian, what's going on with you?' Maggy asked politely. 'One minute you seem as happy as a child in a candy store, then in a blink of an eye a dark look appears on your face, like you have lost a loved one.' She gave me a sad look. 'I've watched you. It happens more when you see children running around. Why?'

I sighed and wiped my brow. 'It sounds weird, but I had my fortune told, and it was said that my fate would tie me with ice and water,' I explained and smiled as I spouted the lie.

'First, I laughed at the idea that a glass of iced water could choke me.'

Maggie smiled faintly. 'But something changed your mind, though the art of fortune telling alone is dubious to say the least!' she said with a chuckle.

'Dubious indeed,' I replied, 'though my mother always heeded their warnings.' That was true. 'But not to the point where it would affect our family.' I remembered one true memory. 'My mother had a reading done, from her old friend, that a green-eyed girl would bring trouble to our family. The next week, my brother brought home a girl to meet them for the first time.' I cracked a smile and so did Margaret.

'Green eyes,' she guessed with a big smile that lit up her face.

'Oh yes, they were beautiful, almost emerald green,' I said and barked out a louder laugh than normal. 'Mum's whole demeanor changed. She was so cold to the point that even Dad and I wanted to move out that day. We never saw that girl again.' The room echoed with our laughter.

The woman who would soon be called the 'unsinkable Molly Brown' waited until broaching the question again. 'So, what changed, Brian? What has you so worried?'

My shoulders sagged. 'A couple of things, actually,' I replied. 'I overheard a man from the White Star company telling the Captain to light the other boiler to hasten the voyage up.' Maggie nodded her head. 'Then, later, a junior officer was talking to another, mentioning notifications on the wireless about iceberg sightings coming from other ships in the Atlantic. It just worries me, that's all.'

Maggie stared at me. 'I heard about the icebergs, but they said this vessel is unsinkable. That sounds to me like a load of baloney. But still, we must trust the Captain and crew.' She smiled and this allowed a silence to creep in again. She yawned. 'It is time for me to retire, Brian. I have enjoyed tonight.' With that, she stood up. Her chair tipped back and fell to the floor, as the rear legs caught in the ornate rug. 'Damn and blast it!' she said and laughed as I helped her lift the chair up.

'I had fun, too,' I replied with a warm smile and followed her to the door. As it opened, I looked at her rugged, hard face. 'Keep warm clothing close by,' I advised her, 'while we are sailing. The wind is bitter and the water even more so.' I placed my hand on hers, which wasn't appropriate behaviour in that time.

She looked at my hand, then gave me a brittle smile. 'I promise, Brian. Now, I will see you at dinner tomorrow at seven, deal?'

I nodded, then headed back to my room. Collecting my heavy coat and hat, I then joined a few people who also liked the briskness of the Atlantic night air. I leant over the railing and watched the bleak ocean flow past the hull of the ship, the waves at times becoming white as they broke against the cold steel. A shiver ran down my spine knowing that, in just over twenty-four hours, people would be leaping to their deaths as the *Titanic* sank to its grave, dragging innocents down with it.

My bed called for me, so I did its bidding and walked back along the wooden deck, nodding at some sailors, wrapped up against the cold, as I did so. Warmth wrapped around me as I finally entered my room and I started to undress, having a small wash using the china basin attached to my bedroom wall. Soon, the bed cradled me into slumber and, as I gave into it, my mind questioned my actions of the evening and whether I should do more to save these people. In the end, in my own time these poor people were already long dead and mourned for. With that thought, my brain closed down for the night.

***

I was woken up by a bark of baritone laughter coming from outside my comfy and warm room. With a jolt, I sat up and, as my faculties came together, I realised today was the day. 14th April 1912, a day that would be etched into millions of people's minds throughout the future, and my history.

I couldn't face the world yet, so I ate some fruit and enjoyed a nice soothing bath. I leant back, with the washcloth resting over my eyes. The peaceful moment didn't last for long, as the faces of my fellow passengers started to flick though my mind – not only the ones I had met and talked to, but those whom I had discovered in my research before coming to this time. Part of me expressed a desire to leave, but I knew I couldn't. I had to see this through. After all, I would be the final witness of this horrific night.

Time crept slowly along. I had my dinner suit all laid out on the bed and the shoes buffed to a fine shine. The rest of my kit was packed away. I had popped out and paid a steward to bring me some lunch, which cost me the rest of my spending money, but the likelihood of me coming back to this time was slim to none.

The day was chilly but clear with a calm sea, so I just stood and gazed out from my small window. It allowed some calmness to pervade my otherwise stormy thoughts. The lunch the steward had brought me was nice and filling. It was a bit too rich for my liking, but it was the normal food for the wealthy – lamb chops and creamed potatoes.

Though heavy, the meal helped me sleep for a time and my dreams were of those from home. I never thought I would miss it, but I was wrong. Next time, the trips would be shorter and less heart-wrenching than this. Maybe a quick jump to watch *Back to the Future Part Two*. That would be fun! Though, I had promised myself not to misuse the machine for such things. *Why the hell not?* I thought. *What harm could it do?*

Soon, the sun began to set. I had to still my nerves and had another quick visit to the bathroom, before getting dressed for the final time in 1912. The black bow tie wasn't a real one; it had Velcro on the back. Not that anyone looking at the tie could tell, which was a good thing as Velcro hadn't even been invented yet. As I gazed upon my form, I must admit to looking quite dapper. If only my family could see me now.

I looked upon my bed, at my bag, heavy coat for later, and the remote that would enable me to get home to safety and warmth. Finally, I looked at my camera, which had fresh batteries and memory card. I didn't intend for anything morbid, I just wanted a picture of the iceberg, the one that cost people their lives and future.

My watch told me that it was time. So, with a last glance, I pocketed the remote, left my cabin and headed towards the first-class dining room. I saw the maître d' who was taking names and directing people to their tables.

I couldn't believe how the dining room looked in the evening; it was full of light, crystal and finery. They had created a posh restaurant on a ship that was already truly mind-blowing. Even the waiters' white coats shone like the stars that decorated the night sky.

'Brian, right on time, I see. Good man!' Mrs Brown called out, waving at me from just inside the dining room, which made the maître d' stand aside and greet me as another first-class passenger, which I was but in false name only. 'Come on, escort me to our table,' Maggie instructed, and she looped her arm through mine as we walked into the world of the rich and famous.

'Where to, Margaret?' I asked as we walked amongst tables of people. They all watched as we headed to our table. The unsinkable Molly dealt with all those who tried to hinder us as we walked to a table by the wall.

I pulled the chair out for her, then I took my seat, the waiter placing the seat under me. Once again, Margaret took control and ordered for the both of us. She liked to be in control, which was a good job really because I didn't know what half of the things on the menu were.

The stoic woman came alive in such an environment. The James Cameron film, which would be made years later, showed her being laughed at, but nothing was further from the truth. Everyone wanted to speak to Mrs Brown, and a few looks and questions came my way, but she fielded them like a professional shortstop at baseball. Soon, our food arrived, allowing her to focus back on our table.

'So, how are you, Brian? Still having those bad feelings?' she asked, though there wasn't any mockery in her tone at all. 'I was worried when I didn't see you about on deck today.'

Margaret waited for my response as she tucked into her plate of oysters, which wasn't my thing, so I had salmon, which was divine. I was glad that Margaret had offered to order the food, as it took the pressure off me for the night, and gave her the control that powerful women desired!

'It's worse than ever,' I replied. 'I heard a steward talking about icebergs again. It didn't help to quell my fears,' I explained and watched the woman swallow the shellfish, which helped with my cover story as I paled.

Silence enveloped us as the plates were taken away ready for the next course. I was surprised that the combined weight of the food stores and the diners didn't cause a problem with the ship's stability.

'I managed to speak to the designer today, a Mr Andrews if I remember rightly,' Margaret explained and took a sip of white wine. 'He says we have nothing to worry about. They have lookouts around the ship at all times, and they all have those spyglasses.' She then leant across and patted my hand.

'I know,' I replied. 'But still, people make mistakes, things can and will happen.' I looked around, making sure no one was listening, but thankfully the room was humming along with the voices of happy people. 'Just make sure you have some warm clothing by your bed,' I said sternly. 'And make sure you and all the women and children get to the lifeboats.'

Margaret's eyes narrowed. 'That's very specific, Mr Partridge. Why the women first?'

I sunk into my seat and looked at her. 'Because children should never be without a mother. Fathers are ten-a-penny, though they cannot love and nurture a young life like a mother can. That's all I meant,' I explained and received a curt nod in reply.

The waiters arrived and cleared our plates. For the main course, Maggie had ordered herself the roast lamb, while I had sirloin of beef with Chateau Potatoes. I didn't really know what that last bit was, but you can't really go wrong with meat and potatoes. It was then that I realised why she had ordered us different dishes, as she skewered a piece of my beef and popped it into her mouth with a 'hmmm' of satisfaction.

We ate in silence, though it didn't feel uneasy at all. She was a delight to be with. Once again, the plates were cleared away, and we cleansed our pallets with a cold, sweet wine.

Mrs Brown looked upon me with what I thought to be mere tolerance. However, her attitude did soften as I believe she had begun to assimilate everything we had spoken about over the past two days.

'I shall do as you ask, Brian,' she said. 'Though, if it does come to pass, I'm not sure what I can do to change things. However, I promise to do what I can.' She looked at me with a faint smile on her lips, a smile that reached her eyes, which warmed my soul.

'Thank you, that's all I ask of you,' I replied. 'And, of course, there must be no risk to yourself. You have a family to care for, and that is paramount.' I took another sip of the wine and the dessert arrived. Once again, she knocked the selection out of the park – peaches in Chartreuse jelly for me, and French ice cream for her good self. However, when we saw the chocolate eclairs being served to the people on the next table, both of our looks were of want. Margaret grumbled something under her breath, though all I heard was 'damn corset'.

At 9 pm, we left the restaurant, arm in arm, with the glow of those who had enjoyed a night of good food, wine and company. Margaret bid farewell to others as we parted and I led her back to her rooms.

'Brian, go and get your coat, let's walk this food off before we retire for the night,' she suggested, though the woman never waited for an answer. So, off I went like a good boy and was back shortly wearing my hat and coat as instructed.

We strolled arm in arm around the deck, the polished wood glinting off the moonlight. No words were shared for a long time. It wasn't until we leant over the railing and looked into nothingness that Maggie spoke.

'One thing Mr Andrews did mention in confidence,' she said quietly, 'was the limited number of lifeboats. The money men wanted us to have more room on deck. He doesn't believe we have enough for all the passengers should anything happen.'

I didn't reply straight away. 'That's what I thought when I counted them,' I lied, as I had known from my earlier research that this was the case before arriving, and that the ship's rudder had caused us to collide with the iceberg. 'I hope I'm wrong, though, and we can all laugh about this tomorrow.'

'I'm sure we will, Brian,' she chuckled and elbowed me in the ribs playfully as the sea mist began to envelope us, as a warning of what was to come. 'Walk me back to my cabin please, I'm cold.'

With a doth of my hat and another elbow to the ribs, I took her back. 'I hope you sleep well,' I said and saw her to her cabin.

'You too, dear,' replied Maggie. 'But I must ask, if such things do come to pass, what part will you play in the drama?' She stopped at her door and turned to me.

We shared a look and I kissed her hand in farewell. 'To my fate, dear lady, whatever that is,' I said with emotion. 'But I will try and be brave and do my duty.' I then felt her silk-gloved hand on my cheek, then saw her heartfelt smile.

'You will, Brian, though I pray that we will meet in the morning for breakfast.' Margaret Brown then turned and entered her room. Though she didn't know it, we would never see each other again to share a meal.

I placed my hand on her door and whispered, 'Goodbye, Mrs Brown.' I then went back to my room to await the time of terror and pain.

I sat on my bed and watched the ornate clock on the sideboard as the hours and minutes ticked by. All my things were ready, as was I. The clock struck 11 pm and my stomach began to writhe, causing me to rush to the bathroom, sending the good food to the depths. The clock echoed through the room. It was almost time. So, washing and drying my hands and face, I headed out to the front of the ship, to wait.

Chapter Four

Taking a lungful of the frigid night air, I made my way up to the bow of the ship. I felt sorry for the two men who were up in the crow's nest as they looked out into the darkness of the Atlantic Ocean. By now, my stomach was as calm as the sea below. However, my mind had been reeling at the thought of the events to come, right from the day I had decided to join these poor people on their last journey.

Tick, tick, tick… Time passed as the ship crept closer to the iceberg, which was surrounded by darkness. From my readings, I knew that the damage sustained to the ship would be caused by the submerged section of the iceberg dragging itself down the side of the ship, popping rivets as it continued on its journey. A simple hole would have been bad enough, but the safety features would have saved the ship. However, the damage that was to come was so extensive that the water flowing in would make the watertight doors and bulkheads null and void.

I checked the time and my heart sank. From my hiding place, I spotted the watchmen leaning out over the side, trying to pierce the darkness with their naked eyes. However, without binoculars they had no chance. Another mistake made.

'ICEBERG AHEAD!' one of the two lookouts suddenly screamed.

I pulled out my camera and switched it on. The display illuminated my hidden position, though there weren't many people out at this time of night. All eyes looked forward, which saved me. I began to record events with the video. Via the small display, I saw something that caught my breath. There it came, the ship destroyer itself. It loomed out from the darkness. As the watchmen screamed, the officers on the bridge began to react and tried to turn this beast of a ship.

The ship drifted to the left, but the story had been well documented in the future that the rudder was too small for such a large, powerful vessel. So, whilst it gracefully moved in the water, it was not fast enough, and the screams of steel on ice echoed into the night. People ran from shards of ice that rained down from the iceberg, littering the deck as I filmed the mountain of ice dragging itself down the ship. People laughed, thinking they had dodged the ice bullet, but how wrong they were.

More and more passengers hung over the railing, gazing at the iceberg disappearing into the night, some still in their nightwear, which was deemed totally inappropriate for this time of night. I saw the officers from the bridge running and I knew it was time to leave. With my camera turned off and placed back inside my coat, I decided to make my way back to my room, trying not to look anyone in the eye. A man still in his dinner suit, who reeked of cigars and brandy, barged past me, asking everyone what had happened. I used that moment to head inside and towards my room.

I stopped suddenly. At the far end of a corridor, I saw the fully clothed Margaret Brown talking forcefully to a White Star officer. She grabbed him and dragged him outside, all the while talking to him – and, if I knew her, she would have been giving him orders. Fortunately, she hadn't seen me, and they moved out of sight, which allowed me to get to my room without any further hindrance. I sat on my comfy bed, contemplating that I was the lucky one. I was about to leave all this, instead of fighting for my life as panic took the ship. With my sunglasses in place, I pressed the return button, but nothing happened.

'SHIT!' I cried out and pressed the red button again and again. With my eyes closed, I steadied my breathing and decided to wait, though the acid in my stomach threatened to burn its way down to my shoes. It was then that I heard the chink of glasses hitting each other as the ship started to tilt, though only slightly. It was the beginning of the end. 'Oh, fuck.'

With a bright light suddenly blinding me, I was torn from this time and back into the booth. My knees were buckling. I'm not sure why, but all the energy had left my body and I slumped forward, catching myself with the palms of my hands on the basement floor.

'I'm home,' I muttered to myself. After what seemed like hours, I dragged myself up and staggered over to turn on the lights, filling the room with a mediocre glow.

In this state, I knew I wasn't going to be up to much, so I shut down the PC and placed the return remote back into its charging unit. Then, leaving my bag, I headed back upstairs, switching off lights as I went. My legs took me to bed, while I tried to push all the faces of the dead from my mind.

That night, my dreams were devoid, thankfully, of the faces of the doomed passengers of RMS *Titanic*, though replaced with Celine Dion singing about her heart or something like that. One has to wonder what your brain does when you allow it free rein.

Having taken off my clothes, just leaving my now outdated underwear and vest on, I crawled into my long-missed bed. The alarm clock advised me I had only been gone a few hours, though my body told me the truth. As I snuggled into the duvet, a smile spread across my face. I had done it.

***

All too soon, the rays of the sun had penetrated the drapes and continued their journey of unwanted savagery. My eyelids weren't up to the task of keeping the light out, having rudely awoken the synapsis in my brain, causing the dreaded chain reaction coursing through my tired body. It finally reached its pinnacle, and I was awoken once more.

'God, I'm tired,' I moaned, turning over and slamming my face into the pillow. Then, casting away the duvet, I sat up and put my face in my hands. Suddenly, the realisation of what I had done came crashing down around me.

'Time travel…' I whispered the words, so that only the spiders that lived under the bed could hear.

With a deep breath, I headed to the shower to begin my daily routine, and I realised how basic and boring my bathroom was compared to the luxury of the cabins I had left on the *Titanic*.

Donning my usual day-to-day garb, I then readied myself for the day ahead. I had a small plate of toast, which I was sure my body would thank me for, especially after my last two meals. How those people ate that many courses was a mystery to me.

Then I headed down into the basement and reclaimed my bag. I turned with a twist, causing my hip to click, an audible reminder to me of my advancing age. I chose to ignore it and headed up the stairs, putting my bag on the kitchen table and beginning to throw all the dirty clothes towards the washer. I hung the suits up carefully, hoping that the creases would fall out before sending them to the dry cleaners.

'Did they have dry cleaners back in the day?' I mused loudly, and realised I had more homework coming my way.

Thirty minutes later, I had finished unpacking and the washer was going through its noisy motions. With practised ease, the laptop was fired up and ready to be used. The memory cards from my trip were all lined up and ready to be downloaded, and I had a nice hot cup of coffee on my desk steaming away. I started to free the memory cards of all the information. One by one, they were emptied and moved onto the secured data cloud, just in case the laptop broke down and the wealth of knowledge was lost. It didn't take long for everything to be downloaded and cleared; the final memory card was the one that had documented the last moments before I had left the ship.

As I sipped my coffee, I marvelled at how all those days spent in England and on the *Titanic* had only been a few hours. It truly was the purest kind of science fiction.

I gathered up all the cards, then picked up the camera and took it to the basement to charge up ready for my next trip, though who knew where or when that would be. After all the emotional experiences I had just gone through, I realised this would influence my choices for future trips.

Back upstairs, I sat down in front of my laptop. The chair creaked mockingly, suggesting that I had gained weight overnight.

'Bloody judgemental furniture,' I chided, making it creak again… Bastard.

Slowly but surely, I sorted through the photos. The smile on my face remained fixed until the images of the last night appeared. The camera had done its job wonderfully well, allowing me to view the videos frame by frame, so that they could be copied and saved as photos.

The iceberg pictures were breath-taking. The dark Atlantic Ocean against the whiteness of the ice, the star-studded sky… It was truly incredible. I wondered how long it had taken to build such a ship, but which sadly would only be famous for the destruction of human life. The quality of the shipbuilders' work could be seen from the many photos of my wanderings.

It took a while to choose the best images to be degraded via an editing programme that I had purchased. It also stripped away the time code from the image, allowing me to sneak it onto the net as newly found archive pictures of that horrid night.

I smiled as I saw an image of Molly Brown. The picture really didn't do her justice. On film, she seemed as if one look from her could kill a horse, though when you got to know her and she revealed her heart to you, you would see that she was kind and welcoming.

I brought up all the websites I had previously visited about the *Titanic* tragedy. The number of the dead hadn't changed. As I said before, the Grim Reaper will always claim his quota, though it's not set in stone who those people are; the deaths of children were down to but a few, the numbers of deceased women were also down. The main casualties were the crew and men in third class and upwards. Generally, the younger ones survived, while the elder men perished.

Finally, the unsinkable Molly Brown had her fame bolstered by being the driving force behind the distribution of the lifeboats and pushing them all to be filled to capacity and in the water as soon as possible. That way, she alone saved so many people that night. I was given a brief mention, as she said a trusted friend had advised her what to do if such a thing should ever happen, though it was down to her to quell the panic.

Sadly, John and Sarah Milton passed away that night. All I could imagine was that Sarah had refused to leave her new husband, because that would leave her alone in the world. It was then I wished we had parted on better terms. With that, I closed the lid of the laptop, grabbed a bottle of water from the fridge and, after donning my dad's old work boots, I headed out and walked around my family's farm.

***

Two days later, I took a quick trip back to 1989 to the city of Boston to watch *Back to the Future Part II*. As it was December, it was cold enough to freeze the balls off a brass monkey. The film was exactly what I needed to bring my mood back to how it was when I started this journey; and so, with milkshake in hand, I headed back home, which was a stupid mistake. I landed with a jolt, making my fist tighten and sending the vanilla shake all over me and the once clean floor.

Over the next few days, I made some purchases to help with my forthcoming trips. The first was a remote-control truck. I attached to its battery a recordable air probe, which would ensure that the air was breathable. I also put a cheap camcorder on the front of the vehicle so that I knew exactly what I was getting into.

One of the more important bits of kit was an emergency air bottle, which would give me a few minutes of air until the emergency remote brought me home again. *Better safe than sorry*, I thought. The smile wouldn't leave me as I threw myself into the plans for my next major trips into the past.

Once the batteries were charged, I placed the truck into the booth and programmed in the location and time for the arrival. I pressed 'enter' to start the countdown. The electrics began to hum loudly as the lights dipped to barely a glow. As the counter showed zero, the whole place was placed into darkness.

'Balls!'

As Tim the tool man Taylor used to say, 'More power!!!' So, after replacing all the fuses, the power was back up and running. However, clearly the system needed a lot more power, so I bought an automatic standby generator of 32k/w and paid for it to be wired straight to the basement, just in case I ran out of power again. The whole thing cost me an eye-watering thirteen thousand dollars – eleven and a bit for the generator, the rest for the electrician to wire it in and keep his mouth shut about it.

After the unexpected electrics delay, I was eager to travel again, but first the truck was to be sent through. With the kit all charged up, the clock counted down. Once again, the lights dipped, though not for long as the generator kicked in and saved the day. The now familiar blazing white light shone brightly, which left spots in front of my eyes. Then it was gone and the truck had left our time. I sat again at the computer and watched the screen. The programme showed the years clicking back quickly. Then, after ten minutes, the message flashed up: 'ARRIVED'.

Excitement ran through me as I watched the automatic return timer count down from five minutes. The truck was there just for stability – and, yes, I played with it a bit outside on the fields, though that was just to check that the battery was strong enough. A notification flashed up on the computer screen advising that the truck was returning. So, I put my shades on, just in time as, with a flash, the truck reappeared, bathing the whole room in white light.

I ran over and took the truck out of the pod. Thankfully, it was in one piece. I carried it to my work bench and took the camera and sensor off their mountings, before excitedly running up the first few steps leading out of the basement until the air and energy left my body. I then slowed to a sedate walk up the stairs.

'Feel the burn,' I joked with myself and placed the camera and sensor onto the dining room table, next to the much-used laptop, and plugged the air sensor in.

It took a while, but I found a website to explain in layman terms what all the information meant. All I wanted was a flashing green light which meant 'okay', or red for 'negative'. In the end, the website said it was okay and that the air was perfect, though it informed me there were some strange readings. However, the air in that time shouldn't kill me, which was a thumbs up from this man.

Next, the camcorder, and all it showed was greenery – not a forest, just a grassy plain, and nothing else.

'Perfect,' I muttered. I closed the laptop down and put it all on charge again, as tomorrow I would, once again, travel into the past.

That night, I barely slept with the excitement of the coming trip; no ghost of the past would haunt me for this trip. The alarm woke me from my broken sleep, and I jumped like an excitable child at Christmas. With the morning cleaning and breakfast rituals done with, I clothed myself in jeans, a thick plaid shirt, my father's work boots and, finally, a leather jacket. An old leather satchel was draped across my chest containing binoculars, sandwiches, a bottle of water and my camera. As I looked in the mirror, I realised that all I needed was a whip and a Fedora.

'Call me Indiana Partridge,' I said and then shook my head, sadly walking away from the mirror, with a little feeling of disgust with myself. What a child I am.

The time machine was humming away calmly as I typed in the same parameters as yesterday's jaunt. I slipped on my sunglasses, stepped into the booth, and watched the brand-new and newly installed countdown clock which adorned the wall opposite. It reached the number one position when I noticed the emergency air bottle sitting upon my work bench.

'Shit!'

With a thump, I landed feet first onto the grass. The air tasted fresh as I took in deep breaths of the life-sustaining air. Although I knew this trip would take me back a greater time distance than the others, it still felt like it was instantaneous. I smiled as I took in the vast plains of grasslands.

There were some animals in the distance, though the binoculars weren't powerful enough to see them in any kind of clarity. That would need to be corrected in the future. Even by using the adjustable zoom on my camera, I still wasn't able to distinguish what they were. So, with a skip in my step I headed that way, being careful not to alert anything – after all, I was the only human being existing in the late Cretaceous period, a whole 67 million years ago.

To say my mind was buzzing was a major understatement. I walked on with the camera in one hand and the return remote in the other. The computer at home was set to bring me home again in three hours – although, as there could well be a T-Rex walking around somewhere, I felt safer with the remote. Sweat coated my back and face, forcing me to sling my jacket over my shoulder, my finger squeezing through the hanging loop. I left the bag where it was as I plodded on.

My thoughts on wearing a hat had changed. The sun was blistering hot, and I was drinking the water way too quickly to last the full three hours. I sat on a small hill to eat my sandwiches and finish off the water, making sure not to litter the landscape – though, it would be funny to see the expression on some archaeologist's face digging up a 67 million-year-old bottle of Evian water.

ROAR!!! My head shot up and I scanned the horizon. The animals I was heading towards were scattering like a scene from *Jurassic Park*. Where's a bloody Jeep when you need it? I downed the last of the water and packed the bottle away. I quickly put my jacket back on and slung the bag across my back, holding the camera and remote in each hand.

Some animals were now heading my way and their footfalls echoed across the grassland. Another roar, this time closer, came again and that's when I saw the huge king of the dinosaurs, a T-Rex – not one, but two of them. I couldn't tell if they were a pair, or what my biggest immediate issue was, but I decided it was the herd of unknown herbivores stampeding my way. I then realised I had nothing to hide behind.

Crouching low, I ran at a right angle to them, hoping they would just carry on their route to nothingness, taking the meat eaters with them. I managed to get to some waist-high grass, which I threw myself into, ducking down. I saw that my had plan had worked and watched the long-necked and legged creatures running past me.

I steeled my nerves and took some photos of the fleeing dinosaurs. The good news was that there were no longer two T-Rexes coming my way. You got it, there was one.

I crouched down in the plush green grass as I watched the two-legged killer come thundering up. In a panic, I pressed the button to return home, and in an instant the big shit stopped and looked around, making me freeze on the spot. Even the rivulets of sweat slowed down.

The monster looked around and then started to smell the air. Now, that was something I had forgotten. Yes, the film told me that the T-Rex couldn't see me if I didn't move. I'm pretty sure they never mentioned my scent. Clearly, eating garlic sausage sandwich and spraying Lynx anti-perspiration deodorant was not doing the trick this time. If he takes more than a couple of steps this way, he was going to be overpowered by a whole myriad of smells, and not a single one of them good.

Despite the massive Tyrannosaurus Rex sniffing around, I was brave enough to hold up the camera using the video function. Like the true show-off it was, the huge creature roared loudly, making me close my eyes in sheer terror. I was now shaking big time, using all my strength to hold the remote and the camera still. Suddenly, the T-Rex received an answering call, causing its head to flick around to where its mate was calling from.

It turned on the spot, giving the air one last sniff. Its eyes seemed to penetrate the thick green grass, my brain and then my soul. My inner monologue declared me a dead man. Every fibre in my body was telling me to run. However, as I would be out of breath by running up a couple of stairs back home, there was no chance of me outpacing a 12-foot-tall behemoth killing machine.

Its hunting partner roared into the air again, echoing throughout the land. Thankfully, this led to my T-Rex friend snorting out a spray of mucus onto the grass before turning and walking off, back toward its mate. As I let out a sigh of relief, I was suddenly bathed in light. Landing in a squat, I fell onto the carpet, leaving a rug burn on my forehead and sending the remote scattering off into the shadows, quickly followed by the camera. At that moment in time, I was quite happy that dinosaurs were extinct.

After shutting the time machine down, I literally crawled up the two flights of stairs, leaving items of clothing as I did so. It is at times like these when living alone is perfect. It took a while and several splinters before I finally made it to my comfy yet boring bathroom and took a shower, scrubbing the scent of sweat and fear from my body, trying not to think too hard about the blob of dinosaur mucus that fell from my hair to my foot, making me kick it down the drain.

I dressed in grey shorts and a T-shirt, then headed downstairs, gathering up the clothes that I had discarded. I then went to where I had dropped my camera and remote. After popping out the memory card from the camera, I put both devices back on charge in readiness for my next adventure. I decided that next time it would be somewhere safe. *Where do the care bears live?* I wondered. *That would be safe enough.*

An hour later, I was sitting at the dining table with my best friend, the laptop, downloading the short, but busy, video. I had a large pepperoni pizza and a can of Mountain Dew to calm my nerves. Some of the video was unusable as the picture was shaking very badly, as if there had been an earthquake. However, there was one image that I thought would look perfect hanging on the wall of what I had now come to call 'The Time Room'.

The image was of the big lizard staring directly at me with his flesh-tearing teeth exposed in a shit-eating grin. Even now, my stomach lurches whenever I look at it, but it is a fantastic picture, whether people believe it or not. I have sent the image away to an online print company who, for a fair price, will frame it in a basic black, wooden frame. I'm sure they will get a laugh out of doing that.

With the remainder of my healthy meal in the trash, I decided to get some online help to decide where to go next. It had to be safe, yet fun. So, I put in a search for the top ten events to witness if you had a time machine, and wow there were some crazy choices.

Find and beat up Jack the Ripper. What makes anyone think they would survive and manage to find Jack, anyway? It's not as if he had been caught on CCTV so they would have specific dates and time of the murders! Plus, London at that time wasn't the safest of cities, especially after dark. Then again, what city is safe, even today?

Now, this was a possibility – watching the Wright Brothers making their first powered flight at Kitty Hawk in North Carolina. The plus point was that there would be no dinosaurs or icebergs, and I'm pretty sure my suits from 1912 would pass muster in 1903. Sounded like fun.

The Hindenburg disaster in New Jersey, 1937 – a bit gloomy, but it was one amongst the most iconic moments of the 1900s. This century didn't work out too well for human beings and the world around them. I smiled as I thought about building a ranch millions of years in the past. All I needed was a T-Rex repellent.

Titanic… done, and never to see or do again.

Witnessing Jesus's crucifixion? 'Don't speak Hebrew,' I muttered and moved on while jotting down some more ideas for later, some plausible, some not.

I liked the idea of watching the launch of Apollo 11 as it rocketed to the moon in 1969, and there would be plenty of places to hide around the Kennedy Space Centre in Florida. That might be one for the future.

But the name Kennedy stuck with me and his assassination in Dallas, 1963. What would happen if I tried to stop it? The Vietnam war might never have happened, many of my father's childhood friends could still be alive, or not so injured, and Dad wouldn't have had nightmares from his stint overseas that kept him up at nights.

I drew several lines under that idea. I know what George Lancaster Jnr had said, but what if it didn't work out this time? Maybe fate and the Grim Reaper had decided that JFK was worthy of having his life spared? Him and thousands of innocents all over the world, just for the sake of stupid policies and money.

For the rest of the day and night, plans upon plans filtered through my mind. The warnings from the author rang out like church bells on a wedding day, but I shook them off and purchased some stylish polyester clothes and some extra money. And a hat. I'm not going anywhere without a bloody hat. No more sunburn and mucus on this man's head.

A week later and I stood wearing a red and blue polo shirt with black slacks and matching shoes, with a nice white Stetson hat and black sunglasses. Perfect. I slipped my camera and remote into a small blue bag, which I slung across my chest.

The time hit zero and, in the now typical light show, I appeared right on target amongst some trees. The sound of people talking could be heard, so I walked in that direction. I stepped out onto the sidewalk and saw a couple of older women shoot me a look.

'A good day for it, ladies,' I said, taking off my hat, and I gave them a winning smile, which seemed to quell their suspicions.

They both wore flowery sundresses that flared out from the hips. One had a blue rinse hairdo, the other was gray as gray ever got. The kindly blue-haired woman smiled.

'Oh, it is, isn't it?' she said. 'So exciting and such a delightful day.' Her friend agreed, and we all turned to follow where the crowds were looking.

Time was running away; things were in motion and nothing could stop them now. Radios blared from many handheld systems of the day. With a nod to the ladies, I moved away to a quieter area, where I couldn't easily be seen. Though I knew exactly how this would play out, my nerves were on fire. I slipped the camera out and switched it on, hearing the familiar whirring noise as the lens zoomed out.

There were family groups enjoying barbeques on the front lawns of their single-storey houses. Everyone could sense the buzz. A child ran over to me offering a cold beer from his father.

'Thank you very much,' I said to the small boy and raised the bottle to the large, barrel-chested man who was cooking chicken on his grill. His wife and baby daughter were sitting on a rug nearby. Everybody was smiling and what a beautiful sight it was! Clearly, I wasn't as well hidden as I thought.

I took a drink from the cold bottle. The boy gave my camera a strange look before he was called back by his mother. The freckle-faced boy, whose name I learnt was Matt, ran off, smiling back to his family as we all waited with bated breath.

Finally, it happened. The radios everywhere crackled to life, and all eyes were drawn to the same location over ten miles away. The funny thing was you could see and hear it with such clarity it unnerved me, though I didn't know why. Then our eyes followed the moving target in the sky. I raised my small camera and let the video roll as I tracked the Saturn V rocket transporting the astronauts and Apollo 11 into space and, finally, to the moon.

This truly had been the days of days. It made you proud to be an American. We all cheered as the rocket flew into the sky and out of sight, even though the smoke from the rocket lingered for some time after. With a smile, I took the now consumed beer bottle back to the family, who kindly invited me to stay and enjoy their hospitality.

It had been a wonderful day as I sat in the sun with baby Cindy sleeping in my arms, watching her parents dancing lovingly as music played from the wireless. Matt was happily running around with his friends from the neighbourhood. To be part of a young family is truly wonderful, something I missed out on with my own family – though, one day, perhaps I could still have one of my own?

***

FBI Headquarters
935 Pennsylvania Avenue, NW
Washington, DC

Unknown to everyone who was, or still is, working at the headquarters of the FBI, there is a room in the basement. The door has a simple aluminium handle without any lock on it at all, and hundreds – possibly thousands – of agents and other workers had walked past it without even a cursory glance. If they did notice it, all they would see was its identifying number T07/04/1776 painted onto the grey door.

What people didn't know was that this was a room out of time, and the computers worked away tirelessly checking the flow of information, making sure nothing in the past had been changed. Nobody knew who had set the room up, or who maintained the computers. The only person who knew of its existence was the Director of the FBI. When the new director had taken on the job, the previous director had shown him the room and advised him that, if there was ever a need, he could be contacted, and the room would open.

At this moment in time, the computers were running checks over the dates of 14th April 1912 to 16th April 1912, and they discovered that something had changed. The software was calculating the differences, and there was an anomaly that set off a silent alarm, which activated a green light that sat upon the wall. Nobody would know of this until more temporal distortion had been traced. It would take another two occurrences for the lights to be illuminated and for anyone to be notified, and in the coming days the alarm would be triggered.

Chapter Five

I am pleased with myself today as, during the trip back to watch the Saturn V rocket launch, I had an epiphany. However, it wasn't until later that it came back to the forefront of my mind.

The breakfast that sat on my plate could only be described as disappointing with undertones of health. Over time, I had come to be more health-conscious and started to eat healthier foods, hence my looking into a breakfast bowl full of fruits covered in natural yogurt. As I ate, I recalled the feeling of national pride as I watched those brave men sit upon all that rocket fuel to be blasted from the world they were born in. Even though so many of their colleagues had perished, they were still in pursuit of their dreams.

'DRONE!' I blurted out, sending a half-chewed grape across the room, and which I never found again. Good riddance.

A drone would be perfect for recording some footage of dinosaurs without putting myself in too much danger. With a skip in my step, I cleared away my breakfast dishes, washed them and let them drain and dry on the side, before heading out to the electronics store. The local one didn't have enough range for what I was looking for, and so I drove into town about ten miles away. The electronics store was like my home, just on steroids. The place had everything electrical I would ever need and, with a smile on my face, I walked around. The drones were easily found, as the display models were hanging from the ceiling by wire.

There was a huge variety, from a mere amateur model for $40 to professional racing machines with prices running into the thousands.

A salesman in thick-rimmed spectacles, and whose name badge announced him as 'Edward', approached me. He was small in stature, I guessed no more than five feet, which made me feel like a giant. *Brian will crush you, puny human.* I smiled at the thought.

'Good morning, sir. How may I help you today?' Edward said, in a clearly practised tone.

We shook hands as men of a certain age do. He seemed to be around my age, which made things easier.

'Good morning, Edward,' I replied. 'I find myself in need of a drone.' I breathed in the scent of electronics. It had always given me a slight feeling of euphoria whenever I was in this shop, with its well-worn carpeting and the huge, flashing televisions.

The man nodded and waddled off on his short legs. 'Is it for recreation, or racing?' he asked in a tone which lacked life.

'Recreational,' I answered, trying to think up a good story, not that I needed one. 'I'm going on safari, and I want to have one to fly around the campsite.'

'Sounds exciting, sir,' said Edward, giving a slight dry cough. 'So you want a camera with the ability to record in night vision?' he queried, looking at me with a faint smile on his lips. It was then I knew what he was thinking. Edward thought I was a peeping Tom, and I just knew that's where his questions were leading.

I shook my head as we passed all the modern mobile phones, which could hardly be called such things anymore. They were more like palm computers.

'No, thank you. It's not advisable to do anything like that in Zambia,' I chuckled. 'How will it record? Does it have a hard drive?'

Edward gestured to a section of the shop where various drones were on display at floor level. It was a techno geek's nirvana – drones and remote toys of all price ranges and styles.

'We have this type,' he gestured towards one area of drones. 'But the air time is low due to the power needed to run it.' I began to wonder if his view of me had begun to shift. 'The popular and best ones are controlled by radio, but the footage is recorded via wi-fi to your smartphone using the manufacturer's app.' He waved to the myriad of toys. 'Take your pick… sir,' he added, sweeping a wide arc with his hand in a grand fashion.

The choice was amazing. I was going drone blind, but after twenty or so minutes I zeroed in on a Mavic drone that had four propellers, a 4k/30fps camera with 31 minutes flight time. It could also be controlled by an app on a smartphone – not that I had one of those. With a big smile on my face and suppressing a girlish giggle, I pointed at my new toy.

'That's the one,' I said, trying to keep my voice serious.

The salesman nodded and turned to walk away.

'Oh, and I need a smartphone,' I added as an afterthought. And, with that simple comment, I lost another hour of my life. When did a phone stop being a phone? Should I get a 4G or 5G? Should it have a camera, or should I get one that could view the moon were I to be hiding in a bunker in the desert? Who cares??

Then Edward asked what call service plan did I want? Tears were almost flowing down my face. Then the paperwork, which included registering the drone with the FAA (Federal Aviation Administration). As I finally wandered out of the store, financially lighter, I wondered how many kids were flying their toys illegally.

I made it home tired yet excited about my new purchases. My first job was to assemble the drone, then charge it along with my new smartphone. I showered and ordered some Chinese food. Not healthy, but I had some major instruction manuals to read and cry over.

As I did so, I thought about the link between the time machine and the return remote. George Lancaster's notes were very sparse when it came to the design of the technology, though it had a manual explaining how to use it and maintain it. So, I wondered if he was the creator of the time machine. Or, like me, had he found it?

With spare ribs and prawn chow mein despatched, I settled down with the small radio playing in the background. The smartphone was up and running quickly enough. I had decided it was just to be used as a camera and drone control. Yes, I could use it as a phone, but that meant using the call plan and the new number. However, that alone would send a wave of panic through my family, especially as my nephew would be called over to my brother's to put the new number into his and his wife's phone, and then the questions would start via very badly written text.

The drone was an easier task and I had it flying around the house quite nicely, with a light hum to it. The only fatalities on its first flight were a cactus that was foolishly loitering on top of the television, and a Chinese plate that my mother had adored and my father despised. You are welcome, Dad. The plate is now at rest in the bin… sorry, Mum.

After putting the drone on charge, I headed up to bed for a good night's sleep with the hope that my endeavours the next day would come to fruition

I awoke the next morning with a plan in mind and fun ahead to be had. And, with clean body and mind, I walked down the stairs to have a healthy, but disappointing, breakfast. My mind wasn't on food, however. It was time to travel. With the drone all charged up and linked to my smartphone via the app, I placed it in one of the pods ready to go. The computer sent it back in time, this time only a few days after my last visit to the prehistoric age. For some reason, you could never go back to the same day after you had been there once.

The counter hit zero and, for a moment, I felt elation as the large grass plain appeared on the camera feed and I could see some herbivores grazing on the long, green grass. However, just then the feed cut out.

'Dang and blast it!' I shouted and pressed the cancellation key on the computer to bring the Traveller back.

In a flash of blindingly bright light, the drone reappeared, though it did take another five minutes before my eyesight came back, only to see the expensive drone broken with what looked like a shit-covered, hoof-shaped hole through it. I had hoped that it would be different to the truck and could be controlled from base via radio waves, but the evidence proved different.

Startled birds scattered from the field outside as swear words finally reached them. They didn't know what such words meant, but I'm sure the meaning even translated into avian.

After having a childish tirade at the broken drone, I threw it and the evidence of dinosaur crap in the trash in my cellar. Then I went back upstairs, throwing myself into a chair and huffing as I fired up the laptop to spend even more money to replace the stupid drone.

I was never going back to the shit-eating grin of Edward at the electronics store, especially as I couldn't claim it was already damaged straight from the box.

After ordering a new drone online, with a heavy heart I decided to scan through the pics from the *Titanic*. I smiled at those of Margaret, and I let the tears flow when faces of those who had perished that night came into sight. Though they were already long dead, they were still alive in my dreams and would never be forgotten.

The next day, the exact same model of drone was delivered by my favourite online store. Once again, with the glee of a toddler at Christmas, I tore at the packaging and got the machine ready to go. I swapped the batteries from the damaged drone to the new one, as they were already charged and, yes, I was impatient.

Within half an hour, I stood upon the lush grasslands of the Cretaceous period, using the binoculars to scan the land. This time, luck was with me and the only signs of life were far enough away not to become a problem… at least, for the time being.

With a smile on my face and my hat at a jaunty angle, I sat on a small rise cross-legged and the drone came to life. Using the smartphone, the machine rose into the air and headed off into the sky in search of my prey. This time, hopefully I wouldn't have to run or have the crap scared out of me by anything.

The aircraft hummed over some herbivores like the ones I had seen last time. Perhaps I should have brought a book with me to identify such beasts. At least the drone was recording everything it saw. Some of the dinosaurs scattered, though many just looked up, giving a surprisingly good show of being confused.

After a while, I had enough footage as there wasn't much to be seen. At least I knew that the drone was working properly. So, after landing it safely and packing everything up, I went for a bit of a walk through the grassland, with the sun blazing away, without the noise of an airplane or any other man-made machine to spoil this young world. I thought how nice it would be if I could build a cabin out here to stay in, though I knew it'd act as a meat eater's lunch box.

The smile didn't leave my face as I walked around. The drone was sent up again as I had managed to get closer to some other types of dinosaurs, but I knew it was too dangerous to linger alone in such a place. Maybe one day I could bring my family here. They surely would enjoy themselves.

Time was getting on and the heat of the day was tiring me out. So, after picking up my trash after a little impromptu picnic and placing everything back into my bag, I stood up and prepared myself for the next step. I pressed the remote button and stood waiting, wearing my dark glasses, bag in one hand and the drone in the other. I waited for the flash of bright light and the journey home.

It took a whole ten minutes for me to return home, which was just in time as I had heard the gut-wrenching call of the T-Rex from the surrounding woods. Then, in a flash I was gone and landed back home. Everything worked out nicely this time.

'Pizza time!' I called out to nobody, and slowly headed upstairs after putting the drone's batteries on charge and shutting down the computer.

Over the next few days, I hopped back and forth in time to collect images of the dinosaurs, knowing that it would be reasonably safe. I took some more images of the T-Rex, then some Ankylosaurus, which were armoured vegetarians. I came close to losing the drone when I came across a herd of Diplodocus; clearly, the alpha male took umbrage at the buzzing noise of my drone, thinking of it as a bug or some other nuisance, and it tried to headbutt it away. After that, I just enjoyed the rest of the day. I sat by the river, watching all the comings and goings of the overgrown lizards, even though I knew that, at any time, death could claim me. But how could I not risk it for such sights?

After that day, I decided I would not travel back in time for a while, especially when the electric bill arrived. Thank the sweet mercies that I had invested well. I swear they thought I was either growing weed out here or making crystal meth. Maybe I should come up with a plan and an excuse just in case the Po Po, as I heard them called on the TV, came a calling.

Days turned into weeks as I tried to decide where next to go. A few ideas took root, but they didn't come to anything. So, as something to do, I headed back to watch the last instalment of Marty McFly in Boston. Maybe a DVD would be cheaper.

One lonely night as I scanned through TV channels, I came across an old movie showing an Egyptian mummy chasing Abbot and Costello. I do enjoy those films so much. They remind me of when my father was alive and when he'd allow himself some time off work to watch a movie with us. So, with that in my brain, I took to the books and maps.

Luckily, after lots of searches, I found the coordinates for the place I planned to visit.

'Khufu, the Great Pyramid of Giza,' I said to myself. Though it was risky as hell, nowadays it was surrounded by the city on three sides, so I had to make sure I stayed well clear of it all and aim to land in the desert. I checked my figures over and over again, not wanting to appear in the middle of the city in a flash of bright light and be hailed the God of Lightning, though it sounded cool.

I hit the online shopping hard, buying desert combat fatigues, a water bottle, a hat and, finally, a sturdy pair of boots. They all took a few days to arrive, but when I tried on all the kit, I looked like GI Joe's special needs cousin. However, I knew it would do the job.

I waited another few days, for the drone batteries to charge up fully, and for my final purchase to arrive – a sand-coloured rucksack. This would be big enough to hold the drone and everything I needed for the trip. The emergency return remote was put inside a ziplock bag to protect it from the sand. However, as a secondary precaution I set the timer at twenty-four hours, which should allow me plenty of time to land and get closer to the Pyramids of Giza. The date I had set the time machine for was what I considered to be the safest and would put me at least a decade after the last pyramid had been built. Therefore, the area should be quiet.

Looking through all my notes, I chose to arrive at seven o'clock in the morning, believing that the flash of light indicating the arrival of the time machine would not be seen so readily – well, that was my thinking, anyway. In my nervous state, I ordered another item that I thought might come in handy – a camouflage netting. Yes, it might be overkill, but better to have it than not.

The day finally arrived and I punched in the coordinates 29°58'31.0"N 31°08'16.0"E 2400bc. There would be no dinosaurs this time, just angry Egyptians chasing the whitest man they would ever see in their lifetimes. That thought reminded me to smear sunscreen over my face.

The truck and camera were sent first, and then brought back. Unfortunately, when I checked the camera on its arrival it showed that it was still night time at my destination. So, while sitting in my combats with the smell of the sun cream invading my nasal cavity, I altered the timings and sent the truck back. I had to send it back to a different day of course, but at least it was daylight and not a person in sight. What did worry me was the lack of images of pyramids, or anything at all, on the camera.

I stood in the pod with adrenaline surging through my system as the counter clicked down, my knees unlocked ready for the landing, the rucksack at my feet. The counter hit zero and the room was flooded with the ethereal white light, and I was sent flying into the past and into…

'SANDSTORM!' I screamed to myself and ducked down, hiding my uncovered face from the stinging sand.

At least it was daylight and I was surrounded by a vast desert. The rest of the identifying markers would be found when this storm blew over – if it ever did. *How long do these things last?* I wondered as my knees started to hurt where I had landed on them. You see sandstorms in films and they just seem to be a hindrance. But this was painful. The sand found its way into any bare bit of skin and punished it by ripping it raw. All I could do was huddle down behind my bag and hope for it to pass.

Thirst was also becoming a problem. Even opening the cap off the bottle would mean disaster, so I waited and prayed that my end wouldn't come. After about an hour the sandstorm had passed, leaving me feeling ill and sore all over. It wouldn't beat me, though. I am here and alive.

I opened my water bottle and enjoyed the blissful feeling of water flowing over my cracked lips, refreshing my mouth and system. Then, an energy bar was shoved down my gullet to help me move. Scanning around, I realised it was still overcast and then the pyramids came into view. I had made it.

As I looked around, I noticed that there were small sandbars, as well as some more rocky outcrops that jutted from the sandy, Egyptian landscape. Walking towards one such rocky area, I held up my binoculars and scanned the now clearer terrain. Not a sign of life behind me or anything to either side of me. But I then realised that, with the end of the storm, came the start of the working day.

The reason for having chosen this period was twofold. Thanks to my research, it was explained that, by this time, most of the pyramids and the Sphinx of Giza would have been completed, so I had hoped that the need of workers in such an area would be lessened. But, like any good contractors, they must have overrun as there was an army of workers walking from nearby settlements. I would hate to get this man's overtime bill.

The workers and, more likely, slaves moved like ants over several structures. You had to feel for them as the heat of the day started to burn away all the residual storm clouds, making workers and their master sweat alike. All I could say was that my underwear and socks would be given as tribute to the fire god that I would set to burn after this journey – though, with the amount of sweat they held in them, it may take some time. The amount of water I had drunk was insane – though, that was something I had expected in this heat.

Hour after hour I watched the workforce, taking time to scan the area around me. The one thing that had stuck with me was the need to be aware of my surroundings, especially as I couldn't claim to be lost. After looking around, I moved slowly but surely from rock to rock, getting closer to the pyramids. Even from half a mile away, they looked amazing, and it was a shame that no one else would see the pictures that I would take – after all, who would believe it?

Time was ticking away as I crept closer and, as the distance was reduced, the sight in front of me became even more impressive. No wonder some people believed that aliens had something to do with building these huge structures. Sorry, my friends, there are no little green men, just thousands of slaves and men with big, bloody whips.

Finally, I made it close enough to see the features on the half woman, half lion statue of the Sphinx. Clearly, the carving of the main stonework had been completed years ago, so now it was just a case of finishing it off and preparing the surrounding groundwork. There were some wooden frames around the base of the Sphinx, which allowed engravers to carve hieroglyphs into it.

I took out my camera and, with the zoom at its maximum, I started to document my journey. And yes, I did take a selfie with my smartphone, with the Pyramid of Giza in the background. Sue me! It was then that I heard the tolling of a small bell, and also a different sound that carried on the wind. It scared me. It was the bleat of either a sheep or goat – either way, I had focused for way too long looking forward, and not checking around me.

Kneeling behind the rock, I turned and saw a herd of goats being ushered past where I was hiding. The man was elderly, wearing an old robe, torn and dirty, with matching turban-like headgear that kept the sun from his head. Though he didn't look my way, the herder seemed to be moving a little quicker than normal, hence why the goats were bleating in annoyance back at him.

It was then that I knew my time here was coming to an end. I also knew that, even though the sights were truly amazing, I would not be coming back here. There was too much risk and, if I was honest, there was too much sand and heat for my liking.

As I watched the man and his herd of goats scuttle off, I unpacked the drone and got it ready. The day was not as clear as I had hoped and, unfortunately, the slight breeze was bringing a certain scent from the city, which didn't match the amazing sights before me.

With a low hum, the drone lifted from the sun-scorched ground and drifted noisily into the heavens. With the smartphone in hand, I watched the drone fly towards the pyramids. There were three of them, all different sizes, and the Sphinx. It flew over the goat herder and towards the cat woman, and I drifted it sideways, getting a nice, slow image of the long axis.

I hoped the drone was high enough, and that the workers were diligent enough in their work that they wouldn't notice it – or if they did, maybe they thought it was either a children's kite, or perhaps a bird of prey. Though, looking through the high-definition camera, it told a different story.

'Shit!' I said, a bit too loud. A worker, wearing what looked like a short skirt, stared directly at the drone with a worried look painted across his work-worn face. He was holding a wooden mallet and a chisel, or some such tool.

The goat herder had almost reached the workers, so my time was short. I moved on, getting as much footage of the Sphinx as I could. It didn't look anything like the pictures I had studied on the web. I was seeing a Sphinx newly painted and looking glorious in reds and blues. In my dreams, it had always appeared to me as being of pure gold, but that's imagination for you.

The workers were starting to scrabble around, and it didn't help that the goat man seemed to be screaming blue murder and scattering his charges near and far, while pointing in my direction. I made the drone gain some height and start to circle the main and largest pyramid, which was the Pyramid of Khufu. The sides were smooth with all the cover stones still in place.

After that, I lifted the drone higher to take a bird's-eye view of all three pyramids – Khufu. Khaftre and Menkaure. There were several other smaller structures called the Pyramids of the Queens. Sounds like a dance club, though that could be my imagination creeping in again.

The drone drifted around, taking in the vast sight. It was then that I noticed a glint of light coming from what I surmised to be the workers' village, or at least the outer part of the city. I squinted at the light, which was quickly getting bigger. I then realised that the reflection was a golden chariot, followed by six others, though plainer in appearance. The front chariot led the charge towards me. I quickly decided that time was finished here, and I brought the drone back to me. If I didn't wrap this up, I was going to be the first American to be attacked by a member of the Egyptian royal family.

My heart was thrumming as quickly as the drone's engine as it outpaced the Egyptian army, which seemed to be about to attack me. Strangely, this had never once crossed my mind in all the nights of planning. Never once had I thought about being attacked by an Egyptian army in chariots.

Taking one hand off the controls, I knelt and searched for the emergency remote. Thankfully, everything else I had brought had been packed in the backpack and was still in situ. Using my teeth, I tore open the Ziplock, allowing me access to the return home button.

As the drone started to drift lower, I readied myself to go, slinging the rucksack onto my front so I wouldn't land on my face on the return. My focus was split between bringing my drone home and the dust cloud, which was caused by the advancing charging warriors.

I ducked as something hit the ground outside the rocky outcropping, which was my castle and my only hiding place. It was then that I saw my first ever Egyptian arrow, though the sight of it made my stomach flip and turned my legs into jelly. I was secretly impressed that they could get that close to me while on a moving platform. That thought was quickly despatched as another possible death bringer shattered into splinters as it hit a rock beside me, making me instantly press the button to go home. If I didn't manage to get the drone back, they could keep the bloody piece of flying plastic. But, as ever, the emergency return home controller didn't work instantly. I cursed the thing as I managed to dodge another incoming projectile.

Panic was setting in. I tucked the remote into my bag and guided the drone back at full pelt. It now remained at head height as more arrows started to fall about me.

'Shit, shit, shit!' I chanted as the horses came closer. The noise of the horses and chariots was loud enough, but the screams and shouts of my possible killers were becoming the loudest.

My eyes settled on the gold-armoured man riding in the front chariot. There was nothing but glee painted across his face.

The drone dropped in height and I jumped up and grabbed it with both hands. Just as my feet hit the earth again, I felt myself beginning to fall backwards and I was bathed in the blinding white light. My knees sagged as I landed home in the pod. The drone and smartphone fell from my shaking grip. There wasn't a single part of me that was not in a state of fear. My eyes dropped down to my rucksack, which had an arrow sticking out of it.

'Fuck!' That's when everything went black.

The real world came flickering back as my brain caught up with the realisation of what had happened. My mind raced as I recalled the man in the golden armour, and I saw again the intensity in the man's eyes as his horse's hoofs slammed into the earth. A smile appeared on my face again as the adrenaline coursed through my system.

The arrow stuck out of the rucksack and, thankfully, I managed to turn slightly as, once again, I fell onto the carpeted floor.

'Best trip ever, but never again,' I muttered.

Slipping the shoulder straps of my rucksack off, I rolled onto my back. Dust, that had hitchhiked from the desert, puffed into the air from my clothes. The sweat, which was starting to dry on my skin and which had soaked into my T-shirt, had started to smell. Nice. With barely any strength, I managed to force myself to stand, my knees screaming with pain from the time spent kneeling. Oh, to be young again. The drone was on the floor, the propellers still slowly turning alongside the smartphone controller, forcing me to bend back down to reclaim the mobile device and turn everything off.

The computers were closed down and I slowly headed up to my bed, discarding my clothes as I climbed the stairs. They could be all gathered up and cleaned tomorrow. All I wanted was my bed, even though it was still daylight outside. My brain and body were tired, though the rush of the departure was still running through my veins.

Bare arsed, I closed the curtains and climbed into bed, the smell of sweat clinging to my body. A shower would have to wait as I slipped into sweet Morpheus once more. Even though the smell assaulted my senses, fatigue was the winner that night.

***

Room T07/04/1776
FBI Headquarters
935 Pennsylvania Avenue, NW
Washington, DC

The bank of computers was at work, analysing reams of data from multiple sources, whether private or corporate, and universities worldwide. Unbeknown to the owners of private collectors, their hard drives were being downloaded and scoured.

A green light started to flash as information was collated and stored in encrypted files, waiting for the right person at the right time to access the information database. At that point, the hunt would begin.

As the final pages were formatted and stored away, the green light remained on, bathing the grey room in emerald green light. The time was near.

Chapter Six

It took two days for my knees to recover enough before I could go for my morning jog around the grounds of my family's land. Pulling on my running shoes, I headed downstairs and grabbed a power bar and a glass of water. After downing both, I looked out of the window before heading out of the door and starting to jog at a slow pace.

As the distance from home grew, so did the pace, just enough to make it worthwhile physically. I waved at a farmer who was ploughing up a recently harvested field. The farm workers always gave me funny looks whenever they saw me running. It was either because of the rumours around town that I was a crazed scientist, or the fact that I was running. Don't worry, I am a Lycra-free zone.

Sweat began to run in rivulets down my face and body as the warm summer sun pummelled me as hard as my feet hitting the New England ground. As I ran, all my adventures flittered through my mind. There were smiles, laughs and, unfortunately, tears.

As tiredness started to creep in, forcing me to turn home sooner than I had planned, I suddenly realised I was missing my family. Mum, Dad and all those that I had pulled away from as I struggled with the issues following my fall from the tractor on that fateful day. Doctors insisted that there wasn't any physical damage – though, from the day that I had hit the ground, my thoughts increased in speed and never once did I seem to have an idle mind. The only way to find peace was through books and films, in an attempt to keep my mind entertained and, therefore, at rest.

Thinking back to that day when I witnessed the launch of the Saturn V rocket, when I held that young couple's baby, I experienced a loneliness in my life that I had never felt before. I missed my parents, but what I was starting to yearn was a family to call my own. On the steps of my home, I sat and watched the birds flutter around the sky and I knew what I wanted and needed to do – though there was no need to hurry, as good things come to those who wait.

My mind rallied as I showered and dressed for the day and headed to a breakfast of fresh berries and bran. The rest of my day was spent running errands in town and picking up a freshly baked loaf of bread, which would be nice with dinner later that night. Then it was home again to start going through all the photos and videos from my Egypt adventure. I would be careful to throw away only those that showed nothing but sand, or my panicked face as I leapt like a salmon to grab the drone from mid-air.

It made me chuckle a little when I took the arrow that had lodged into my rucksack to have it mounted into a display case. The man in the shop thought I was crazy spending good money to put a newly made arrow in a case. And, yes, I could see his point. Even though it was thousands of years old, technically it could've been made only yesterday. In the end, he agreed because, after all, money is money.

The pictures of the Sphinx in all its glory looked amazing, displaying its freshly painted stonework. If only I could show someone, like my nephew and his wife, Tabby! But could I trust them not to tell? Some of the writings from Lancaster's journeys warned that you can't change things in time and, if you do decide to do such things, prepare for the chase and to leave your life behind. He never went into any depth about that. Was it a temporal governing body? Or the men in black?

Later that evening, when I was sitting at the dining table eating soup and fresh bread, I began looking through the family photo album. I gazed at my mother when she was a farm girl, all dirty and holding a piglet, and my dad on his tractor. Then, I looked at several other images of him and his Marine buddies before heading into battle in the city of Hue in 1968. The Tet offensive cost many lives and Dad lost a lot of his friends as they fought, street by street, against the North Vietnamese army, along with the Vietcong. As kids, we even heard him cry out some nights as he suffered from vivid nightmares.

Then I looked at pictures of my parents on their wedding day and all of us on our holidays. The latter ones always made me sad – the divide between my brother and I was always there, and it was clear in the photos.

The next morning, I managed to run a bit further without even a hint of pain in my knees, of which I was grateful. So, after a shower and breakfast, I packed a small overnight bag and put on clean jeans, some new boots, a plaid shirt and a leather jacket on top to finish off the look. With the details typed into the computer for my next foray back in time, I paused for a moment to think about what I was doing. It would be hard, but I needed to say goodbye. And so, with a flash of light, I disappeared, back to the summer of 2018.

I landed in the middle of a cornfield at noon. I could tell from the look of the crop that it had at least another month of growing before it was time for harvesting. I swung the bag onto my back and headed off towards a group of outbuildings and a single-storey house.

As I got closer, a big green tractor appeared as it pulled out from one of the outbuildings. Even from where I was standing, I could see it was my older brother Jacob driving it. It looked like he was off to plough a field. He looked just like my father – tall, broad, with sandy blond hair. I picked this particular day to go and visit my family because it was a week before my parents would take up the offer from a neighbour of a free flight down to Miami. They would never make it, as the small single-engine plane would crash into a forest when the engine cut out.

Jacob saw me walking up the road and waved. I knew he would be surprised to see me as we hadn't talked for over a year now, and our family didn't even work this farm anymore. However, I remember Jacob saying, after the accident, that the farmers had in the past needed a hand, so he and my parents had always helped them out. That was the last time they had been together as a family before Mum and Dad died.

I could see worry on Jacob's face as I got closer. I could tell he was already thinking about how to act with me. After all, we were men from New England and farmers to boot. I was the same height, yet slimmer with a runner's physique, and my mother's black hair.

'Hey, Jake! I heard you were down here,' I called out. Then, when I got to him, I pulled him into a hug. He stiffened slightly, but soon his muscles relaxed.

'Hey, Doc, it's been too long,' he said with a slight tremor in his voice, no doubt worrying about upsetting me and watching me run off in a temper, which I was once prone to do. However, I was so happy to see him again.

'It's good to see you, Jake,' I said.

'C'mon, you're in luck, Mum and Dad are here, too,' he announced, releasing me from the hug and slapping the new covering of dust that he had given my clothes.

We walked down the dusty track towards the farm.

'So, what are you all doing here? Thought you'd be relaxing and enjoying your early retirement?' I said with mirth and saw a smile creep across Jake's face.

He barked out a laugh. 'You know how it is. I'm busier now than I have ever been. If it isn't Alison asking me to do things around the house, or Adam needing a hand at the store…' Jacob explained, loving the fact that he was still needed. 'Then Frank Kingston called, saying he got let down by some contract workers, so we jumped at the chance to help out. It feels good to work on the old homestead again.'

'I bet Dad is loving it and Mum is hating it,' I said happily as I saw my parents and Alison, my sister-in-law, in the distance. The heat made their outlines shimmer and I knew this would be a hard, but fun, day. I waved at them. Mum, even though she was in her late sixties, started to walk quickly towards us. Her wrinkled face broke into a grin and she threw herself into my arms. My breath hitched as we reconnected after five years since my last visit.

Mum pulled away, placed her hands on my cheeks and looked at me. Her eyes matched mine in colour but were now shiny with moisture. She looked directly into my eyes, making sure her wayward child was okay.

'Oh, Brian, what a wonderful surprise!' she gushed and looked me up and down. 'You are looking so well.' She looked at my brother. 'Doesn't he, Jake?'

'Sure does, must be all that healthy living and running he does, Ma,' Jacob chuckled and once again slapped me on the back. 'I'll leave you with the folks, Doc. I'd better get to it.' With that, he trotted off back to the tractor.

We carried on our walk, with Mum hanging on to my arm.

'I've missed you, Mum. How have you been?' I asked, knowing I hadn't kept in touch with them for a good month or two as I was struggling with dark thoughts.

Her grip on my arm became tighter. 'We are good, thank you, dear,' she replied. 'We worried about you, of course, but that will never change.' She gave a weak laugh. 'Are you okay? Any nice woman in your life?'

'Aww, shucks, Ma! Not yet,' I said and pulled her into an even bigger embrace than the first. 'You're the most important woman in my life, you know that,' I continued, making her giggle like mad.

'Silly boy,' she chuckled and pulled me along. Mum's state of dress was much like the farm girls all over the country – jeans and a plaid shirt, with her grey hair covered up in a blue scarf. 'You need a good woman, Brian. And a family, dear.'

I sighed as she went on with her normal diatribe and we continued walking up to my father. He finally put his glasses on so he could see me better.

'Hi, Pops! You're looking well,' I said.

He nodded at me. 'How do, son. Long-time no see,' he replied in gruff tones, but that was just Dad being Dad. 'You here long?'

'A couple of days, Dad,' I said. 'I can stay here or in a hotel if you want?' I knew that my mother wouldn't let me out of her sight, and even as I said that Dad started to shake his head.

'Now, son, you will bed down with us while you're in town,' he said. 'Your mother has missed you.' He looked over at another waiting tractor. 'Got to get on,' he said and slapped me on the shoulder, which felt like being hit with an iron bar.

Mum kissed me on the cheek. 'He's glad to see you, dear, you know how he is,' she said.

I hugged Alison, my brother's wife, who had just joined us. 'He's a grumpy old git, and his son is just as bad,' Alison chuckled.

My father used to be a bundle of fun before the war, but then the pressure of the world and family commitments had made him a quieter man. However, his old self would return whenever he met up with one of his few remaining war buddies.

Alison slapped me on the chest. 'And you aren't that much better, running away and doing who knows what,' she said and gave me a pointed look, though there was mischief in her eyes. 'When are you coming back home, Doc?'

I shrugged. 'I'm thinking about next year,' I replied. 'Maybe this place, if no one is using it?' I watched the joy spreading over my mother's face. 'If that's okay, that is?'

Both women tried to hug me at once. Clearly, the news had the desired effect.

'That would be wonderful,' said Mum. 'Your father was worrying about it going to rack and ruin, as the Kingstons just want to rent the land.'

'I'll have a word with Jacob when he comes back in,' said Alison. 'It'll be nice to have the family back together again. They don't say it, but they truly do miss you, Doc.' I just nodded. I then went back to the house with them both and helped to prepare some lunch for the family.

My immediate issue was that I did not know how to stop Mum and Dad from taking that accursed flight next week. I couldn't believe that any kind of paradox or problems would come about as a result of them surviving.

The day was getting on and we were all sitting on the grass, enjoying the summer sun. Jacob was over the moon about me moving back, mainly because it gave our parents such joy. Though if we were stuck in a room together, things would be very different between us. Dad was just sitting quietly as he ate his overflowing sandwich and gazed at the scenery.

'So, any plans on holidays?' I asked the group. My brother shook his head and Alison pouted.

'Cheapskate!' she said with a frown.

Mum leant over, took my hand and beamed with childish glee. 'Finally, after all these years, I have managed to get your father to take me on vacation,' she announced with a giggle, making my old man groan and roll his eyes. 'We are off to Miami,' she finished and clapped her hands together rapidly.

My heart turned to ice as I knew how their future would plan out. 'Wow, really Dad? You're leaving home? Have you told the police?' I asked earnestly, before laughing and dodging a half-eaten bread roll that was sent my way, though it did make my family chuckle their heads off at our interplay. This hadn't happened for years; it even brought a rare smile to my father's face. 'How are you getting there?' I asked. 'Plane, train or automobile?'

'Plane,' Mum said.

'Car,' Dad said grumpily. 'Flew enough in the war!'

For the next few minutes, the family discussed the right way to go to retirement heaven, which apparently was Miami.

'Why don't you rent an RV and drive down?' I suggested. 'There is no hurry, so enjoy yourself and see America.' Those words struck a chord with my aging parents as they stared at each other, having a silent conversation as they had always done. It was weird when they seemed to know exactly what the other one was thinking.

Soon, Alison broke the silence. 'So, husband of mind, Brian is looking to come back to the heart of the family,' she announced, making my brother and father both snap their heads towards me. 'He could move in here and take care of the place, save it from falling down.'

'That's true, Brian? You wanting to come back?' Dad asked in his typical gruff tones, though his eyes showed hope. I nodded and he tried to grin. 'What would you do for work? There isn't much around here.' He waved his calloused hand around the place.

I took a sip of cold lemonade. 'I have made enough money from my wanderings and buying and selling. Plus, I can always work from here on the computer,' I explained, and that's when I lost my parents. Their eyes glazed over, but I would let my brother explain further to them some other time.

Jacob grinned, but much like my father he was a man of few words, so he just nodded. Then he looked at his wife and gave her a wink.

'So that's settled, then,' Alison said and looked around. 'We shall take care of the household bills.' When I tried to refuse, I was shut down by the two women of the family. 'You can pay for food, TV and internet,' added Alison, 'and we shall pick up the rest. And that's final!' The tones she used left nothing left to be said. Sometimes, you just can't argue with family.

Jacob and my father stood up and stretched their backs, almost mirroring each other.

'Right, back to it,' Jacob said and gave his wife a kiss, while my dad just squeezed my mum's shoulder, which said a thousand words in their relationship. What surprised me was that he also did the same to me, before striding off to the tractor.

My brother shook his head and bounced his balled-up fist off the same shoulder that had felt my father's warming grasp.

'Wow, Doc, that was almost an emotional outpouring from the old man!' he joked and, with another bump of his fist, he followed in my dad's wake to continue their day's labour.

Mum pulled me up from the grass and linked arms with me.

'Come on, son, take your old mum for a walk,' she said in tones that were meant to be obeyed. Alison gave us a wave as she tidied up the remnants of lunch. Clearly, this had been planned between the women, though aren't most things. Men are just puppets in the game of life.

We strode in silence on the sun-dried ground, looking around to watch the two tractors in action. It was Mum who spoke first.

'Thank you for coming home. We miss you so much.'

'It's okay, I'm sorry it took so long,' I answered, and saw concern flash across my mother's weathered face. 'Nothing is wrong, and I'm not in any trouble,' I added, knowing how parents' minds work, and that they are generally right to presume such things.

She laughed. 'I would never think such a thing of my baby boy,' she cooed and placed a kiss on my cheek, trying to cover up the fact that she spoke with a forked tongue, as the native Americans used to say. 'It'll be nice to have the family back together again. Adam missed you. Tabatha won't put up with his comic books – he needs a place to hide them, I think.'

We laughed together. Adam's wife was fun and easy to get on with, but science fiction or fantasy was not her thing. Being an engineer, her mind was like that of a computer.

'I miss them both, too,' I replied. 'How's his brother, Jeff? Still doing the whole contract farming work?' I asked, even though I knew the answers. Jeff was like me and preferred to wander, though he didn't have the mild bouts of depression I was sometimes prone to. Whilst my travelling adventures did seem to help, over thinking had become more of a problem.

'Oh, he phones me and his mum regularly,' Mum replied, giving me a little dig about the lack of contact between us all in the past. But this was the now and I was enjoying the time I had with my family. I hoped that my parents would survive their trip to Miami by taking on my idea about the road trip.

We shared a bottle of water that I had brought with me. Conversation started and stopped at regular intervals, though the silence was never strained, and soon enough we arrived back at the place where I would make my home.

'So, you'll stay with us tonight, and your father will fire up the grill,' said Mum. 'I bought some nice thick steaks the other day. Oh, here they are now' She indicated to the tractors that my brother and my father were masters of, returning after the day's tasks.

Mum pulled me over to their battered old Jeep that they used on a daily basis around the farm. Most people would say it was a pile of junk, though Mum and Dad claimed it had character. However, sitting in the back, as I soon would be, I knew which way my choice of descriptive words would swing.

'JACOB! WE'RE DOING COOKOUT. ARE YOU COMING?' Mum called out, making my father wince. I wasn't sure if it was the noise or the realisation that he had more work to do tonight.

'WE'LL BE THERE, I'LL SEE IF ADAM AND TABBY ARE ABOUT!' Alison called back as they got in my brother's newer and cleaner 4x4. We followed them down the old farm track until we hit the tarmac main road and headed towards town.

Mum turned around to look at me. 'How did you find us, dear? I don't see a car.' Mother was always a quick one. My eyes flicked to the rear-view mirror and saw my dad's twinkly eyes looking back. He always liked it when Mum questioned somebody else.

Ha, the life of a time traveller. I had time to prepare plans and backstories, though right now I was just having the best time of my life, and long may it continue.

'I came on the train from Boston,' I replied, 'and thought I would just have a walk around the old place before coming to see you and Pops.' I saw my dad wink back. 'Just a bit of luck, really,' I added. 'Never knew Dad left the cabin!' I saw the mirth disappear from the old man.

Mum giggled at the light-hearted digs her loving husband was receiving from her kids. Our journey continued with my mother wittering on about friends around the area who were alive or had passed on. I just hoped that they took my idea of driving down to Miami seriously, and that fate wouldn't chase them down the interstate.

We pulled into their little homestead – well, that's what they called it. To me, it looked like one of the old ranch homes from the TV series 'Bonanza'. It was surrounded by woodland, though between the cabin and the woods there were about three acres of grass. So Dad, it seemed, had given up farming to be a full-time gardener.

'Hell, Dad, do you ever finish cutting the grass?' I asked, as the engine was finally turned off and started to ping as the metal began to cool down.

He barked a laugh. 'Son, you have no idea. It's like those men who paint the Golden Gate Bridge – once they finish, it's time for them to start again!' That was a long chat for him. 'It never ends.'

Mom slapped his bare forearm. That was another thing with Dad, his sleeves were always rolled up and his shirt always had three buttons undone that showed off his chest.

'That's why I have so many photos of your father, Brian,' said Mum. 'Otherwise, I wouldn't recognise him when he final finishes in the garden.' She had a playful lilt to her voice. She then stepped out of the vehicle, followed by my pops.

With my bag in hand, I followed them into the house. From outside, it looked like an old bunkhouse, but inside it looked like any other home. It was clean and tidy, just the way my parents always liked it – Mum, for being raised like that, and Dad all thanks to the Marine corps.

They showed me where I would be sleeping and the bathroom, which was down the hall. Then Dad went out to fire up the grill, while Mum took me by the hand and showed me around.

'This looks great, Mum,' I said. 'So quiet.' We then watched Dad swearing at the grill that didn't want to light.

'You wait until the morning, dear,' said Mum and she looked up at me. 'The animals are early risers, just like your father.' She smiled. 'If you still run, why don't you join your father. He jogs slowly around the boundary, it would be nice for you to meet up with him tomorrow. Please, he would like it.' Her look intensified.

'Sure, Mom, no problem,' I answered her request and kissed her on the side of her head, before she walked off to the kitchen.

While my mother prepared salads and other dishes for our enjoyment, I found my way to the wall of photos. There were more on display than the last time I had visited. All the families were together, though obviously I wasn't in them. This was something to this day I will always regret. I allowed my insecurities to run riot in my mind.

I lingered on a set of black-and-white photos intermingled with some old, coloured ones. They were from the Vietnam war. I gazed at the photos of my father and his squad, lounging about in the country smoking with their M16s at rest. Some photos were more up to date, which showed some of the same men but looking older and a lot worse for wear. One photo showed a date and a place – 'HUE, 1968'. The floorboard creaked behind me. My dad was standing by my shoulder.

'Oh, hi, Dad,' I said and pointed at the war photos. 'Haven't seen those before.'

He sighed. Dad never spoke much about his time in 'country', as he called it. 'Well, you know I had nightmares, it's no secret,' he stated sadly, to which I nodded. 'I spoke to a guy who had a bad time in Afghanistan. He had his problems, and he warned me that hiding the past and refusing to talk about it just causes more issues.' He looked at some of his long-lost comrades.

'When I told your mum, she did all this. You know what's she like when she has a cause.'

'Don't I just,' I said and laughed lightly.

Dad tapped one of the early photos of his squad. 'That was our first patrol in country, so scared and not a dammed clue what we were doing,' he explained, and I knew better than to interrupt him in mid-flow. As I said, he didn't talk much. 'We lost Mikey three days later to a mine…' I saw the man himself in a picture Dad pointed at, tall and skinny wearing thick-framed glasses.

'We were lucky the rest of the time,' he continued. 'Other squads got hit, but ours were always the lucky ones, until the Tet Offensive when we were sent into the city of Hue.' Dad pointed to the later photos. 'It was hell on Earth, never knew who VC or innocents were. They sent us in with tanks, which worked for a bit down the streets…' He stilled for a moment. 'That's when the nips realised, they could use the tanks to ricochet their bullets at us. We lost Douglas, Adams and Stevie in one day.'

I turned and saw his eyes were glistening. 'Was that where you were hit, Dad?'

He nodded. 'The very next day. I was lucky, really. The RPG hit the tank. Me and one other was hit by the fragments. I was taller than Jonesy, so I got it in the upper chest. He wasn't so lucky.' He pointed to a short, but strongly built, African American man holding an M60 machine gun. 'In the end, there were only three of us originals left. Now I'm the only one.' He bumped his fist off my shoulder before heading to the kitchen, where Mum waited with two cold beers and a warm smile on her face. We shared a look that I had never noticed before, a look of gratitude.

When I spoke to Mum later about it, she said Dad had talked to the others about some of the things that went on, but he really wanted to tell me more. That's what he had now done and he seemed to relax around me a little. Soon, my brother and his wife arrived and apologised that Adam and Tabby couldn't be there. They were heading out of town for a dinner party but would meet up with me when I moved back home.

The night went on in good style. Many a bridge was built that evening and I had never remembered my parents laugh so much. My mum especially laughed the hardest when Alison, in her wine-induced state, tried to feed what she thought was a squirrel. It was left to my dad to tell her it was a rat from the wood pile and Jacob ended up with the last of the potato salad on his head. Sleep came easy that night and the next day I would bring up the RV idea again.

'Jesus,' I muttered, as Dad and I jogged around, and saw him smiling to himself on the dew-covered grass. 'You're enjoying this, aren't you, Dad?'

He didn't answer for a few more steps. 'Oh yes, son. I learnt many years ago in the corps, never overindulge food or drink. Our drill sergeants pulled that on us one too many times for it not to stick in my mind. Five-mile runs with a full belly and bladder… No thank you, son!' We then made our way back to the cabin. 'When are you heading back, son?'

'In the morning,' I replied. 'The sooner I get back, the quicker I can move down here.' I saw his mouth crease up into a smile. 'Hopefully, I'll be here when you get back from Miami.' Finally, we stopped in front of the kitchen door. 'You going to rent the RV then, Pops?'

Dad put his hands on his hips and drew in a deep breath. 'Sounds like a good idea, kid. Better than sitting on one of those planes.' He opened the kitchen door and we were encompassed in the smell of bacon, eggs and coffee. 'Now, just to sell it to your mother.'

I slapped him on the back playfully. 'I'll work on her, Pops, don't you worry,' I said and followed him in, making sure to stop the conversation so that Mother's radar-like hearing wouldn't pick it up.

And try I did. Dad went back and continued to work with Jacob on our old homestead to help the leaseholder, while I worked with Mum around home, cleaning and preparing some more food for that evening's get together with Jacob and Alison.

As it happened, it was one big happy family, which meant the camera came out, producing more photos for Mum to add to her wall of pictures. At the end of the night, I embraced my brother and his wife and told them I would be back soon. They promised to clean up the old family home ready for my return. The plus point was Mum agreeing to travel to Miami by road. That lightened my heart, knowing that, finally, I had managed to do some good with my time travelling.

The next morning after a run and breakfast, Mum and Dad took me to the train station in town, where I purchased a ticket to Boston. Really, however, I would just hide in the toilets and head home from there. I gave Dad a big hug, which, for once, he returned. Mum received the same and then I just took in her loving face. Though I did respect my dad greatly, it was always Mum's loss that hurt me the most. Our eyes locked and we just smiled at each other while holding hands, though all to soon Mum and Dad were gone. I waved as they disappeared into the distance.

'Love you, Mum and Dad!' I called out and headed off to the restroom to head home again.

Chapter Seven

My vision was alive with the blinding white light from the journey home. I schooled my breathing and excitement at what I had just attempted to do – save my parents. Stepping from the pod onto the carpet cellar floor, I cast away my bag and instantly started the shutdown on the time machine, following the correct steps so that nothing was lost or corrupted, as computers were prone to do.

As the hum of the machine slowly died away, I collected my bag and headed upstairs, turning off the light as I went. I made time to drop all my dirty clothes in the laundry basket before placing all my clean clothes back in the drawers and wardrobe where they came from.

With tort nerves and a clean shirt on, I locked up the farmhouse. I didn't want some farm worker playing with my toys or somehow transporting himself to medieval England and calling the king a poof for wearing fancy clothes, though that had played across my mind from time to time. Then I got into the truck and fired it up. The thrum of the engine reverberated in my ears and the sound of the tyres hitting the join in the tarmac almost matched my heartbeat. My thoughts were racing. Had it worked? Had I managed to convince my parents to drive and survive their trip? After my parents had died, my brother sold the cabin to a family called the Johnsons, a husband and wife with three little children. I needed to know if my parents had survived.

'Please, please be there…' I begged as I turned into their long driveway.

'NOOOOOOOOOO!!' I screamed, as I locked up the truck's brakes and slid sideward down the road, in a mist of dust and stones. Tears filled my eyes, blurring my vision. My head pressed against the hard plastic of the steering wheel, my eyes blinking the tears away. The Johnson family were all outside the cabin. Nothing had changed. Luckily, I was far enough away that they couldn't see me clearly, especially the state I was in.

Taking a deep breath, I slowly turned the truck around. I gave them a friendly wave out of the window, which the husband mirrored, but slower. After my parents' deaths, Al Johnson had allowed me several times to wander around the property, so hopefully he knew I was just having a bad day.

The journey back home went in a flash and, before I realised it, the truck had arrived in front of my home. Shutting off the engine, I headed inside to take a shower to wash away the grit and sadness that had eclipsed me.

After a bite of lunch, I sat in the living room of my old family home, tears setting up permanent residence on my face, especially seeing all the pictures of my parents that looked down at me from the lounge wall. It was obvious that they had been a happy couple, though Mum did confide with me that Dad struggled after he came back from the war. That made me scour the war photos of the men who fought in the Vietnam war, a war that nobody wanted. These men were sometimes hated by the folks back home because they fought, even though they were forced to enlist.

As my attempt to save my parents had failed, I decided not to try again. They had lived good lives and they had family, including grandkids. But maybe there was something I could do that would change things for a lot of people. I couldn't stop the war from happening – America's involvement had started in the 1950s, be it political or financial. There wouldn't be a thing that I could do to change that. But, after Kennedy was shot, the new president, Lyndon B. Johnson, increased the number of troops in Vietnam and escalated the war, even more than JFK, and then came Dodgy Nixon. All throughout my childhood, people discussed what would've happened had the assassination never happened. Would JFK have increased the troops to the levels that LBJ had? Some say yes, as he had hated communism that much, especially with the failed Bay of Pigs episode. Others said that he wouldn't, and that was why JFK was killed.

My brain reeled as years of our country's history flew through my mind along with the consequences of what I was about to plan – though, at the moment, it was just an idea in my head as I sat in solitude on the sofa. A small smile appeared on my face; I could go back in time and stop one of the darkest moments in our history. If this worked, maybe I could save other people? Malcom X, Pearl Harbour? Yes, I know the writings of George Lancaster warned me about doing such a thing, but you had to try… didn't you?

There was no point going to bed yet. The grief of the day had been quashed under the force of excitement and hope that my next trip would be for the betterment of mankind, or at least for America. Yes, it was a risk, but a risk worth taking.

There were so many different accounts of the day in question. Was JFK's assassin a lone gunman? The one and only Lee Harvey Oswald, firing from his vantage point at the Texas School Book Depository? Or were there multiple shooters, and Oswald was just a pawn in a much bigger plot? Whilst each theory had merit and some proof, I wished I could go back in time and see which one was the true story. But that would mean I couldn't return to the same day to alter the outcome.

There were two ways to stop the assassination. The first would be to stop the shooter, or shooters, which meant I would have to become Jason Bourne and run up the flight of stairs and take out Oswald. Then, using the sniper's rifle that they said he used, despatch the other shooters, wherever they may be.

Or, in the second method, I would redirect the motorcade to take a different route and stop the President's car from heading down Elm Street and away from Oswald and the grassy knoll. Maybe I could create a diversion to force them to go down Main Street – which supposedly was the original route but was changed for some reason. However, it is said there was no paperwork to prove that it was ever changed.

The next morning, I ran around the fields as plans were made and then dismissed in my head. One great idea I came up with was to walk into the road and force the motorcade to stop. That was a real gem. How long would it be until the police or Secret Service dragged me away? And, if they took away my emergency getaway remote I would have serious problems. The next idea was even worse… walk into the road and fire blanks at the motorcade. We all know how that would end up... it's Texas, for heaven's sake.

The warm shower washed away the sweat after my run, and then it hit. I had thought of a way to redirect the traffic without killing myself. The towel did its job, then the search was on to find my polyester clothes that I had worn to watch the rocket launch.

Within the hour, I found myself standing by the grassy knoll after appearing in a carpark a few blocks away, at 6 am on 20th November 1963, two days before the assassination. Even though it was Texas, there was still a chill in the air. Well, how could I have known, since I had never been there before?

The area was so quiet as I walked slowly up Elm Street. The roads were wide, so even if I could steal a large truck and trailer and block the whole street to force the cavalcade down Main Street, I wouldn't get away in time. Plus, I couldn't drive the big rigs. My only worry was hurting bystanders – that would be something that would haunt me till my dying days.

My shoes echoed on the concrete sidewalk as I walked around, searching for crucial locations that were familiar from the history books and films. I looked up at the book depository, remembering the documentaries I had seen, where police and FBI had surmised how Oswald would have pointed his rifle out of the window. They had argued whether Oswald could successfully have used such a clunky rifle so well and accurately. The final lethal shot was supposedly able to go through tree branches – which, at that time, were still covered in leaves. Even today's law enforcements can't agree whether he could or could not have made those shots.

I made my way up Elm Street and, once more, studied the junction I intended to block, before carrying on my journey deep into the city, looking for anything that could help me with my plan. I stopped at a diner close by, where it was all abuzz with excitement about the President's visit. Sitting by the window so I could view the city streets, I caught the attention of a mid-forties waitress who walked up to me with a tired look upon her face.

'Hi, sweety. Coffee?' she asked in a typical Texas drawl, her name badge informing me of her name.

'Thanks, I think I will, Jennie,' I answered and watched her pour the hot and potent beverage into a white cup. 'Are you looking forward to tomorrow?'

'Sure thing, honey,' she replied. 'I'm working, but the boss says we can see him as they go past.' Her eyes suddenly sparked with life as she spoke. 'You ready to order, honey? Or do you need a minute?' She smiled, showing off tobacco-stained teeth.

I looked at the menu. 'Blueberry pancake, with a side of bacon, please,' I said and watched the poor woman walk away. Not a healthy breakfast, but it would do as I'm on their time. I watched people walking past outside. Life seemed to go at a lot slower pace than at home in the cities.

The diner was busy, but the food came quickly. It turned out to be nice, though it might take a few runs to burn off the carbs. After the meal, I waved goodbye to Jennie and left the bill and a larger than normal tip on the table, then headed back onto the streets of Texas with a plan forming in my mind.

After a while, I headed down into an underground parking garage and made sure I was out of sight, then pressed the emergency home button and waited. It did seem that the closer I was to my own year, the quicker it worked, hence the reason why it took so long with the bloody dinosaurs.

When I eventually arrived home, I shut everything down and made my way to the bathroom to shower and change. I felt a bit stuffed with the pancakes weighing me down, but I wouldn't run till the morning, just in case the added weight shattered my ankles or I barfed up all the good food.

Afterwards, I took the laptop outside with a cold beer and made some purchases that the mainstream online seller just didn't have – not that they were illegal, but for what I was going to use them for it was a grey area. Once that was done, I watched birds swooping down catching bugs in the air, while I sipped the cold beer.

That night, sleep did not come easily. The shooting of JFK ran through my mind repeatedly and, no matter what I tried to do, the President still died. Was my subconscious telling me not to try changing the past and let sleeping dogs lie? I had changed the outcome of the *Titanic* tragedy so that nothing but good could come from that act; and, if this also worked, it would lessen the blow for thousands of people… hopefully.

The next day's run was a hard one. The sweat poured off me and maybe even the blueberries as well. I had stopped planning, as I was waiting for my purchases to arrive – a new set of clothes and matching sunglasses for the trip to Texas. I would hate to have my picture captured, as that would cause a lot of problems, especially if they managed to track me down in the future. 'Excuse me, sir, but is this your time machine?!'

Finally, everything was ready. I stood in front of the mirror as the idea of cancelling the whole thing crossed my mind. What would happen if the changes I was planning on making went wrong and I made the future even worse? I shook the negative thoughts away and took in my disguise – black slacks and a Dallas patrolman blue shirt with the silver and blue police badge. I also slipped on the common light brown overcoat to conceal the uniform.

Heading downstairs, I decided on leaving the hat behind. I could take one from my unwilling helper, along with his belt and gun – though, the latter would never be used unless it was to save my own life. With my heart pounding, I typed in the coordinates, the date and time for my arrival, along with a return time of seven hours later. I would be arriving at 6 am and I would be back home at 1 pm their time.

With my 60s sunglasses in place, I watched the counter, and with a flash, I found myself in the same underground garage as the last trip. With a briefcase in hand, I headed out into the Texas early morning air. The streets were already buzzing with excitement, and families were lining the route ready for JFK and the first lady.

I headed deeper into the city and found a nice shady park that was out of the way of the hubbub. I took a seat on a bench and watched as dog owners walked their pets. Strangely, there weren't many runners around. Perhaps they used other parks closer to the residential areas?

Time was moving slowly, and my nerves were stretched. So, to keep myself focused, I went through in my mind the plan I had devised, and went over the route. That helped for a bit. Of course, the looks that came my way from the early risers were worrying. Did they know I wasn't of this time? Or was this mere paranoia on my part? I moved on through the now awake city.

It was nearly time. Thankfully, with the internet you can find out almost anything, and everything about this day of days was well documented. That was how I found my first target; there, parked on a side road, was a black police car with one single occupant, who seemed to be enjoying a quick snooze before the storm of the day encompassed the city.

My pace slowed as I neared him. The plastic of my weapon felt cold in my hand, despite the sweat that leaked from my pores. The policeman was a blond, rugged-looking man with a crew cut, maybe ex-military and, unfortunately, he had the bluest eyes I had ever seen. That last snippet of information came from the fact that he sensed danger and his eyes sprang open.

'What the hell…!' he shouted as his eyes dropped to my hand. Those eyes widened as I raised the gun. 'Don't be stupid!' he said and tried to get his own gun out from its holster, but it was too late. I pressed the trigger, sending two metal barbs into his chest.

The two connection wires sent a pulse of 50,000 volts into the man's body, making him convulse in a way any break-dancer of the 90s would be proud of. I sent another couple of pulses into the man to make sure he wouldn't put up a fight. Drool dripped from his mouth as I pulled the barbs from him and put the stun gun back into its case.

I leant into the car and took the keys from the ignition, walked to the back of the vehicle and opened the trunk. There was room for me to enact the next part of the plan. Looking around, I was glad that the area was still quiet. This was why I had picked this man, as his report that I had read on the web said he was stationed here when he received news of the shooting, before heading off to hunt down the shooter.

Opening the driver's door, the big man fell out with an audible thud. Patrolman McAdam did not bounce well. I released his gun belt and rolled him over to free it from him. Luckily, it fitted around me. Taking his wrists in my hands, I dragged him to the back of the patrol car; then, sitting him up and coming up behind him, I put my hands under his hot armpits and, joining them together across his chest, I hoisted him up.

'Fuck!' I groaned as the bones in my back nearly fused themselves together. This man was solid muscle. Somehow,

I managed to get his top half in the trunk, though it cost me most of the skin on my knuckles. Taking his tree trunk legs in either hand, I finished the job, and the twitching patrolman lay there in the boot.

'Sorry, man,' I said genuinely and used his handcuffs to secure his wrists together.

I took off my coat and threw it over my shoulder, then picked up my briefcase, opened it up and brought out a small bottle of chloroform and a rag, before stuffing my coat into the soft-sided briefcase. It was a tight fit. I poured the potent fluid onto said rag and pressed it to the man's face, making sure it covered his mouth and nose. It stayed there until his breathing changed and his body relaxed, although a slight tremor still shot through his slumbering form.

I closed the trunk with a loud thud and walked back to the driver's door, putting the briefcase on the passenger seat. I placed the man's hat onto the floor, and then started to repack the briefcase, leaving the emergency home remote on top. I was hoping that no one would come my way and the gods of time must have been with me, as it seemed that the whole of Dallas had turned out to watch the motorcade go through the city.

Judging by my watch, I had thirty minutes to stop the assassination, so I started up the police issue Ford Galaxie cruiser. The engine sounded rough, but it was oozing power. As I slipped it into drive and moved away slowly through Hord Street, the radio crackled to life, startling me somewhat. I didn't know if they were calling for this car or others, but crunch time was nearly here.

After pulling onto N. Houston Street, I stopped the vehicle. The engine idled, which added to the heat in the car. People walked past, trying to find a good viewing point along Elm Street or on the grass at Dealey Plaza. I checked the time again. Fifteen minutes to go. The plan was to drive onto Elm Street with sirens blazing, which would either force the motorcade down Main Street, which would make the shot a lot harder, or down Commerce Road, which would take them out of range. Otherwise, the President's motorcade would take the right-hand road which was closest to the Texas School Book Depository.

That's the one thing that always struck me as strange when I studied this event at school. The easiest route was to travel down Main Street all the way to where it split Dealey Plaza and then proceed straight onto Commerce Street; but, for some reason, the motorcade turned right and then left again onto Elm Street. It just didn't make sense, unless you had shooters in place and you wanted JFK dead. My plan would force them away from the crucial location.

The radio squawked again. Just five minutes to go. Clearly, despatch was keeping up to date with the President's movements. My hands gripped the steering wheel and I put the vehicle into gear. The windows were open and I could hear the sound of cheering getting louder and closer. I drew my sleeve across my sweaty forehead, then I put the flashing lights on and pressed the accelerator pedal gently. POP.

'WHAT THE HELL!' I screamed as a small hole punched itself through the windscreen, the cracks in the glass spider webbing away from the hole. A thud came from behind me as whatever had hit the car hit the back seat. POP! Another hole and my body screamed in pain as something hit the top of my shoulder, my shirt quickly beginning to soak up the blood.

Though in pain, I scanned the crowds, checking whether anyone had noticed the gunshots. There had been no sounds from the gunfire. I moved the gear selector into reverse and floored it as another hole appeared where my head once was. The side rear window shattered. I slammed the brakes on and instantly went into drive. As I pressed the accelerator, gunshot holes began to appear in the hood, sending paint flecks flying up into the air. Steam began to escape from the dying engine.

It was then that I saw two men in dark suits wearing shades, much like mine. They were crouching behind a car, firing what looked to be silenced automatic pistols at me. That's when the real gunfire started. I knew then it was time for me to get out. Both men turned sharply towards the plaza. I used up whatever life my car had left and floored it back the way I had come, only minutes before, and into inner Dallas.

A couple of blocks later, the vehicle died. Grabbing my briefcase, I opened it quickly and pressed the return home button before jumping out of the car. The two men turned the corner and shouted; then, even before their voices reached me, their guns were raised and the noise of bullets zipped past me. My eyes flicked to the trunk of the car where I had deposited the police officer. The keys were in my hand, so I quickly ran to the trunk and tried to open it with my sweat and now blood-slicked hands.

The two men were running towards me, but no longer shooting. This allowed me the time to open the trunk up before escaping up another side street. Once again, I did this just in time, as another police car screeched to a stop alongside the vehicle I had just left. The men shouted, but there was no gunfire. I turned again down another back street, panting for breath. I stopped long enough to see the police swarming over the steaming wreck of their comrade's car. At least he was safe.

My vision was blurry, and I was becoming dizzy. Looking down at my arm, I realised it was still dripping blood from the wound on my shoulder, though the pain was manageable. The area I had stopped to rest in was quiet and so I took the opportunity to gather my thoughts. I was stunned. Who were those men who had shot at me? I slumped against a wall as another wave of dizziness hit me.

There was an alleyway across the way. I stumbled into the rubbish-strewn alley and saw an overturned trashcan, on which I sat down in order to get some respite. My body sagged as all the strength left me, my head dropping to my chest. My vision began to darken into nothingness.

Pain. It pulsed through me, closely followed by a terrible thirst. I tried to open my eyes, but they were resistant.

'Shit…' I groaned as I tried to move. There was a closeness to the place, of stale air. I heard a low crackle. A singular eyelid opened and all I could see was carpet, and it was of a familiar colour. Then I discerned the slight, electrical hum in the air. *Home.*

It took a full five minutes before I could open the neighbouring eye. I guessed I had toppled out of the tube face first… again. Any attempt to move caused the pain to fire up in my shoulder, making me wince, though I continued to rock myself from whatever was restraining me to the floor. It hurt like hell, but I finally managed to roll onto my back, using my good shoulder to lever myself over.

'Oww!' I looked down at my hand and realised it was covered in a mixture of dark blood and carpet fibres.

Slowly but surely, I managed to get myself sitting upright. Looking around, I could see that the computer was in standby mode, but the power was still flowing. I sighed at the thought of the next electricity bill. I was glad that I had taken on paying that bill from my brother, otherwise questions would be asked.

Using my good arm, I managed to get onto my knees and then, with the aid of a helpful nearby desk, I slowly got to my feet, albeit shakily. Using one hand, I shut down the computer. It was a miracle that I had managed to keep hold of my briefcase, with the remote in it, otherwise I wouldn't have made it back. The marksmen would have caught up with me in the alley, while the remote and the briefcase would be sitting in the pod, eventually to be found by my family.

Like a cat burglar from any book or television programme, I crept upstairs and made my way to the main bathroom, where I could finally examine the damage. Button by button, I took off the shirt which was firmly adhered to my arm by my blood. I grimaced as I pulled the blood-soaked material away from the wound. It looked nasty, but there was good news; it was just a deep graze on the top of the shoulder, by the neck. I had been very lucky – a couple of inches closer to my neck and it would have been lights out.

Being a bit of a health nut and a total loner, I always kept a well-stocked first aid kit, including antibiotic tablets and cream. After cleaning the wound and the surrounding area, I added some of the cream, then covered the wound with a sterile dressing, before swallowing some antibiotic tablets to stave off infection. With a waterproof covering over the dressing, I stood in the shower to finally scrub my body clean, which was tricky with only one working hand, but I manged well enough and then went to bed.

Sun streamed into my room, awaking me with a painful groan. My shoulder hurt, but not to the same extent as yesterday. Slowly, I went through my morning ablutions and carefully dressed my shoulder, before dressing myself and making my way downstairs for breakfast. It was a simple mix of oats and berries – boring, but easy to make and eat, especially as I was sporting a sling to protect my shoulder.

With a full belly of breakfast and tablets, I fired up the laptop and investigated the JFK folder that I had created when planning my failed trip into the past. It opened and displayed links to relevant police and other information sources which had helped me in my research. I needed to know – *Who were those two men?*

There was a short note about Patrolman McAdam being beaten, drugged and thrown into the trunk of his car. They thought Oswald might have been the culprit, as the car would be a perfect getaway vehicle. There were witness reports of two men in suits shooting at the police car, who were thought to be Secret Service or FBI, just as I had thought. However, scouring through the files, it was becoming clear that they were not from any branch of law enforcement.

At the time, the police had freed McAdam from the trunk, and had then approached the two gunmen, who had turned and walked back into the crowd and disappeared. Reports had stated that one was a middle-aged Hispanic male of medium height, while his partner in crime was a blond, tall, well-built man.

Nothing had changed after all that mess. JFK was still shot and killed by whomever you dare to choose as the murderer. I closed the computer down and wandered over to the photo of my father and his army friends. I placed my fingers onto the frame and looked at my father's face.

'I'm sorry, Dad,' I whispered. 'I tried everything I could think of.' As my fingers shook and rattled the frame with emotion, tears rolled down my cheeks.

I vowed, then and there, that I would no longer play around with time. I stumbled to the fridge in the kitchen and pulled out an ice-cold beer. What harm could drugs and beer do!

***

Room T07/04/1776
FBI Headquarters
935 Pennsylvania Avenue, NW
Washington, DC

The nondescript room on the ground floor, that normally went unnoticed by most of the employees, suddenly came alive, as all the computers went into overdrive crunching data. Reams of information were filtered through terabytes of historical documents, listed and collated. Suddenly, the third of three green lights flickered for several seconds before staying alight. The computer hard drives froze for a second and then all three lights on each computer changed to red. An emergency light on the wall began to flash.

The main PC was connected to the FBI server and generated a very rare email to the Director of the FBI. Jonathan Walker was a tall, grey-haired man, 52 years of age and only three years into his ten years of service at the Agency.

Jon, as he was known to his friends, through many walks of life, from school to political, had tried never to make an enemy, though that was hard to do in the businesses he had been in. From training and working as a lawyer in New York, to becoming the director of a three-letter agency, it meant that he saw his wife of 21 years less than he wanted.

His two children were in college, leaving his wife Sofia to her charitable work in the local community.

Luckily, today was a light workday, being Friday, so Jonathan just had a few quick catch-up meetings with department heads about ongoing operations. Over the weekend, he was hoping for a whole two days of family time and working through the list of chores his wife would have made for him.

Jon leant back in his leather office chair with a groan and looked out over the City of Washington DC. His family hadn't been all that happy about moving here, but, as he had said to his wife, the FBI doesn't have an office in the Caribbean. The smile that adorned his face at the memory of his pouting wife was wiped away as he heard his office door automatically seal. All the blinds closed – not only on the main window, but also those that closed him off from his PA, Sharon.

He sat up. 'What the hell?' he muttered and picked up the handset on his phone. As he pressed the handset to his ear, he realised that it was dead. Then he saw a notification on the PC alerting him to a priority 1 message. Most things were priority 2 or higher, the latter meant war or something equally as serious.

Jonathan Walker typed in his password to open the email, which was strange in itself. The sender was someone from this building. He thought he was being pranked when he read the information about the 'Temporal office'. The email was brief and to the point:

To Director FBI

Three temporal distortions have been logged at this time, activate Special Agents Marcus Martinez and Avery Saunders for the duration of this investigation. No information should be passed outside of Room T07/04/1776. Any communication between yourself and agents should be in said room.

This priority one status notification will be deleted in the next ten seconds.

Director Walker snatched up a pen and wrote down the agents' names. Never in all his years had he known anything like this. The email then disappeared. All the blinds opened and the door unlocked, revealing a very confused Sharon, who walked into his office.

'Everything okay, sir?' the blonde woman asked, while looking around nervously.

'Fine, thank you, Sharon,' replied Jonathan. 'Just tech geeks going overboard, as usual.' His tone of voice was confident, though he knew his face showed differently. He passed his handwritten note to her. 'Please recall these agents back here immediately. Doesn't matter where or what they are doing. Tell them to come here to see me instantly.'

Sharon read the names. 'Of course,' she said and looked up. 'No weekend for you, then, sir?'

With a sigh, he picked up the phone. 'I guess not. Let me know their ETAs as soon as possible.' He then dialled his wife's number, just to warn her. He noted the sad smile on his long-term PA's face. 'Hi Sophia, now don't be mad…' He sat back and listened to his wife's tirade. After all, they hadn't been together for a weekend in months.

Chapter Eight

Special Agent Marcus Martinez had finally made it after eight years on the job, being everything from a desk jockey to pretending to be a homeless junkie. The previous role had lasted way too long for his liking, as his bosses said he had 'the look' for it. His parents had moved from Mexico City in the seventies, so he was American born and bred and fluent in Spanish.

His job progression had been the typical one for a special agent: Army as a teen; joined Los Angeles police department; then, having finally passed the interview and tests at the FBI, he became an agent. And, like any job in law enforcement, the hours were long and hard. His wife of ten years, Loretta, suffered in silence as she raised their twin girls, Adonia and Laura, whenever he worked away from home.

Unlike other children of immigrants, Marcus was luckier than most, as he had inherited a small plot of land in Bentwater, Montgomery, Texas, after the sudden death of his parents in a car accident. After leaving LA, he and Loretta had enough money to build a house along with a small annex for Loretta's mother to live in, after the passing of her husband due to cancer.

Marcus – or Marc to his friends – worked as part of a task force to crack down on drug and human trafficking through the ports of Texas City at Galveston Bay. It was jointly run with the DEA. They, of course, kept tabs on the bosses of the local crime syndicate. Marcus and his partner, Stan

Lamington – or Lamb for short – sweated their arses off in a blacked-out bread van, keeping an eye on the comings and goings of a local Italian sandwich shop, where the aforementioned gang liked to congregate. He had never been happier.

Looking at several monitors that were linked to cameras inside the deli, as well as the security cameras on the street, with coffee in a Styrofoam cup and half-eaten doughnuts still waiting to be cleared, Marcus was in hog heaven. His wife would be well pissed if she'd known that he and Lamb continued to eat nothing but junk.

'Aye, Lamb, Fat Tony is talking to Alan Limpy Johnson,' said Marcus, reminiscing back to all the mob films he'd grown up on that filled his desire for the three-letter agency.

Stan, who was five years Marcus's senior, rolled his eyes and wiped the sweat from his bald head. His partner was enjoying this shit life, but he was not. Give him an air-conditioned office any day and he'd be happy.

'Marc, I told you, stop making up names. What are you, a child?'

The Mexican's beaming smile brightened up the badly lit interior. The paint alone seemed to drink in all the light, and sap one's will and happiness.

'Where's the fun in that, buddy?' he asked and pointed at the monitor. 'Oh look, Anthony Gallo is talking to Alan Johnson!' He threw his hands up in mock anger, which sent a small piece of glazed doughnut to the floor.

'You do know we have to clean this up before the next shift take over?' said Lamb. 'They were pissed last time when you left a chicken bone in their mission brief.' He sighed at the memory, though he had found it funny at the time. '*Stakeout* this is not,' he said. 'Richard Dreyfuss and Emilio Estevez, we are not.' He stood up, brushing crumbs off his slight paunch. 'I'm going to grab some more coffee. You!' He pointed his strong and hairy knuckled hand at his over-eager partner. 'Clean this shit up!' he ordered before climbing out of the rear of the van, letting the hot summer air flow in.

Marcus pouted, though he knew the man was right and he started to clear the van up. However, not too well, as he was a professional and he had a 'person of interest' log to keep. Soon, the van was looking as clean as his kids' room – after he and Loretta had given up asking the twins to clear up and did it themselves. Those cute girls owned them.

His phone pinged, indicating a received message.

He sat down and wondered if it was from his wife, asking what time he would make it home that night. Luckily, they lived not too far away, so he managed to get home every night. That's why the DEA used the local FBI – it saved on hotel rooms. It also meant that their DEA boys could upgrade their hotel rooms, as some of their men were from out of town. They all stayed together, their reason being 'just in case we are needed'. They had sent all of the local agents a 'thank you' card with a photo of their rooms.

Stan returned to the van after a while with two cups of coffee and a selection of pastries. Just as he sat down with a contented sigh, his cell phone rang.

'Yep?' he answered. 'Okay, I understand… first thing with SWAT… Okay, sir.' He hung up, then handed out the coffee and pastries to a gobsmacked Marcus, who eagerly awaited the news. 'Coffee?'

'What the hell, man. What was the call about?' Marcus demanded and took a Danish and the proffered beverage.

Lamb looked puzzled for a second, his forehead crinkling up like a walnut shell. 'Oh, that… It was just my wife,' he answered and carried on munching on his bear claw. It was tricky, as he was forcing down a laugh in reply to his excitable colleague.

Marcus placed his hand on his Glock 19m. 'I'll do it, man. Just fucking tell me.' He watched as his partner almost fell about laughing, coffee spilling and crumbs going everywhere.

'The boat is coming in early hours and we are joining SWAT to raid your friend, Fat Tony,' replied Lamb. 'Once they catch the ones at the docks. It'll be one busy day.' He knew Marcus would be happy with that. Just as the grin appeared on Marcus's face, his cell phone pinged.

'Shit, Loretta won't be happy,' he chuckled and opened up his flip phone, reading the last message to have arrived. 'What the fuck…' Marcus stared at his phone and handed it to his partner.

Lamb read it. 'Damn, what did you do?' he asked as he read the message again, this time out loud. 'Agent Marcus Martinez, reassignment immediately, report to Director Walker directly on arrival. Priority one.' He looked at Marcus and frowned.

'What do I do? Can it wait until the raids are complete?' Marcus asked, hoping that it was a yes and he could finish the job.

The bald man did feel sorry for him. 'Sorry, bud, but it's priority one and the Director himself. You must go. Pack and be on the first flight to DC,' Stan said slowly, and watched his partner deflate. 'I'll keep you in the loop, okay?'

'Yeah, right,' Marcus grumbled and looked at Fat Tony laughing away on camera. 'What a pisser!' he snapped, then stood up and shook his friend's spare hand before stepping out into the insanely hot day.

Closing the door of the van behind him, he walked away to where his car was parked. There, glinting in the sun, stood his personal car. Yes, the agency offered an official vehicle, but his family preferred the Honda CRV. It was comfy, like sitting on a couch. Starting it up and shifting it into drive, he headed home to give his wife the bad news. Unfortunately, the twins were away staying with friends, but that opened up the option of a much nicer goodbye, depending on his darling wife's mood.

***

'It's not my fault,' Marcus cried out as he saw his favourite coffee mug fly past his head. His darling wife looked feral. Unbeknown to him, Loretta had organised a huge anniversary get together for the next weekend; all the family and friends had been invited and, yes, he had forgotten it. Loretta knew and had come to terms with that, so she had done all the organising. She then sent a vase his way, which, thanks to Marcus's FBI training, he managed to deflect away with a kick.

The next few sentences were mainly Mexican slang swear words, so he was particularly thankful that his little girls were not there to witness their mother say such things, especially about what part of a donkey's anatomy he was.

'I'm sorry honey, I truly am,' Marcus pleaded. 'The Director of the agency has requested me. Even my boss can't stop this…' He showed Loretta the text, which allowed him inside her guard and would prevent another ceramic projectile coming his way.

'Why?' Loretta said in sad tone as the fire left her dark eyes. Slowly, she slouched to the ground, her bronzed legs folding up underneath her, looking from the phone to her husband. 'They promised that you could have next weekend off!'

Marcus sat in front of her and pulled her into a hug, which she came into willingly. He let his flip phone fall to the side, bouncing silently upon the carpet.

'I know, my little paloma (dove)' he murmured and placed a kiss on her forehead. 'Like I said, this is from the Director of the FBI himself. You can't just say no and expect to keep your job,' he explained and placed his lips on the secret pleasure spot on her neck that he had found many years ago.

'Oh, Marky,' said Loretta. 'What could it be about? Have you ever even met the Director?' she asked, as his ministrations started to work, making her grind her curvy body against his. 'How long will you be gone, do you think?'

He nibbled her neck, making her moan. Maybe this goodbye would be nice, after all, and not a trip to the emergency room. That had only happened once, when he'd bought a Harley Davison motorbike for them to use at the weekend. Clearly, spending 25,000 dollars was not a good thing to do. He recalled that his wife played softball for the college team at the time – she had one hell of an arm on her. Marcus always wondered why their home was littered with keepsakes from their travels, all of which were suspiciously the size of said games ball.

In between kisses on the special spot, he answered, 'No… but… I… hope... it… wont... be… too... long… Mi Tesoro (my treasure)…'

They said farewell in style, though they did make their way to the bedroom as the lounge was covered in glass and China.

While he showered, his wife packed for him and booked a night in a hotel by the airport.

In dishevelled clothing, Marcus and Loretta drove to Montgomery airport. There, a ticket would be waiting for him on American Airlines flight #4774 to Baltimore International leaving at 4 pm in the afternoon, landing about eleven-ish the next morning. He had a two-hour wait.

The Honda slid into the off-loading bay and they exchanged a look of love, the kind that many couples had shared over the years on this exact spot.

'Call me when you have landed, Markey,' said Loretta. 'And stay safe… you hear?' She pulled him into another embrace.

'I promise, and I will try and get back for the party,' Marcus promised with a soft smile on his face, before they kissed again. 'Say goodbye to the kids, and I'll call as soon as I can.' With another shared smiled, he opened the door and retrieved his suitcase along with a spare suit from the back seat. With a wave, he disappeared into the air-conditioned airport as his wife and mother to his children drove off.

'Well, here we go…' he said to himself and headed to the checkout, showing the boarding clerk his credentials. He hoped they didn't get too jumpy about his sidearm on the flight.

The trip was uneventful, and the hotel was like many others he had stayed in for work. He would have to claim the money back, and if you spent too much the bean counters would get twitchy and then only reimburse you what they deemed to be the necessary expenditure. Always much less than you spent… gits!

Before closing his eyes for the night, Marcus received a text from Director Walker's PA, informing him that they expected him at the Director's office at 8.30 am on the dot. He was not to speak to anyone about the reason for his visit. He still didn't understand why he was there, but that's the government for you, and he slipped into slumber.

He awoke just after six, the sun invading his eyes. Normally, Marcus would go for a run, though the likelihood of this place having a gym was zero – unless it involved running away from gangbangers. So, he showered, shaved then dressed in his best suit. Then, after packing up the rest of his things, he checked out of the hotel and grabbed a cab to 935 Pennsylvania Avenue, the headquarters of the FBI.

***

Marcus arrived at the FBI headquarters at 8.20 am. The building was surrounded by heavy-duty plant pots which would stop most cars from ramming the building. He found his way to the waiting area. Apart from the PA, who was sitting at her desk, there was only one other person waiting. He was a taller and younger man, who looked for all the world like the poster child of the Bureau; 6 feet tall, athletic, blond, with blue eyes. Marcus thought that, in contrast, he must have looked like the gardener, for fuck's sake. However, the poster child had a bored look on his face, and Marcus wondered what he did.

The door to the office opened and Director Walker leant out. 'Martinez? Saunders?' he asked and waited for confirmation with head nods. 'Good. Get in here.' He then looked over at his PA with a smile. 'Go for a chat, Sharon. I'll call you when it's time to come back.'

The blonde woman nodded. 'Yes, sir. I'll go and see Carol in Personnel. You can reach me there,' she said, collecting her small leather handbag and phone before heading off.

The Director pointed to the two chairs opposite his desk as he settled into his bigger and better chair. 'Sorry to call you off your assignment, Marcus. But just to bring you up to date. They cleared the whole gang up, along with the women they had smuggled in. Good job.' He congratulated Marcus and then looked at Avery. 'Where did you come from, Avery? Sharon never said.'

Avery Saunders sighed. He always hated this part of the job, having to be social and playing the game. He glanced at the man next to him who had a Hispanic look about him. He hoped they weren't going under cover. That would be like a living hell to him. His father, may he rot in hell, always called him a coaster, amongst other things. His mother died at childbirth, which bought him a lot of leeway in his life with school, work and women.

Unfortunately, his father was right – he *was* a coaster. But not in the way of a stoner who would just wasting his life away with chips and weed. For Avery, ever since his first day at school, everything came easily to him and, to people from the outside, he looked bored, which brought with it other problems.

His teachers and his father, whenever they saw him like this, would push him to be all he could be. The former wanted him to become a teacher or lecturer at a topflight private school or university. His father, however, wished him to follow in his footsteps. However, the more they pushed Avery to succeed, the more he played up and refused.

That was, until the episode with his maths teacher who, for some reason, thought it would be a good idea to manhandle the boy. Thanks to his father's self-defence lessons, the teacher was sent flying through the air.

Avery then found himself at Military school, which was linked to his father's Army base. This forced him to focus more, though the discipline pissed him off and he grew to hate it. He would be trapped unless the idea of running away became more appetizing – not that he had anywhere to go.

So, once again, he walked the training and exams. It was only Avery's attitude that upset the leader of his training platoon, then Company, and finally the General, who ran the whole school. This brought his father to the Colonel's office for many a meeting about his son's manner.

Avery managed to graduate third in his class, and of course his father took the plaudits, telling his Army buddies it was tough love that steered his son straight and true. And so, after graduating, he enlisted.

The Army had difficulties finding the right post for him. Judging by appearances alone, the blond man looked like the right stuff, and had the brainpower to match, just no get up and go. So, during his five-year term of service, Avery was bounced from unit to unit, ending up in Army intelligence doing a desk job and learning everything about cybercrime. That life was perfect, as it was just him and a small group of fellow tech nerds. Fortunately, the episode with the Commanding Officer's daughter was hushed up and he was asked not to re-enlist.

Then came his time in law enforcement, when he went straight in as investigator of Miami Police Cybercrime department. Once again, he was surrounded by likeminded individuals. Yes, there was the odd one who kissed arse to rise up the ranks, but mostly they were all happy just tapping away during the day, then heading home or to the local bars for a few drinks.

As the years clicked by, Avery became increasingly bored, and eventually thought about doing something different, especially after his breakup with his girlfriend and supervisor, Alex Anderson. She soon turned out to be a spiteful and angry woman who brought their personal life to work with her, making his life and the life of the young intern, whom he was caught in bed with, a living nightmare.

It was during one of his investigations of medical insurance fraud that Investigator Saunders was liaising with a local branch of the FBI. The lead agent was Samantha Ivanov, whose family was from Russia, though there was not a hint of an accent when she spoke. Avery started to chat with her about the pros and cons of government work, though the pros didn't sell it to him straight away. No, that was when he found all four tyres on his BMW slashed outside his apartment with a dead rat shoved up the tail pipe. A year later, he became a trainee FBI agent.

Though his father wanted him to be a career Army man, he was just as proud when Avery passed top of his class, becoming Special Agent Avery Saunders. He was fast tracked to the Agency's Cyber Division in the fraud department. Avery wanted to go back to Miami, but he had to disclose the brief liaison he'd had with Samantha after leaving his police job. And so, in the end, he ended up in San Diego, which was still warm enough and by the ocean, which fuelled his desire for bikini-clad women.

***

At the same time that Marcus Martinez was sitting in a truck sweating his arse off while making up names for gang members, the toned and bronzed Special Agent Avery Saunders had just finished his morning ritual. He saw the little note from last night's conquest. He smiled and read it. All it said was 'Call me' and her phone number and an imprint of her lipstick-covered lips.

With a slight laugh, he threw the note into the wastepaper bin and headed out the door to his job. All the while, he was trying to remember the girl's name.

'Brittany? Bianca?' he mused loudly and walked to his Beamer, which thankfully still had all its tyres inflated. He had stopped thinking about relationships thanks to one spiteful woman in Miami, so he sufficed with one-night stands when he could get them – for now, at least. Most importantly, there would be no workplace hook-ups – well, apart from Samantha. He'd finally found a job that he really enjoyed, and the people there accepted him for who he was.

The drive in his air-conditioned German beast of a car was a short one and he parked up feeling happy about the workday ahead. Avery decided to sit down at his tidy desk and fire off his regular emails to his father and Samantha. She still worked in Miami, and they met up from time to time when their diaries allowed it. The tall, slender Russian woman was like Avery in many ways; family and marriage were for later, when their bodies and life started to slow down.

He walked through the building, imagining being the type of guy who bumps fists with a few of the black-clad Tactical guys that he occasionally drank with, all big and muscly and donned with enough armour and weapons to start a war. But that wasn't him. He walked past one particular group of guys; they must have just completed a positive operation, as they were high fiving each other like mad. They were looking at him with scorn and threw a few misplaced words, which he found funny, and yet they did not.

Avery winked at a few secretaries, even though that was breaking his own rules. But hey, today was going to be a good day, he could feel it. Settling down at his desk, he sent off the planned emails. Sam would answer within the hour, his father would get back to him when he found someone to open the damned email for him. The leader of men still couldn't work a PC for shit.

Avery started opening files for a group that had been strong-arming pensioners to put claims in via a corrupt doctor's office. He was linking them with three other infirmaries in different states. It wasn't complicated – all the key players chatted via texts and email, so it just meant collating them all together.

'Hey, Avery, how's tricks?' a voice came from down the office, making him look up. He saw Agent Adam Thornberry.

'Not bad, good night last night,' he replied, smiling at the tall, skinny, red-haired man, who was at least five years his junior and classed himself a lady's man, though the evidence was somewhat lacking. 'How did you fare?' Avery gave him a knowing look.

Adam sighed. 'Not as good as you, evidently. How was Suzie?' He grinned, while giving Avery a wink.

So that was her name. 'Yeah, she was nice,' replied Avery. 'Didn't see her leave this morning, which made it easier.' He couldn't hold back the shit-eating grin on his face. 'Don't worry, you'll have some luck soon, buddy.' He then noticed the little yellow post-it held in the man's pale and thin fingers, which always reminded him of Mr Burns from *The Simpsons*. 'What's that about?' he asked and pointed at the note.

Adam's freckles were almost eclipsed as his pale skin reddened into a blush. 'Dude, I don't know what you have done, or to whom,' he said with mirth dripping from his thin lips. He then handed Avery the note. 'This is from Director Walker's office; they want you to call them ASAP!'

Avery looked at his sometime wing man – it was more like crash and burn, but he made Avery look good whenever they headed out to the bars together. He read the number written on the post-it and recognised the Washington area code (202). He looked up and blue met hazel eyes.

'What the fuck?'

The ginger-haired man started to cackle insanely. 'Buddy, you'd better call them,' he said before turning away to head back across the carpeted office. 'You are so boned. Let me know when your retirement party is.' Adam looked back over his shoulder and laughed some more, making half the office look up and gaze at the pair.

Avery rubbed his forehead, now slick with sweat. Taking a deep breath, he dialled the number on the note. The phone rang twice before a bright voice sang down the line.

'Director Walker's office, how may I help you?'

'Errrr, good morning, this is Agent Avery Saunders from the San Diego Cybercrimes department. I was asked to contact you?' He spoke politely, though with a distinctive tremor of nerves. Could this easy-going job have come to an end? He wouldn't admit it, but he was worried.

'Ah yes, finally,' replied the woman. 'You have been transferred here for an undetermined time. Please reassign your caseload to other personnel and make you way here asap. You have a meeting with the Director tomorrow morning at eight-thirty precisely. This is a top-secret meeting. Your superiors have been notified.' She spoke in a quick and precise manner. 'Do you understand, Mr Saunders?'

'Errrr, yes,' Avery said, trying to work out what was happening. 'It might take me longer than a day to get there, I'm afraid,' he added, playing for time.

There was silence on the other end of the line. 'No, Mr Saunders, it won't,' replied the woman coldly. 'If the Director of the Agency wishes you here, then you will make it on time, do you understand?'

'Yes!'

'Perfect, otherwise this time tomorrow you will no longer be an agent … Good day, Mr Saunders.' The woman then hung up, the phone line mocking him.

Instantly, an email notification sprung up on his phone. It was from his boss, telling him that he should close his computer and leave without talking to anyone. His cases would be either frozen or handed over to another agent. Then, at the end of the message, two words seemed to resonate with his predicament. GOOD LUCK!

Avery's breathing matched his heartbeat at this moment, racing like a stock car at the Indianapolis 500. He was never like this… ever. Slowly, he closed his computer and gathered his personal items from his desk, which weren't many – just a picture of Samantha, soppy he knew, and another one of his parents when his mum was pregnant with him.

With his belongings put away safely in his soft leather brown bag, Avery stood up and pushed his chair in, then headed out. His boss threw him a salute.

'AVE!' Adam shouted from across the office, but Avery didn't turn back. He had orders.

'Agent Thornberry, this is not a high school kegger. Saunders has his orders, as do you,' the department head said slowly, but his voice carried weight, making everyone duck down and get back to work.

Saunders made it back to his apartment quickly, threw open his personal laptop and checked on flights to DC. The early ones had already gone. The next was a Delta Airlines flight leaving San Diego at 11.20 am arriving at DC 22.24 pm, with a stopover at Detroit.

'Fuck! Long day,' he muttered and booked a seat. Then he booked a local airport hotel, where he could take a brief sleep before the meeting.

Within the hour, he was headed via taxi to the airport, with the one suitcase. Anything else he needed could be obtained while he was there. Avery closed his eyes and tried to sleep in the comfy business class seat. Sod money, he was going to travel in comfort. If they didn't reimburse him, so be it, but his ass would not be punished for this job. In transit, despite what the text message had told him about keeping the assignment secret, he sent his father and Samantha a quick text to say he had been called to DC and would contact them when he was able.

It was almost midnight when he checked into the hotel room. His face bounced off the overused mattress springs and his eyes closed instantly, despite his concerns about the upcoming meeting. What was strange for Avery was the lack of female company. Back home, he was often alone, but if there was ever a trip and a hotel involved, then there was always a warm body next to him.

The next morning came too quickly. Yawning, he showered and shaved and dressed in his best suit – a nice charcoal Hugo Boss suit. He wore matching shoes, with a crisp white shirt, cufflinks and a silk tie. Avery didn't know what this meeting was about, but if he was going down, he was going to look good. Placing his credentials in his inside jacket pocket, sliding his service gun and holster in his waistband, he headed out to his doom.

With the suitcase by his side, he headed to the FBI headquarters, the wheels of the suitcase running smoothly over the tiled floor as he headed upstairs to the Director's office. The young man calmed his breathing as the elevator door opened. A blonde, petite woman was sitting at a desk. She had a small smirk on her lips as he walked closer to her.

'Good morning, Mr Saunders, I'm glad you managed to make it,' Sharon, the Director's PA, said warmly, but with a hint of steel in her voice. 'Please take a seat. We just have to wait for one other.' She pointed to one of the chairs by the wall.

Avery nodded, placing his suitcase by the chair and checking his watch. It was 8.10 am.

'I hope he's not too late,' Avery said playfully, making the woman look up. Her eyes were cold, like those of a great white shark clamping its teeth down upon an unlucky surfer, and he was that surfer.

'Indeed, Mr Saunders, but shall we give him some leeway?' the PA replied. 'After all, he was on assignment trying to arrest some traffickers – who, if I'm correct, were bringing drugs, guns and women into the country,' she added and looked at him coldly. 'I'm sure your computer is in safe hands while you are here.' Avery looked her over, trying not to snarl back at the woman's words. After all, they all worked for the same government here.

Just then the lift door opened, and a stocky Hispanic man rushed in. His suit was okay, but ruffled from his cab journey, which proved the cheapness of the fabric. The man sat down hastily next to him.

Avery then watched as the 'she wolf' pressed a buzzer on her desk. The door opened and the Director himself appeared and leant through the door and called them in, then told his PA to leave.

'Agents Martinez, Avery,' said the Director. 'Thank you for coming so quickly.' He proffered them to empty seats opposite his desk while sitting back down. 'So, Marcus, you were part of a trafficking task force, yes?'

'Yes, sir,' Marcus answered.

The Director smiled. 'Yes, that did end well. Sorry to pull you away.' His eyes then rested on Avery. 'Avery, what was your department?'

The young agent sighed. Whatever he said was just going to sound lame. 'I was working in cyber fraud,' he replied and received a nod from both older men.

'Good, good,' said the Director. 'You should both work well together. Avery with your computer skills,' he said and then looked at Marcus, 'and you, Marcus, with your fieldwork. And, of course, you have both served in the armed forces, which will come in handy.' He smiled again and went to get up.

'What's this about, sir? I haven't received a brief,' Marcus asked and looked at his new partner, who also shook his head.

'We can't speak of it here, gentleman. Follow me and bring your luggage with you,' Walker instructed and walked to the door.

It was Avery's turn to ask something. 'Where are we going, sir?'

The tall, grey-haired man smiled. 'Room T07/04/1776. Follow me,' he replied and headed off at a fast pace to the elevator, which was already waiting for them.

Chapter Nine

Marcus and Avery swapped confused looks as they stood behind the boss of the FBI. Silently, they shook hands and watched as the elevator counted down to the depths of the building. They had both thought it wise not to talk about anything – not that they had anything to discuss at this time.

Bing. The lift doors slid apart, revealing a long corridor with large utility pipes running down the length of the nondescript corridor.

'Follow me, gentlemen,' said Walker. 'You will have to swipe your ID cards to enter this lift from now on.' He gestured to the card reader on the wall as he strode away.

Avery noticed there were several doors running down the left-hand side of the corridor. He found it strange that there was only one door on the right, and that was where the Director stopped and swiped his ID card through the black card reader, which bleeped and opened the door. The other doors on this level just had the typical key locks set into the aluminium handle on the door, with no elaborate card readers.

'Make sure you both swipe in too, okay?' Walker instructed and headed into the room.

His movement triggered lights, which automatically came to life and flickered onto the walls of the corridor. The two agents both swiped their ID cards and walked in, carrying their suitcases as they did so.

'Welcome to your new assignment,' the Director announced, taking a seat that leant against one of the workstations. 'Please sit,' he said, pointing to two other chairs.

Marcus and Avery took in the room. It was large with just three workstations adorned with top-of-the-range computers humming away quietly. There were also banks of servers with lights flickering away madly.

'Wow, this is all top-of-the-line kit,' Avery admitted, noticing the three red lights that sat upon the far wall.

The Director nodded. 'Indeed. This room is top secret, to the point that I only knew about it yesterday,' he explained and saw the shock on his agents' faces. 'I'm not lying. Although I knew of the existence of such a room, I didn't know the location.'

Agent Martinez, like his new partner, was taking in the equipment. 'How can that be true, sir?' he asked. 'You *are* the Agency.' He was glad that the young man next to him agreed with him. 'Somebody must either clean this place, or maintain the PCs.'

Walker smiled at the men. 'Yep, it pissed me off, too. When I was told about this place, I couldn't believe it. Only certain cleaners come in here, and they don't mix with the others. In fact, they are employed by a totally different firm.' He ran his fingers through his hair, messing it up slightly. 'IT maintenance is done remotely. If hands-on work is needed, then a random person from our department does the work. The non-disclosure agreement we have to sign is the harshest I have ever seen.'

The two agents took the documents that Walker handed them. They knew they should've read them first, but under the eye of the Director himself, you don't hesitate. They signed, though they had to share a pen as Marcus had left his in the stakeout van. He recalled his partner stirring a coffee with it.

'What is the assignment?' asked Marcus. 'Something this secret has to be something which could cause ripples if the information got out.' He watched as the Director tucked away the signed paperwork.

'Those two workstations are your new homes, for however long this will last,' he replied. 'It's not for me to say what the timescale is, the programme will tell you when the mission has been completed.' He pointed towards the three red lights on the wall. 'When those are green, you are doing something right. If they are completely out, you can go home. You oversee your own time.'

'All information is to be relayed to you, sir?' Avery asked.

'No, just do your job as stated on those two computers,' Walker said and chuckled at the look of shock on the agents' faces. 'If you need to talk about it, call me and I will meet you here. The files will give you all the information you need to work with. I must stress that not a word of what you do in here leaves this room.'

Marcus saw a door beyond the banks of servers. 'What's through that door, sir? The break room?' he asked with a smile. He noticed the door had a black card reader on it, like the one that they had used to enter the main room.

The Director shrugged. 'That is a mystery, even to me,' he replied. 'My card will not open that door, but if I'm right, yours will. I do not know what is in that room, though my imagination is running riot at this time.' He chuckled and stood up. 'Across the hall, you have two bedrooms with en-suite bathrooms, and a kitchen diner. If you have laundry, leave it in the baskets and the cleaners will have it cleaned. If you need groceries, leave a note on the refrigerator door, and they will pick it up for you.'

He headed towards the door. Opening it, he looked back at the two agents. 'Read your briefs, do your jobs, and don't talk to anyone. Good luck. I will visit tomorrow.' With those words, he turned and walked out, closing the door behind him. The agents just looked at each other in amazement.

'What the hell is going on?' the blond man hissed and, once again, offered the older agent his hand. 'Avery Saunders, Cybercrimes and totally confused. You?' He shook the older man's strong, rough hand.

The smaller man barked out a laugh, then collapsed down into a chair with a thump. 'Marcus Martinez, or Marc for short. Organised crime. And if *you* are confused, whatever I am feeling right now doesn't even have a title!' Both of them laughed out loud. 'Let's check out the rooms, and see if there is any coffee, shall we?' he added.

Saunders nodded. 'Hell, yeah! I'm buying,' he replied, and they headed straight out, leaving their bags in the computer room.

The door opposite was the kitchen/diner and was possibly the greyest room they had ever seen, though all the cupboards, refrigerator and freezer were stocked full – and recently, too. Avery watched as his new partner started work on the coffee, putting the powder into the filter.

The bedrooms were identical – a double bed, a bedside table, one chest of drawers and a wardrobe. The bathrooms were stocked with all the items they would need for a prolonged stay. The two men made their way back into the diner and poured themselves a cup of the toxic brew, then sat at the round, wooden dining table and took their first sip.

'So, this doesn't seem like a quick assignment, does it?' Avery said in a downcast manner.

The Mexican shook his head. 'Nope. My missus is going to be pissed. Our anniversary party is this weekend.' Marcus took another sip of the rich, brown beverage. 'You married, buddy?' He had noticed that the man didn't wear a wedding band, but lots of agents didn't for one reason or another.

'Nope, free and single over here,' Avery answered and winked. 'But I do have someone that could fill that place in the future. It's just not the right time.' He thought back to the long, one-sided conversation he'd had with Samantha, about how he was part of her life. That was a long weekend.

Marcus liked the man already, although he did have this bored look about him. Marcus thought that perhaps that was just his normal look.

'Can't say I blame you, my friend,' he said. 'Though, it is nice to go home to someone you care about at the end of the day.' He took another sip of the coffee and then checked out the time. 'Right, I'm going to call my wife, Loretta, and warn her about this weekend. Then let's get unpacked and read the brief!' He stood up and went to walk out with mug in hand. 'You better get some more clothes sent here. I don't think they want us shopping.' He then headed out to be shouted out in the peace and quiet of his own room.

A small spike of jealousy hit Avery as he heard Marcus speaking rapidly in Spanish to a clearly upset wife. He wasn't great at languages, but he did hear Marcus asking his wife not to call him that, whatever that was. He grabbed his coffee, claimed his bag and headed back to the room he'd picked out, closing the door after him to block out the sounds of domestic bliss.

It didn't take him long to unpack, so he sat on his bed and took out his phone. He scrolled down the list of contacts and went to his 'go to' girl.

'Agent Samantha Ivanov speaking,' came the strong voice.

'Hey, Sammy, it's Avery,' he said.

'Ave, what's going on? Where are you…? Are you okay?' she asked quickly. 'Your supervisor wouldn't tell me anything.'

Avery fell back onto the bed. He was surprised by how clean the room smelt, not musty at all.

'Yes, I'm okay,' he replied. 'He wouldn't know, and I'm not allowed to say anything. This is real top-secret stuff.

The NDA alone is a bitch.' He paused for a moment. 'I was wondering if you could send me some clothes from your apartment. We aren't allowed out.'

Samantha's tone went deadly. 'What the hell have you got yourself into, Avery Justin Saunders?' She spat the words down the phone, and he knew he was in trouble as she had used his full name. 'I will not have my possible future husband, and baby's daddy, disappearing off the face of the Earth!'

'It's fine, Sammy,' he said, trying to remain calm. 'Anyway, your plan was that we had another ten years until you want to get married. I'll be back by then,' he joked, which was a mistake. The growl that rumbled down the line scared him, and those things that classed him as a male of the species were pulled back into his body for safety.

'It's my plan,' shouted Samantha, 'and like all women I can change it at any time I want, even though I don't wish to!' She snarled like a pissed-off lioness. 'Avery, I will do as you ask and send you some clothes, but with one condition. After this, we go on holiday together… okay?'

He knew then that this little jaunt to Washington DC had her spooked for some reason. There often had been rumours of black bag operations where the agents just disappeared, though that was mainly the CIA. But clearly something had rattled her normally stoic exterior.

'Of course, Sammy, whatever you want.'

The silence on the line lasted only seconds, but it felt longer. 'Okay, Avery, where do I send your stuff?' she asked. Avery told her to send his things to the Washington DC office and he gave her the room number. 'Well, I better go. Some of us have real jobs to do,' she said and giggled.

'Thanks, Sammy,' said Avery. 'Speak later, if I can.'

Silence again. 'No problem. Love you!'

He stilled that time. They never said that. Yes, they called each other 'love' sometimes though it was rare, but never expressed such a thing. What should he do or say? His mind ran through so many scenarios, but he knew that the silence between them was going on for too long. He wanted to scream, then his mouth took over.

'Love you, too, Sammy. Take care.' And then the phone clicked off. 'What the hell was that?' he exclaimed and then he smacked his forehead with the phone.

There was a knock on his door. 'Yeah, come in,' he groaned, still lying on the soft bed as Marcus came in.

'Well, it looks like your call went as well as mine,' Marcus joked. His ears were still ringing from his wife's tirade, though she had apologised via text seconds later.

'Sammy never really wanted to be tied down,' said Avery. 'Neither did I. That's why we were so perfect together,' he added, not knowing why all this emotional stuff was happening. 'But me being brought here and not being able to tell her… well, it has set her off.'

Marcus smiled. 'Thing is, she knew where you were, and you were both happy in your little world,' he explained. 'Now, suddenly you are out of her comfort zone, and she's worried.' He walked over and grabbed the younger man's hand, pulling him upright. 'Now, let's find out why we are here. The sooner we do this, the sooner we can get back to our lives!'

'Hell, yeah! Let's do it,' Avery replied and followed his partner back to the control room.

Once they were back, they both looked around at the computers, not sure where to begin.

'I'll take this one,' said Avery, pointing to the furthest workstation, before looking at the files on the screen. 'Temporal brief,' he read aloud and they both looked at each other.

Marcus walked over to the workstation and sat down next to Avery. They both read the message on the computer screen:

> **Welcome to the Temporal Investigation Department. You have been chosen for this task due to your personality and professional abilities. This department was created in 1972, in this very room with equipment way beyond the current level of today's computers and electronics. This room and its computers and equipment are out of time; they do not exist on our timeline, and they are programmed specifically to you and your partner alone. If somebody else tries to enter this room to use the time machine, it will immediately close and all personnel will be ejected, and new agents will be assigned. You have been activated, as**

the software, which repeatedly scans information on past and present events, has detected significant changes. If you look at the wall ahead of you, you will see three red lights. The fact that they are red denotes three changes of said timeline, caused by a person or group, which is drastic enough to warrant investigation. Your assignment is to track and investigate said changes and take action to reset the past events back to the original timeline, where possible or necessary. When this has been completed, the lights will turn green. Once at least one of the lights have been extinguished, you will then leave, and you will never discuss this assignment again. Please update this brief if any new information comes to light.

Avery shook his head at all the information that was dumped on him. *Time travel? Are they serious?* he thought and clicked on the file to close it. It was then that he saw a small text file attached to the brief, which he opened. It was an unofficial report from an agent, so Saunders decided to read it, as you can never have enough insight.

He couldn't quite believe what he was reading:

My partner and I decided to write this brief to put you in the picture about what you are going to be tasked with. We were picked for one of these tasks, by whom we do not know, though we guessed it was someone within the Agency from the future, and that they were able to come back in time to set this all up. This department has updated hardware and software from other governments around the country, which cannot be traced to a specific department, or state. We did try and identify all the sources that had contributed to the information stored in this room, and the message we received back was strongly worded, telling us to back off, that we were to do our jobs or be replaced. This job is unbelievable and a lot of it will blow your mind. Enjoy yourself, but stay safe – and remember, you are in charge and no one else. Good luck, Agents.

Avery and Marcus both finished reading around the same time. They were only a few feet apart, but their silence spoke volumes. They both pushed back on their swivel chairs, which moved soundlessly on the tiled flooring. They turned to each other.

'What the fuck!' spat Marcus.

Avery looked at his partner. 'Time travel? This must be a joke,' he laughed and looked at the list of other files. Travel pod instructions, past incident and agent reports, recent temporal incidents...

Marcus sighed. 'I don't think so. Take your pick – agent reports or the recent incidents?' he asked and saw his colleague chewing his bottom lip.

A simple game of rock, paper, scissors was the deciding factor on which agent actioned what. The loser was forced to take the agent reports. Marcus was pissed and started to read them.

'Stupid game, stupid scissors…' he mumbled. 'Puta!' He clicked open past episodes and reports.

They had decided to spend the morning going through all the reports, then have lunch and discuss whatever they thought was relevant, as there was no need to submerge themselves in information that was not important. There were occasional utterances of 'bullshit!' and 'I don't believe it!' In the end, however, they both came to believe it. The proof was there in written word and photo evidence.

The minutes turned into hours. They had fallen into silence and it was only their breathing and the hum of the computers that could be heard in the room. Avery checked his watch and realised that they had been working for four hours without a break.

'Marcus, I need a break… How about some lunch?' he asked and saw the older man rub his eyes with his fingers.

'Oh, yeah, my man,' Marcus replied. 'This shit has got my mind reeling. I don't even know where to start.' He stood up and stretched, his back giving an audible crack. 'A coffee and a bite would be a good start, my friend,' he said and followed Avery out. It was then that he noticed the clock in the kitchen. According to the clock, it was only nine in the morning, whereas his watch told him it was 1 pm.

'Avery, check out the clock. This room is truly out of time!'

The younger agent checked his own watch. 'Jesus, you might make your anniversary meal after all,' he chuckled and saw the smaller man's eyes widen. 'You make the coffee, I'll make lunch,' Avery instructed and walked away to retrieve the fixings for their meal.

'This is good,' said Marcus a few minutes later, eating his ham and salad sandwich. His partner nodded as he pushed his plate away. 'So, what caused those lights to appear?'

Avery leant back in his chair and took a sip of a chilled bottle of water, placing it back on a coaster. The condensation had made a pool on the table, which he soaked up with a napkin as he formatted his thoughts.

'Well,' he began, 'in order of calendar years, the first one was back in the Egyptian times. New hieroglyphs appeared in a temple depicting a man grabbing an eagle from the sky as the pharaoh fired arrows of lightning at him. The man then disappeared in a flash of blinding light.'

'Hijo de perra,' Marcus cursed, which brought a confused look from Avery. 'Sorry, it means son of a bitch,' Marcus explained. 'That's one place we can't go.' Avery nodded in agreement. 'What else?'

'*Titanic*, 1912,' replied Avery. 'Same amount of people lost their lives, but more women and children were saved from all decks, not just the first-class occupants. So, that one is to be left alone. It would be too problematic with that many people.' He looked over at the Mexican, who was cradling his head in his hands.

Marcus looked up and shook his head. 'I agree, but what is this person doing? The first one must just be someone doing a bit of sightseeing. But the *Titanic*... That's just madness. And how did he manage it on his own?'

Avery nodded. 'According to the files, the Unsinkable Molly Brown had more to do with it in this timeline, than the past one,' he said and took another sip of water.

'Okay,' replied Marcus, 'she must know who this person is. So, if this is all real, we should go and ask her a few questions about that night.' He shook his head in frustration. He was a man of action and disliked analysing facts and data. 'But I agree, we shall leave these events as they are. What's the last one?'

Saunders chewed his bottom lip. 'JFK. He saved him,' he stated. Marcus stared at him in amazement. 'I know, he died in Dallas, but that is because we will stop this man. I don't know how it knows we are going to do this, but it does!'

'What if we don't, though?' Marcus frowned. 'What I read in my files is that we can only go back to the same day once.' Not knowing how the hell all this stuff was done, his mind was struggling with all the information. He just wished he could sit down with his wife and talk through it, just like he did with everything. Yes, if the FBI ever read her mind, he would be in trouble. The amount of top-secret information she knew would send them both to prison for life.

Avery was fighting off a migraine. He sifted through some sheets of computer printouts in front of him on the table. 'According to this, he managed to divert the motorcade away from the shooters.'

'The shooter. There was only one… Oswald,' Marcus corrected earnestly. That was what his parents believed and that's what he believed, too. His parents would never believe that members of a government of the free world would do such a thing.

'Okay, that's what I meant,' Avery said in a sing song voice and internally rolled his eyes. Though he knew his partner wasn't the only one who believed it, some even believed the magic bullet theory. 'Well, anyway,' he continued, 'the motorcade was away from the Texas School Book Depository, so he survived the day.' He sighed. 'The President's plane, along with the President, first lady and all the retinue, were killed. The fallout was even worse than the shooting.' He closed his eyes, trying to retrieve the information. 'It was a messy job, hundreds were linked to the plot and arrested.'

Agent Martinez paled slightly. 'What is this man? A terrorist?' He was shocked to his gills. If that many people had been caught for the bombing, how many were involved in such a complicated shooting? Things just weren't adding up to his beliefs.

'I really don't know,' replied Avery. 'It must be the same person, but you don't save people on the *Titanic*, only to change the way the President was killed. Who knows what he was thinking? Maybe to keep JFK in office? That could have changed the escalation of the war, but it's hard to know.'

The room went quiet as they let the information sink in.

'So, let's talk to this Brown woman,' suggested Marcus. 'Maybe get a lead on this crazy man, then stop him from trying to save JFK.' He gave a low chuckle. 'Sounds backwards to me, but if it means we can go home, then we shall do it.'

Saunders nodded. 'But we do have to find this man and either stop him, or take away his equipment, as I don't think there is a court in the land that could convict him,' he stated and finished off his water, before launching the bottle into the air, where it flew straight and true to gain him three points in the non-existent game he was playing. 'So, what about yours?'

Marcus rubbed his face, then slowly walked to the fridge and grabbed a cold can of Pepsi.

'Want one?' he offered the other man, who shook his head. After opening the can up with an audible hiss, Marcus sat back down. 'Well, it seems the last time this happened was in the early nineties. It was tracked to a sci-fi author called George Lancaster Jnr – who, like this one, just did the hopping around. But the major thing that sent agents to this room was a big one.'

'Kidnapping the Lindberghs' baby?' Avery guessed with a smile.

'Nope,' replied Marcus. 'He killed Hitler in April 1941, shot him and his aides with a silenced handgun on a train on the way to Graz in Austria.' He sighed sadly. 'The author lost family members in the deathcamps later on in the war. But when army generals took over the running of the war, they made peace with Britain and the US, and cut ties with Japan and helped us defeat them.'

'Wow, that doesn't sound too bad to me,' said Avery. 'What went wrong, then?'

Marcus took a sip of the fizzy drink. 'The Russians were pissed and refused to agree with the Allies,' he replied. 'The war never really ended. They had small fights constantly along the borders of Poland and Austria.' He paused and then his shoulders sagged. 'Behind closed doors, they built an atom bomb. In 1952, bombs were dropped on Berlin and London. We were hit by planes from Cuba with smaller bombs, which brought on World War Three.'

'Holy fuck,' exclaimed Avery. 'Whoever built this time machine didn't know the cost of playing with the timeline.' He had felt the pressure building, given what they were being asked to do. 'Any idea who built or designed this thing?'

'No, just rumours,' Marcus replied, frowning. 'They think Orson Welles got together with Einstein after the war, and, with the latter's links to the best brains in the world, worked on it over the years. The other theory was that someone came back with the plans and gave them to Lancaster to build, and use.'

Avery walked around and loosened his tie. 'What about this Lancaster guy? What happened there? Did they get him and his equipment?'

'The agents caught him trying to board the train to kill Hitler,' replied Marcus. 'They didn't want to kill him, so they made a deal – he stops using the machine, strips it down and destroys it, and they won't come after him.' He knew how highly strung authors could be and how easy they were to scare. He had done it himself when someone wanted to write a book about an operation that he had been part of. Somehow, he had gotten hold of the list of agents and targets, the book was never written.

'Lancaster wrote about time travel until recently,' Marcus continued, 'then disappeared off the face of the Earth.'

They remained silent for a while, allowing their thoughts to be processed.

'So maybe, whoever is using this, bought it in an estate sale when Lancaster was declared dead?' snapped Avery. 'But, obviously we can't leave here or task other agents to hunt this man down.' He felt angry, knowing his hands were tied. 'And these things are normally cash only, unless you are buying the property... FUUUCCCKKKKKK!'

Marcus stood up with his hands up, trying to calm the young man down, though it was quite nice to finally see some passion in the man.

'Hey, hombre, take it easy,' said Marcus. He saw Avery's eyes flash in anger, but they were soon calmed again. 'Let's just get back into the work,' he said. 'Your choice – either learn how to travel in space or find out where this Brown woman can be located.' Then he proffered a round fist, ready for the game to start again. 'ONE, TWO, THREE, ROCK... Pendejo!' (arsehole) and stomped away as the flat hand of Avery mocked him all the way back into the control room.

He sat down at his computer and clicked open the file containing the instructions of how to operate the time machine. This was difficult to do as his partner was now smiling away happily.

'Vete al demonio' (go to hell!).

Agent Avery Saunders was concerned for a moment when he felt the flash of anger rise up inside. That was rare indeed. Even when a psycho bitch of an ex had messed with his car, he didn't lose his shit. Instead, he would stay there in the computer room until the job was finished – which had been done already, but he and Marcus had to complete it so that it came to pass. Crazy day!

However, beating a rough and tough field agent in two games of rock, paper, scissors was strangely uplifting, and he started to whistle again to drown out what he believed were Spanish curse words. Maybe he should learn some phrases so at least he knew what he was being called – and, of course, to swear back.

'Now, Mrs Brown, where are you?' he said loudly, bringing another tirade from his new friend.

Finally, the tasks were done. The time travel aspect was easy enough. Marcus stood up and checked his watch. It was now 6.45 pm.

'Right, let's check out the other room,' he said. 'Did you find the woman?'

Avery nodded and asked his partner for his clothing dimensions so that they could get some outfits delivered by morning for the correct era.

'And remember,' he said, 'there will be no SUVs, or sunglasses like you field boys like to use. It's quiet in and out.' Avery laughed as he saw Marcus pout like a little schoolboy. The email to an unknown person was sent and the files were closed down. 'Marriott Hotel in DC, June 1926. Her husband passed away four years prior, so we will go in gentle.'

'Sure, no problem,' Marcus replied and swiped his card in the black plastic reader to the second mysterious room. With a beep, the door unlocked. The action was repeated by Avery, causing the second and final lock to disengage and the grey door swung open.

The twin fluorescent light tubes in the room flickered to life and the two temporal agents stood there, feeling quite underwhelmed. All that was in the room were two tube-like things and a computer on a small table. The screen indicated where to input the information – coordinates, time, date. There were also two small cell phone-like boxes. Avery picked one up.

'What's this?'

'That is what we use to come back,' replied Marcus. 'Flip the cover up and it sends you back here.' He sighed in exhaustion. 'Just don't lose it, otherwise you are stuck in that time period,' and he watched the young man place the device back into the charging port. 'It says we should aim for a clear area in daylight, as we will apparently arrive in a big flash of light. So we need to check that before we leave.' Both agents lapsed into another bout of silence as their minds tried to comprehend what they were about to do.

Without another word, they headed back out to the kitchen/diner. Despite their watches saying 7 pm, the clock in the kitchen still said 10 am.

'This is going to mess with my head,' Avery sighed. 'I want to eat, speak to Samantha, then sleep. But I can't, because it's under two hours since we spoke last.' Like Marcus, Avery was also tired, and his words came out harsher than they were meant to sound. He stomped over to the fridge and pulled out two sodas and handed one to his partner. 'There's a takeout menu here. Chinese?'

Marcus settled down at the table and opened his can after throwing off his jacket. 'Sounds good. Go wild and order lots. They have us stuck here; they can pick up the bill.' He pointed to a tablet that was resting by a small door in the wall. When opened, it revealed itself to be a dumb waiter, which would allow food to be delivered without interacting with anyone on the outside.

Within forty-five minutes, they were tucking into a feast of Chinese food. They were not sure where it came from at ten in the morning, but they did not argue. And anyway, who said the clock on the wall was correct? These clandestine deals always fucked with the agents under them. The two men then spent the next few hours watching rubbish TV before hitting the sack at 1 pm kitchen time.

It was 8 pm kitchen time when they met up for breakfast of Captain Crunch and coffee, the breakfast of champions. Their delivery had also arrived. On the dining table were boxes filled with everything they would need – suits, hats, shirts, and shoes. But what surprised them the most were the ID and badges, holsters and revolvers, with six bullets already in the cylinders.

'Wow, they know their stuff,' Marcus said, gathering his outfit up and heading off to get ready to go.

They laughed at each other as they walked towards what they had chosen to call the tube room.

'I'm not really a hat man, but I guess back in the day they all used to wear them,' Avery said, clipping his badge to the leather belt, following the very helpful diagram that told them how they should look. 'And remember, Marc… we are the Bureau of Investigations. The FBI doesn't exist yet.'

Marcus nodded as he typed in the coordinates that Avery had calculated. They would appear just as the sun rises in the grounds of the hotel.

'Hey, they might not even let me in,' said Marcus with a laugh. 'They might think I'm a posh gardener!' Even now, he got strange looks in certain places. 'Right, get in the tube and bend you knees slightly,' he instructed Avery. 'They say you land with a bump.' He then watched Avery as he stepped into the cold, plastic tube and closed his eyes, relaxing his body.

Both of their hearts were pounding. Marcus pressed the 'go' button, which indicated that he had twenty seconds to get into his tube. It was then that he saw the two 'home' remotes still sitting in their chargers. His stomach flipped at the thought of being stuck there. He pocketed both remotes and hurried to his receptacle. Then, like his partner, he closed his eyes and flexed his knees. Then the light shone through his eyelids.

Chapter Ten

They landed with a slight thump on the well-maintained lawn and looked at each other with wide eyes.

'Holy shit! We're time travellers!' Avery joked and placed his hat on his head.

'Hell, yeah. Let's get into some cover,' Marcus replied, standing up straight and walking away slowly towards the main road that passed the Marriott Hotel, which looked glorious in the summer of 1926. 'We'll look better walking than standing in the middle of the lawn.' The grass was crisp underfoot from the morning's dew, which was starting to cover their shoes in moisture.

They made it to the road just in time, as several gardeners had started to notice the two well-dressed men standing like gnomes, looking around them.

'Where to now?' the younger agent asked. 'They didn't give us any money, so breakfast is out of the question.'

'Let's just move on from here in case they've called the police,' Marcus replied, looking back at the gardeners and continuing to walk casually away. 'Oh, and make sure you know where your return remote is. There is a slight time lapse from pressing it to disappearing.' He heard panic and frustration from his partner.

Avery was patting down his suit. 'Oh, shit! Shit! Shit!' he chanted. He had forgotten the remote. What was going to happen to him? *Calm down, idiot*, he thought. *Maybe Marc can come back in the morning? That's it, there are ways around this...* But that would mean admitting to such a blunder.

'You okay, homey?' Marcus asked, stopping and turning around to see his panicking partner. 'What's up?'

Avery's head dropped. 'I forgot the remote. What with everything else going on...' he said and the words died on his lips as he saw Marcus twirling one of the remotes with his finger. 'You shit!'

The older man smiled at Avery's reaction, then tossed the device towards him. Avery only just managed to catch it before it hit the sidewalk.

'You're welcome, my man,' said Marcus. 'I nearly forgot mine, too. That would've doomed us all!' He waited for Avery to catch up with him. 'No one else is overseeing us, so it's just you and me, buddy.'

They walked in silence together along the streets of Washington DC.

'So, Marc, how do you cope with twin girls?' Avery asked kindly, as they both took in the early morning rays that were starting to dry out their shoes.

'Not too bad,' replied Marcus. 'They were nine last month, and I managed to be there for the whole weekend.' He recalled what his wife had vowed to cut off him if he wasn't there – in jest, he had hoped. 'I am blessed, they are good girls. Loretta managed to get an office job locally, and her mother is happy to look after the kids, so things are working out well for us.'

The blond man nodded. 'That's good. Most people don't get on with their mothers-in-law,' he joked and saw the other man flinch. 'Not all clear sailing, eh?'

Marcus shrugged. 'It's okay, but you upset one of them, then you have all four women pissed at you. That's a lot of disapproving looks for one man to cope with.' He laughed lightly and kicked a rogue stone into the road. 'Even my little angels have that disappointed look down to a fine art now. The house is sometimes a scary place to be, but I love them to distraction.'

They walked for a few blocks before another word was uttered.

'So, does your mother-in-law live close, then?' Avery queried. 'That's handy.'

'Loretta is very traditional,' replied Marcus. 'When my parents passed and we moved to our new home, she brought her mother to live with us. She lives in an annex on the house. So yes, very... close.'

Marcus missed his parents very much, even more so now he had the power to visit their younger selves with this time machine. What would be the harm in that? Like the men who had already altered time, he would want to do good things himself, never realising the effect his meddling would cause to the timeline.

'So, what about you and yours?' he asked.

Avery chided himself for having started this conversation. But he was right to have done so, as they needed to work together, so they had to share things about themselves.

'Lost Mum at birth, and grew up with just Dad, who we call the Colonel. From childhood, he pushed me to follow his lead, but we were always moving homes, with different babysitters caring for me, and it fractured our relationship,' he explained sadly. 'Unfortunately, things came easy for me, which grew into arrogance, then boredom.'

'I did notice that look when the Director was talking to us,' admitted Marcus. 'You need to hide that.'

Avery just shrugged. 'I do try. If something interests me, like this…' He waved his hand around. 'Then I'm good. But it's the whole power trips that people higher up like to play, just like my dad. I don't play that game,' he added coldly. 'Same thing with women, I'm afraid. They push, I walk!'

The clicking of their new shoes hitting the sidewalk echoed as the two men walked.

'But you seem to like this Samantha, though,' said Marcus. 'Your eyes brighten when you talk of her.' He tried steering the conversation, then pointed to a bench over on a patch of grass, away from the road. They sat down and took off their hats.

'Sammy? Yeah, she's the only woman I've met who hates the games as much as I do,' Avery smiled happily. 'She has this plan in her head and won't deviate from it – well, until now.'

They fell silent as a police car drifted by. The two police officers inside nodded at them and Marcus and Avery nodded back, which seemed to pass muster, though they looked upon Marcus a bit longer than was necessary.

When the car passed by, Avery continued. 'Us being spirited away like this has unnerved her.'

Marcus chuckled. 'She's not the only one, my friend. But we have a plan and, if we stick to it, we might be home making them angry in mere days.' That made them both laugh.

They continued chatting about their past histories, professional and personal, as they walked around the city. They also decided that, if they had to do this journey again, they would remember to ask for the appropriate currency. Coffee makes everything better.

It had just turned 10 am and the two agents began to head back to the Marriott Hotel on Woodley Road. They entered the clean, well-polished lobby and saw three suited and well-groomed hotel employees. It was agreed that Avery would talk to the men, being mindful of the prejudices of that time. Behind the reception desk, the small, slender man with a pencil-thin moustache and slicked-down hair looked at the blond man, and only him.

'Good morning, sir, how may I help you today?' he asked with his eyes locked on the white man, whilst the other two hotel employees had eyes for Marcus only.

In a well-practised move for all law enforcement professionals, both agents flipped out their badges for the little man to see.

'Bureau of Investigations,' said Avery in a no-nonsense tone. 'We believe you have a Margaret Brown staying here?'

The man stared at them for a moment. His gold badge stated that he was the manager.

'Yes, we do,' he replied. 'Can I ask what this is in reference to?' He spoke in a sickly and clipped tone.

Agent Saunders placed his hand on the polished rosewood counter, leaving oily fingerprints. All eyes fell on him. 'That is between the federal government and Mrs Brown,' he said. 'So, please contact her and tell her we would like to see her… now.' Avery's eyes never shifted or blinked as both he and the manager fought for dominance.

The seconds drew out until the manager picked up the phone and turned his back on the two agents, who had now removed their hats. There was a muffled conversation, then the phone was put down.

'Mrs Brown will receive you in her suite,' the little rat of a manager spat with a cold look. 'Third floor, room 352!'

Marcus walked over and put his big hands onto the wooden surface and gave the manager a hard stare, showing him his badge. 'Agent Martinez. I would like both yours and your colleagues' names and home addresses, please. Just in case we have to do a follow-up investigation, and especially as you have been so welcoming.' He spoke with a smile that didn't reach his eyes and watched as the pale trio almost went translucent under the Mexican's steely glare. He did enjoy this part of the job.

Two minutes and thirty-three seconds later, they found themselves going up in the elevator, trying to hold in their laughs in front of the lift attendant.

'Well, that was fun!' said Avery.

'Hell, yeah! Sometimes, it's good to be cop,' replied Marcus, making them release their laughter and causing the lift attendant to gaze at them strangely. As the lift rose to their desired floor, they both stepped out onto a plush, carpeted hallway. The attendant told them that Mrs Brown's suite was at the furthest end.

'So, how are we doing this? Good cop bad cop?' Marcus smirked.

They knocked on the door and it was opened by a maid wearing an old-fashioned uniform consisting of a black dress and a white lace pinny. She was devoid of a smile.

'Good morning, gentlemen. May I see your badges… please?' she said coldly as the two agents towered over her. Her hazel-coloured eyes flicked over them, reading their names off their identity papers. A smile graced her lips as she looked up and tucked a rogue blonde lock of hair over her ear. 'Please, come in and take a seat,' she said and gestured to a couple of ornate chairs with flowery cushions upon them.

'Thank you,' both men replied in unison as they once again took off their hats and sat down.

The maid brought over a trolley with tea and coffee pots, along with several china cups and saucers. 'Would you care for tea or coffee?' she asked.

They both had a black coffee with sugar as they waited for the unsinkable Molly Brown to appear. The maid refused to be drawn into any long conversation – clearly, she had been well trained. A door at the far end opened and in glided the one and only woman, causing the two agents to stand up and bow slightly. They didn't quite know why they did that.

'Good morning, gentlemen! Please sit,' Mrs Brown said.

She was a well-built lady with a hard look, dressed all in black in remembrance of her husband, who had passed in 1922. Molly Brown was an intimidating sight, even while she was being served a cup of tea from her servant.

'That will be all, Cynthia. You may go and have breakfast,' Molly said, and the maid curtsied and left. She took a sip of her beverage and then carefully set the cup down. 'Now, what can I do for the Bureau of Investigation?' she asked with a smile.

This time, Marcus took the lead. 'I hope you don't mind, Mrs Brown, but we have a few questions about your time on the *Titanic*.' He saw her face still, then her smile fade and her eyes harden.

'Go on,' she replied icily. 'Though, I don't like speaking of that night. Such a terrible loss of life.' She dabbed at her eyes with a handkerchief. 'I will try and answer your questions to the best of my ability.'

The agents looked at each other.

'Firstly, we admire you for the help you gave all those people on that terrible night,' Marcus said calmly, and he received a curt nod in return. 'We have been tasked to speak with survivors and ask questions about the tragedy. They want to write the finite account of the night.'

'It seems strange to me that you would be a part of such a thing,' Molly queried while frowning at the two men. 'Isn't your remit to investigate crimes and those who carry out such acts?'

Avery stepped in this time. 'I believe somebody high up in the government wants this information and has pressured our bosses to loan us out,' he said, making it up on the spot. Who knew she would be so suspicious?

Mrs Brown gave a bored roll of her eyes. 'Fine, fine, ask your questions,' she stated.

Marcus pulled out a pad and pencil. 'You boarded the ship on your own, yes?'

'Yes, my grandson fell ill, so I headed home early,' she replied, wondering where this would be going.

Marcus made a note. 'From the reports we had, you spent some time with a youngish gentleman, who was not known to your shipmates. Is that correct?' he asked and saw Mrs Brown's quizzical eyebrow rise up sharply.

'Hmmm, such a question to ask a widow,' she replied calmly. 'But I will answer your probing question. He was a handsome young man called Alfred Gwynne Vanderbilt. Not sure why people didn't recognise him, though.'

Even though both agents came from different backgrounds, they both knew a lie when they heard one.

'I see, and do you know where we can speak to this gentleman?' Marcus pushed.

Margaret dropped her head. 'The poor young man was destined to die at sea. He sank on the *Lusitania*, just two years later. Such a nice young man.'

Avery wanted to move this along. 'Molly, people said they never saw Vanderbilt board the *Titanic*, and this man was a stranger to all but you.'

'DON'T call me by that name, young man!' she snapped. 'Especially if you are calling me a liar, then I am Mrs Brown to you. The man I spoke to said he was Alfred Vanderbilt, and he kept me company on the journey, which is not a crime I believe.'

The younger agent cringed at her abrupt response but was determined not to back down. 'Was it this man that pushed you to make sure that the lifeboats were filled with women and children?' he asked. 'All witnesses said that you were single minded in your task and were heard saying that you were told this would happen.' Avery hoped she wouldn't notice he had lied.

Molly's eyes widened as she recalled the night in question. 'Well, I can tell you that only the Captain asked me to do such things. The poor man was beyond breaking point at the time and bumped into me on the way to the radio room.' Mrs Brown lied wholeheartedly. She knew it and they knew it, but what could they prove?

The room stilled and then they all exchanged smiles, albeit false ones.

'Well, thank you for clearing that up, Mrs Brown,' said Marcus. 'You did a wonderful thing that night, whoever it was that asked you,' he added with a smile. 'Hopefully, we can find some photos of you and Alfred together, just for the book.'

'Alas, there are none,' replied Molly. 'I have searched and asked all those I knew that were on that ship, but no luck I'm afraid.' She checked her watch. 'Do you have any more questions? The day is moving along, and I have many things to do while I am here.'

Marcus and Avery looked at each other.

'No, I think that will be it today, Mrs Brown,' Avery said, signalling for both men to stand up with their hats in hand. 'Hope you enjoy your visit to the capital.'

Molly nodded and stood up. 'Thank you, I will. I look forward to seeing this supposed book gentlemen,' she replied with added sass as she walked the men to the door, her eyes sparkling with mischief. 'Good day,' she said and closed the door.

The two agents walked towards the elevator in silence. They were passed by the maid, who was coming back from breakfast. Her eyes tracked them as they passed, but never a word was said. The two men remained silent until they walked out into the Washington DC sunlight. They looked at each other.

'Well, that was a load of bullshit,' said Avery with a laugh as they headed away.

Back up in room 352, the stoic Madam Brown was standing at the window watching her visitors walk away. She was then joined by her maid.

'Are you okay, Madam? Did they upset you?' the maid asked.

'No, Cynthia,' replied Mrs Brown. 'They just asked questions that brought forth some of the nicest, and some of the darkest, of memories.' She smiled briefly. 'Have you ever known of any member of the law enforcement to walk anywhere, and to ask questions for the contents of a book?'

The maid watched the two men walked away up the street. 'Not that I have dealings with them, but I would guess they wouldn't do, either' she replied and saw her mistress nod. 'Shall I call for your breakfast, Madam?'

Molly continued to watch the men as they disappeared in the distance.

'Yes please, Cynthia,' she said softly, walking back into her bedroom and straight to a small travel case that she took everywhere. She sat on a chair as she opened the case and looked in it to find one of her many prized possessions. She had photos of family and friends from all over the world. She continued to leaf through the images until finally finding the one that made her heart pump with excitement. The picture had been taken by a photographer who frequented the first-class restaurant. Margaret ran her finger down the man's cheek in the photo. They had been laughing at some shared joke, which her memory had lost the details of along the way. The photo brought the emotion back, just not the words.

'Who are you, Brian Partridge?' she said quietly. 'Your story was weak to begin with, and all these years later questions are now being asked. What have you done, my mysterious friend?' she whispered and kissed two fingers before pressing them against his photo. The feelings she held for the man confused her, but he was long gone and so was her husband, and neither one would be seen again. Tucking away her photo, she left her bedroom to start her day again, properly.

The temporal agents landed into their separate pods after leaving Mrs Brown. The younger man stumbled forward a couple of steps and then he turned to see his partner smiling happily. He wondered what he had to be so happy about.

The words his partner had said as they had pressed the buttons to return home came flooding back. It was a line from the damned show *Star Trek*. *Why are there so many geeks in the Bureau?* Avery wondered. He looked at Marcus pointedly.

'What did you say?' he asked.

'Beam me up, Scotty,' said Marcus. Avery rolled his eyes. His partner was tricky.

'You enjoyed this, didn't you?' he said.

'What? Time travelling?' Marcus asked and received a nod back. 'Hell, yeah! At least we didn't have to pick up some whales!' The Mexican laughed and walked out of the travel room and to his quarters to change. He hummed the *Star Trek* theme all the way there.

His partner just sobbed in mock despair. 'Why me!' he cried out and made his way back to his own quarters to change and text Samantha. It wasn't the fact that he hated Trekkies, or science fiction – he simply didn't understand the devotion these people seemed to have. Maybe it was just a fault he had ingrained in him, he concluded.

They both reconvened in the kitchen to make some coffee, which didn't taste as nice as the one they'd had with Mrs Brown.

'So, what shall we do now? Clearly, she was lying,' said Avery, trying to ignore the time showing on the kitchen clock. He took it down and placed it in a drawer.

'I don't think there is any point checking her story,' replied Marcus. 'Going back and telling the real man that somebody pretended to be him on the most famous maritime disaster going, it might make him change his future choices.' He gazed thoughtfully into the steaming hot cup of coffee. 'I suggest we look through every photo we can from the passengers, and maybe check if there were any photos left by family members after Molly Brown's death.'

And that is what they did for the rest of day, hoping to find just one photo of the time traveller, whoever he was. However, they never did find a picture of the man and Margaret Brown. At the end of their day, they were sitting down eating a takeaway, this time from Marcus's fellow countrymen.

'So, what do you want to do now, Marc?' asked Avery. 'Shall we go back and stop his attempt at saving JFK? Or shall we just try and find him and take away his equipment?'

Marcus thought for a moment. 'The thing is,' he replied, 'if we stop the major event in Dallas, but don't catch the person who is messing with the timeline, our job here will be over and this place will shut down. But we need to identify the target to negate any future problems.' He took a sip of his orange soda. 'How about we loiter around the boarding area of the *Titanic*, and see if we can see him? Then we'd know who we are tracking.'

'Sounds like a plan,' said Avery. 'Remember our credentials won't work in England, so all we can do is look about.' He smirked slightly. 'It is something that would be amazing to see though, and we already have suits contemporary to that time period.'

'Okay, I think we need to have a kip, then let's go travelling,' Marcus said as they went back to enjoying their meal. Once again, they chatted casually about their lives and what they would love to do in the future.

The next day their nerves were taut. They had picked some waste ground outside the docks in Southampton as the location to 'land' in. They wrapped their coats around them and followed the map that Avery had printed off for them.

Avery was grumbling about the chilly, damp weather. 'Bloody England and their shitty weather,' he moaned as they walked onto the cobbled streets. His shoes slipped on some horse manure. 'Fucking hell!'

Marcus snickered, but he wasn't the only one. Some locals walking nearby were having a good laugh at the posh-looking gents, who were clearly lost.

'That's what I respect about you,' Marcus began, making his blond-haired partner turn towards him. 'It's your ability to blend in wherever you go.' He felt his world lurch as the fellow agent tried to push him into a puddle by the side of the road.

With laughter ringing in their ears, they made their way to the docks and the home of RMS *Titanic*. The amount of cart, automobile and foot traffic increased the closer to the ship they got. A few minutes later, they were standing out of the way of all of the people, just staring up at the iconic ship.

'Jeez, what a vessel,' Avery exclaimed, his eyes roaming over the hull of the ship, gazing at all those rivets that were driven in by hand. 'How in the hell did this thing ever sink?'

'Bad design, rudder was too small. Very bad luck,' Marcus commented, though they both knew there were many reasons why the big ship sank and so many people died. Standing on tiptoe, he scanned the crowd. 'We don't have a chance, buddy. He could be here or on the ship already. We just don't have a chance in hell of finding him!'

Avery agreed with his partner. 'Let's just take five and watch the ship leave, man. At least this is something that we can chat about that only a handful of people still alive have witnessed.' They both fell into another comfortable silence as they watched the passengers from many countries and backgrounds follow their dreams and head to America, though most of them would never make it.

After watching the large luxury liner depart, the two agents walked away with the other onlookers to find a safe and quiet place where they could return home. Once again, they landed in their pods and the science fiction fan could not wipe the smile from his face.

'Right, want to sleep on it? Or shall we just move on the trip to Dallas?' Marcus asked.

'Nope, let's get this done,' Avery replied. He wanted to get home. 'Email the Director and ask him for new suits, and anything you think we'll need.' He looked at Marcus. 'Do you agree?'

Marcus was torn. He wanted to spend more time visiting places, maybe visit his mum and dad. It was then that he realised the trap of doing these sorts of trips, the power of going anywhere and at any time, including seeing his parents again. No wonder this unknown man had tried to change things.

'Okay,' said Marcus, 'I'll email him with a plan and see what they will provide us with.'

Marcus clapped his hands together and started to work on the plan and the email, then made some coffee.

This was it, the final mission, as they saw it – though, it was twenty-four hours later than they had wanted. They were ready, but would their actions be enough to stop the last temporal event in Dallas? They were given black suits in the fashion of the day, but with a Kevlar weave added into the lining. It added to the weight, but it was tolerable, as the mission brief explained that the target had kidnapped a law officer and taken his weapon.

A full-on combat bulletproof jacket would easily be noticed and could cause other temporal issues. They wore hats and dark glasses of the day and looked like any other man of the city. What amazed them was the weapons they were given. They were .45 Colt semi-autos with suppressors. Although the bullets were from 1962, they were reloaded with up-to-date combustibles to make them quicker than the old powder that was used back in the day.

Marcus glanced at his partner, who looked overly focused. 'You okay, Ave?' Avery gave a brief nod in return. 'Ever fired one of these away from the range?'

'No, born desk jockey, I'm afraid,' Avery replied with a brittle smile on his face. 'Does it show?'

His partner nodded. 'Isn't a problem. Keep the safety on, and the gun out of sight until we engage. The job is to scare him off or to apprehend him. We aren't there to kill him,' Marcus explained and slid the hefty weapon into the holster that hung by his ribs. 'He'll be in a police cruiser. I'll put a couple of shots in the windscreen to scare him off. If you are confident as I move, you shoot a few into the engine, okay?'

'Got it,' Avery shot back, though he hadn't intended the harshness of his tone. His time at the firing range had been limited and, although he had fired a good range of weapons in the Army, they both knew his talents lay elsewhere. 'I won't let you down, I promise.' They shared a look and walked through to the travel room, where the coordinates were already typed in. Remembering their remotes, the two men settled into the pods and, in a flash, they were gone.

They landed in a small patch of grassland that wasn't detailed on the maps that they had been using. An instruction from their computer had detailed how they should go about stopping the Traveller from disrupting the timeline. They frowned, because it had directed them to arrive just thirty minutes before the assassination attempt.

Their plan was to arrive early and have breakfast, so they had asked for the currency of the day. That request had been instantly quashed by the Director. At the same time, an email had arrived ordering that they should not engage with any other members of law enforcement or the public.

They intended to stop the man before he stole the police vehicle. Avery was shaking with nervous energy as they walked among the crowd of people heading towards the plaza, to watch the President and the first lady drive past. They were getting strange looks, but they just guessed it was the dark clothing, which matched the Secret Service attire. Soon, they allowed the public to pull away as they reached their destination, N. Houston Street. Looking at the diagram they had been given, they judged they were about a hundred yards away from where the car would pull up.

They moved closer to the very last parked car on their side of the street, which cut down the distance.

'You okay, Avery?' Marcus asked, his eyes not leaving the junction where the target would come from.

'Yeah, but this information… how did they get it? It reads as if I'd written it myself.' He tucked the paper away, nodding at a pretty blonde woman who gave him a strange look. You couldn't blame her, as they were standing stock still as the crowds flowed around them, like a rock in a river.

Marcus saw the police cruiser turn onto the road and park up. They couldn't quite see the man who was driving.

'The report was written by us in the future, I guess,' said Marcus. 'That's how they knew we would stop this.' He slowly pulled his weapon out, flicking the safety catch off in a well-practised movement with his thumb. 'Avery, get ready,' he instructed quietly, his eyes locked on the target. It was a long shot, but they had cover.

Avery followed his partner and readied his weapon. The flow of foot traffic had finished, which meant it was nearly zero hour. The engine revs picked up and, as if that was the audible key, Marcus brought his gun to bear and fired. In a second, the vehicle windscreen was hit and had spiderwebbed badly. Another cartridge flew out from the gun's chamber as Avery punched another hole into the destroyed windshield.

The car shot backwards, making both agents fire their weapons into the retreating car's engine block. Fluid began to pour out as it stopped and Marcus saw a bullet fly into the driver's side windshield. Luckily, it missed the driver. Suddenly, they heard gunshots and screams coming from the street behind them.

'What the hell…' he said and realised the assassination was in progress. It felt dirty to let such a crime be committed. 'Let's go!'

They started to run as the police cruiser disappeared. By the time they had turned the corner, the Traveller was blocks away.

'STOP! POLICE!' Avery screamed and fired some rounds down the road, missing the man.

Marcus shook his head as they started to run again. 'Put your weapon away. Too many civilians!' he called out and watched as the target struggled at the trunk of the car and, after popping it open, he ran. He was quick, despite carrying a bag. 'Shit! Let's go. We aren't going to catch him.' As Marcus spoke, he pointed to an alleyway, just as another police unit arrived.

They were a few blocks away. Both agents were bent over, breathless, as the remotes took them home again. They had lost their hats and sunglasses in their endeavour to capture the target and then to evade the police, who had turned up to save the stricken policeman still incarcerated in the trunk.

'Thought I had him when he was running,' Avery panted.

'Never shoot a man without a gun, my friend,' said Marcus. 'We were there just to scare him.' He stretched his back, his blood still pumping fast. He couldn't blame the kid – it was, after all, his first time in the field. 'But we did the job, now the paperwork,' he added. With that, they walked out of the travel room and looked at the three lights on the wall. There were only two lights now.

Avery jumped up in the air. 'Wooohooo, baby!' he said and turned to his partner in time. 'Reports, then beer! What do you say?' he said, sporting a huge smile.

'Sounds like a plan, buddy,' said Marcus. 'Let's get this done.' They high fived and made their way to the diner. All in all, he would make it back for his anniversary party. 'Hey, Ave, wanna come to a party this weekend? You can bring your girlfriend.'

The tall, blond agent turned and smiled. 'Sure, sounds like fun!'

Chapter Eleven

It had been a month since I had even gone down into the basement. It wasn't the fact that I had failed again – it was mainly due to the two men who had shot up the police car and, to a lesser extent, me.

Where had they come from? Was I being watched? Or was my browser history being monitored? All the sites I had used were above board, so I decided it was probably best to go cold turkey for a time while recovering from the bullet graze. During that time, I ordered a large greenhouse, which has only just been installed, thank you workmen. That meant I had lots of work to do in terms of getting it ready for planting, so I would have access to plenty of vegetables during the winter.

Also, using my poor woodworking skills, I turned one of the unused outbuildings into a chicken house, with plenty of roosts and access to the grass area outside. I made it especially fox proof, or any other predatory animals come to that.

The next day, a big noisy rooster called Karl was delivered, together with eight clucking ladies to lay eggs for me. The number of eggs would lessen through the winter months, but hey, at least it would keep me busy, along with my running and looking after the garden.

During the evenings, I looked through George Lancaster Jnr's notes about his trips. Not only that, but I re-read his novels just in case there was anything hidden in his writings

– and there it was. I had totally forgotten about the scourge of one of his books, where the main character gets followed throughout the novel from time jump to time jump, all the while being tracked by the men of shadows, who seemed to work for the government.

Even in his personal notes, Lancaster skirted over his jaunts into the past, just noting times and dates, including the events he had witnessed. Mainly, however, he wrote in short bullet points which lacked any concrete facts, unlike his books in so many ways. One night, however, I did notice a passage written in very small, chicken-scratch writing:

7th December 1941, 8 am Hawaiian time

Pearl Harbour, Akupu Mountain.
21°21'54.0"N 157°57'00.0"W

Found perfect view to see the attack by the Japanese.

Just as attack starts, two men, possible shadow, were spied creeping towards me.

They wore camouflage, which is not of this time.

Took photos and then moved away and returned home.

There was a photo attached of two large males walking up a narrow track towards him. They were carrying M4 carbines. Then, later, in pencil there was a note:

I am being followed; the shadows have found me!

Shaking my head, I chided myself for not going through these documents properly. All I was focused on was the time travel machine. How could I be so careless?

The rest of the evening was given to working out a plan to view these agents of shadow in action. I must admit to liking the name, though. While in bed, troubling thoughts travelled through my mind thanks to my imagination. What if they were watching me? If they were, why weren't they bashing down my door? Or just putting a bullet in my head? After all, they quite happily ran after me, firing at me in Dallas.

The night was troubling, as every creak was a black-clad agent coming to despatch not the time tourist, but the Evil Time manipulator – not a great name, but I was asleep. The next morning went on as usual and I had a run after feeding the still disgruntled chickens. The rooster was ready to fight me, but he was never going to win that battle.

After breakfast, I finally made it down into the basement and I started to clean the place up. The carpet had some blood on it, but it didn't look too bad. I then cleaned the desks and computer. Satisfied that everything was shipshape, I then looked at the coordinates that Lancaster had used for his trip back to 1941.

After setting up the plans, I popped into town and picked up some food supplies. I also bought a digital camera with a detachable long zoom lens. This was not only to take pictures of the agents, but also the act of aggression by the Emperor of Japan. On the way home, I bought some camo gear from the Army and Navy store, along with matching boots. Might as well at least try and hide from these people. After all, they would be armed.

I was still getting funny looks from the town people. Clearly, the electrician was still gossiping his heart out about working for the mad scientist. Maybe I should go back in time and kick him in the balls.

So, the rest of the day was spent washing my new clothes, then taking the camera out and getting used to the basic functions so that I wouldn't fumble it on the day. It took a while, as I wasn't Andy Warhol reborn. I swear Karl the Rooster sneered at me when I immortalised him and his harem. Who would have thought chickens could be so judgemental?

The next day after my morning chores, I dressed in my new kit. GI Joe I was not, but this camo gear would help to keep me hidden within the green woodlands of Hawaii. With a bag filled with water attached to my front, I also had snacks that I had placed in sealed plastic ziplocked bags, camera, binoculars and the emergency remote, while everything that needed to be charged was charged. Slipping an olive-green beanie on my head, I set the machine to count down.

Placing my sunglasses on, I was once again thrown into the past. I then promptly fell over, face first, into a bush, scratching my face asunder.

'MOTHER F…!' I cried out, but quickly stopped myself, aware of the danger I was in. The bush was easy to escape from and I noticed the reason for the fall. I instantly felt foolish, as this is what happens when you land on the slope of a hill or mountain.

Slinging my bag onto my back, and with map in hand, I began to walk forward. The time machine had placed me a short way from the trail where the agents would walk along. According to Lancaster's notes, he would have been to my right and, only slightly lower in a small, flat clearing, is where he would make camp.

I knew that George Lancaster Jnr would turn up at around 7.30 am. I guessed he was not the patient sort. For me, waiting wasn't a problem as it allowed me time to wipe my face with a wet wipe, making my skin sting from the multitude of scratches from my landing. I then readied the camera, while taking on some water and food. It was such a gorgeous still morning, but that would soon end.

A flash of light made me jump out of my reverie. Lifting the spyglasses, I look down the path. They were far away, but I could see two figures making their way up the game trail. Moving into cover slowly, I waited for my favourite author to arrive – and, with another flash, there he was. Lancaster arrived with a big smile on his face, a long-lensed camera hanging from around his neck on a thick sling. He also had a small chair for him to sit upon.

The drone of the Japanese aircraft started to drift in, though my eyes were flitting from the strangely excited writer to the agents slowly making their way up the hill. Everyone jumped as gunfire and explosions rocked the harbour, which was a fare distance away, but you could see flames and plumes of smoke rising into the once blue sky.

Lancaster swore loudly and I watched as he lowered his camera down to the game trail.

'Bastards!' he shouted, then instantly pulled the remote from his pocket and pressed it. He then placed it in a pocket and started to walk away slowly, while taking pictures of the horrifying scene below.

Just after the biggest explosion, which seemed to make everything get pushed back in the blast, the writer disappeared in a flash, causing the incoming agents of shadow to swear. They continued to the spot where Lancaster had been sitting, where they both took off their sunglasses and scanned the area, giving me the perfect opportunity to take photos of their faces.

Then the world went crazy. It felt like the air was full of lead, sending myself and the agents to the ground and scurrying to find cover. A big boom sounded as a white plane flew over us. The red sun adorned the underneath of its wings. Then a flash appeared, announcing the fact that the agents had bugged out, too.

Then it came to me. The flash of light was announcing to the battle that something was up here.

'SHITTTT!' I shouted as I dug out my remote and pressed continuously, like a game of whack a mole at the fair. That's when I heard another drone of an aircraft. I dived behind a large tree, just in time as machine gunfire tore the ground up in the surrounding area. Clamping my hands over my ears, I screamed in fear.

VROOOMMM! The plane sped over in a nano second, finally finishing off my ear drums. Shaking off the dizziness, I picked up the return home remote from the ground. Thankfully, it was still in one piece and within reach. My thumb did its job and pressed the red button to take me back to safety. I placed the remote in my pocket and then slung my backpack on my front. That way, it wouldn't launch me from the pod and cause me to fall, face down, onto the basement floor… again. I headed back into some cover and continued to take photos of the slaughter below.

And that was why I never saw the plane coming at me. Focusing so much on the view finder and the din of the battleship, my ears were buzzing so much that I didn't notice the hum of the plane. Dirt was flying up below me and creeping upwards, trees and bushes being shredded. Wide-eyed, my arms sagged, causing me to drop the camera to my waist as the plane came into view. They had me dead to rights and the bullets were nearly upon me.

I thought that my last living act was to lift the camera and begin to click away. My eyes closed, though I kept the button pressed. Then, thankfully, I was enveloped in light and I found myself back in my basement, covered in sweat, dirt and foliage. Standing stock still, laughter started to come, followed by tears that created clean patches upon my checks.

'Fuck!' I said to myself.

Stumbling from the pod, I managed to sit down as my legs weren't ready for any kind of long journey. The adrenaline that was coursing through my system felt like it was at a fatal level, as my heart nearly tore itself from my chest. Raising the camera, I flicked through the last few images – the white plane, flames coming from its wings, and the focused look of the pilot, though that could have been my imagination. I turned the camera off, placing it onto the desk, then closed the computer down and enjoyed the thrum of electricity dying away slowly. I then sat there in the gloom, with my eyes closed, as I tried to centre myself.

It took two hours for me to make it upstairs and strip down in the kitchen, throwing the newly purchased clothes straight into the washer. Then I made my way to the bedroom and then to the shower. But after all that had happened, a smile remained on my face, as the excitement alone was like a drug.

The clock on my bedroom wall told me it was time for dinner. There was some cold chicken and salad already prepared in the refrigerator. And so, with that and a cold beer, I sat in front of the TV and watched some of my favourite shows – though, in my mind, the image of the Japanese pilot firing away at me played again and again.

As the sun started to go down, I headed out and locked up the chickens. Karl was being a bit of a dick, which meant I had to chase the little red bastard in. Once they were all safe, I popped my earbuds into my ears and, with my iPod on, I headed off for a run, hoping the exercise would cause me to burn off the excess energy I was feeling.

The running shoes kicked up dirt during my circuit of my family's property and, as I ran, ideas flowed through my mind. I had checked all of Lancaster's works and notes. But what I had not done was read the partially written books that he'd not had time to finish before his passing. My running pace slowed, and the last rays of the New England sun began to disappear.

'Did they find his body?' I muttered.

I kicked off my shoes as I entered the old farmhouse and walked instantly to the laptop, searching for Lancaster's obituary on the internet. It took a while to find the official cause of death.

With my chin resting on my hand, I read the webpage. It appeared that two years ago, Mr George Lancaster Jnr and his good friend, Siobhan O'Keeffe, had passed away when their yacht went down in the Atlantic during a storm. Wreckage was recovered, but no bodies had been found at the time.

That painted so many pictures of how George, or someone else, could have faked their death. So, search teams had decided that the likelihood of them being alive was zero and the family sold off his estate. Now, did he use his remote to take them both back home? And did he dismantle the time machine ready for the sale? Or had somebody in the family been asked to do that? Maybe he had made another machine and placed it in a secondary location? Which would give him all the time in the world to relocate himself anywhere and anytime.

Leaning back in the chair, I groaned as my back popped. *Maybe he had it right?* I thought to myself. If the shadow agents were after him, why not disappear? Was that something I now had to do? It would hurt my family. Yes, my brother and I do get on better now after my trip back, but we don't talk or search each other out.

Frustration was pouring off me. So many things I did not know. What if these agents were after me? Would I ever get to finish all that I wanted to do? After wiping my search history and closing the laptop down, I gathered up Lancaster's unfinished books and settled on the couch with a cold beer and read into the night, until exhaustion took me as its own.

'EUREKA!' I screamed the next day, while reading the unfinished novel called 'The Shadow of Normandy'. The main character was called Alexi Trebuchet, who was a time travelling mercenary and who, in this story, had been paid to cause havoc behind the lines the night before the Normandy invasion. And, when he started his blood-thirsty rampage through the sleeping soldiers of the Wehrmacht, the agents of shadow appeared and chased him into the countryside and all the way to the coast, where he fought them off while he waited for his temporal return belt to spring into action.

For some reason, this made my pulse race. Could it be true? Was he chased? I couldn't believe that he fought off the agents, though running away and hiding sounded about right. And, while it sounded dangerous as hell, to see D-Day for myself would be scarily amazing. But dare I risk it?

The rest of the day and evening was spent looking over maps of the Normandy beaches on D-Day. According to

Lancaster's notes, the invasion initially started out at Pointe du Hoc, with a plan to wipe out the garrison and the big guns the Germans manned – which, of course, I had read about on the net. On the actual day, it was found that the garrison was not at full strength, as the guns had not all had been fitted, and the ones that had were not safe to be fired. Plus, there were just a few soldiers guarding the cliff edge.

So, I concluded that a little distance away from that point might be the place to appear. It was surrounded by a wooded area. Plus, at that time, the German soldiers would all be looking towards the beaches and the mass of Allied forces, not backwards. The coordinates were about a mile behind the gun emplacements in the wooded area. The troops would start their attack just after seven that morning, when they would attempt to scale the perilous cliffs under fire. So, I planned to arrive just as the poor soldiers had started their climb.

For once, I was not nervous. After all, facing down a Japanese fighter plane was harder than this. I would be playing hide and seek behind the lines, hoping to see Lancaster and the shadow agents, and maybe even get to see some of the invasion first-hand. However, I wasn't too hopeful about that.

In preparation, I made some purchases – a camouflage ballistic helmet, along with a plate carrier vest, which had better stopping power than the normal bulletproof vest, though heavier, and finally a large camo coat that covered the vest easily. Waiting for these to be delivered would give me enough time to get everything ready, including writing a new note for my nephew, just in case.

I looked at endless pages of documents and photos of the Pointe du Hoc. For safety, the remote would be in my hand always. Not only that, but the stun gun would be coming with me. It was charged up and ready to go. I went over the timeline once again to make sure everything was correct:

06.39 – H-Hour. D, E and F companies of 2nd Ranger Battalion approach the Normandy coast in a flotilla of twelve craft.

07.05 – Strong tides and navigation errors mean the initial assault arrives late and the 5th Ranger Battalion, as well as A and B companies from 2nd Battalion, move to Omaha beach instead.

07.30 – Rangers fight their way up the cliff and reach the top and start engaging the Germans across the battery. Rangers discover the casemates are empty.

08.15 – Approximately thirty-five Rangers reach the road and create a roadblock.

09.00 – Five German guns are located and destroyed using thermite grenades.

The likelihood was that this was going to be a short trip, but that's good in a war zone. It took three days in total for all the new toys to turn up, which now included a matching water bottle and belt, which would allow the taser to be holstered. Once again, the mirror mocked me. Though the vest did make me look more buff, it took a bit of adjusting to get it to sit right. That done, I started on the rest of the kit. Rambo I was not, but it would do.

This trip was going to be done after lights out. And so, just in case something happened, the chickens were safely locked up with a few days' worth of food – unless the gutsy rooster ate it all in one go.

I sat in the basement, nerves and adrenaline building, my fingers tapping against the desk while my foot tapped even quicker than Fred Astaire. I could not waste any more time. This was it. Standing up, I grabbed the small digital camera and placed it into a pocket, securing it with the Velcro. It would not do for someone to find a top-of-the-range digital camera. That would be awkward.

The timer ticked away and, as it did so, my hand twitched, rattling the stun gun, the remote sitting tightly in the other hand. Suddenly, I was blanketed in light, and then even more quickly the light was replaced by noise. Instantly, I ducked as my sight regained some clarity. The trees were exactly where they were meant to be, the trouble was that they had soldiers running through them. Cracks of gunfire were everywhere, while leaves and branches fell, covering me as I crouched behind the tree.

'Shit, shit, shit,' I muttered and headed towards the open area behind the gun emplacement, running in a crouch from shell hole to shell hole. It was like the surface of the moon. Not a blade of grass was left. Bodies were strewn about, all wearing the dark German Wehrmacht uniforms. Helmets and weapons lay about the place. German re-enforcements were also jumping from shell hole to shell hole to try and fight the US Rangers off the cliff.

'SCHNELL! SCHNELL!' a voice cried out from a group of German infantries as troops raced across the wasteland. With my stomach clenching, I ran, stooped over, towards a shell hole furthest away from the soldiers. Just as I jumped in, half of their number was torn apart by an explosion, causing blood and flesh to fly out, covering the Earth in gore. Screams from the Germans were drowned out by machine gunfire, which cut a young man in half, his blond hair flicked backwards by the force.

As soon as I landed in the hole, the button on the remote was pressed by accident as panic took hold of me from the assault on my senses. It was the screams that worried me. Bullets were zipping past, though you couldn't see them, just the noise. And then it hit me. The smell was awful – could it be from the bombs, or the bodies as they were torn apart?

After placing the remote in a pocket and zipping it closed, I dared to move above the lip of the shell hole. Pop, pop, pop. Bullets hit the ground at the top of the crater, sending me backwards and dirt flew into my face, making me cough loudly. It was time to go.

It was hell. The noise was deafening. Men were screaming, and explosions threw everything you could imagine into the air, but what came up had to come down. I looked again after steeling my fortitude and saw the olive-green infirmed men of the US Rangers fighting their way from the top of the cliff, bodies dropping on both sides as they clashed.

A loud thump, and then stones being scattered behind, made me turn around.

'Oh, shit!' I said as my eyes locked upon a German soldier. He was in his twenties, eyes wide. His helmet and main weapon were missing, he just had a dagger and a pistol holster attached to his belt. He had slid into the hole on his back, blood oozing from the many gashes in his uniform. I pointed my taser at him.

'SURRENDER!' I shouted, not knowing what else to say.

The man turned to me, a sneer forming on his face. On his breast were pinned a few medals that I had seen on TV. He looked like a hardnosed front-line soldier. His right hand slowly edged towards the pistol that sat on his leather belt. I gripped the taser harder.

'Don't fucking try it!' I screamed at him, just as a shell narrowly missed us, covering us both in filth.

'Yankee schwein,' he spat and jerked his gun out and pointed it towards me, moving forwards as he did so. I pressed the trigger, sending the two barbs into his body. The man went rigid, eyes rolling back into his head. Then his chest exploded as massive holes made a pattern across his chest. Next, all I felt was pain and, once again, light.

The pain was blinding, and it forced me to drop the taser. I could see that the barbed part of the taser had come back with me, flesh still attached to it. I looked down and saw the soldier's gun on the floor; it must have flown out of his hand when the Rangers shot him. However, it was strange that the barrel had wisps of smoke coming from it, and where was my pain coming from? That's when I registered the blood pooling on the floor. My eyes traced up my leg to my thigh and I saw the bloody gash.

'Shit!' I said and then my face hit the carpet.

Boom, boom, boom, sounded in my ears.

'What the fuck is that?' I muttered to myself sleepily, not knowing if I was coming or going. Boom, boom, boom! It was then that I realised the sound was coming from me. It was my heart beating. 'Well, that's a start,' I said and tried to move, which caused a scream that sounded like a little girl and brought on a wave of nausea. That's when it all came flooding back: the blood, bodies, noise. No wonder soldiers have so much trouble after a tour in whatever hellhole their leader sends them to.

Trying to get my fingers to work was hard enough. Finally, however, my helmet rolled away and, as it settled, I could see gouges cut into it. Not only that but blood, too. Luckily, not mine – I hoped. Forcefully, I rolled over onto my back and screamed the house down as the pain in my leg caused my sight to darken, though light could still be seen through the blackness.

As unconsciousness was kept at bay, the jacket was unzipped. That took a lot out of me, as breathing was difficult. Slowly and painfully, I managed to take the jacket off and the Velcro straps of the body armour were released. Every movement was excruciating, and my brow was awash with blood and sweat. It must have been over an hour before I managed to sit up, my back leaning against the desk.

My eyes took in the state of my leg, but all I could see was a bloody mass. Somehow, I managed to shuffle my ass over towards the door that led upstairs, and that alone made me pass out. I awoke, finding myself with the door open a crack. I was leaning sideways, and blood was still leaking from the hole, making me dizzy again.

Step by step, I moved upstairs towards the first floor. The pain pulsed with every move. Time didn't exist, as right then it was survival, and every second felt like a minute. Yes, I should focus on what to do with a bullet in my leg. Was I expecting to have the agents of shadow burst through my door to drag me off to some federal prison somewhere? Or could it be a very angry Karl the Rooster, pecking me to death for payback?

Bump. 'Ow!'

Bump. 'Ow, shit!'

Bump. 'Jesus, help me,' I sobbed, as the blood still oozed from my damaged leg, a trail of blood showing my slow progress up the stairs. I felt as if I was teetering on the edge of unconsciousness.

Sitting on a middle step, I was feeling fatigued. Sweat had now drenched my body and I had also started to tremble, which didn't bode well for my future. Was it because of blood loss, or shock? All I needed was to have Dr House and his crew from the TV show to barge in and declare that I had lupus.

With a hint of irony that my time was running out, I considered that I could well be the last combat fatality of World War Two. The climb up the stairs took what seemed to be forever, and then I had to open the door at the top, which was especially hard as my strength had long since left me. With a blood-curdling roar and using my good leg, I launched myself up, slamming against the door while turning the handle. Darkness claimed me as gravity slammed down hard. The pain alone shut my body down, then there was nothing.

Once again, the world had become dark. The only thing that gave any light was a small lamp that sat upon the sideboard illuminating the phone and the bowl, which contained the keys to the truck. Not only that, it was the resting place for my smartphone. It was only a waist-high cabinet, but at this moment in time it could have been a hundred feet in the air. I had no energy.

Slowly, I moved closer to the Everest-like sideboard while pain racked my body. Two choices came to mind: try and get to the phone and call anyone to help me, or just lie here and die, and decompose until a family member decides to check up on me and then proceeds to have nightmares for the rest of their lives. I decided. Phone it is.

I opted to use the same lunge technique that had worked so well before. Yes, I blacked out, but it was worth a go. After screaming a few times, I found myself sitting on the floor with my good leg underneath me. That way, I could balance on the knee and use my arm to pull myself up and rest against the furniture, while calling my rescuer.

That's why, five minutes later, I found myself on the floor, covered in keys, the home phone somewhere in the darkest corners of the house, and the smartphone screen shattered. It was then that the decision was made to just fucking give up and die.

Chapter Twelve

'Bloody hell, I wish they would get this road fixed,' she cursed to herself as the bumpy farm track leading to the Partridges' home attempted to send her through the roof of the Land Rover. Okay, so it wasn't an American vehicle, as all the farmers liked to mention at every visit, calling her a Limey lover, even though she was a born and bred local girl.

Dr Dana Lea Thompson had gone to school with the Partridges' youngest son. They'd both been loners who chatted occasionally about their need for all things science fiction and books, but peer pressures and different goals in life had pulled their friendship apart, if you could call it such a thing.

Like so many families in the county, she chose to sign on with the Army so that they would pay for college and train her to be a doctor, which had always been her dream. Well, if she was being honest, her first choice was to be a muppet – though, with the death of the god who was Jim Henson in 1990, that dream came crashing down. So, doctor it was.

Her plan was to work out her enlistment in the Army, travel a bit with them, then take up a post in a hospital in Boston to be closer to her folk. The final part of her vision for the future was to open a small practice in her hometown, settle down and have some kids. But, like everything else in this world, plans fail – or, in this case, they blew up in her face, not once but twice.

The tall, slender doctor was halfway through her second tour of Afghanistan when she received the heart-breaking news that her parents had passed away in a car crash one snowy night. The report said that her father had hit a deer head on, sending the animal into the windscreen and then the car into a tree. Her parents were said to have died instantly, though she would always have her doubts.

As Dana – or DNA to her friends, or Princess Leia to the people who wanted to feel her wrath – didn't have any siblings, she tried her best to organise the funeral from her camp in Helmand Province, and with the help of family friends it was achieved. She was unable to make it back in time, however, as her medical bay had been hit with mortar fire, killing several of her colleagues and putting her in a bed with concussion, a broken arm, fractures to a shin, and multiple shrapnel hits.

The shrapnel had left her with a permanent limp and, following a medical discharge, Dana had to decide what to do when she got home. She felt fine about the discharge, as she couldn't face working on people anymore, especially after seeing her friend's body all bloodied and broken beside her, eyes open, though they showed not a single flicker of life. She couldn't face the possibility of another moment like that. When she arrived states side, she decided that her next chapter was to become a vet, and she did just that.

The years went past too quickly. She had partnered at a local veterinary office in Boston, though that didn't last long, as the hustle and bustle of city life wasn't for her. Instead, Dana started her own practice in her hometown.

There were hard times, but over the years and, with her family name, her client list grew. She was then able to employ others to run the office while she went from farm to farm in her trusty Land Rover – which, as a young doctor, she had gotten use to during a stint at Camp Bastion with the Brits.

A fellow doctor from somewhere called Leeds had taken her for a drive in one – well, until the Military Police found them upside down in a ditch. But, that day she fell in love with the truck, and every time she drove it a smile creeped onto her face, and then a laugh at the memory of her drunk driver, Liza, punching out a Military Policeman before running away, never to be found by them. Dana denied all knowledge of her and was sent back to her own base the next day. She and Liza still correspond often.

On this day, the blonde-haired vet had been driving through town when she noticed the local farming supply shop. It was the family business of one of her old schoolmates. Dana knew that Brian had disappeared suddenly a long time ago. His upbringing had been hard, and then, like her, he'd gone through the trauma of the death of his parents. She hadn't heard any news about him for a while, so she pulled into the parking lot and decided to go for a snoop around. She also thought perhaps she could place a card in their window. You always need more clients.

Luckily, it was a warm day, so her damaged leg wasn't paining her too much. Slamming the door on the truck, she headed in. The store looked much larger on the inside than the outside had suggested, very much like the famed Tardis. Dana looked around for a while, but boredom soon kicked in and she began to seek out someone to ask about her placing an advertisement card in the window.

It was then that she saw a man who was quite obviously a Partridge, so that was her goal. He was quick on his feet, but she was ex-Army and managed to cut the man off by some chicken feed bins. The man looked startled as Dana stepped in front of him.

'Ah, just the man,' she said. 'Would I be able to put this up on your advertisement board, please?'

The man nodded his head briefly and took the card and read it. 'Dr Dana Thompson, Veterinary Practice' he said slowly. For a moment, he had a vacant look on his face. Then his eyes opened wide, just like his smile. 'You wouldn't be known as Princess Leia, would you?' He flinched at the look she gave him.

'Only by those who wish a painful death. Why?' Dana snapped and squinted her eyes.

The man gave out a nervous laugh. 'Oh, I remember my uncle telling me about a friend of his from school. She wanted to be a doctor, and you were called Leia,' he said and stuck out his hand. 'Adam Partridge. This is my store.'

Dana shook his hand and her face relaxed into a smile. 'Did Brian tell you how many times I hit him for calling me that accursed name? Well, did he?'

'Nope, but he did flinch when he told me about it, though,' Adam chuckled. 'I'm sure he didn't mean it. Not a harmful bone in his body, that one. He didn't have many friends, so take it as a compliment.'

Dana scoffed. 'Well, I haven't seen him since our schooldays, and I heard he moved away. So if you ever see him, tell him I'm gunning for him.' She went to step out of the way of a big, burly shopper.

'I will, but you can threaten him yourself if you wish,' said Adam with a smile. 'He's living at the old family farm. We kept the house but rented out the land.' He then looked downcast. 'Haven't had time to visit him yet, time just gets away from you, sometimes.'

'Hmm,' Dana said and tapped her cheek with her long, slender fingers. 'I might just do that. Is he married? Or a girlfriend? I wouldn't like to intrude.'

Adam barked out a laugh and pretended to wipe a tear from his cheek. 'Old Doc? Married?' he joked and smiled. 'Not a chance. I think he's allergic to people – always has been since the fall, Dad says.' He then looked closely at the woman. 'Did you know about that?'

Dana gave a curt nod. 'Yes, he said he slipped from a tractor and banged his head,' she lied, knowing that Brian had actually been pushed off the tractor by Adam's father. However, this was the lie they cast around, as the man in question didn't want to upset his family in any way.

This man could not lie, but he did try. 'Yep, that was it, we were quite close. We both shared a passion for sci-fi, but life moved on... You know how it goes,' Adam stated. 'But please, if you have time, just pop in and see him. He would be over the moon to see you, I'm sure.'

Dana took a hairband from her wrist and tied her straggly blonde hair back into a ponytail. 'I'll see if I have time this week,' she replied. 'Thanks for the chat and for putting my card up,' she added and flinched as her leg pained her. 'See you again soon.' She waved, walking off with a pronounced limp.

When she finally made it to her truck, Dana settled in and gave her old wound a rub. The surgeons said they had taken the shrapnel out, but she swore that some of it was still in there. She started the engine and filtered back onto the road.

'So, Brian, you're back in town,' she said to herself and turned on the radio. 'Question is, should I visit?' She continued the drive back to her office while musing about her old school friend.

A couple of days after meeting Adam, Dana was sitting at her office desk. Her thoughts had been muddled as she re-evaluated her history with Brian. They had been close once, enough for him to share the troubles with his brother and the fall from his father's tractor. Then he had felt disjointed, not part of the family, and that had hindered his time at school.

It was the last two years of high school when they'd seemed to drift apart; her pursuit of becoming a doctor had encompassed her, and Brian's insecurities spiked, and so that was it. They had smiled and waved at each other, but their true friendship was over. Her other classmates, who swarmed around her as they all grew into young women, always joked about the two of them having a secret affair, to which she always responded with 'He wishes!' And then Dana remembered that he had heard the gossip one day, and that was the last day he was seen at school.

While checking on the day's call sheet, Dana saw that one job meant having to go past the old Partridge Farm. Her lips quirked slightly at the thought of seeing him again and she wondered how he looked nowadays.

'Oh, shut up, Dana!' she chided herself, while gathering up her paperwork in readiness for the working day. 'You are no longer a teenager.' She kicked her office door open before stomping out into the reception area, totally ignoring her employees, who watched her exit, leaving mutterings and laughing in her wake.

The first call was a simple one, just to check if a horse breeder's chestnut mare was pregnant, which she was. So, they were all happy and hugged her while the male owner kissed both of her cheeks. Dana half expected him to call her darling and mince away, but she was wrong.

The second call was not as much fun. A breeding sow had died from internal bleeding. Age had caused it in the end. The farmer held back his tears as they discussed the plans for collection and disposal.

She drove away from the farm deep in thought. The road curved around the trees nicely, the leaves almost ready to change. That would herald the influx of tourists to gaze at the myriad of colours which the season brought about. It truly was a sight to behold.

'FUCKKKKK!' she screamed and locked the brakes, leaving rubber on the road. Dana watched as the driver of the large John Deere tractor waved an apology, albeit half-heartedly. An old sign lay on its side at the junction of the turning the vehicle had come from. It was for the Partridge family farm. Could this be a sign?

With a deep breath, she changed gear and pulled up onto the old farm track. Clearly, it had only seen heavy-duty farm machinery for some time now. Maybe he had left and never told his family where he was going?

'Oh, shit!' she cried as her head collided with the roof after hitting a particularly large rut. 'Bloody hell, I wish they would get this road fixed,' she cursed as her whole body seemed to become weightless for a second at every bump, during a long and painful half a mile drive.

The track levelled out and she saw that there was a fork in the road ahead. Left was nice and flat and the farmhouse could be seen in the distance. Dana therefore surmised that turning right would take her to the fields – and her possible doom, if the road ahead was anything like this one.

The butterflies in her stomach were making the breakfast Burrito a bad choice for her first meal of the day, but the engine needed fuel, right? Just maybe not such a spicy one. An unladylike belch escaped her mouth, scaring some crows from a dying tree that stood next to the road.

'Yuck, it's fighting back,' she joked, then stared as the farmhouse came into view ahead. The shutters were open, which was a good sign, plus the beat-up old Ford truck added to the positive vibe.

Slowly, Dana parked next to the faded red truck. She glanced around, but there was no sign of life anywhere, all apart from a small outbuilding with a chicken run attached. It seemed as if Brian hadn't made it out of bed that morning, leaving the poor birds locked up. So, doing her duty as a vet, she opened the door to the run, making sure to close it behind her and pulled up the sliding door. The chickens poured out like a feathery tsunami.

Dana looked around and saw a galvanised food bin by the door. It would cause the chickens to go mad knowing the food was so close, yet so far out of their reach. Picking up the lid for the bin, she delved her spare hand into the feed. It was the typical brown pellets, and with a flick of her wrist the food was cast over the pen, making the hens go crazy.

She scattered a few more pellets around, then checked the bowl for water, of which there was plenty. It was then she realised her mistake. Dana turned around and saw a huge Rhode Island Red Rooster strutting out of the hut. The look it gave her was alike a master to a slave. If a chicken could sneer, this one would.

'Good chicken, nice chicken,' Dana muttered as it looked coldly upon her. In her job as a vet, many animals had looked upon her with ill favour, but this one seemed to have planned this. He had waited for her to enter fully, before cutting off her escape route. It stood tall, up to the top of her knee. In that second, she felt for the hens, who did look a bit glum.

'Come on, boy,' she said. 'Don't be a dick, now.' She wondered if Brian ever had this trouble. Maybe he had been killed by this feathery bastard?

The rooster suddenly took a pose like that of the Diloposaurus in *Jurassic Park* that spat poison into the face of the double-crossing computer nerd. Never trust a man who just tells you to turn your PC off and on again when you have flames coming out the back of it. She shook her head to focus, which had always been a problem since the explosion in the service of our country that had sent her through a surprisingly thin wall.

Dana dodged like an NFL running back, making the dick of a rooster miss and take out a couple of hens with his bulk. He recovered quickly, but just not quick enough as the ex-Army doctor was out of the pen and slamming the door shut, while flipping the bird the bird.

'Fuck you, birdy!' she screamed, then thought what kind of impression this would make on anyone.

She decided to leave the Mexican standoff that the rooster had decided to start and headed for the farmhouse. It had been many years since Dana had been here. It had only been the once, but they'd had fun reading comic books until his brother broke it up, sending Brian into a funk. His mother had to take her home, apologising as they drove. It was strange how things like that kept popping up now and how your perception of friendship can change over time, Dana thought.

The wooden steps up to the house creaked. Clearly, Brian hadn't maintained this place much while he was here.

However, there was a nice new greenhouse set up, so at least that was a start. *Unless he's growing drugs*, she thought, which she couldn't see happening. Dana opened a newly fitted screen door and knocked on the front door and waited. No answer. She tried again and put a bit of weight behind it.

Her brow creased in annoyance. She knew the bedrooms were on the ground floor, so where was he? With a rattle, Dana tried the door handle just to prove to herself that it was locked.

'Damn it!' All that build-up and he wasn't here. So, with a last try, the vet walked to the little window next to the door and squinted into the gloom that was the house.

'Brian, you there?!' she shouted. On the floor, she could see items scattered around, but it was too dark to see properly. 'Briannn, it's me… Dana… from school!'

Just then, she heard a noise. It was only slight.

'Brian, is that you?' she barked again and heard the same noise. Dana started to push on the door, making it flex and then rhythmically pounded on it. 'Brian, please come to the door. You're scaring me.'

Dana was now breathing heavily. It had been a while since she had felt this way, scared and angry at the same time.

'Fuck this shit!' she cursed, knowing her parents always hated her foul language. However, her father did know that Army taught you how to fight and curse the best, and she took those lessons to heart.

Gritting her teeth, she stepped back, causing the boards underneath to groan, making her wonder if she had a weight problem. Moving quickly, Dana kicked the door, hearing both the door and something in her knee crack.

'Fuckity fuck!' the vet cursed again loudly. The next kick shattered the door lock, sending wood shards and metal flying into the hall. 'Oh, shit!' she exclaimed when she saw the camouflaged man lying amongst phone parts and blood. It was Brian.

'Brian!' she cried and ran to his side, kneeling beside him, not bothering about the pool of blood that now coated her well-worn jeans. Her training kicked in and she absorbed all the available information – pale, laboured breathing, gunshot wound to thigh. Her fingers traced the back of the leg and found the lack of an exit wound. Nothing serious had been struck, otherwise he would be dead. Dana calmly cupped his cheek.

'I'll get you help, Brian,' she said and went to pull away, but stopped when bloody fingers grasped her wrist, making her jump.

She looked at his face, but it was devoid of any signs that indicated he was conscious.

'Brian... Brian, wake up!' Dana said and gave his cheek a slight slap. Nothing happened. 'What happened to you?' she asked and scanned his army gear for any unit patches. The boy she knew would never have made it in the Army. Picking up her phone, she was about to call the emergency services, but then something told her not to and she cancelled the call.

She could see that the bleeding had stopped, and she chewed her bottom lip and looked at his face, sighing.

'Don't make me regret this,' she said and ran outside to her truck, pulling out her first aid kit that was always kept filled and ready to use. It always surprised her how many accidents she witnessed during her rounds.

Dana lugged the large case into the kitchen, took out some alcohol spray and wiped the kitchen table. Then, from her stock of veterinary equipment she laid a plastic cover over the wooden surface and attached it using straps around the legs. She looked around and saw that the equipment was all spread out ready, but now for the hard part.

'JESUS!' she hissed, while trying to lift her old friend. Yes, Dana was strong, but lifting a deadweight was always difficult.

Dragging him into the kitchen was easy, although this left a trail of dark blood on the floor. After several attempts, she managed to get Brian sitting upright on a chair next to the table, sweat drenching them both. It took thirty minutes to finally get him lying on his back on the table.

'You're a lump, Bri,' Dana panted with a smile. She took out some scissors and then began to cut off his clothes, all except for his undershorts. She could not bring herself to do that… yet.

Firstly, she wiped down his body, as there was too much old blood around the wound. Then, Dana placed an IV fluids to stave off dehydration. Finally, it was time to get the bullet out. She could see it in the wound. It surprised her that it hadn't gone through his leg. That was a bit of luck.

Dana cut away some of the burnt flesh caused by the heat of the projectile hitting his leg and forcing its way into the tissue. Brian moaned a bit as the forceps were pushed into his damaged leg.

'Come here, you little shit!' she muttered angrily. Wiping some fresh blood away, she went back on the attack. The bullet resisted, but eventually it came out. 'Hmmm, that's weird…' Dana commented as she looked at the bullet. It didn't look like the ones that had been used during her tours.

Within the next hour, Brian was cleaned and sewn up, while a new bag of fluids began working their way into his bloodstream. If only he could have had a transfusion, she thought. But they didn't match types and getting bags of blood was impossible, unless he fancied having rooster blood.

Brian remained unconscious, so Dana took the opportunity to finish her jobs quickly and advise her office that she would be unavailable for the next few days. This caused many rumours to be whispered around about affairs or a new boyfriend on the scene, and many a bet was made that day. She made time to nip home for some clean clothes, then on to the medical centre to pick up some more IV bags.

Brian was still lying unconscious on the table when she arrived back. To her surprise, all his chickens had gone back into the hen house early, so Dana locked them away for the night before heading in and locking the front door, with the help of a dining chair to keep it closed. She really had done a number on the thing.

Dana decided to get a mop and bucket with strong disinfectant and start to clean up the blood trail on the floor. It really looked worse than it was, due to how it had smeared as Brian had dragged himself through the house. Soon, she worked her way down the cellar steps, cleaning one by one.

'What a hard bastard,' she said to herself, and thought how much it must have hurt trying to get up those steps on his own. 'What the hell…?'

Dana looked around the room and was confused and yet amazed at what she saw. There was a computer on the table, and two large plastic bathtubs that stood end up and attached by what looked like sensory tanks that some high-end boutique would rent out for people to have some kind of vision quest. That sort of thing always sounded like bullshit to her.

That was where she found a helmet and body armour which matched the rest of Brian's uniform. This sent her thoughts reeling. *What was he doing down here?* she wondered. Dana stilled when her foot connected with something metallic. Looking down, she saw a gun. As she was still wearing yellow washing-up gloves, it was safe to pick it up.

'A fucking Luger?!'

Sitting down on a chair, Dana popped out the magazine, cleared the chamber and saw that it was missing just one bullet. The others matched the one she had dug from Brian's thigh.

'Have you been playing war games, Bri, and shot yourself?' she asked herself, though that didn't seem right considering the angle of the wound.

Dana placed the gun down onto the desk, next to the inert computer, and took in the photographs that littered the walls.

'What the hell!' she joked and stood up to have a better look. 'Is that a T-Rex?' She then saw an image of the *Titanic* in a high-definition colour photo. She shook her head in disbelief as she looked at more photos of dapper gentlemen and posh, lace-covered women on said ship.

She laughed when she saw three ticket stubs from a theatre in Boston, for all three *Back to the Future* films. He did like those films. She was equally baffled by photos of a rocket launch – which, she thought, looked like the one that had gone to the moon. She had seen it so many times, though the definition of these photos was sharper and much clearer than the old ones in history books. Then she saw a picture of Brian dressed in old-fashioned clothes holding a giggling baby, surrounded by a family. It wasn't his child, by the looks of the other male in the picture.

The last one did it. Dana was now very confused as she looked at photos of Pearl Harbour that she realised must have been taken during the Second World War. There was one image of a fighter plane with the machine gun blazing away. *Were these just copies that had been modified to look new?* she wondered. *Is he a graphic artist?* If he was, then she was impressed. Trouble was, there were too many questions that needed to be answered.

Shaking her head, she carried on her cleaning, hung up the helmet and vest, then headed back upstairs to pour away the now bloodied water. Dana heard Brian moan and groan as he shifted on the table, but not once did his eyes open. The Army doctor knew he was low on blood, but the bags of fluid should do him some good. His pulse and heartbeat were stronger than before, which pleased her.

Dana helped herself to some fresh fruit and a cold beer, then turned on the TV. All she had to do now was wait. Wait and try not to think about what Brian had been up to.

The evening crept into early morning. Her patient would groan now and then, but his breathing was better, as was his heartbeat. Dana had added painkillers and antibiotics to his drug regime, which she hoped would stave off any infection.

She dozed for a bit, but nothing substantial. There were too many questions to be answered, mainly why hadn't she phoned the paramedics? And what the hell was going on here? Finally, at four in the morning she gave up her pursuit of sleep and picked up a black ring binder, which was full of pages. It looked as if the words had been typed, which made her laugh as most people these days used a computer to write and a printer to print their work.

'The Shadow of Normandy… Good title,' she muttered and manoeuvred herself into a comfortable position. Clearly, the story had not been finished as the text was covered in red pencil, suggesting changes. She had seen such things on programmes about newspapers and how the editors reworked reporters' stories. This story was of a time traveller, obviously not like from *Quantum Leap*, where Sam Beckett, played by the wonderful Scott Bakula, hops around doing good. No, in this story a man had been killed for money while being chased by some federal agency, and this was set in World War Two.

Dana caught her breath as she began putting things together. The time machine that the author described was scarily like the one in the cellar. Then there was the Luger, which looked almost new. Then there was Brian wearing army gear, including a bulletproof vest. Dana threw the folder away into a corner.

'Bullshit!' she spat angrily, not allowing her mind to believe such things. 'This is all just make believe.'

The vet jumped up and stomped away, making her way back down to the basement. Then, standing in the middle of the room, she slowly turned around, taking in the full room.

'No, it can't be…' she muttered, looking at the photos that had made her laugh earlier. Dana saw, on a shelf, a camera with a long lens. She picked it up and could tell that it was a new Canon digital camera. Pressing the power button on, she took a seat and waited for the display on the back panel to come alive.

'No, I can't believe it,' she whispered to herself as the photos flicked past in the viewing aperture. 'Pearl Harbour…' and she watched a video of some men walking up a path. Then the attack started with big plumes of smoke, planes diving and buzzing around the skies. Next came an attack at the cameraman himself. The very last photos were of a blazing bright light. The final nail in the coffin was the picture taken of this very room, taken from over by the wired-up pods.

Putting the camera down, Dana stared at the photos again, this time wide-eyed in astonishment. She had witnessed war and death first-hand, but this... It just couldn't be true, even though all the evidence proved otherwise.

Suddenly she realised her world had changed. Again, Dana looked through the photos in the camera, loitering on the men creeping up a path through some woods. Would this change to her world be good or bad? And would it tie her to the man upstairs? Yes, that was the dream, when they had first become friends. But they weren't those kids any more – and to be honest, all those thoughts and memories at the time had been quashed to make her life easier at school.

Dana sat there, gazing into nothingness, her eyes unable to focus. She was zoned right out. Even her pulse was dangerously low as her mind struggled to comprehend what had been going on at the Partridge family farm.

'Hey, Princess!'

Chapter Thirteen

'Brian! What the hell are you doing?' Dana growled like a pissed-off lioness. Her cheeks glowed red, though, knowing that I had caught her snooping. 'You're going to ruin all the work I did on your leg,' she said and looked at the small, red dot that had appeared through the bandage.

I gave her a small smile. 'Sorry, but the table was killing my ass something fierce,' and I watched her put the camera away. A sigh escaped my dry mouth. 'I think we need to talk. But first... thank you.' My old friend nodded and came over and I put my arm over her shoulder so that she could help me walk up the stairs. Clearly, the Army had made her strong.

Dana helped me to the sofa so I could stretch out, then she checked my leg and the IV site that I had pulled the needle from. Her mutterings were interlaced with swear words, cussing me for ruining her hard work. She then threw a blanket over me and stomped off. Within a minute, I had a glass of water and apple slices on a tray, while she had a cold beer and sat cross-legged, staring at me.

'So, what the hell happened here?' she demanded, waving her arms around the place.

'Firstly, I want to say I'm so sorry about what happened to your parents. I wasn't here when it happened,' I explained and saw her nod and take a drink. 'And I understand you couldn't make it to my parents' funeral, either. It's just the way of things.'

Dana barked out a quick laugh. 'That's life, Bri,' she said and gave me a watery smile. 'So, firstly, I want you to explain what that thing is downstairs. I'm really hoping it's not what I think it is.' She took another sip of her beer. 'Secondly, why did I find you almost bleeding to death on your floor, with what looks like a bullet wound from a German gun?'

That did make me laugh. 'I have missed you, Dana,' I said warmly, leaning back onto the sofa so that I could look straight at her without lifting my head. After all, I felt exhausted. 'It depends on what you think it is. Most people around here think I'm a crazed scientist.'

She rolled her eyes. 'Nothing new there, Brian,' she said. 'Now, spill it, or I will call the cops on your scrawny ass.' She raised a warning 'don't fuck with me' eyebrow, which she had done as a kid, ordinarily followed up with a dead leg.

'Fine, spoilsport,' I smiled. It had been so long since I had felt this comfortable with someone. Yes, we had drifted apart, but that's what people do at a young age. 'It's a time machine, though you knew that already by looking through the camera and the photos on the wall,' I surmised and looked at the unfinished book strewed on the floor. 'And the book over there,' I added and pointed at the binder.

Her eyes pierced my heart and soul. 'You're serious, aren't you?' she laughed, though her face painted the truth. She did believe me. 'But that's impossible…' she added, then shook her head hard enough to damage some brain cells. 'Even if it was possible, why you?'

Yes, I could take that as an insult, but she did have a point. Why me, indeed?

'Firstly, it isn't impossible,' I replied, 'though I do understand your scepticism, Leia.' She rolled her eyes at me again. I liked her middle name, though I pronounced it as the namesake of the wonderful Princess in *Star Wars*. And, whilst her real middle name was spelt differently, audibly there was no difference. 'I do have proof, not just photos. I have video and, once I'm walking again, I can take you with me.'

'Fuck that! Are you crazy?' she shot back and finished her beer off in a single draught. Her eyes searched my face. 'You believe it, don't you, Brian?'

I nodded my head and dared to smile at her. Then came the sound of a muffled cockerel crow, making us look towards the covered window to see daylight forcing itself through the drapes.

'Oh, by the way,' she added, 'your rooster is a dick.'

'Don't I know it!' I laughed. 'Could you let them out for me, please?' I asked and saw her squint her eyes. '*Pleeeease!*'

Dana looked at me with a sneer. 'Fine,' she said at last. She stomped into the kitchen and brought back a pitcher of water and some energy bars, then left the room again before returning with my laptop. 'I will fight with that bird, again. After that, I'll go home for a wash and a change of clothes.' She walked to the door and opened it, showing me that it was well and truly fucked. 'Drink, rest and eat,' she said.

'I'll be back at lunchtime.' She waved her hand at the computer. 'I want to see proof, Brian. Get to it!'

'Yes, Leia, no problem,' I answered and gave her a smile. The door made a hell of a bang as she left, shouting swear words as she did so. Seconds later, there came a scream of frustration and pain. Clearly, Karl the Cockerel had claimed another victim, the little shit.

After drinking some more water and then managing to swallow down the apple slices, I closed my eyes and tried to sleep, thinking how lucky I was that Dana had chosen that time for a visit. My school friend and first and only crush had saved my life.

'Shit, she will never let me forget it, either,' I muttered as sleep claimed me.

The dreams were not nice ones. The face of the German soldier as the taser caused him to go rigid into the air, the large bullet holes that tore into his flesh… It was truly horrific. You see films or TV programmes and you think that's how war is. But they don't tell you about the noise, smell and the sheer amount of carnage. They don't tell you about the months and years of training those boys went through, only for their lives to be snuffed out in seconds by people they can't even see.

I was torn into consciousness as the front door was slammed closed, and there was Dana with a couple of large, filled sandwiches from the local deli. She had lodged a chair against the front door handle to stop it swinging open on its own. I would have to ask her about that. What surprised me was the outfit she wore. It was confusing;

normally, she dressed as an overworked farmhand, but this was something different. She wore some white linen trousers, sand-coloured work boots, and a New England Patriots jersey.

'Looking good, Dana,' I said and shot her a wink.

'Laugh it up, McFly,' she shot back and walked straight past me to the kitchen. Unfortunately, the deli bag was at head height. Albeit by plan or accident, it smacked me right in the face.

'Heads up!' came from the kitchen and that answered my question.

The pain wasn't too bad in my thigh today. It throbbed in time with my heartbeat. Dana came back and set the food down on the coffee table, each sandwich set on a tray.

'Let's check that leg out,' she said and pulled back the blanket, then peeled away the adhesive bandage. 'Not my best work, then again not my worst, either' she concluded and put the cover back over it. 'I'll clean it up and change the bandage later. First, though, let's eat.'

We ate in silence for a while, then swapped questions about our time away from home, where my friend had dedicated herself to the service of our country, and then for animals. I shamed myself by hiding away from life.

'So, how did you find me? Was it your Army training?' I asked.

She choked out a laugh, sending a chewed-up piece of pickle my way. 'Oh yeah, Jason Bourne you are not! I bumped into your nephew at his store, and he told me you were here,' Dana explained while retrieving the rogue filling. Thankfully, it was binned and not eaten. 'He apologised for not coming to see you, but he said he will soon.'

We carried on eating for a time, then I had to take the tablets that were placed next to the soda.

'Jesus, are these horse tranquilizers?' I complained as the chalky, unpleasant-tasting pellets scoured a groove all the way down my oesophagus. My comment resulted in another clip around the head, this time by her iron-like hand. 'You have a great bedside manner, Doc!'

I could hear things being cleared away in the kitchen while she mumbled something under her breath.

'I'll have you know,' she called out, 'that my bedside manner is delightful and professional to all those who deserve it. Also, I tend to work my best in a surgery room, not a dirty farmhouse.' Dana then walked back in and sank to her knees next to me.

'There is no need to beg, I know you're sorry… ARRRGHHHH!!!' I screamed as the bitch/Doctor tore the bandage straight off. She always did have a vicious streak. To be honest, the wound didn't look too bad. She prodded it, which made me wince, then slathered it with cream before wrapping it back up.

'How is it looking, Doc?' I asked.

'It looks okay,' she replied, 'though only time will tell. Keep it clean and take your meds. That should stop any infection, especially as it was from a battlefield, where any number of nasties can get inside the wound,' she stated. 'And then the fact you dragged yourself all the way up here.'

Dana sat on the floor crossed-legged and smiled up at me. 'I have missed you, Bri. But hell, what a way to come back into my life!' She allowed a little girlish giggle to come out. 'So, lay it on me. What is all this stuff?'

So that's what we did. I talked and she listened. Dana didn't interrupt once. I kept a few things out, but mostly told her everything and her jaw seemed to drop lower and lower.

'Okay, so what about these men in your photos?' She waved her hand at the ring binder that held the unfinished book. 'Shadow agents, or something. Who are they?'

I shrugged. 'I'm not sure. Lancaster seems to think they are from some government agency tracking temporal activities.' Dana nodded, indicating she understood. 'I read in his notes that he had seen these men at Pearl Harbour, so I did my homework and made a plan.'

'You... homework? Yeah, right!' she mocked, until I sent a death glare her way, which didn't have much of an effect. 'Sorry, continue,' she said with a smirk.

'Well, it worked, partly,' I said and chewed my lip. 'I took the photos, then Lancaster went back home, which caused a bright flash of light. I'm guessing the Japanese pilots thought it was a gun or something, so they decided to say hello... with machine guns.'

The look Dana gave me was unreadable. 'Hello with machineguns,' she said. 'Well, that's new,' she joked and shook her head. 'Is that how you got the picture of the Japanese fighter coming straight at you?'

'Nope, that was the second one,' I said. 'The agents zapped out, causing another flash.' I paused to take another sip of my drink. I hadn't talked so much since the rocket launch. 'So, either they saw it, or it went over the radio. They came right at me, but I didn't see it as my focus was on the attack itself. I had pressed the remote to go home, so I was just taking as many pictures as possible before I returned.' I gave a faint smile. 'Then I heard the gunfire and the ground, lower down on the hill, started to explode. That's when I saw him. I had no time to run, so I just took photos. Luckily, I got out just in time.'

I picked up the laptop and showed Dana the pictures of the attack, as well as the ones of the author and the two agents. 'I was hoping to find out who these people are,' I explained as she flicked through the pictures.

'Makes you wonder how they found you in Dallas, and him at Pearl Harbour,' she mused aloud. 'Do you think there were reports of the flashes? Especially this time, as you were another visitor?' She carried on flicking through the images. 'Why attack you in Dallas, though? You only went there to watch, right?'

There was an uncomfortable silence. 'Brian, you only went to watch and take pictures, right?' This time, Dana demanded an answer, and the truth. I lowered my head.

'Oh, Bri, of all the films and books you have read, what do all of them tell you? What are the rules?'

I exhaled. I knew she was right, as usual. 'Never try and change the past, because fate will always try and find a way,' I replied, wishing the sofa would swallow me up. 'I know, but when you go to these places, it's tempting to try and make the world a better place.' I pointed at the laptop that Dana was still holding. 'We have a wealth of knowledge at our fingertips. It all sounded so easy.'

'What about Lancaster?' Dana asked. 'In his writings, did he warn not to meddle with time?'

I stared through the window. 'Yes, but he must have done it, too,' I replied with a pout and shrugged. 'I just thought, being younger, I would be smarter.'

'How did that work out for you?' she asked sarcastically and raised that well-used eyebrow again. 'So, tell me what you tried to change, and why?'

My head dipped. 'I played the market to make a bit of money.' Dana smiled and nodded. 'I made sure more women and children were saved when the *Titanic* went down…' I saw a warmness in her look, something I hadn't seen since we were young. 'I made up with my brother, and tried to convince my parents no to fly in the neighbours' plane…' That caused a tear to roll down my cheek, and Dana massaged my good leg. 'I tried to stop the assassination in Dallas, hoping it might change the timing of the coming war.'

'Oh, Bri,' Dana sighed. 'Deep down, you must've known it was never going to work,' she said softly, while massaging my shin. 'But you did good helping those kids. How did you manage that, though?'

I took back the laptop, opened up a secure file and found the picture. 'She helped me, the unsinkable Molly Brown.' I beamed at my friend, who instantly took back the laptop and stared at one of the photos I had taken secretly of the stoic woman. 'She really did give the sailors hell.'

Dana looked up. 'Did she know who you were, and where you came from?'

I shook my head. 'No, but she knew I wasn't the person I had claimed to be, though she bought my cover story, I think.' I chuckled at how easily Molly had broken my cover. 'It was a good time, but sad seeing all those faces, knowing they were going to die.'

'But you do that every day,' said Dana. 'We all die, Bri.' I knew what she meant, and I knew she was right. 'I understand, though.' She put on her thoughtful face. 'So, I presume they have a way of knowing if you attempted to change time? Then the government can stop you.'

'Yep, and the fact we can't go back to the same day, hinders it,' I replied, pausing for a moment. 'Though, I think now that's for the best,' I added sadly.

Dana stood up, stretched her legs, and started to walk around the room. 'What made you think it was a good idea to go to Normandy? It's a bloody war zone,' she asked with some emotion. 'Was it because of the book?'

'Yeah, I hoped I might see those agents again, and the battle of Normandy always intrigued me.' I shrunk under Dana's glare. 'I thought I had picked a quiet sector, but I was wrong.'

'Fucking hell, Brian!' she shouted. 'A quiet sector of the invasion of Europe? Are you touched or something?' Once again, she cuffed me around the head. I began to think I would need an MRI scan after she had left. 'In war, people still die in a quiet sector, so how did you get shot, genius?'

I told her the story about how, as soon as I landed, the mission went south, making me want to leave. Then I described the taser episode and what happened to said man.

'It wasn't a great idea, I must admit,' I added and watched her pace again, back and forth.

Dana turned around like a pissed-off cobra. 'Right, I need to go,' she said and walked to the door. 'There is another sandwich in the refrigerator, but refrain from moving around too much.' She stopped at the door and looked at me, then suddenly walked back and gave me a peck on the lips. 'I'll be back tomorrow morning. And you will not be using that thing alone anymore…' She poked me in the chest. 'You got me, buddy.'

'Yes, dear,' I replied and that got me another kiss, before she walked out slamming the door shut, and somehow securing the door. I listened, waiting for her truck to fire up. Nothing happened for a while, then her rage came through the wall like a hurricane.

'FINE, FUCK YOU THEN! YOU CAN STAY OUT HERE FOR ALL I CARE!' she screamed, and a few moments later the engine of her truck started, and the front of the house was peppered with stones as she burnt away. Clearly, she had a run with Karl the Rooster. He really was a pain in the arse.

With laughter in my heart, I slept for a good few hours until my bladder decided it wanted to be emptied. Thankfully, the bathroom was on the same level, but everything still hurt like hell. Not only the leg, but it felt like I was passing liquid fire. In the end, though, the remainder of the night went well.

***

'Wakey wakey, eggs and bacey,' sang an off-key Dana, making me wake with a start. 'Wow, you stink, Bri,' she said. 'That dressing is waterproof, so how about having a shower, Mr Stinky?' She started to unpack some groceries. 'Come on, breakfast in ten!'

I groaned and forced myself to stand up. That was when I discovered she had brought a crutch for me.

'Cheers, Leia,' I called out and promptly received a wave back. It was a difficult ten minutes, but I managed to wash and change into shorts and a T-shirt, and eventually I made it back to the sofa.

'How's it feeling, Bri?' she asked and brought over a plate of bacon and eggs and placed it down on a tray for me. 'There you go, eat up.' She stepped back and sat on the seat opposite. Today, Dana had chosen jeans and a T-shirt.

I rubbed the sleep from my eyes. 'It's okay, pains me some when I move it,' I replied and tucked into my food. 'Oh, thanks for locking up my chickens for me.'

Dana dropped her fork onto her plate. 'We will talk about that when you are healthy. You owe me big time for that alone, Brian,' she said and picked up her fork again. 'But I see a nice roast chicken dinner in our future.'

That did make me laugh, especially as Dana loved animals so much. That rooster did have some personal issues – maybe he was dropped as an egg?

'Sounds good,' I replied. 'Did you have a nice evening?'

She nodded, devouring the eggs in an unladylike way. Maybe it was from her days in the forces?

'Yes, thanks, lots of ideas and questions,' Dana said calmly, then finished the bacon with one swipe. Placing the tray on the floor, she gazed at me. 'We have to plan for the future. You know the government won't stop looking for you?' She looked around her. 'This place has been in your family for years, so they will come here first.'

'What do you suggest, then?' I asked. 'I can't give up my family home.' She nodded in agreement. 'I paid cash for the estate sale. All Lancaster's readers are anti-social types, so only the delivery company knows the address, and that was cash as well.' I pushed my plate away and dutifully took the tablets once again. 'None of the computer parts for the machine were bought by me. It came with the sale. The only things I bought were the pods.'

Dana's eyes were glistening. 'That's good,' she said. 'What we need is another site, a traceable one with fake details. And a money trail, one that even a blind illiterate can follow.' She laughed. 'You know what? They are like, if the evidence fits, that is it.' Happiness was already pouring out of her. 'How much money do you have?'

'I tweaked my investment a little before trying to kill myself, so I have done quite well,' I replied and chewed my lip. I had always promised myself that greed would not be a driving force. 'Ermm, 1.4 million in multiple accounts. Most is in gold, though.'

Dana stared at me, open mouthed. 'Holy shit, Bri. How come the government has never traced it? With that amount, they should be over you like flies on shit.' Dana spat and laughed. She had always been a delicate flower.

My face flushed red. 'I have a very well-paid, dodgy accountant. When I started this, most things were done on paper. He made up multiple names, the IDs of which I have in a drawer over there.' I pointed to a drawer.

She ran off and looked at my portfolio. From the look she then gave me I could tell she was both amazed and impressed. Dana sat down and worked her way through it.

'Does your accountant know what and who you are?' she asked.

'He does, that's why he went above and beyond,' I admitted and took in the look of worry painted across her face. 'It's okay, it sounds bad, but I chose him for a reason. He was good, and he would die in a bank robbery that went wrong two years later. That was enough time for him to organise it all.'

Our eyes locked. 'That's pretty dark, Bri,' Dana said and looked down, taking out a set of IDs from the pages of the portfolio. 'Do you trust me, Brian?'

How could I not? 'Of course, always have, always will,' I replied, and I saw a blush appear on her cheeks. 'The money is just sitting there and growing. I don't need much – well, apart from a new rooster,' I added, making us both laugh.

Dana stood up and cleared away the breakfast things. 'Okay, I have some plans in mind. It will cost quite a bit,' she called out from the kitchen, 'but, as you're minted, that's okay.' She started to giggle away like a toddler who had learnt a swear word. 'I need to sort work out and maybe employ someone to take over my duties while we work on this,' she continued. 'You need to heal, anyway, so we have time, hopefully.' It seemed like her mind was going in a hundred different directions at once.

She came back into the lounge and I looked at her. I was surprised that her eyes weren't twirling around in different directions.

'Well, don't burn yourself out,' I said. 'Like you said, I need to heal first.' She nodded and gave me a longer than normal kiss on my cheek.

'I'll be back later with food,' she said. 'Just rest and read.' She went to open the front door. 'Oh, I've bought a knew lock, by the way. I'll fit that later, though we should plan on replacing the whole door.' And, just before the door closed, she blew me a kiss and then turned away. I heard her outside shouting 'FUCK YOU, KARL!'

I was intrigued at the plans she had thought up. A woman's mind is a wonderful, yet scary, thing, and now I had handed her the keys to my future. It seemed like we had re-awoken our past friendship, but dare I hope for more? I had last time and that was snuffed out by events.

Sleep was easy to come by as the sun warmed my body. The dreams were just like the sun; they were memories of my parents, and even my brother when we were happy, though there hadn't been many of those moments. My moods didn't help. But I knew, in myself, that things were getting better for me.

A cockerel crow woke me, and for once I was happy. My bladder was at full capacity and so, with the aid of the crutch, I hobbled and swore my way to the bathroom. I noticed that the bathroom cabinet was open slightly, so I pulled open the mirrored door and was stunned at what I saw. A woman's deodorant and toothbrush. They were still in their packaging, but it was the intent that interested me. The bleakness that loitered in the recesses of my mind warned me not to hope for too much; it was just common sense that Dana kept those things here. After all, we were sharing a meal most days.

Picking up the laptop, I ordered myself another smartphone, as the original had been damaged when I knocked it off the sideboard. That would be arriving tomorrow, and I left a note in the delivery instructions to put it through the open window by the front door. I didn't really want to have to move when they knocked.

I decided to have a look at the photos of the agents from Pearl Harbour. I had to know where these people came from, what agency they were from, and, more importantly, what time they were from. They weren't the same ones who had shot at me in Dallas. So, I looked up a private detective agency in Washington, knowing that was the best place to start as it was the seat of the government. I sent them an email from an account of one of my other identities.

I explained to Michaels & Sons detective agency that I had found a photo amongst my late father's papers, and I wanted to know who the men in the photo were (I lied). I also requested that, as money wasn't a problem, please would they discover the men's identities without them knowing. The agency came back with several more questions and a price. I paid a deposit up front, the remainder to be settled when the job was done and I had the information.

After all that, my body had started to shut down. So, before taking a nap, the tablets were despatched and I cuddled down into the sofa and slept the afternoon away. I thought about going to visit Molly Brown just one last time before she died, just to say thank you for all the help. I'm sure Dana would have agreed.

***

'I FOUGHT FOR MY COUNTRY, YOU FEATHERY JERK. I CAN BEAT YOU!' came the angelic tones of my friend. The door was kicked open and Dana staggered in under several brown paper shopping bags.

'Hey, Bri! You are looking well,' she said sweetly and blew me a kiss.

I smiled at her. 'I feel it, too. I hear you and Karl are getting on.' I heard a muttered swear word and felt a bag of chips hit the back of my head as she went into the kitchen. 'Did you have a good day?'

She was wearing the same clothes as earlier. 'Not bad, actually,' she replied. 'I put some feelers out for my replacement, had a few calls back.' Dana handed me a small bottle of orange juice before sitting down in what had become her usual chair and unscrewed the top off her drink, which seemed to be pineapple. 'Doug, who is the small animal vet, fancies having a go, and he knows a few people who aren't happy at their surgeries,' she added and gave me a thumbs up.

'You don't have to do that, you know,' I said. 'You worked so hard to get that practice up and running…' I was stopped by a glare and a hand in the air demanding me to halt.

Dana placed her bottle down onto the table, leant back and crossed her jean-covered legs, some dirt falling from her work boots.

'Yes, I worked hard and still do, so it's time for me to sit back and enjoy the fruits of my labour,' she said in the type of logical tone that scares all men. 'I'm not leaving for good, though. I am taking time away to help my best friend, who foolishly not only let our friendship lapse, but then disappeared into the ether.' I could see the emotion in her eyes. 'Yes, I could be to blame as well,' she added, 'but I am the woman, so it's the man's fault.'

I nodded. 'Yes, but...'

'I haven't finished yet. We are having a moment,' Leia stated with the edges of her lips twitching as she fought a smile. 'After you, all I had were girlfriends – and not in the "let's experiment type", Brian, so you can get that idea out of you mind.' She pointed her strong and deadly finger at me. I really hate it when people read my mind. 'You knew I wanted to be a doctor, but, like you, my family just didn't have the money to send me to college. So, the Army was the way to go – and yes, I did have a few relationships, though none of them clicked.'

'I get that,' I replied. 'The world is full of people, yet only a few matches. Strange, isn't it?'

This time, I received a bottle cap to my head. 'My story, your turn in a minute,' Dana shot back with a smile. Her aim was way too good for my liking. 'After my experience of being blown up, and when my parents died, I decided to retrain. Having to see injured human beings, day after day, became just too much for me.' Once again, a pointed look came my way. She ran her fingers through her loose hair. 'So, I came home and, in the end, started my business. Yes, I may have pushed you to the back of my mind, but you always had a way of popping back up. All it took was a joke, a book, or even a film...' Her cheeks flushed red. 'My last boyfriend left after I called him Brian when we were in the bedroom… and please don't get a big head about that. We had just watched *Back to the Future*.'

Dana picked up her drink, finished the rest of it and launched the plastic bottle across the room, where it landed in the little trashcan, not even touching the edge.

'Then I heard a rumour about you being back and I meet your nephew,' she said and sighed, wiping a tear from her cheek. 'And here you are. We are standing on the edge of a great adventure, and we will do this together. Whatever happens in the end, so be it. I will never leave your side again, be it friend or more… What do you think?' Dana looked at me hopefully, her heart on her sleeve.

'Wow, that was a hell of a speech. Did I tell you I bought a new phone?' I said and smiled at her. 'Shit.'

Chapter Fourteen

Laughing and joking together, FBI Special Agents Marcus Martinez, a burly 38-year-old of Mexican parentage, alongside his 30-year-old temporary partner, Avery Saunders, had just finished their stint as temporal agents. Their mission reports had been written and sent away to whoever would read them.

Finally, it was time for them to leave, and they carried their luggage down the corridor and back to the real world. After leaving the FBI building, a trip to a bar was decided on, then the airport. For Marcus, it would be home to friends and family. In Avery's case, he would be returning to a hot Russian fellow agent.

'Ready, Marcus?' Avery asked, gripping the aluminium door handle and holding his ID card in the reader.

'Oh, yes, my friend. Let's get that beer,' Marcus answered eagerly. 'I'm buying!'

Avery swiped the card to access the elevator to freedom, but the little LED light blinked red.

'What? Come on, you shit!' he muttered and started to press the call button in frustration, before trying his card again. 'Oh, for fuck's sake… What's going on?' The anger was building.

'Calm down, Ave. Let me try it,' Marcus suggested to his friend, but the same thing happened, causing Avery to throw his luggage down the length of the corridor in frustration. It made the smaller man chuckle at his antics. Avery obviously thrived on pressure. 'Okay, there must be a reason for this,' continued Marcus. 'Let's go back to the control room. Maybe something there will tell us.'

Agent Saunders slouched against the wall. 'I thought we were done with this,' he said in despair and stood back up, following Marcus back to the computer room, swiping his card to gain entrance. The green LED appeared, which brought a Russian swear word into the mix. He had always been multilingual when it came to swearing.

Avery pushed the door open. The room, once again, was bathed in red lights. 'What has he done NOW!' he shouted and walked back to his bedroom to drop off his belongings.

Marcus sagged slightly and went back to his room and unpacked. This was precisely the reason they had decided not to let their significant others know they were coming home. That was the best thing about the time room – the longer they stayed in there, the less time passed, so he could still make the party at the weekend and keep his wife happy.

They both sat in the kitchen area and drank a coke from the refrigerator.

'Fine, let's do this,' Avery spat, wishing a most painful death on this time traveller, who seemed to enjoy messing with his life. 'If we see him, though, we will take him down,' the young man snarled.

Marcus looked at his partner sadly. 'We'll see. Let's find out the reason first,' he said, trying to defuse Avery's anger.

He then led the young man out and into the main control room.

He noticed that the three lights, that had once been green, were now red, as was the flashing light on the ceiling. 'Just have a seat and I'll take a look,' Marcus instructed. The moody younger man nodded and threw himself into his desk chair.

Marcus opened the folder that sat in the centre of the monitor. The title surprised him: 'Normandy, France 1944'. He looked at his partner, who was staring up at the ceiling as he began spinning around on the swivel chair. 'Ave, will you act your age! You *are* a federal agent, after all!' he chided and saw the young man pout.

Avery pushed with his shoes on the floor to stop his rotation, leaving black scuff marks on the tiles. 'Fine. What we got, Marc?' he said and leant in to look over his friend's shoulder. 'Shit, what has he done now?'

Marcus opened the file. It still amazed him that someone, or something, could tell them how to go about the next mission by the reports that they were to write after said mission. It was truly crazy. He brought up the map files, along with what the time terrorist had done. They read the report out loud:

Temporal target appeared in the woods behind the coastal batteries of Pointe du Hoc, just as the American forces climbed the cliff to capture and destroy the mounted gun, which had been taken away prior to the invasion.

Target ran from shell hole to shell hole, trying to keep away from German forces, who came to reinforce the garrison on the Bluff. No idea what he wanted to do here, but as he took cover in a shell hole, a German corporal jumped in. This was the pivotal moment.

Target would be taken back to the forward command post. Then he would be moved on to Berlin and SS Headquarters, where he would be tortured for days, until he gave up what was a false name, though also the remote control which could be used to send himself home.

A month later, an SS sergeant along with a scientist was sent. They manage to work out the basics of the time machine and move groups back and forth before reporting their findings.

Hitler and his henchmen were assassinated, and the German high command sued for peace. Then, Germany and the Allies turned their forces against Russia, winning by April 1945.

In June 1955, German atom bombs, that had been created for use in the Second World War, were used against New York, Washington, Los Angeles, England, and Canada. Other cities were also targeted.

Germany, Russia and other European countries turned on their once Allies after the financial demands of USA and UK following the Second World War, nearly bankrupted them.

The two agents looked at each other. This guy, in one move, had fucked the world without even knowing it.

'Jesus, what has he done?' Marcus groaned and rubbed his palms into his tired eyes. 'Now what are we going to do?'

'You any good with a rifle?' Avery asked, as he fired up his own workstation and pulled up reports and maps. He stopped to turn to his partner as he hadn't received an answer. 'Marc, did you hear me?'

The Mexican sighed. 'Yeah, I've hunted all my life,' he replied. 'Not sniper quality, but I can hold my own.' He knew what Avery was suggesting they do, but only because his mind was going the same way. 'It's going to be a tough job, all those bullets and bombs, soldiers from each side.'

Avery smiled to himself. 'It's risky, but what choice do we have?' he said. 'If we don't do it, we are never getting out of here,' and he continued checking over the reports. 'We know where and when he arrives. We can arrive safely and hide up in the woods, somewhere that doesn't get obliterated if possible…' He pointed to a circle on the map where the Traveller would arrive. Then, he pointed to a small copse that, according to photos after the invasion, was relatively untouched.

'Hijo de las Mil Putas,' said Marcus and swore. 'Killing people isn't an easy thing to do, my friend. That shit stays with you.' He gave his fellow agent a haunted look. He had killed in the Army. And, as an agent, when a homeless man pulled out a gun during an undercover sting, both situations left him no choice.

'My father said the same thing,' replied Avery, 'but someone has to get shot. If we kill the German, then our target gets away.' He gulped. 'Then again, if we shoot the target, all of this will stop.'

Marcus stood up and stretched his back. 'I'm going for a coffee. Can you write up a plan with timings? I'll have a look at them and see what we need.' He then went to walk out of the room.

'Marc, I am sorry, I just can't see any other way. Especially with all that's going on,' Avery explained and watched his partner slouch out. He turned back to the computer and let his fingers dance across the keyboard. He focused hard, as he didn't want to think about the fact that he had to appear in a war zone in between the two opposing armies. What scared him most was the fact that his grandfather would be landing on Omaha beach.

It took the young agent a good hour to write down the plan, with timings. If he got this wrong, he would be sending them into a world of hell. Avery gathered up all the paperwork and headed out to the kitchen, but his friend wasn't there. The sound of Marcus's voice came from down the corridor; it was a mixture of Spanish and English. Clearly, he was making sure he spoke to his family before embarking on the mission.

Avery placed the files on the kitchen table, went back to his room and pulled out his cell phone. Flipping it open, he went straight to the list of contacts. He saw her name and, sitting on his bed, he pressed the dial button; it rang three times.

'Hey, baby, how's the secret mission?' Samantha chuckled, trying to make light of the situation. However, what Avery didn't know was that, as an FBI agent, Samantha had been bombarding all her sources to find out what the man who she had decided to marry was doing in Washington. Though she had found nothing.

'Hey, honey, it's weird all this secretive stuff,' Avery replied in a light tone. 'But it is nearly over, we just have a final, short mission…' The phone went silent for a few moments.

'What do you mean… mission?' she asked sharply. 'You're a computer geek, you don't do missions. You track a money trail while playing solitaire and you beg for naked pictures of me.'

Avery knew he had said too much. 'Hey, the latter wasn't just me. The boys at work wanted some, too,' he said, hoping to change the subject. 'Anyway, when I'm back we'll have a nice break together, what do you think?'

Another bout of angry breathing. 'What mission, Ave?'

'I can't speak about it,' he replied, 'but it won't take us long, I promise.' He paused for a moment. 'Should be home before the weekend, and we've been invited to my partner's anniversary party. Think you can make it?'

There was an exhalation of air at the other end of the phone. 'Yeah, sure,' Samantha replied. 'It'll be nice to meet your new partner, who seems like a *proper* agent,' she said with a chuckle. 'When is it?'

'This weekend,' replied Avery. 'I'll give you a call when I'm about to leave here, then we can arrange the weekend,' he added hopefully.

'Sounds like a plan, Avery. Now, you be careful and bring your sweet ass back to me, you hear? Whatever it is you are doing,' she said in loving tones. 'Love you!'

That stunned him. It really did seem that she meant it. He had been thinking about her in a more permanent way lately since being here. 'Love you, too,' he replied. 'See you soon.' Then, with a click, they were once again alone. And, if he was honest, that hurt.

Avery stood up, placed his cell phone in his inside jacket pocket and headed back into the kitchen area. The conversation between Marcus and his family had finished, and he was sitting at the table with all the paperwork scattered around.

'Hey, buddy, family okay?' Avery asked and took a seat opposite him.

Marcus nodded without looking up. 'Yes, thank you, my friend,' he replied. 'They are looking forward to having me home again.' However, his darling wife had said that, if he got hurt, she would find a healthy spot and hurt that a bit more. 'Loretta and the kids can't wait to meet my young, handsome partner – the twins especially.'

Avery laughed. 'Well, I'm bringing Samantha. She says it'll be nice to meet a *real* field agent, not just a computer geek,' he said, making them both laugh. 'But if I do get hurt, she better not find my body. I think she would stuff me and use me as a punch bag.'

Marcus looked up. 'Damn, Ave, I don't think we should let Samantha and Loretta talk. It could mean a most painful death for both of us,' he joked and looked back at the paperwork. 'This is good work, my friend. The aerial pictures prove that small copse is still standing the next day, so no heavy guns were used on it.'

'That's what I saw, too,' said Avery. 'The target will come from our right, from another group of trees and bushes.' He showed the best-guessed route the man would probably use. 'It gives us good cover and line of fire on both men, our target and the German. I'm guessing we wait till they are in the shell hole together, then we can hit whichever one feels suitable?'

Marcus turned some pages over and took a sip of his coffee. 'I suggest we request German paratrooper camouflage uniform and helmet. It's the best, all bar the Waffen SS, but I can't bring myself to wear theirs.'

'Studied much?' Avery joked, and saw a photo that his partner had grabbed off his tablet. He had to admit, it did look good. And as they were going to be coming from the German side, it would be for the best. 'What about weapons?'

'Can't be anything new,' replied Marcus, 'so I would go with a Garand M1, with attached scope. Most sniper rifles of that time were bolt action. We will need more rounds, just in case I miss the first time,' he explained and flicked more paperwork over. 'We shall both carry MP 40 machine pistols, just in case. They have thirty-two rounds in a magazine, so spray and run if we get cornered.'

Avery felt ill. The thought of having to use such a weapon did worry him. 'I haven't used guns like that before,' he admitted and felt foolish for it.

'It's okay,' replied Marcus. 'We'll take the kit and do some target shooting at a suitable time and place in the past. It won't take you long to get the hang of it.' He was now sporting a huge grin. 'Maybe they will send us some old potato mashers,' and saw the confused look on the other man's face. 'It was a nickname for the Nazi grenades. They looked like a potato masher.'

'Do you think they can get all this stuff? It must be hard to come by?' Avery asked.

Marcus just shrugged. 'We shall see, my friend. If they want the mission done, we need the equipment. I'm not landing in a Normandy field wearing a suit and tie while flashing a badge. That might work on an old lady from the *Titanic*, but not the German Wehrmacht.'

Avery barked out a laugh. 'Yeah, though I'm not sure even that worked on the old girl. She knew we were bullshitting. I felt her eyes on us as we walked out of the hotel. Did you?'

'Yeah, but I like to think we outwitted an old lady, otherwise it could dent our pride a bit,' Marcus said with a small smile on his face. 'Right, let's get the request in and get some food ordered, too. It feels like a fried chicken type of day.'

It took a whole day in real time for all the equipment to be sourced, even though they had changed the firearms requested.

'Ah, the MP44,' Marcus said with a happy smile as he withdrew the magazine. It was a thirty-round magazine. He slammed it back home and pulled back the charging bolt to send a round into the chamber. Then he took out the mag and cast out the bullet from the chamber and dry fired it a couple of times. He repeated the process with the other gun. 'Looks good.'

Avery agreed. 'Looks like we have two machine guns, with four magazines each.' He looked through all the kit. 'No grenades, though.'

'I'd be surprised if there were any,' said Marcus. 'They won't want us to have too much fun.' He continued to examine the MP44 with the attached scope. 'Right, let's go to the travel room and go on a trip to check these bad boys out,' he said, a shit-eating grin adorning his face.

An hour later, Special Agents Martinez and Saunders stood in the Nevada desert, years before the thought of Las Vegas was even dreamt of. They stood in the baking heat, dressed as members of the elite Fallschirmjäger. Marcus taught his partner how to load and unload the MP44 – including the most important part, the safety catch, so he didn't kill himself or, more importantly, his partner.

During their time in the desert, they practised moving with the rifle, such as moving forward taking a knee and covering for the next man. Marcus had used these tactics in the Army, but Avery picked them up quite quickly. Then, they put a full magazine of thirty rounds through the guns, single shot and rapid fire. They ended the training, smiling and happy, as the sun began to go down.

They landed back in the travel room and instantly took off their helmets and downed bottles of water.

'How do you think that went, Ave?' asked Marcus, looking across at the red-faced man.

Avery nodded, the plastic water bottle to his lips. 'Yeah, it was good,' he said as he gulped the water down. 'Guess it will be different when we get there,' he added, with a look of concern creeping across his face.

Sitting down in the kitchen with the rifles placed on the table, they looked at each other.

'In answer to your question, my friend,' Marcus replied, 'all your senses will be affected. Being in a battle is like hell on earth,' he admitted. 'It'll be worse for us, as we are non-combatant. If it gets too bad, we'll just have to come back and try it again somewhere down the line, though that will be harder.'

Avery scoffed. 'Harder? Bloody impossible, I would say. We have to get it done.' He finished off his water. 'And the fact they gave us the German weapons, that says to me they want the target dead, not the German.'

'We'll see,' Marcus replied, though he didn't like the idea of shooting this man, whoever he was. The Traveller obviously had no idea of the repercussions of his actions. If only he could sit the bloke down and talk him through it. He looked at the real-time clock – it was 8 pm local time.

'Did you want to get this done now? Then we can rest overnight, and travel fresh in the morning?'

The older agent watched as his partner suddenly got up and ran back to his room, where he heard the young man empty his stomach. Marcus couldn't blame the kid; he was feeling the same. This mission was like something from a film. He did wonder how the Traveller felt, who was also involved in this mess. It didn't matter how well you planned something: in war, no plans survive first contact.

After a few minutes, Avery came back, his face red and wet. Cold water was a wonderful thing.

'I'm okay, I won't let you down, Marc,' he said and grabbed his gun off the table, leaving the one with the telescopic sight for his partner. 'I just sent Samantha a text to say… goodnight.'

'Good idea,' said Marcus. 'Go and get things ready, and I'll meet you in there,' and he jogged off to his room. He wished he had thought of messaging his wife first, even though Loretta would be very suspicious.

They stood in the travel room, dressed in their paratrooper kit.

'Right, we have a full magazine in the gun, check?' Marcus asked.

'Check.'

'Two full magazines in your pouches?'

'Check,' Avery confirmed, patting said ammo pouches.

Marcus nodded. 'Water bottles, and return remotes?'

Red faced; Avery nodded. Just to make sure, they both looked at the charge stations and saw they were empty.

'We're good to go, Marc,' he said shakily. Marcus took his partner's hand and shook it.

'Remember, safety on, keep your weapon pointed away from us,' Marcus instructed and moved over to the computer, which had already been set up. 'When we land, hit the deck straight, and then move to cover.' He pressed the enter key to start the countdown. 'If I'm hit, just leave me. There is nothing on me that will alter the time, okay?'

Avery nodded, only because he was worried that he would puke again so couldn't risk talking. They both stood in the pods, waiting for the counter to reach zero hour. They would arrive at 06:45 UK time. His world suddenly turned bright white as they travelled back in time, then the world came alive with noise. Without even thinking, he dove forward. He saw Marcus to his right; he was pointing to some bushes to the left. At a low crouch, they ran towards cover.

Soil was flung high in the air as shells from the ships hit the coast of France.

'Fuck! You forget how loud this shit is,' Marcus screamed into Avery's ear, whose eyes were as wide as saucers. 'Let's move to that bunch of bushes over there,' he said, pointing with his hand. They both ran, crouched over. Then the shellfire seemed to stop.

Avery looked around, while trying to hold his panic at bay. He checked his watch. Time was running out.

'We have to get in position,' he said, just as a few shells made them both fall flat on the ground. Shrapnel cut the foliage above them, covering them in it. 'FUCK!' Avery screamed as machine gunfire came from somewhere near the cliff. He was pulled to his feet by Marcus and they ran full pelt. Eventually, they made it to the position they had picked out on the map. It was a shell hole with some bushes hiding their backs.

Marcus pointed towards the German lines. 'Watch them,' he called out. 'Paratroopers weren't in this sector, so they might get suspicious, especially if we don't move.'

Avery shuffled around, keeping his eyes on Marcus. He could see movement in the trees. 'Why did you pick this uniform, then? Wouldn't it have been better to blend?' He poked his gun barrel over the lip of the hole.

'It's the best,' shouted Marcus. 'Plus, they might think we are on a special ops.' He scanned the area. There was heavy smoke rising from most of the mainland. He thought about all the men who would be coming ashore, straight into the sights of the machine gunners. 'Keep your eyes out for the flash of light,' he ordered, just as he saw a group of Wehrmacht disappear in a blast from a ship's guns.

Avery was watching a group of Axis soldiers. They were huddled up, as if they were working out which way to get though the grassland towards the cliff, perhaps to try and drive the US Rangers back into the sea. They all turned their heads as bright light appeared in the middle of some trees.

'He's here!' Avery called out, just as machine gunfire started up somewhere, creating more fountains of earth.

'Okay, keep watching him,' replied Marcus. 'I'll track him when he gets closer to the shell hole we marked out.' He made sure the safety was switched off, and that it was set to semi-auto. The battle was getting fierce all around them.

Just then, Avery spotted the target. He was dressed like he was going to war, but he didn't appear to be armed.

'He's running!' he called out to Marcus and saw more German troops getting killed. 'He looks shit scared. Can't blame him.'

'Got him,' Marcus said, getting his rifle ready. 'When I fire, press the return home button, okay?'

'Got it,' replied Avery. 'German just been blown off his feet, lost his gun. He's following our man.' He watched the man as he jumped, hole to hole. It was then that Avery saw a group of eight soldiers creeping up through the trees, their eyes following the man in front. Avery's stomach almost flipped as he readied his gun with one hand and placed his spare hand on the homeward bound remote, his thumb hovering above it.

Marcus saw the target jump into the shell hole, a look of panic on his face. Clearly, he hadn't planned for this. Marcus took in the man's face with the scope. He was tall, Caucasian, fit looking.

'Why the hell would you come here unarmed?' he muttered. Then he remembered that the man had never shot back when they were in Dallas, and the changes he had brought about on the *Titanic* only saved more women and children. 'Who are you?'

Marcus centred the crosshairs on the man's sternum. He didn't want to kill him. He calmed his breathing, just as a German soldier slid into the shell hole. The only shot he had was of the target, who seemed to be grabbing for something.

'Is that a fucking taser?' he said to himself. Suddenly, the soldier moved in front of the scope. 'Bingo!' Marcus pressed the trigger rapidly, three times in succession. Then, he closed his eyes as the scene was painted in a bright light.

'SHIT!' Avery called out. The group of German soldiers had just seen the man that Marcus had shot, and where the bullet had come from. 'Incoming fire!' he yelled and pressed the go home button on the remote, before shouldering his weapon as the group spread out. He beaded in a pair and sent several rounds at them; however, in his haste, he had missed. That caused the earth in front of their hole to erupt, including the whizzing of shots that flew overhead. He fired again. This time, a man with dark hair was flung backwards, blood spurting from his neck. His helmet rolled away into another shell hole.

Marcus scanned the shell hole and saw that the German was dead. His back had been ripped apart. He pressed his return home button, then went to help his partner, and instantly saw the problem.

'What did you say to them to piss them off, Ave?' He sighted in on a man with a rifle. With a recoil, the man lost half of his face, covering his companion in brain and gore. The companion scrambled away from the man in a panic, which allowed Marcus to send three rounds into his chest.

'They were watching what had happened to the other soldier,' said Avery. 'Guess they didn't like what they saw.' He sent another man to join his ancestors in Valhalla.

Marcus laughed, and knocked the helmet off another one. This one, however, kept his head.

'That would do it,' he said. 'I took the shot just as the soldier jumped up, tagged him in the back, then target disappeared.' He gave a grin. 'Shot the same one in the ass, teach him to retrieve his helmet like that!' He looked over to Avery. 'Right, go full auto. Let's make them keep their heads down.'

There was an explosion of noise as they sent their ammo down towards the German lines. Avery suddenly saw the bright light. He took his finger off the trigger, though he dived to the floor as one round rebounded off the concrete chamber.

'Shit,' he said from the ground, relieved he was home. 'Marc, that was close…' he smiled, looking at where his partner should be. 'Oh no!'

'Well, that's not good,' Marcus said to himself as Avery disappeared along with the familiar bright light. He loaded his last magazine and changed back to semi-auto and then stopped firing, hoping to bring the German heads back up. 'C'mon… bingo!' He sent another to hell.

Then he saw reinforcements making their way through the trees. There had to be another dozen coming his way. He took the leader out with a bullet to the chest, making the world erupt in noise and lead.

'I love you, Loretta…' he muttered.

Marcus popped his head over the top of the shell hole and took another man down, shooting him in the shoulder. That was when he saw the grenades flying through the air.

'Fuck.'

Avery ducked as his friend suddenly appeared in the room and fell, face first, on the floor.

'Shit, man, you okay?' he said and helped to turn Marcus over. 'Fucking close, wasn't it?' he laughed, helping Marcus up and brushing him off.

'Understatement, my friend,' replied Marcus. 'They had friends, and those friends had grenades!' He made safe his weapon, taking the magazine out and the bullet from the breach. That was mirrored by his partner, who had clearly forgotten to do any of that.

'I need a coffee, my friend,' said Marcus and headed out for the kitchen. Two green lights illuminated the room.

Without another word, they both departed to their separate bedrooms to shower and change, each reliving the trip, one better than the other. Avery stood under the hot water with his head resting on the now warming tiles. In his mind, all he could see was the empty German helmet rolling across the ground, as its owner was thrown backwards with a gunshot to his neck.

'Am I a murderer?' he muttered to himself.

Marcus sat at the dining table, thinking about the Traveller. Somehow, he needed to talk to him without Avery knowing what he was doing. His partner was ready to put a bullet in him, just so he could go back to his cushy computer job. And that was something else that was bothering him; would the Bureau really let them split up and go their separate ways after this mission?

He looked up as Avery walked into the kitchen. He was wearing shorts and a T-shirt, looking like a disgruntled teen who had just had their game console taken away. The blond man threw himself onto a chair and sipped at the hot beverage, which Marcus had already made for him.

'You okay, my friend?' Marcus asked.

Avery's first thought was just to shrug and say nothing. But then he thought of all the stories of service men and women, suffering in silence when they arrived home from combat, many of whom had no one to talk to about their experiences. Here, he had someone who was now a friend, and who had shared the same shell hole with him. If Marcus didn't understand, who would?

'I'm struggling with what we just did,' he replied. 'I killed men. We killed a lot of people today, all because of one man.'

'I understand, though we are here doing a job because of one man,' replied Marcus. 'The Director ordered us to, plain and simple. But yes, we killed.' He dipped his head slightly. 'It was either them or us. Plus, the likelihood was that those men never made it through the day, anyway. They were going to fight the Rangers, and they are the elite.'

Avery just sat, quietly nursing his mug of coffee. 'I understand that, but I've only ever shot a weapon during range time. Now I have killed at least two people,' he said and allowed tears to form in his eyes. 'How can I face people knowing that I have taken lives? What will Samantha say?'

The older agent had asked himself the same questions during his service for the US Army. 'You did the job ahead of you,' he replied. 'Not only did your actions save my life, it saved yours as well.' He placed his cup forcefully on the table. 'While I don't know your Samantha, she is a federal agent, and if she was in that situation, I'm sure the young woman would do exactly the same. You didn't murder anyone. Those people died over seventy years ago. There is no one now to grieve over them, so neither should you.'

'I understand, it'll just take some time to get my head around it,' Avery sighed and then looked into his friend's eyes. 'I just hope the target doesn't do anything else as stupid as this. I want to go home tomorrow.'

'Me too,' said Marcus. 'We have a party to go to, my friend. Now, go and rest and I'll see you in the morning.' He bid his fellow agent goodnight as Avery did as he was advised. As the door closed, he thought about how he could get to the Traveller. He preferred to call him the Traveller rather than the target. Then a smile appeared on his face.

'Gotcha!'

Chapter Fifteen

There was snow on the ground around the Partridge farm. Parked outside was the two now familiar 4x4s. It had been almost three months since I had fallen out of the pod after being shot. It was not the best day to begin with. I stared out over the snow-covered farmland as I did the dishes; it was so serene. My mind played back the last three months. It all started when Dana managed to find a replacement to cover her while she took some time off to look after her little wounded soldier. Her words, not mine.

One evening, we sat opposite each other following a nice, healthy meal and after she had changed my dressing. Dana was very happy with the way the wound was healing, though there was a heaviness in the air between us.

'Bri, we need to talk,' she said softly. We locked eyes and she saw me gulp. 'Where do you want this to go between us? We both have issues from our past, so it might be best to lay things out, so we know what this is.'

I nodded. 'Don't we just. Honestly, I am so grateful to have you in my life again, you have brought stability back to it.' When I said this I saw her smile slightly.

'I know I'm a control freak, but that's the Army in me. And then setting up the practice on my own, it's just the way I am!' Dana explained and laughed. 'But I'm sure you remember how I was as a teen?'

'Scarily focused, but that's why I fell for you back then,' I admitted. 'You were my north star. You gave me direction when needed it.' I saw her head drop.

She sniffed. 'Then I disappeared…' She looked up again with teary eyes. 'But I am back now and would like to see where this leads between us,' and she gave me a hopeful look. 'What do you say? Can I be your north star again?'

It was my turn to nearly succumb to tears. 'I have been alone for so long,' I said. 'You can see what happens when I am left in control of my life.' I gestured at my leg, making her snort with laughter. 'But it would make me beyond happy to see where this goes. And yes, I like and need your drive and control, though I will tell you if you go too far, or I start to feel uncomfortable, okay?'

A voice brought me out of my silent reverie at the kitchen sink.

'What are you looking at, Bri?' Dana said from behind me, as a pair of thin arms wrapped around my waist and a warm pair of lips kissed my neck. I looked around and smiled. Dana was wearing her ever-present New England Patriots jersey, which she now wore to bed after I had threatened to throw her out for wearing my shirts to sleep in. It had been a risk worth taking, but I survived the night.

We shared a brief kiss.

'Just enjoying the day,' I answered and gave her rump a slight pat.

I don't remember when Dana moved in, or the point where we started to share a bed together. I'm not even sure I was part of the decision making, but the end product had made me the happiest man alive.

'So, you've checked my leg out, and you say I'm nearly fixed?' She nodded her head, then cuddled into my chest before walking away.

'Yes, but that doesn't mean you can go running about on it yet,' she clarified and moved out of sight. 'And, as promised, I will fill you in on my plans. I just want to wash the night's grime off me first.'

And then her top came fluttering back into the room, which, even for my male dull-witted mind, was code for 'wash my back'. She was teasing me, as we still hadn't made that leap, especially after the talk we'd had.

Later that evening, while I lay in my bed, she started to read all of the late George Lancaster Jnr's books and paperwork. As she was doing that, my finances were taking a bashing, though I never saw any reason or evidence for this. All Dana would say was to wait until I was better.

A month later, Dana did her first (and solo) trip in the time machine. For the first time since leaving the Army, she put on her uniform, and damn it did look good on her. Leia gave me a kiss on the cheek and walked away from me. Several minutes later, when my old friend came back, tears were streaming down her face and no words were shared. Dana undressed and climbed into my bed and asked me to hold her and never let her go again. Two days later, we officially changed from being close friends to lovers. We broke the bed, but that was her fault as I wasn't allowed to move.

It turned out that Dana had decided to travel back in time to visit her parents, pretending to be home on leave. It was only weeks before their horrific car accident and, unlike me, she did not try to stop it happening. Everything that had happened served as a warning. Fate will always win and the Grim Reaper never goes without. At least my Princess Leia finally had closure, as did I.

After that, she disappeared for a few trips here and there. But I didn't mind the fact that she went on her own. Finally, I had someone in my life whom I loved and missed dearly when she wasn't around.

One morning, we sat down together and had a nice, warming breakfast of oatmeal and ginger tea, which was something that dear Dana had brought into the house.

'So, what is this great plan then, Leia?' I asked as the last remnants of oatmeal were scraped from her bowl.

Dana shot me a wink and wiped her mouth with a napkin. 'Well, my dear Brian. Using one of your wonderful fake IDs, you, Brian Johnston of Boston, are now a proud owner of one Titan II Missile Complex 571-1, located in Benson, Arizona,' she said happily and walked off with our breakfast things, coming back moments later with a folder containing all the information and pictures. 'It's perfect.'

Flicking through the paperwork, I saw that the complex had been buried by the previous owner to stop vandals breaking in, as he lived far away. It was attached to the local water, power and other services.

'Jesus, dare I ask how much?' I asked and opened the file again. 'It needs a lot of work, honey.'

She tucked a strand of her dirty blonde hair behind an ear. 'At today's prices, it was just under half a million dollars.' She watched as all the blood left my body to places unknown, but happier. 'So, I went back a decade, and offered the owner three hundred thousand in gold, and he nearly tore my hand off!' She giggled as my head just nodded under its own steam. My mind visualised a man dressed like Yosemite Sam running off with my gold.

'Okay,' I answered hesitantly, knowing I had not spent even a small percentage of my legal but ill-gotten gains. 'Right, so we have an evil lair, mwahahaaa!' and I pretend to stroke a white cat.

'We need a secondary location, just in case those shadow arsehole agents turn up,' Dana explained. 'And that thing downstairs isn't just a time portal. You can use it as transport – and, as you aren't travelling through time, you can go to the same location multiple times,' she added happily. 'Not only that, I've had contractors in to make the new place habitable. That was just after the purchase, and then I travelled five years later and managed to get permits in your name to build a nice, three-bedroom ranch-style home over the top of it.'

'Holy shit!' I muttered as I looked at the photo she slid across the table, showing a very rustic, old-style ranch made from logs. 'It's wonderful,' I said and looked up to see her walking around, moving my chair away from the table. Leia settled onto my lap.

Her lips were warm when we kissed briefly. 'Bri, this is your family home, but it holds too many bad memories for you,' she said softly. 'And, if I'm honest, for me, too.' She looked over to where she had found me on the floor, nearly bleeding to death. 'I won't force you to leave this place. Just know that we have a home ready and waiting for us, somewhere where we can't be found, and we can enjoy our life together.'

I knew Dana was right. A day didn't go by without a grimace at the past. 'What about the time machine? How do we transport that there?' I asked, even though I knew she probably had planned for that already.

The smile on her face became brighter than the summer sun. 'What do you take me for, Bri? We have the exact same time machine set up there as we do here, with several rows of solar panels, plus an emergency back-up generator.' When she explained it like that, I realised how intelligent Leia was. 'When we travel from here, we walk out of the pods in Arizona, so no worrying about the flash or people seeing us. Plus…' An evil grin appeared on her beautiful face. I held up my hand to stop her.

'What did you do? And how much will it hurt?' I asked and watched her flutter her eyelashes at me.

She placed her fingers to her chest. 'Moi?' She slipped off my lap and swayed her way into the kitchen, opening the refrigerator. 'Do you want some juice?' she called out to me.

Her voice echoed through the house. 'What did you do?' I shouted in return, alarmed at this distraction. I then saw her smirking visage come walking back in with two glasses of orange juice. I took mine and watched as Dana sat back in her original seat. 'Come on, what did you do?'

'It cost a bit,' she replied. 'For security reasons, the door from the time room has a fingerprint scanner, and a number keycode, too,' she said with an evil grin, which would befit Lady Dracula herself. 'And, if they fail to leave or put too many incorrect codes in, then the computers shut down, and they are stuck.'

Pinching the bridge of my nose in frustration, I let a blast of air out. 'So, what then? We have people locked in our home but how do we get them out?' I asked.

I saw a quick flash of anger in her eyes, that disappeared as quickly as it arrived.

'Easy, now Brian,' she said and gave me a 'you're on thin ice' kind of look. 'It will notify us that someone has arrived. We can see and talk via the computer, or the video phone. If they won't piss off, then we have the gas grenades,' she added and smiled happily.

My mouth dropped, and whatever I was about to say just disappeared. 'Gas grenades?' I asked weakly.

'Yep.'

I blinked slowly. 'Real… gas grenades?'

Her jaws ground together. 'Yes, gas grenades,' and it was said with force.

'Okay, I love you, and you know that, right?' I said, making sure I had a free run to the front door. 'But, where in the bloody hell did you get gas grenades? And why?' I tensed my legs, ready to flee, though my injured leg still ached.

Her cheeks blushed. Maybe it was because this was the first time I had properly said that I loved her.

'And I love you, too, Brian,' she replied in softer tones than before. 'The gas grenades came from some prepper types back in the eighties, and why…' Dana added, 'you have pissed of the federal government.' She pulled out the well-read file from Michaels & Sons detective agency. 'FBI agents, Adam Walker and Danny McDonald, who are senior agents working out of the New York office. They were the ones at Pearl Harbour, so by your description it's a different pair chasing you, oh changer of time.'

We then had a long conversation about the reasons for not changing anything in history, including watching the film *Butterfly Effect*. Dana, when she had a point to make, man does she drive it home.

'Okay, I'm sorry,' I said and thought about the report. They did good work, it seems. The agents had worked separately, at either ends of the country, until November 1996, when they both moved to Washington. Then, three days later, they were transferred together to New York, where they partnered up, and moved their families down for good.

Dana packed all the paperwork away and stood there with her arms crossed. 'Now, come on, I won't bring that up all again,' she said and took my hand. 'Unless you balls it up again,' she added and kissed me on my blushing cheek. 'Let's go and have a nice look around our knew home.'

With my interest piqued, we ran downstairs, but then I pulled her to a stop. 'I haven't done the chickens. Karl will be pissed!' I stated and saw her eyes narrow. Even now, they didn't get on, and as I had been injured, Dana had been their main caregiver. And there wasn't that much care given to the cockerel.

'Fuck him,' she said. 'They have enough food inside for today… *We* shall clear them out tomorrow,' she growled in tones which would make a grown caveman make a run for it. 'Now, let's go.' and she pulled me down the stairs.

It had been a while since I had been down here, and I noticed that more pictures had been put on the wall. I smiled when the photo of me and Molly Brown came into view, then Dana and her parents. They were so happy in that picture.

Standing in the pod, I watched my beautiful girlfriend tap away on the console. By now, she had done a few trips on her own; she visited the launching of the *Titanic*, and the dress she had worn was wonderful. But, unlike me, Leia only went to watch the famed ship sail off into the history books – and, after all the trouble and heartache I had experienced before, I wished I had as well.

The light blinded me slightly, and then we were in a large, tubular room that was so tall it seemed to go straight up for miles. It was not surprising, as this used to be home to nuclear missiles.

'Guess they didn't leave us the weapons of mass destruction, then,' I chuckled.

'Penis envy, Brian,' Dana teased and scuttled away as I leapt at her. 'Piss off, before you hurt yourself!' She quickly put herself in a fighting stance. Yeah, that would hurt.

'Fine, lead on,' I said, smiling and watching her walk to the large steel door. She pressed her finger to a glass pad, which glowed green. Then the keypad lit up, but white this time.

Dana looked over her shoulder. 'It's a five number code. The computer program will generate you one when we put your fingerprint on the file upstairs,' she explained as the door clicked loudly, allowing her to turn the overly large locking wheel. It looked like it had come from, well, a missile silo, or submarine. 'Follow me,'

We walked and climbed and walked. 'Jesus, how big is this thing?' I called out, my voice echoing in the steel-walled stairway. It had been four levels by now, and my leg had started to throb.

With a little sweat on her brow, Dana turned and smiled. 'It's a missile silo, Hun. They aren't meant to be small,' she said honestly. 'But we are having a lift put in. It works on compressed air, so it's cheaper than the typical type with all the gearing.'

'Thank you, otherwise this would kill me,' I said as we continued the climb. 'Hang on, won't they see the time machine, Leia?'

'Nope,' she replied. 'I've looked on the internet and found a place that has been making these types of lifts for the last five years. I will just need to pop back and place an order for them to do it before the pods get delivered.'

By now, we had finally reached the top. With another fingerprint and code for the door, but without the big wheel, the door opened into a small office.

'Here we are, our little house above ground,' Dana announced and waited until I was in before closing the door behind me. The room was homely and warm. 'Come on, luv,' she said and took my hand, leaving the computer-adorned desk behind.

It was a beautiful house, all wooden structures and modern appliances, and the furniture matched the walls, which made it just perfect.

'This is amazing,' I said to her as we stepped outside into the Arizona winter sun. There was a light dusting of snow on the ground, but nothing like the snow at home, which was a blessing. There was also a two-door garage. 'So, will we drive our cars down here, then?'

Once again, Dana rolled her eyes at me. She tugged me across the Stoney surface and straight to a secure, heavy-duty wooden side door. This had a keypad lock. With a click, it opened. Dana looked at me. 'Close your eyes,' she purred.

I stopped dead. 'Last time you said that, you walked me into a post!'

She huffed. 'That was an accident. Now, close your bloody eyes… please Brian.' Dana gave my hand a knuckle-popping squeeze and my resistance gave out. I followed her lead into what, I hoped, was the garage. The sudden noise of electrical lighting being switched on attacked my ears. 'Now you can open them.'

'Well, holy shit!' I stated as I took in the sight of two brand-new trucks. Of course, Dana had a top-of-the-range Land Rover, while mine was the Ford F-150 Raptor. Giving out a girlish squeal, I ran to the truck. It was jet black and oh so big. 'I don't know what to say… Thank you, honey.' I grabbed hold of her and spun her around, which sent my spine into panic, but it survived the trip.

'You're welcome, baby,' Dana replied. 'We both paid half on them,' she added and walked me around. 'We have a local cleaner who comes around twice a week. Her husband checks over the vehicles for us, and also takes them out for a run. He didn't want to, but you know what happens when they aren't run.'

I nodded as I massaged her butt. And that was how we christened the garage. There wasn't the whispering of sweet nothings, or roses. It was in the back of my truck, and not even on the back seat. Nope, on the truck bed. After all, we were in cowboy country now.

All red faced and happy, we walked back into the house and to the office, where Dana fired up the computer. She took a green glass tablet from the wooden desk drawer and linked it to the PC.

'Okay,' she said, 'put your finger and thumb of your dominant hand on the pad, one by one. When it flashes green, take them off.'

'Yes, dear,' I said slowly, which brought forth another look. Did all couples have this much fun? I hoped so. Doing as instructed, we finally managed to get my prints on the PC. It felt like I was going to prison. *I hope I don't have to work in the laundry*, I thought to myself with a shudder.

Now with my prints on file and with a super-secret number issued, we headed back into the complex, this time heading towards the living room. So, with thumb outstretched, we made our way through the maze. It all stopped when I received a slap to the back of my head for humming the *Mission Impossible* theme tune. Now, where else would you sing it? The deeper we went into the living quarters, the more space age it felt.

'I love it, it's amazing,' I said. 'Not to live in all the time, but if we are attacked by the federal government, I could see us living here.'

We cuddled as she showed me the kitchen and the three bedrooms. They were nice, just not as nice as the bedroom in the little house above ground, but it was the perfect hideout.

'I'm so glad you like it,' said Dana happily. 'Like you said, it'll do at a push. The lift will make a huge difference when – and if – we decide to move here.' She then led me over to a nice settee, where she grabbed the remote control and turned on the large wall-mounted TV for the local news.

'You did so good, Dana,' I said. 'I am so proud of you for doing this for us.' I pulled her in, making her cuddle even deeper into my side. 'After this, fancy going for a nice trip into the past?'

We sat in silence for a while as ideas were mulled over.

'Well, I have several ideas,' Dana said eventually. 'Some are a bit dark and I'm not sure about it, but I'd like to watch the Hindenburg crash. I know people died, but it's just one of those things,' she admitted, although her cheeks reddened.

'Hey, I went to Normandy, and the sinking of the *Titanic*, so who am I to judge?' I replied and tried to laugh off the bleakness of those events. 'What's the other?'

'Chicago in the 1920s,' said Dana excitedly. 'We could try and get a hotel and sneak into a speakeasy.' She looked up at me hopefully. 'What do you think?'

I did have to laugh. 'Why not? Maybe we can see Capone?'

'Oh, that would be so cool!' said Dana. 'And maybe go back and see Bonnie and Clyde do a hold-up. Pleeeease!'

We kissed for a while, just to stop her pleading. Well that was my plan. 'Okay, Hun,' I said. 'We'll start the research when we get home, then order some clothes so that we blend in. Maybe stay for a few days, if we can get the cash.' And then I found myself being pushed and pulled all through the titan complex by a strong ex-Army doctor. How the world changes.

I woke the next day to an empty bed. I knew that Dana had wanted an early jump on the day ahead.

'Bloody Army people,' I mumbled as I got up and walked sleepily to the bathroom, where I had a shower and washed the sleep from my body. As the orders still stood, there would be no running for me until the summer. Even now, I felt my body changing and not for the better. I decided to buy an exercise bike. At least we'd have something to hang the washing on later.

'Hello, Sleeping Beauty,' she called out happily, but not looking up from the laptop. 'Sleep well?'

I placed a kiss on her cheek. 'Yep, like a dead thing. You?'

'Okay, just my mind was buzzing all night, so I needed to get to work,' she said as her finger moved down the touchpad of the laptop. 'Got a plan done for the Hindenburg trip,' she said. 'Very easy,' and she waved a file at me, though I had already moved past her.

'I'll be back, do you want anything?' I asked and she lifted up her juice glass. And so, turning into a waiter and serving her more orange juice, I sat down with my breakfast, and I took the file. It was full of maps, photos and times, along with coordinates. Reading while eating, I realised Dana was right. It would be one of the easiest visits.

'We don't need money or outfits,' she continued. 'It'll be daylight, so they won't notice the flash, especially if we time our arrival as the Hindenburg arrives.' Dana tapped a cross on the map. 'It's a large, open-grassed area, and it'll be far behind all the press and onlookers.'

I was impressed, her mind was even more beautiful than her face. Give her money and power, this woman could take over the world, or at least England. Start small.

'Yes, it seems almost too perfect,' I replied, 'but carry on with the other projects and order what we'll need. I'll go and say hello to the chickens.' I took away my breakfast things before slipping on some work boots and a coat, to head out into the New England weather, where the wind cuts you to the bone.

Karl and his hens barrelled out of the hot box of a coop and ran around picking up all the corn that was scattered across the ground. The rooster watched me as I shut the coop door and headed inside. That bloody bird needed its own theme tune, like *Jaws*.

It took a while to empty the coop of old straw and droppings. Then I collected the day's eggs, which at this time of year amounted to only two. After throwing down clean straw, I headed back outside and started to shiver instantly.

'Sodding weather!' I grumbled as I opened the coop and watched the hens run in, while the rooster just slowly strutted pass, his jet-black eyes never wavering from me. 'Dick!'

There was a pot of tea ready for when I came back in. Dana had already poured herself a cup.

'How was the feathery Grim Reaper?' she asked, once again her eyes not leaving the monitor.

'The norm,' I replied. 'Luckily, he was too busy looking after his wives to hassle me, so I managed to clean them out and collect the eggs. I've put them in the kitchen.' I took a sip of the ginger tea. 'While you're on there, could you order me an exercise bike? I need to keep fit.'

At last her eyes moved from the screen to mine. 'Already done. Will be here tomorrow,' she advised and then a smirk appeared on her face. 'And by the weekend we'll have a place to hangs your shirts on.' I replied by going all British on her by blowing a raspberry and showing her the reverse peace symbol.

'Nothing but class, Brian,' she replied. 'Now, drink your tea and get into the camo jumpsuit and boots. It's time to fly!' With a bark of a laugh, she ran off to get changed, followed by the still limping me.

'Once more unto the breach, my dear, once more,' I quoted as I stood in my pod, holding the camera, while Dana inputted the data for us. It still amazed me how, while I was ill, she sent the return home remotes away to a friend of hers, who copied them and added a longer life battery and sent back another four, plus the original. I feel quite superfluous at times.

Dana looked at me. 'You've been very British today. As you know, I have nothing against them, but coming from you it feels wrong, so stop it!'

I fired back a wink. 'Alright, treacle,' I said in my best cockney accent, which caused magic to happen.

And, with a flash of light, we were gone.

NAS Lakehurst, Manchester Township, New Jersey

The ground was slightly uneven, causing my legs to fold and sending me to the ground, which was the plan anyway. Dana looked down at me.

'You alright down there?' she asked as her head moved with the binoculars against her eyes. 'We're okay, everyone is looking at the airship.' She sat down cross-legged, wearing the same kind of jumpsuit that she had bought me.

My watch told me it was 7.10 pm and the Hindenburg was just turning above the landing area. I was taking photos and, with the long lens, I could get in close. Not only that, I could use the lens to make sure we weren't being watched. I snatched a look at Dana; the smile on her face was huge. We knew we couldn't stop such events, so we put the loss of life out of our minds. This was just an event in history.

'You okay, honey?' I asked.

'It's amazing, Bri,' said Dana. 'I don't have the words to describe it.' She lifted up the small video camera that had once been attached to the remote-controlled truck. 'I can see why you got hooked on it,'

It was 7.20 pm when the mooring ropes were dropped from the airship. Then, just like in the reports that were written after the event, a flap of material came loose upon the top of the ship, then flames appeared on what I had learnt was the port side. Within seconds, the airship was totally engulfed, and it dropped to the earth. We could hear the screams and shouts of the onlookers, the sounds of the steel frame collapsing on itself. It was truly something out of Dante's inferno.

Dana moved closer to me and wrapped her arms around me. 'That was terrible,' she said with tears trickling down her face. 'But yet, just so incredible.' I could feel her shivering. 'Let's go home,' she said and stood up, then helped me to my feet. Together, we pressed our remotes.

I looked down at her. 'It's hard to watch, I know, but they have been dead for years. All the grieving has been done, and we shall grieve for them a bit more out of respect. We owe them that.' She looked up at me with a wet grin. Then we disappeared back home, and we went straight to bed and held each other and made passionate love into the night, to feel the love we had together.

The next couple of days were quiet. Dana left to do some paperwork at her practice. She wanted to make sure everything was running okay – which it was, given her constant contact with employees and customers.

While Leia was away, I managed to keep myself busy, planning for other trips that I wanted to make. The exercise bike had turned up, so I enjoyed exercising a bit more. It did take a toll on the wound, although by now it felt like it had healed. I felt that building up the fitness slowly again would make things a lot easier, especially when we left for the Silo.

We talked in the evenings while watching the TV, curled up under blankets like so many do during this time of the year. It seemed that my wonderful girlfriend was still struggling with the images of the disaster and the flames. It took her back to the bombing and being surrounded by flames and screams.

'It's okay, just take your time. We are in no rush to do anything,' I said softly and kissed her on the top of her head, as that was the only part of her I could reach.

Finally, she looked up at me. 'Bri, we still have secrets, don't we?' she said sadly.

My head dipped. 'Not bad ones, I hope. But yes, we do.' It was then that I knew it was going to be a long, sad night.

Her long fingers intertwined with mine, and then she looked into my eyes, as if she were piercing my soul.

'Where did you go when you left home? What did you do?' Dana asked, never once losing eye contact with me. 'Nobody knows, not even your family. Jacob and your sister-in-law came round to my parents' house looking for you. You had just disappeared; it was only because you packed that they didn't call the police.'

I sighed. It was bound to come up one day.

'It was on a Friday,' I began. 'I was meant to be at college, but I bunked off to buy some new comics, and I heard my family talking about me. Mum was in tears, Father and Jacob were arguing. Dad wanted to give me a go on the farm, but my brother refused, saying I was damaged and lazy.' I paused for a moment. Tears had filled both of our eyes. 'Dad went silent, and then agreed. But he said I was his son, that I may well be a drain on the family, but it didn't mean I couldn't be part of it. Mum ran to the bedroom after that.' I sighed deeply. 'Something in me broke that day. I sold all my comics and left town. I left Mum a note saying I was sorry, and that I loved her.'

'Oh, Brian, why didn't you contact me? I would've helped,' Dana sobbed.

'You were at university, and we hadn't spoken for ages. Your friend's boyfriends warned me off, because their friend wanted you, and I was in the way. So, I had no one and left.' I held her tighter. 'During my travels, I was robbed and badly beaten. I had no ID, nothing. The New Orleans police had nothing to go on, as in those days their computers weren't linked to the national database.

'The beating sent me into a spiral, and depression got the better of me. But I struck up a friendship with a doctor, whose brother ran a fishing fleet. I worked on their docks in exchange for food and board, plus some spending money. I made sure that I contacted Mum when I could. She kept it secret from the men of the house, knowing how they would act. After a time, I moved closer to home to work so I could pop in and out of my parents' lives. I was travelling when they died, and I couldn't be contacted. That was when I came home. Jacob didn't mention me leaving, neither did I, and he let me live here free of charge.'

Dana began to cry, then kissed me, smearing tears over both our faces.

'We are so mad for each other,' she smiled. 'That bloke who wanted me, he attacked me when I said no. He was a dick. I wondered why your name was mentioned in his rant before he punched me. He tore my trousers and top off, but before he could do anything else the dormitory security was called, and he was gone.'

'What a shit,' I said. 'Where is he now?' I felt her hand crush mine, making me wince.

She turned and sat on my lap. 'He is in prison and won't be coming back. Later that year, he attacked and killed a prostitute after keeping her hostage for days. I was a witness for his prior offences.' Dana gave me a sad smile. 'But that, isn't my secret. When I was injured in the bombing, some shrapnel hit me. Remember seeing all those little scars when we played name the scar?' I nodded. That was a fun day. 'The one on my bikini line, the one you called Kathy Ireland, that's the one that robbed me of my chance to have a baby. I had to have a hysterectomy. I'm sorry, Bri…' And then she sobbed the most heart-wrenching cries I had ever heard.

I pulled her face to mine and kissed her. 'Marry me.'

Chapter Sixteen

The words 'I do' will be forever etched onto my mind. As we knew that the FBI were hunting me, we travelled back to Las Vegas, July 1970. The IDs were easy enough to find and, after a short ceremony on the Strip with paid-for witnesses, Reverent Danny Brown pronounced us man and wife.

The witnesses took plenty of photos to show my family when we could; they were poor quality, though Dana reminded me that they could be cleaned up on the PC with a decent software program. My now wife, Mrs Brian Johnston, lay happily on the queen-size bed wrapped in nothing but a white sheet, which only just covered her modesty. It had been a fun night of drinks and dancing. And then we watched, along with thousands of people, Elvis singing out hit after hit. We continued the night of drunken abandonment, and my head was banging while Dana snored like a pig beast from hell, but I couldn't love her any more than I already did.

We had brought some gold coins with us, which we swapped for chips in the casinos, and we lost them all in a week-long honeymoon. I placed my head against the hotel room window, letting the coolness sooth my aching head.

'Hubby,' a groggy voice called out.

'Yes?' I mumbled back, though the vibration of the noise made hurt my head.

She groaned. 'Firstly, you're never touching me again,' she announced, with a wince.

'Gotcha. Secondly?' I replied, softer this time.

'Can we go home? I think we have celebrated enough, don't you?' She tried to move and failed. 'I'm broken, Bri.'

My stomach rolled from the debauchery of the previous evening. 'Yes, some healthy food would be nice, and peace.' I tried to move away from the window, but it was just too soothing.

'Thirdly… you're naked,' she said and giggled.

I shrugged, which made a joint crack somewhere. 'What happens in Vegas, stays in Vegas, baby,' I replied with a forced smile.

I looked out the window and noticed a person pointing up at me from the sidewalk and that won the day.

'Darling, the natives are restless, time to go,' I announced and moved like an iceberg thanks to my abused body. I collected up clothes and personal items, not knowing whether to leave things behind. 'What do we actually need to take home?' I asked, desperate for help to organise my thoughts and actions.

Still under wraps, Dana waved her manicured hand around the room. 'Purse, wallet, photos… wedding dress,' she listed without even opening her eyes. Her makeup was still intact from the night before, though slightly more spread out than it was at the start of the evening.

Moving quicker than before, I packed all the things into one bag, including Dana's thigh-length white wedding dress. It was stunning yet daring, but not for the 70s. That and knee-high platform boots, it was this decade's finest. Finally, everything was packed and ready. I left thirty dollars on the nightstand and picked up the two remotes, and then tried to pick up my wife.

'What the fuck!' she shouted out. The new wife had fallen asleep again.

'We have to go,' I said. 'Get your ass up!' I dodged a fist.

'Fine, just press the bloody button!'

I smiled at her as she wrapped the sheet around herself and held her hand out for the remote, pressing the red button at the same time I did. Dana held it in the air and shouted, 'Goodnight, Las Vegas!' Then, in a flash we disappeared.

'Ow! That hurt,' I muttered and not for the first time, as my new wife sank to the ground, baring herself to the world. Luckily, we were in the cellar. 'Come on, you, let's get to bed,' I told her and, with the walk of the shamed, we made it back to our bedroom and collapsed.

We lay there, facing away from each other, as sleep took us hostage. It wasn't because of a disagreement or an argument; it was the fact that, in our fragile states, even a soft breath across our skin would irritate the micro hairs, which sent pains shooting to our brains. So we deemed it fit, just for this moment, not to touch.

Day slipped into night, then back into day again before we made a move. I allowed my clenching wife the first turn in the bathroom.

'What a week!' she shouted out from the bathroom with perverse glee. 'Can we go back next year? They certainly know how to party!' She shouted out something else through the door but was drowned out by the flush of the toilet.

We met at the bathroom door and I pecked her on the forehead as we both had bed breath. Things were still tender, so my wife showered first while I headed downstairs to start breakfast and feed the evil chickens, though my mind happily reminisced about the fun we'd just had. I also thought about the heartache that Dana held onto about not being able to bear me children. There had to be a way somehow, sometime.

I stilled in mid-act of throwing feed to the fowl. *Dare we try it?* I wondered. After checking the water supply for the chickens, I walked back into the kitchen. Dana was at the sink and I kissed her on the neck, making her sigh and lean against me.

'Dana, I have an idea,' I said. 'It's a challenge, but if you're up for it, then I am.' She turned around and linked her arms around my neck.

'If it's that Tequila challenge we did two nights ago with Elvis, then no,' she chuckled. I was thankful that no cameras had been allowed in the King's after-show parties. We were high rollers and bad ones at that, thus the invitation. Best night ever!

'No, it's about the Kathy Ireland problem. I know it hurts you,' I said gently and had to stop her from turning away from me. 'Please listen. Why don't we look to the future? We don't know what's there and what they can do,' I explained. Dana stood still and stared at me in confusion.

We didn't talk for over a minute. Then again, we didn't move, either.

'That's so dangerous, Brian,' Dana said eventually. 'We don't know what might happen as a result. That's what Lancaster always said. The risk of doing it is too much. I don't want to lose you, not again.'

Her chest was heaving against mine as she cried.

'I'm sorry, I just thought it might work,' I whispered into her ear.

She looked up at me. 'Let me think about it. You work out a plan, while I ready the other trips, okay?' She kissed me quickly. 'Now, go brush your teeth, death breath.' She then pushed me away to continue her work.

Soon enough, parcels turned up making Dana happier than ever. Clothes, money and identity papers arrived. She had picked some waste ground in Chicago in early July 1926. When Al Capone was at his best, we would appear right around the corner of the hotel that he and his men occupied from time to time.

I dressed in my suit, though Dana didn't allow me to wear spats as they did in the movies. With my hat donned at a suitably roguish angle, I went in search of my darling wife, who was changing in the other room. Pushing the spare bedroom door open, I saw her wearing a knee-length skirt, which for her was unheard of, apart from our wedding day. She also wore a short jacket and hat.

'What do you think, stud?' she purred and spun around, showing off her legs.

'Beautiful, but one problem, Princess,' I stated and scanned her up and down.

'What?' she replied quickly, looking down at her skirt and frowning. 'It's fine.'

Shaking my head in disgust, I sat on the spare bed and took off my hat and twirled it around with my finger. 'It is my understanding that they do not wear pantyhose in the roaring twenties. Are we not trying to dress correctly to mirror the era we are in?' I gave her a loving smile.

She gasped and then smiled. 'This is what I am wearing. No one else will be seeing my underwear, not even you if you keep this up!' She raised her skirt to show off her thighs. 'During my years on this planet, I've tried garters and stockings only once, and the bloody strap nearly took my eye out. So no, I will *not* be wearing them, not for you or Al Capone. Got it?'

I lowered my head. 'Yes, dear,' I said and looked up. 'You look great, though.' I picked up the suitcase with some other clothes for hopefully a night out. Then, arm in arm, we went down to the cellar and into the past.

'Now listen, if we see Capone, don't accidently knock him into any traffic, or trip him up so he breaks his neck,' Dana warned, while pushing me into my pod. 'There will be no changing of history, okay?'

Putting down the suitcase, I held up my palms in defence. 'Hey, it's me you're talking to, here!' I shot her wink which, once again, brought her salty language out for an airing. Though the word she called me, just as we disappeared, hurt my feelings, I didn't hear it properly, and therefore I let her off this time.

We landed on some waste ground that was awaiting building permits for an office building, which I knew would be built the following year. This time, it was Dana's turn to stumble, thanks to the heels she was wearing. Scanning around, checking there were no onlookers, I took my grumbling wife by the hand and led her to the sidewalk. I then followed the instructions, which were ingrained in my head. We walked towards the Metropole Hotel, which was known to be Capone's and his associates' hangout from 1925 to 1928.

Arm in arm, we walked up the polished stone steps into the foyer. The building was situated on a corner plot. It had seven floors and was built in pale-brown brickwork. It was nice, just tired looking. As we headed towards the reception desk, I noticed a few men watching us. They wore smart suits, though it was the marks on their faces that told a story of a different side to life.

'Good morning. Welcome to the Metropole Hotel, do you have a reservation?' asked a sickly, thin-looking man, whose badge announced him as the Manager.

I put the suitcase on the floor and gave him a small smile back.

'Morning,' I replied. 'We have just gotten in from Boston, and I didn't think to phone ahead for a booking. Do you have any rooms available?' I watched the man as his weaselly eyes looked us up and down, spending way too much time lingering on Dana. Then he opened the guest book.

'How many days are you looking to stay?' the manager asked. His voice was slimy, like his hair.

I looked at Dana, who looked back thoughtfully. That was the only thing we hadn't discussed.

'Two nights, please,' said Dana. 'Hope we can find some fun tonight, just like home,' she said with the biggest and naughtiest smile in her repertoire.

The man nodded. He checked my ID, then asked for Dana's before pushing them back across the desk.

'Room 121, first floor,' the manager said in a monotone voice, while pushing the key towards us, which had a gold disc with the door number etched upon it. 'The elevators are over there, and breakfast is being served now, if you would like it. The cost can be added to your bill since you are just booking in.'

I swiped the keys off the desk and nodded at the funny-looking man. 'Thank you, but we have already eaten.' Then Dana linked her arm with mine and we headed to the elevators. The lift was already there, so all we had to do was walk straight in and press the button. Within minutes, we found ourselves in the most depressing room ever.

'Well, this is shit,' Dana chuckled, throwing her hat onto the bed, which gave a strange thud. She gave it a test by sitting down; then, locking eyes with me, she bounced up and down on it. 'Whose bloody idea was this?' she cried out. 'This bed is worse than the cots the Army gave us to sleep on.'

I thought about reminding her that this whole adventure was her idea, though her steely eyes suggested it was not the best thing to say right now.

'Well, we don't have to stay the night if you don't want to,' I said cheerfully and joined her on the bed. It was akin to sitting on a slab of iron. 'Holy shit, they don't want repeat business, do they?' I exclaimed and stretched out my back.

'Pussy, but you're right,' said Dana. 'Let's go for a wander around the city. If we don't get a whiff of speakeasy, we'll head home.' She then went to powder her nose before heading out.

It seemed that all the black-and-white photos were quite apt for this city. Despite what the films tell you, life was hard and boring in the twenties.

All we saw of Al Capone was his henchmen, who had faces not even a mother could love. Not to be disheartened, we headed into Chicago – and, yes, it was gloomy. We took in the sights and snuck a few selfies in as well. Well, you can't blame us. Dana showed off her scandalous thigh for a picture in front of the Cubs baseball park, which is now known as Wrigley Field. We were actually New England football fans, but we felt we should support the Boston Red Sox. So sod the Cubs, hence the photo of my beautiful and slightly crass wife, who was now mooning said stadium.

After that, we had a brief lunch in a diner, which was full of body odour and cigarette smoke. That made our minds up and we headed straight home again to our time. Clearly, if you wanted to have fun in this era, you needed to know people.

Down in the basement, my darling wife's grumbling never stopped as she reinputted coordinates. I was forbidden to leave my pod or talk. Soon, the light flashed again, and we found ourselves in the 1930s.

During my time travel experiences, I have spent more time in alleyways than I would care to mention. This time was no different as, once again, I walked out into the daylight with a smiley wife on my arm. It looked like your typical small town of the time, shops and businesses lining a long, straight, dusty main street.

'Do you have the camera, Bri?' Dana asked, as we both noticed, on the opposite side of the road, a man sitting inside a parked car idling beside the kerb outside a bank. She pulled me behind a vehicle on our side of the street and pointed towards the bank.

'This is it!' she whispered and giggled, staring up at the bank's exterior. We couldn't see much of the goings on, so we just waited for the fun to start.

That's when we saw a small group of people come running out of the bank. We could see clearly that one of them was Bonnie Parker. I raised the camera above the car roof we were hiding behind and pressed the button. The flash went off. The place went silent as all the gang members looked our way.

'Damn!' I exclaimed under my breath and looked at my stunned wife.

'What the fuck!' Dana snapped and was just about to blame me for something that clearly was her fault, since she had readied the camera before coming here. The silence was shattered as quickly as the glass window of the car, as firing broke out in response.

'Think this was a great idea then?' I shouted as bullet holes appeared through the thin-skinned car we were hiding behind, opposite the scene of the crime.

Dana's expression was a picture. Glass had cut her face and blood was dripping down her cheek into her mouth, but I had never seen her happier.

'Can you believe it? We are getting shot at by Bonnie and Clyde!' She actually clapped her hands together as the car was being turned into Swiss cheese. 'Did you get any photos?' she asked, totally forgetting about ongoing events caused by the camera flash.

I nodded. 'Yes, now let's get the hell out of here,' I replied desperately. I received no response; instead, my giggling wife ran past me, crouched over, as bullets kicked up chips from the road.

We made it into a deserted alleyway. Then, together, we pressed our return home buttons, just as the getaway car sounded like it was being driven away. I was being kissed furiously by my wife as we were dragged back into the future; dirty, grazed, and covered in blood, but at least my little Dana was happy.

While Leia was out with a work thing, I sat in the basement looking at all the photos I had taken during my time travelling escapades. There were three that truly scared me. The first was of a Japanese pilot firing at me. The second was the iceberg. The third was an image of the one and only Bonnie Parker and Clyde Borrow trying to shoot at us, all because the flash went off on the camera. They were not happy.

My only regret was not telling Molly Brown the truth. I knew that she suspected my story was bullshit. With a faint smile, I went upstairs and put on my suit from the Chicago trip. We had only just gotten it cleaned. Putting on my hat and coat, I stepped into the time machine for my first solo trip since my injury.

Once again, I appeared in a bright flash in an alleyway in New York, on the night of 26th October 1932. Slipping off my father's shades, I walked around the dark corner and passed some people running towards the source of the light. Thankfully, it was a miserable night; cold and wet.

It only took me another five minutes to reach my destination, the Barbizon Hotel, 140 E. 63rd St., Manhattan. Stepping into the foyer, I was lucky as there was a woman talking to the receptionist. So, with my head down and my hat pulled low, I managed to ghost my way past them and, dispensing with the elevator, decided on stretching my legs instead. So I climbed the stairs to the fourth floor. It was amazing that someone had documented her life to the point that I could walk directly to her room. I looked down at my watch; it was now 8 pm. With a deep breath, I walked to the target door and knocked.

'Who is it?' came a weak voice from behind the door. 'It's late. What do you want?'

I took a breath. 'It's Brian, Brian Partridge,' I replied, and I heard her gasp.

'It can't be…' she exclaimed. 'When did we last meet?' she demanded, though her voice still sounded weak through the closed door.

'On the deck of the *Titanic*,' I replied. 'I convinced you to harass the crew into doing their duty, though it cost them their lives.' I heard the door being unlocked clumsily. The door opened and there she stood. 'Hello, Margaret,' I said. Her old, tired eyes looked me over, then a cold hand reached forward and cupped my cheek.

'I know my eyes are older than my body, but how is it possible that you haven't changed at all?' Margaret asked and then she backed away into the darkened room, drawing me in with her and closing the door behind me. I averted my eyes as the once stoic woman climbed back into her large bed. 'Sorry, Brian, but I'm not feeling my best tonight.'

After tucking herself in, she patted the edge of the bed for me to sit. The mattress squashed down as I balanced upon it and I let my hat drop to the floor.

'How have you been, Margaret? I've missed you,' I said kindly.

A warm smile adorned her face. 'Thank you, Brian. Even though our first meeting was a brief one, you have always held a special place in my heart, one that no one else could possibly fill.' She leant back against the headboard. Her hair was a lot greyer now, which glistened in the lamplight.

'I know, I felt it too,' I said with a smile. 'That's why I had to come and see you.' I took her hand, then my heart stilled as I saw a photo of us both on her nightstand. 'Is that us?' I asked.

Margaret gave out a dry chuckle. 'The only one in existence, my friend!' She leant across and plucked it off the polished wood and handed it to me. 'You take it. I feel that time is short for me.' Her eyes met with mine and she visibly paled. Her hand touched her chest. 'I feel weak.'

I tucked the picture away into my pocket. 'Shall I get a doctor? Maybe they can do something to help?' I suggested, but she merely shook head slowly. I patted the pocket that I had put the image of us both and said, 'I shall treasure this photo, for ever.'

'As I have done since that night,' Molly replied and then gave me a smirk. 'You can tell your wife that I will not challenge her for your affections.' She laughed again, though there were signs of pain in her face. Her grip on my hand tightened briefly. 'What's her name, dear? And, while we are at it, what is your *real* story? It will be safe with me and the angels, I promise.' She looked at me with watery eyes.

I knew she was a clever one. 'Well, Margaret, if you really want the truth, then you shall have it,' I announced and noticed that her mouth had dropped on one side slightly, though this was no surprise to me. 'My name is Brian Partridge, and I am just recently married to Dana, who was in the Army as a doctor, then retrained as a vet. I was born in 1976.'

One of her eyes opened wide with surprise, though the other eye above her drooping mouth did not.

'I would call you a liar, but the proof is in front of me,' she said. 'It's nice to hear that women can hold such jobs in the future. Dare I ask how you came to be with me on the ship?' she asked, her interest still piqued, despite her rapidly failing health.

'It is one of the most famous maritime disasters in the world,' I explained, 'and I wished to see it with my own eyes. I hoped that I could change something about the events to save more lives.' I held her cold hand even harder. 'With your help, it worked. Though the number of the dead didn't alter, more females and younger passengers fared better following your help, which made it easier to bear.' I kissed her hand as I saw the shock on her face. 'I used a machine to come back in time, though it causes me some trouble.'

Margaret nodded sleepily. 'Trying to change things was always a foolish quest,' she said. 'Two men came to see me a few years back. They said they worked for the federal government, and I believed them. But the questions they asked me were strange. They wanted to know about you, my sweet Alfred... sorry, I mean Brian.'

'I'll always be Alfred for you, Molly,' I reassured her. 'Can I ask you to describe them?' I probed but saw that the tiredness was taking her away from me.

She stilled for a moment, then started to say something. However, the words came out in a slight slur, her hand still upon her breast.

'Mexican, shortish, and the younger one was tall and blond, I think,' she muttered and closed her eyes. 'Be careful, dear. God doesn't share control of the heavens and Earth.' Molly nestled down into her bed. 'I'm tried. Will you stay with me until I fall into a slumber? Don't leave me again, I don't want to be alone.'

I leant over and gently pressed my lips onto her lips and pulled her hand to my chest. 'I'm here, Margaret. You rest and I will always be by your side. Now, to sleep, Mrs Brown,' I whispered soothingly and rubbed her hand against my cheek. A tear rolled from her eye to her chin and over the very last smile she would ever have. I was there for a full hour with Molly when her heart failed, and her soul left her to re-join her friends and family.

'Rest in peace, Margaret,' I said solemnly.

With one last look at the unsinkable Molly Brown, with the photo in my pocket and tears in my eyes, I slipped from the room, making sure my hat was back in place in an attempt to leave the building unseen. The receptionist did call out for me, but nothing was going to stop me leaving this place forever. It was still raining as I made my way back to the alley.

I stood behind a dumpster and reached into my pocket for the remote. That's when I felt something cold and metallic pressed to the base of my neck. The click of a hammer being drawn back on a gun echoed in my ears.

'Who are you? I don't have any money!' I said quickly.

'That is good,' a voice behind me replied. 'Keep your hands away from your return home button, and we will be fine.' My breath was caught in my throat. 'My name is Temporal Agent Marcus Martinez, and I have been looking for you… Traveller.'

I forced out a laugh. 'Are you mad? What are you talking about?' I felt the gun nudge the back of my head again.

'Keep your hands where they are, my friend, and turn around,' the voice instructed, while the man stepped away out of lunging distance. I turned around and instantly recognised the man. One of the men of shadows was standing in front of me.

'I have watched you in Dallas. You can run pretty fast, and then also in Normandy. That was a foolish trip. You were nearly killed, or worse,' Marcus stated.

Sagging, I leant against the rain-sodden wall. 'Fine. What do you want?'

The man took the gun away. 'I just want to talk,' he said. 'It is just me, and this is definitely not official.' He pointed to a coffee shop that was still open. 'Come on, I'm buying.'

He walked past me to the mouth of the alley and now I had two choices – see what he wanted, or run. I decided that gaining information about his role would be beneficial and might help me to remain safe. We walked across the road together, where we found a booth far away from anyone else. We each held in our hands a cup of dreadful coffee.

I decided to start the ball rolling and get some answers. 'How in hell did you track me here?' I asked. 'Molly Brown said you had talked to her a few years ago.'

The agent laughed. 'I knew the old bird had rumbled us,' he said with a warm smile. 'It wasn't easy to find you, but as she willingly helped you on the *Titanic* and you held a connection, given that today is her last day on Earth, I hoped the event would draw you here.'

Dipping my head and gripping the cheap porcelain mug until it creaked, I sighed. 'I had to say goodbye,' I explained. 'I didn't want her to die alone, you see.'

Marcus nodded and continued. 'I know that the changes you tried to make weren't for personal gain, not really…' He took another sip of the coffee. 'That's why you are getting this chance. A selfish man wouldn't be here, and an evil man would've been shot in a shell hole in France instead of some German.' He picked at his fingernail before looking me straight in the eye. 'Stop changing things,' he said firmly. 'You have no idea of the ripple effect it causes. Just the Normandy trip that you made was bad enough.' He shook his head and handed me a sheet of FBI headed notepaper with some print on it.

I scanned the document, almost throwing up as I imagined the fallout. Then I read it more slowly, taking in all the details of what I could've caused to happen. My eyes scanned over the Normandy trip; if they hadn't stepped in, I would've been caught, tortured and then taken to Berlin. This one event would put in motion World War Three and the end of not only America, but our allies, too. I looked up.

'My God, please say this is a lie?'

'Sorry, but it isn't,' Marcus admitted. 'I will tell you this, though. Our investigation is currently concluded, but that doesn't mean my partner or somebody else from the Agency won't come after you.'

Pushing the paperwork back to him, I wiped the tears from my eyes. It had been a tough night. 'I have really pissed your partner off, then?' I asked.

The agent nodded his head. 'He's a poster boy, who enjoyed his easy life sitting in an office, then was thrown into a death-defying mission. It scared him and he seems to blame you for it all – which, for the most part, is correct.'

I took another sip of my coffee. 'Maybe, but I never meant to cause this. The machine wasn't even created by me. I found it in an estate sale.' I noted the look of surprise on the man's weather-beaten face. 'When I realised that it actually worked, I couldn't resist.'

'Have you travelled through time a lot, just for fun?' Marcus asked.

I smiled. 'You haven't lived until you've been chased by a dinosaur,' I said, making us both chuckle. 'I went back in time to watch the *Back to the Future* films, too,' I added, and that made the man roar with laughter.

'You know that your image is painted on a pyramid, right?' Marcus announced with a knowing grin and pushed colour photos across the table. 'You're a part of history, my man. Though, I am envious about it all. I wish I could just go visiting places.'

I raised a quizzical eyebrow at the man. 'Well, why not? You're doing it now, aren't you? Why not just go to other places?' I queried, but he shook his head.

'I wish I could,' he replied. 'I'm not even sure yet how much heat this little jaunt is going to bring on me. This whole situation, as you can guess, is highly classified.' Marcus pushed away his coffee. 'They won't be happy if they find out about this. It will be for the best when my partner and I go our separate ways after this assignment.'

I decided to share some of the knowledge about the agent's chances of gaining a new partner.

'The man who owned my equipment wrote about being chased by agents,' I said, 'but in his book he called them agents of shadow!' That made us both chuckle again. 'I found a notebook about the time he saw these agents, and I saw them myself at one point. Then I did a bit of digging. I found out that they were forced to partner up and move to a different part of the country.'

The agent leant back and cracked his back. 'Jeez, I didn't plan on that. Avery, my partner, will be doubly pissed when he finds that out.' The man took out a business card and slid it towards me. It had a cell phone number on the back. 'Just a warning,' he added. 'Disappear if you can and leave the machine so they won't chase you… hopefully.'

'Why are you helping me?' I asked, sliding the card into my wallet. 'It could cost you your job, surely?'

The agent paused for a moment to drink his coffee. 'I just thought that, if you knew the disastrous change that you had already made to the timeline, maybe you would stop the time travel jaunts before a government agency stops you themselves. I figured that you deserve to know the risks you are taking and the possible end that you are racing towards. This is a friendly warning, putting the control back into your hands, rather than taking it from you forcibly.'

The FBI agent then stood up, signalling an end to our meeting, and left some money on the table for the bill with a tip.

'Thanks for the warning, I owe you one,' I said sincerely, standing up and shaking his hand.

'Maybe one day you can take me and the family to see those dinosaurs,' Marcus said and smiled. 'The twins would claim you as their hero for that.' He looked out into the cold, dark night. 'What's your name, my friend?' he asked.

I smiled and slapped him on his back. 'Brian,' I replied.

We waved goodbye to the waitress and headed outside, then back to the alley. We both pulled out our remotes and pressed them to head home. I suddenly had a thought and I turned to Marcus.

'Give me a few days, and I'll send you my number,' I said. 'When you are out of the FBI, drop me a line, and maybe you can see a dinosaur or two. What do you think?'

The man laughed and tucked the remote back into his coat pocket. 'Sounds good, my man,' he said. 'But firstly, take my advice and run. If they find out I am here, then they might guess why. I might be out of the FBI quicker than I thought,' he added with trepidation. 'Good luck... Brian.'

'Good luck, Agent Martinez,' I answered, and we stood there nervously waiting. 'Never takes you when you think it's going to…' I began. And then, in a flash I was back in the cellar, only to be confronted by a very concerned-looking wife.

Her hands were on her hips. 'And where the fuck have you been...oh husband of mine?' The question was devoid of any warmth.

I sighed and handed her the photo that Molly had given me. 'I didn't want her to die alone, so I sat with her until her time came,' I explained and walked to sit on a chair before throwing off my wet hat. 'She's a good woman and sends you her greetings, and wished you could've met each other,' I added. I watched as my wife's hard exterior crumbled as she knelt on the floor by my feet, resting her head on my leg.

'Oh, Bri, why didn't you tell me? I would have come with you,' she said, stroking my cold hand.

I shrugged, which had seemed to become quite a habit for me lately. 'Wasn't planned, just thought it was the right time. Though, I did have a visitor before I headed home,' and I handed the FBI card to her.

'What the…' exclaimed Dana, this revelation making her sit up straight. 'How? Why?'

So, I told her the story, and what we should do, even though I wanted to see if we could go into the future to help her have a baby.

'Okay, let's look at your plan for seeing into the future,' I said. 'But we have to start moving things, okay? I believe him when he says they will find us.'

'I agree,' replied Dana. 'Let's get started.' We both closed the machine down and headed upstairs.

Chapter Seventeen

Marcus smiled to himself as he hung up his hat and coat. At least the Traveller was receptive to his plan. Clicking off the light, he walked back into the corridor.

'Need a coffee,' he mumbled to himself while rubbing his tired eyes. Then he stilled as he registered a shadow sitting at the dining table. 'Ave, is that you?'

The light flickered to life to show the youthful man sitting there, tired looking and dressed in a white T-shirt and boxers of the same colour.

'Where were you, Marc?' he asked flatly, then took a long sip from his mug. 'I couldn't sleep, and found your bedroom empty?'

The older agent walked over and poured himself some of the potent brew before sitting down in front of his partner. 'I just had something to finish,' he replied with a yawn. 'I wanted to check that the Traveller hadn't done anything stupid.'

Avery stared at him. 'Why do I feel like you are lying to me?' he asked. He quickly stood up, swaying slightly. 'That's fine, just hope the people upstairs don't find out. They will crush you,' he said and headed out of the room.

Marcus pinched the bridge of his nose and closed his eyes. 'That's why I lied, my friend,' he mumbled and took another sip of his coffee before heading to bed. He was looking forward to seeing his wife and kids, and at this rate he would make the party.

As the sun rose outside the FBI building, the two latest temporal agents showered and prepared themselves for their meeting with Director Walker. They hoped that, following the meeting, home would be their next destination. After their showers, they both sat in the kitchen, opposite each other, not willing to be the one to start a conversation.

'Well, my friend, it has been one hell of a ride,' Marcus said with a roguish smile, watching Avery munch on a bagel. 'What day is it, anyway?'

'Friday, so you'll be home for your party,' Avery said and looked at his phone. 'Sammy is looking forward to meeting your family, as am I.'

Marcus nodded as he read the text from his wife. She was happy that he would make it home, yet still pissed about the whole running away to Washington thing. 'Loretta and the kids want to meet the tall, blond, handsome partner,' he said with a grin. 'They have been sorely disappointed with my other partners.' That got a laugh out of the younger man.

Avery checked his watched and saw it was time. 'Shall we go, Marc?'

'Sure, let's get it done and head home,' Marcus said with a sigh, taking their plates and cups and putting them in the sink for the unseen cleaners to take care of. 'Hope the PA is in a better mood today.'

Avery barked a laugh. 'You were okay, she liked the genuine agent rather than this keyboard-tapping one.' He pointed his thumb at himself, then pulled the handle from his travel case. 'Then again, everybody is happy on Fridays, aren't they?'

'We shall see,' Marcus admitted and carried his case out of the kitchen, down the corridor and back towards the busy offices of the FBI. Together, side by side, they headed to the elevator and were taken to their possible doom.

As they arrived at their desired floor, the elevator doors opened and they saw the stoic form of the Director's PA, Sharon. Not a word was passed between them. The long, talon-like nail pointed at their luggage, then to the seat area. Then, using two fingers, the woman gestured for them to go straight into the office. The agents swapped a look that suggested that not everybody was happy on a Friday.

The Director stood up, smiled and shook their hands, gesturing for them to sit. 'Well, congratulations, gentlemen,' he said. 'I have read the preliminary report detailing that it went as well as it could, though the target did cause us some added problems in the end,' Walker admitted with a smile.

'Indeed, he did, sir,' Marcus agreed. 'We were just about to leave the room, when another event occurred…' He paused, knowing not to share specific details here. He saw the haunted look that flashed across the younger man's face, and so did the Director. 'Yes, it was a rough one.'

'I understand,' Director Walker said. 'However,' he continued sternly, 'I must reiterate that it is absolutely essential that these matters are not discussed outside of the room downstairs,' and he rifled through some paperwork. 'You will both get a bump in pay grade, as well as a commendation on your file.' He stood up and shook their hands again, as a sign that the meeting was concluded. 'Now, take the next week off and reconnect with your families. You will be contacted again after your reports have been reviewed. But, once again, well done.'

The two men bid the Director farewell and headed off. This time, Sharon nodded.

'Goodbye, Agents,' she said, and they took that as a win.

They grabbed the first cab they could hail.

'Well, that went okay,' Avery commented, surprised. Marcus just agreed with an incline of his head.

'Let's see what our overseers have to say,' he replied. 'But first, let's go home and get ready to party!'

As soon as Marcus exited the airport, he was attacked by his darling twin girls, screaming happily that he was home. Loretta was there waiting for him, along with many extended family members.

'It's going to fun, huh?' he said as his little girls cuddled him, and it was.

While this was happening, Avery was reconnecting with his now definite girlfriend, and was spinning her around making her squeal like a schoolgirl. They had decided to meet in Austin Texas airport, so they could have a nice break and yet be close for the Martinez's party.

Avery and Samantha turned up fashionably late the next day and were an instant hit with the twin girls, who dragged the young couple from person to person, introducing them to everyone. It was a whirl wind for the fresh-faced agent, but it gave him an insight into a type of family life that he had never known.

However, life came crashing back down for him the following Tuesday morning. Avery was sitting in his apartment, just about to have his midmorning beer, when his cell phone rang. It showed an unknown number. He pressed the screen to answer it, while putting down his bottle of beer.

'Hello, guv, you got yourself Lord Avery MuckityMuck, from England,' he announced down the phone. 'What you want, mate?' he added happily, as the early morning beers had done their jobs nicely.

'Agent Saunders, this is Director Walker. Are you alone and, dare I say, sober enough to talk?' The voice boomed down the phone, instantly pulling Avery back into the world of sobriety.

He sat up quickly and coughed. 'Yes guv… I mean, sir,' and slapped his forehead. 'What can I do for you?'

There was a moment's silence. 'Open your door. I will be there in a moment,' the Director instructed, before ending the call, making Avery instantly panic. He ran around picking up food wrappings and empty beer bottles. In his haste, he caught his foot in what his now committed girlfriend Samantha classed as a 'beautiful rug', sending him to the ground, scattering all the recently gathered-up rubbish far and wide. If he was prone to crying, it would be happening right now.

Knock knock!

'Answer the door, Saunders!' the Director called through the door. *Hardly James Bond, shouting my name through the letter box*, Avery thought. He jumped up and ran to the door, kicking a full bag of chips into the corner.

'Good morning, sir. I wasn't expecting you,' he stuttered, trying to decide whether it was drool, blood or beer he could feel dribbling down his chin. Then he opened the door wider. 'Sorry about the mess, sir,' he added, panic galloping through his body.

The Director rolled his eyes, which Avery was sure he had learnt from the witch of a PA.

'It's okay,' he replied, 'we are all young once. Now, will you please let me in, we need to talk,' he ordered, walking straight in and scanning the room. 'Ah, *Family Guy*,' Walker said with a ghost of a smile, as he registered what was on the TV.

Avery saw a positive result here. Maybe they could bond. 'Funny as hell, sir. Do you watch it often?' he asked, as he moved a training shoe off a kitchen chair, while offering the other chair to his boss of all bosses.

'No, but the children next door seemed to enjoy it,' Walker said dryly and shot down any hopes Avery had of them bonding. 'Anyway, please sit, time is short, despite the job you have done for us.' He gave a dry laugh, pointing to an unoccupied seat.

The young agent wiped his mouth and saw the translucent fluid on his hand. It was just drool, he realised with relief, until his mind registered the fact that his boss has just seen him watching cartoons in shorts and a T-shirt, while dribbling. *Shit*, he thought.

'What can I do for you, sir?' he asked.

'As discussed at our last meeting,' replied Walker, 'I was awaiting the report about your mission from whomever was running this bloody op. Well, it has finally come back.' He paused for a moment and then looked around. 'For the most part, you did good work and the Bureau is proud of you both.'

'Why do I get the feeling there is a but around the corner, sir? For you to have come down here from Washington, it must be bloody big,' Avery said.

The grey-haired man picked at his recently manicured hand. 'Quite. Did you know that, the night before we had our last meeting, after you had finished your mission, your partner took a trip back in time to New York, 26th October 1932?' He watched his young agent go wide-eyed at the realisation. 'Did you know about his little jaunt, or why he went back?'

Agent Saunders' face went blank, and then he picked up his phone and searched the date that Marcus had chosen to travel to.

'Can't be his parents,' he said. 'Then, it must be something to do with the case, and the only thing near that date is France. But that can't be it…' He tried to figure out why Marcus had found the need to pick that particular moment in time.

Director Walker leant forward. 'We can't talk about the details, but it must be something personal to either Martinez or the target,' he said, knowing he was close to breaching his brief of the temporal unit.

The young man tapped on his phone again, then dropped it onto the glass-topped table. 'Shit, it's the unsinkable woman! She died on that day,' he said carefully, tiptoeing around the specifics, knowing it sounded crazy to him and anyone else who heard him. 'Marcus thought she was lying when she told us that no strange man ever spoke to her while she was on the *Titanic*.'

'What do you think your partner was doing?' the Director asked sternly.

Avery shook his head. 'Wish I knew. Is he in trouble, sir?'

Walker leant back again and rubbed his face. 'This is a grey area. It wasn't an officially sanctioned mission. The overseers, as I call them, didn't mention anything about it. But I want to know why he did it, and why he went without you!'

'The only reason I can think of,' replied Avery, 'is that he thought the target might go to see the woman again on her deathbed. Marc thought they had a connection.' He gazed out of the window. 'Either he tried to capture the man or warn him about the consequences of making any more trips.'

Walker wanted to smash the table. 'Okay, this is now official,' he announced angrily. 'You and Martinez will be made permanent partners. Your new posting will be Boston.' He held his hands up to stop the protests from the young man. 'It was always going to happen, I'm afraid. It's part of the brief. I only found out when I received the report. It's standing orders with that department. It keeps you together, so it's easier to make sure you're not talking about the operation.'

'Fuck, but why Boston?' Avery muttered. Sammy had been talking about moving in. She really was going to hit the roof.

Walker nodded. 'Yes, It's Boston. Out of my hands. Whoever runs this bloody thing has chosen the posting.'

Avery sighed. 'What about Marcus? Are you going to tell him, too? And what do I tell him about this trip he took?'

Walker ran his fingers through his hair. 'I am going to his home next to discuss everything with him,' he said and then chewed his lip. 'You are coming with me so I can brief you both about your working situation.'

Avery didn't say anything. He just stood up and walked off to get changed. In his bedroom, he texted his girlfriend to let her know that he was going on a road trip with the Director of the FBI. The reply was one of suspicion and swear words, including some in her mother tongue, which he would look up later.

Avery came back into the living room, dressed for work in his suit with his badge and gun. 'I'm ready, sir,' he said.

The older man laughed. 'Ease up, kid. Martinez knows we are coming,' he advised, and led Avery out of the house and down to the typical generic federal black SUV.

'Bit of a long drive, isn't it, boss?' Avery asked and again realised he had made two mistakes. First, *never* call the Director 'boss', otherwise you get a look that would have the Grim Reaper himself calling for his mummy. Second, only stupid people think you drive from San Diego to Texas. That comment alone made for a very quiet journey to the airport, where they boarded the FBI jet to travel to Marcus in Texas.

***

Marcus knew this wasn't going to be a good meeting, so he had asked his wife to take her mother out to do the shopping. Making that last trip had been a risk, but something told him it was the right thing to do. Brian wasn't a bad man, he just wanted to do good things and you couldn't blame a man for that. After all, Marcus himself would go back and talk to his parents again if he could, just for old times' sake. And, likewise, Brian's actions on the *Titanic* just weren't something a selfish man would do.

Marcus had been surprised when he got back from the DC mission, though. Loretta had received a call from a company about an old investment that his parents had made in his name after he was born. The company had called to ask if Marcus wanted to change the strategy. Loretta was surprised about the money, but she just accepted it as a gift from the gods. He mused it had to be the Traveller's way of saying thank you. $250,000 was one hell of a thank you. However, Marcus's conscience did argue with him for a time because, whichever way you sliced it, it was a bribe. In legal terms, however, it was a decision that his parents had made. There was no way that he could alert work to this, or even his wife. How could he explain what Loretta now considered their little darlings' college fund was actually a payoff from a rogue time traveller? So, he had decided to keep it and maybe get a jet ski out of it, Loretta willing.

Eventually, he saw an SUV coming up the road. When it pulled up on the gravel driveway, he opened the front door.

'Good afternoon, Director Walker, welcome to my home,' he said warmly, then saw his miserable-looking partner. 'Hello again, Avery.'

'Afternoon, Agent Martinez,' said Walker. 'Let's get on, shall we?' He spoke abruptly and walked straight into the house. 'I trust we are alone?'

'As you had requested, Director. Please come this way,' Marcus replied and led them into his office, offering them both a seat on either a small sofa or chair. The Director took the chair and Avery slouched on the sofa. 'Care for a drink before we start?' Marcus asked looking from man to man.

Walker shook his head and Avery nodded, so Marcus walked to a hidden fridge and brought out two ice-cold waters for Avery and himself, then he sat in his leather office chair.

'So, I take it this is about my little solo trip?' he asked calmly, which took the surprise from his boss's argument.

'Yes!' the Director snapped, losing his cool. 'You knew it wasn't allowed, but you still did it. We can't speak of the details, but why, man?'

Marcus relaxed and took a sip of water. 'I spent a lot of down time reading old reports. The last agents chased an unknown man all over the place and they were nearly killed at Pearl Harbour. Yet, they still never found their target,' he explained, stopping to take another gulp of the crisp water. 'These agents were chasing a man named Lancaster. He was an author. In the end, he just disappeared.'

'That doesn't explain why you went alone, Marc. You could've told me,' Avery cut in quickly.

Marcus looked at him calmly, refusing to be rattled. 'You were a mess after France,' he reasoned. 'All you wanted to do was kill the man.' His friend looked angry but nodded in agreement. 'This man didn't mean to hurt anyone, he wanted to save his family some hurt,' continued Marcus. 'He knew nothing of the repercussions that he had caused. So I found him and explained to him that his actions had caused huge changes in history – skirting around the exact details, of course,' he added, though he knew that was a complete lie. 'He's not a bad man. He just played with something that no one should have power over, even though it was for the betterment of his family.'

Walker frowned. 'You disobeyed orders and there is no excusing that. If these were normal circumstances, I would have your badge,' he said coldly. 'Luckily for you, I can't.

Just be careful and keep your mouth shut!' He stood up abruptly. 'Agent Saunders, Agent Martinez, you are being transferred to a new posting, where you shall be working as partners for the foreseeable future. This is not negotiable. Your transfer papers will be drawn up within the week.' He walked to the door, as if to go, but then turned back. 'The car will be leaving in ten, whether you are in it or not, Avery!'

He stomped out and slammed the door closed. The two agents then heard the slam of the car door.

'Well, he's in a piss,' Marcus chuckled and went to the fridge and brought out two beers. 'I'm sorry, my friend. I didn't want to get you involved.'

Avery took a long pull of his drink, then checked his watch. 'Well, I am involved. They are sending us to Boston. We have to work there as partners,' he said and finished off the bottle. 'And they want us to find this target and take his equipment.' Then he stood up. 'We don't have a choice, Marc. We have a month to relocate and start the search, or we are in the shit, and he means it.'

'Yeah, I knew that was going to happen,' admitted Marcus. 'They did the same to the previous agents who worked there. They got moved to New York.'

Avery's eyes widened in shock, then narrowed with suspicion. 'There weren't any agent names on the reports, they were redacted. So how did you find all that out?' he fired back at him.

Martinez stood up and started to walk out of the house, quickly followed by Avery. 'The Traveller did his homework. Loretta is pissed, but a change is better than a rest, you know. Going to be chilly, though,' he said with a smile, before shaking his partner's hand.

'What's this guy's name we are looking for? So, I can do some searches while I pack and hide from Sammy,' Avery queried, opening the front door of the vehicle just as the SUV engine fired to life.

'Brian. That's all he gave me, I'm afraid,' Marcus said. 'I think if we try the Lancaster link, we may get him that way. That's where he got the equipment from.'

'It's a start,' said Avery. 'Be seeing you, Marc.' He climbed into the passenger side of the SUV and headed off for a long trip in angry silence.

Marcus laughed. 'Not if I see you first,' he smiled, watching the SUV burn out of his property. 'That Walker needs to chill,' he commented to himself and headed back in for another beer while the house remained quiet.

A month later, the partners found themselves looking over the Boston skyline. They shivered, even though the sun was shining brightly outside. They came from places that the sun burnt hotter and for longer!

'So, you all settled in?' Avery asked, taking their normal beverage of strong coffee.

'Yeah, Loretta is looking at some homes out of the city. She doesn't want to swap schools for the kids yet, so her mother will take care of them for now while she's here,' Marcus explained. 'How about you, my friend? You comfy? And what about Sammy?'

The blond nodded. 'Yep, all in and unpacked. Samantha has put in for a transfer here, so we shall see.'

It had been a hard month for them all. Once Avery had managed to track down one of the previous temporal agents in New York, who said very little but confirmed they had been partnered up and forcibly transferred, Avery knew it wasn't all his partner's fault. They now shared a tiny office, and even this workplace kept them segregated from the other agents, though Marcus was a walking welcome wagon.

'So, we had better start work then,' said Marcus. 'Something tells me Walker will be on our ass for updates.' They both settled down on their better-than-average office chairs. 'What's the 411 on the estate sale for George Lancaster Jnr's estate?' he asked. The younger agent gave him a look. 'Hey, my kids use the phrase, why can't I?'

Avery tapped away quickly on his desktop computer, which sported two monitors. His partner could only cope with one, as too much information made his head spin.

'Yes, the Lancaster estate was settled last year by Windle & Merrythorpe Associates,' said Avery. 'They weren't totally forthcoming with details, but what they did say was that a developer bought the site, and a single person bought the contents. And, surprise surprise, it was a cash sale, the signature unreadable.'

Marcus chuckled. 'Hmm, no doubt they took their cut of the profits, which would be larger if they fudged the paperwork, sales taxes and all,' he said and knew it wasn't unheard of in such circles. Estates sales were big money for online sellers and thrift store owners. They'd rather use cash, and it was only the property that needed paperwork. 'Maybe we should ask around local hauliers? He would need help to move the stuff, right?' He started to slowly pound on the keyboard, making Avery wince.

It took a morning of internet searches and a multitude of phone calls to find out the actual firm who had transported the goods. The agents had realised that, once said companies knew that there was not a booking or money coming their way, they quickly lost interest in helping.

'Found them!' Avery shouted out. 'The Broccoli Brothers. It took nearly their whole fleet to transport it.'

'Cool, do they have a name and address for the buyer?' Marcus asked, looking over his monitor, bleary eyed. He really needed eyeglasses for this shit.

'They aren't fans of talking about clients without a warrant,' replied Avery. 'But they reluctantly said that they would email me the booking form with his signature and place of delivery!'

It took until 5 pm that afternoon before Avery received the email.

'Finally, it's here!' he shouted and clicked it open to see the image they had sent of said document. 'Oh, for fuck's sake.'

Marcus chuckled. He always enjoyed hearing other people swearing, especially when it was not aimed at him. 'What's up, my friend? What does it say?'

The younger man thumped the desk with his fist in frustration. 'It's signed Brian, but address just says NEW ENGLAND. Bastards.'

'At least we know it's New England, buddy, that's a starting point,' Marcus said and smiled at the younger man. 'C'mon, it's beer o'clock, and Loretta is heading back home, so it's just you and me.' Marcus shut down the PC, then picked up his coat from the stand in the corner. 'I'll introduce you to the Tactical boys and girls. They are drinking at a bar around the corner,' he continued and showed off his pearly whites.

Avery shut his desktop down as well. They'd only been in this place five minutes and Marcus had made friends with most of the staff, whereas they all gave Avery a wary look, calling him 'poster boy' behind his back. Thankfully, being Marcus's partner, they allowed him some dispensation.

'Sure, sounds fun,' he replied. 'But, if they have talked to the Tac team back in San Diego, we might have a problem.'

Marcus groaned and leant against the door frame. 'Why? What did you do?'

The young man placed his forehead on the cool surface of his desk. 'I thought it was funny,' he began. 'All I said was, all they were good at was opening closed things. I threw them a jar of peanut butter and told them to open that!'

'Did anyone laugh, Ave?' Marcus asked with a straight face.

'A few in my department,' Avery responded defensively. 'Next day, I found my locker full of peanut butter, then my car was filled with whole peanuts, it was never ending,' he said, taking his own coat off the rack. He received a slap on the back from Marcus as they left their office.

They walked out of the building and to the Irish bar O'Halloran's.

'Deep breath,' advised Marcus. 'I'm sure they haven't spoken to anyone else. New city, new chance, my friend!' he said as they walked into the loud pub. The room hushed and a group of sporty-looking men and women raised their drinks to them.

'Marc and Peanut!' they all chorused. They were both handed a beer and Marcus was hugged by a tall, athletic-looking blonde woman.

A burly agent, well over six feet tall, whose call sign was 'the Opener', approached Avery and whispered in his ear, 'Got any jars, little man?' That's when he knew he was doomed, again.

Marcus found out later that night that FBI Tactical Units were a very close-knit department, mainly because of multiple groups going through training together, and outer state operations. Whilst they were not openly hostile towards young Avery, they did keep him on his toes, and their filling his locker full of peanuts was funny. That is why the older man always treated people like a friend until it was time not to. *Maybe they should teach that at the Academy,* he mused to himself, as he held the refuse bag which was being filled with peanuts by his partner.

'Bastards,' Avery muttered. His suit trousers were covered in dust from the peanut shells. The bloody things had managed to get everywhere. Deep down, he knew it was his fault, but that was covered up by anger. 'Finally!' he said as the last shell-covered peanut hit the sack. He stretched out his back and slammed his locker closed.

'What we going to do with all this, Ave? Donate it to the zoo?' Marcus asked with a chuckle as he shook the bag. 'I'm sure the elephants would just devour you and it,' and they heard other muffled laughs from the depths of the changing rooms.

Avery grabbed the refuse bag and tied it secure. 'Nope, going to dump it in the Tactical Unit Humvee. Payback is a bitch!' he scoffed. A sneer appeared on the young man's face, until a cough woke him from his revenge-fuelled daydream. And there stood the Opener, in full battle rattle, which made him look even bigger. 'Okay, I'll take it to the zoo in my lunch hour!'

'Good choice,' Marcus said as he walked past him and slapped Opener on the back. 'Morning, big-un,' he said and shook the numbness from his hand as he laughed. That man was all muscle.

The big man grunted, staring at Avery. 'Hey, Marc, how's tricks?' the man mountain grunted again, before forcing himself through the door to the garage. 'You find a home yet?'

They paused where their routes would part. It had been a couple of weeks since their night out, and the job of tracking Brian had stalled thanks to lack of evidence to get the much-needed warrants. Very few judges would sign off just because they were the FBI nowadays.

'Yeah, Loretta is a force of nature when she has my wallet,' smiled Marcus. 'She bought a small place in Holliston, an old farm. The kids will love it.'

'I look forward to the moving-in party, my man,' Opener hinted and gave the much smaller man a hardy slap on the shoulder, separating some bones from their long-term resting places. 'Later,' the gravelly voiced wall said and headed off to fight crime single handed.

Avery and Marcus finally made it back to their desks. The former was still pissed about the whole affair, but a coffee and a bear claw from the shop down the way had perked him up somewhat.

'YES!' the blond man shouted and punched the air.

'Good pastry was it?' Marcus asked and snickered like a toddler saying a swearword for the first time.

'Well, yes,' replied Avery, 'but we finally have a warrant for traffic cameras covering all of the routes from the estate sale towards the New England area, in a twenty-miles radius!' He started to send off emails with the warrant number included.

Marcus rested his chin on the palm of his spare hand as the other was taken up with a particularly good coffee. 'So, what's got you all hot and bothered, my friend?' he asked and watched Avery's fingers dance across the keyboard, almost silently. 'Why traffic cameras?'

Avery stopped what he was doing for a moment. 'The Broccoli brothers refused to give us the destination, or even the route they took,' he explained and clicked away with his mouse. 'But we do have a list of their haulage fleet's licence plates, and he did say it took most of his fleet to move the contents of the house.'

'Ah, I see, so we can track the vehicles leaving the sale to their destination – and, therefore, to Brian?' Marcus asked and saw the smile appear on his partner's face. 'What do you want me to do? Check a few cameras?'

Avery stopped typing and looked up. 'No,' he said firmly. 'Walker is watching us. He doesn't trust you, and is looking for a way to can your ass!' He was also still on the fence about what his partner had done. 'You'd better keep out of the way of this for now,' he advised and went back to typing. 'Go back to searching for hits of Brian's identity in that area between the ages of thirty to fifty years of age, okay?'

'Sure thing, my friend,' replied Marcus. He looked at his colleague. 'Don't worry about me, I know I made my bed. It's time to lie in it,' he added and slowly went to work. It was a long and laborious job; in fact, he was only doing it half-heartedly as, unbeknown to Avery, he was texting the Traveller an update. It was going to be a long, boring day.

For Avery, this had been a long time coming. To be able to put a stop to the ridiculous actions of this man was so important to him. The target had put him in a position where he was forced to kill and was almost killed himself. He understood Marcus's thoughts on the subject, but when push came to shove the target had caused the events, not Lancaster, or anyone else. It was squarely on this man Brian's shoulders.

Avery had found the line of trucks leaving the Lancaster estate deep in rural Pennsylvania. There were so many cameras, but luckily the men stayed on task and the vehicles headed straight to their destinations minus fuel stops. This must have cost the target a small fortune, and all in ready cash, too. He tracked the legion of white trucks all the way to Connecticut, then a town called Winstead. *Got you now*, he thought when he realised that the trucks hadn't made it to the next camera. Going backwards, there were not that many residences, mainly farms, about half a dozen at most. Some large, some small enough just for a cow and a chicken.

He pulled up the registry for births and death covering those farms alone. Brian was a popular name in that area, but one did pop out.

'Brian Partridge,' he said quietly, then dug in deeper on the family – parents deceased, no wife or dependants, one brother with dependants who lived away from the family farm. Avery then brought up another screen which showed that the 160-acre plot was rented out to a local farmer, though the family kept control of the house.

Pulling up purchases and bills of sale and utilities for said property, Avery noticed that the electricity bill had spiked, and Brian had bought some expensive kit to regulate the power supply. This had to be the target. Avery looked up and saw his partner twirling his tie quite happily.

'Found him!' he announced. 'Brian Partridge, Partridge Farm, Winstead, Connecticut, New England.'

Marcus looked up from his work, surprised. Then he clapped his hands together. 'Perfect. Let's get the warrants and go and say hello!'

Avery received a high five from his brother in arms. 'Hell, yeah! You are dead meat, Partridge,' the blond agent said with determination. He then put his head down to fill out the forms to ask for said warrants. 'You're going down, Brian!'

Chapter Eighteen

'So, this is your plan, is it, Bri?' Dana asked, looking at the myriad of different writings. On one page, there was even a crayon drawing of Jesus Christ with a speech bubble saying 'You're cured'. 'Are you serious?' she said in disbelief and frustration. 'I think you have been pushing yourself too much.'

I just shrugged. 'Maybe the drawing went a bit far,' I said and chuckled before throwing the drawing into the bin. 'The only way to make sure the future is safe is if we jump forward in increments of five years,' I suggested. 'That might work.' I handed to Dana my last-ditch attempt of a plan, which had a marvellous coffee stain upon it.

We sat on the sofa later in the day as we talked about our plans. We had decided to travel into the future, using the Boston cemetery as our landing point, where I had landed before to watch the *Back to the Future* movies. Appearing locally would be dangerous, particularly if we were recognised and looking so much younger than we should for that year.

The farmhouse was already looking quite empty, as we had moved some of our personal items to the underground compound. Thankfully, the lift had been installed. Time was marching on, days were turning into months and we found ourselves in May. Luckily, there was still no sign of the agents of shadow – or the FBI, as they are commonly called.

'The downside is that there isn't a map or any information on the future, and with Trump in the White House who says there is a future?' Dana suggested with a dark chuckle. 'So, when and where shall we appear?'

I scratched my head as I thought. 'What you find is that cemeteries remain unchanged, and we can send the little truck forward to investigate, like I did before my trip to see the dinosaurs. There is an oxygen meter to make sure it's safe,' I explained, not mentioning that one truck had been stomped on.

Dana nodded, but she looked sad. 'Listen, this is a.trip to help your nephew's wife, not me,' she said and lifted her hand to stop me from talking. 'My time for children has passed, and I am okay with that. Let's bring some happiness into their lives, it's the least we can do.'

'I understand, and thank you,' I said, and I took her hand. 'But whatever happens, let's be safe and happy.' I leant across and captured her soft lips with mine. We parted and smiled goofily at each other then, hand in hand, headed downstairs. I had put the mini truck on charge yesterday, as any trip to the future would necessitate using it. Arriving in a nuclear, apocalyptic world without any idea what we were letting ourselves in for would be a big 'no thank you'.

My wife worked at the console happily. 'I'm sending it to July 2030, then we shall do it again to 2040. You agree, Bri?' she asked with her head down again.

'Yep, sounds good,' I replied. 'Just put the timer on for five minutes, that should be enough. Early morning, too,' I added as I was struggling to refix the camera and oxygen meter onto the radio-controlled truck.

Dana giggled. 'I hope there isn't a funeral going on. That would bring a few strange looks,' and she went back to her programming.'

The basement was now looking bare. All that were left on the walls were copies of photos that I had taken. None were showing our faces, as my family didn't know that I was now married. Placing the truck into one of the pods, I gave Dana the thumbs up. She replied with the middle finger and pursing her lips into a kiss, so I started up the camera and meter and, in a flash, the truck was gone.

We stood, arm in arm, with nervous excitement coursing through us. 'I hope they are all wearing silver Lycra catsuits,' I said with a smile, and then my face straightened. 'Though, you may rock in it, but it's not my thing!'

Dana's face paled. 'Can you imagine those of a weighty disposition rocking one of those?' she grimaced and gave me a squeeze in an enjoyable place.

We waited out the five minutes. Then, with a flash, the equipment returned from the very same cemetery in Boston that I had visited to watch a movie – this time, from the future and not the past. With a smile, I collected the camera and meter, placed them onto the desk and plugged the camera into the desktop computer, while my darling wife brought the recording onto the screen. I checked the meter.

'Air is good quality,' I confirmed.

'What about the video? How does it look?' I asked and turned around to view it. 'Oh, well, that's not good,' I said, with a voice that conveyed utter disappointment.

Dana lowered her head. 'You got that right. Five minutes of a tombstone and, what makes it worse, we can't even see whose it is.' She slammed her fingers on the computer keys, making them wish they had never been created. 'I'll change the coordinates slightly, then send it again.' She gestured frustratedly with her hand for me to move the camera back to the pod. Then, just as I put it in place, it disappeared.

'Wow, easy girl!' I exclaimed, standing up. 'You nearly sent my fingertips into the future,' and I saw the laughter playing over her face. That's the thing with the ex-armed forces, they have a dangerous sense of humour. But, hey, I love her to bits, always have, always will.

'Sorry,' she purred and went back to watching her screen, which counted down to the return of the camera and, hopefully, some better pictures. With a flash, the camera returned again, and this time I took out the memory card, handed it to Dana and left the truck in place.

'There we go, no hover cars or Lycra-clad pandas. Hasn't changed much,' I said with a smile and took the card back out.

I placed the card back into the camera. 'Shall we move it a decade later?' I suggested and, with a nod of agreement from Dana, that's what we did. The oxygen meter stayed about the same, while cars seemed to just glide along with hardly any sound at all. 'What do you think? Shall we go for it?'

Dana chewed her bottom lip. 'Yes, why not? Let's take some gold coins, and maybe that little digital camera. If there is an antiques store, we might be able to make some cash.' She walked off and grabbed the camera. Dana made sure the card was cleaned and restored to factory settings before slipping it into her handbag.

'What about the clothes? How much could fashion change over twenty years?' I asked. However, Dana was concentrating on tapping away at the PC again.

'We'll just take the remotes with us,' she replied, 'and if we cause too much of a distraction, then we come home again. Agree, luv?' She looked at me, a finger loitering over the enter key to start the counter.

We were dressed in just our normal day-to-day work clothes, comprising of jeans and flannel shirt for me, jeans and a blouse for Dana.

'Yep, let's go,' I agreed and I heard the click of the keys being pressed. We both donned our sunglasses and, the next second, we were flashed away.

'Fuckkkkkk…!'

Landing in a graveyard is bad enough, but Dana had landed on some uneven ground and fallen sidewards. I ducked down, even though it was still early in the day.

'What you doing down there, little Miss Falling Over?' I asked her, chuckling, and I received her favourite salute in response.

'Ouch, that bloody hurt,' she said, rubbing her shin while pointing at a raised slab surrounded by a small stone wall. Dana looked around. 'How's it looking? Have we been seen?'

Lifting my head above the headstone, I saw that the area was devoid of any foot traffic. 'No, we are good, Hun,' and I helped her up and watched her settle on both feet. 'Ready?'

Dana pulled her blonde hair back into a messy ponytail. Let's be honest, she had the type of hair that can't be tamed. 'Yep, let's go, hubby,' she said and linked arms with me as we snuck out of the cemetery. 'Hasn't changed much,' she voiced quietly.

The view resembled a scene from the *Demolition Man* film, with cross-branded shops and advertisements as we looked upon McDonalds King. All the shop fronts seemed to be silvery metal and glass, while being all light and airy. As we walked, we agreed that people's attire hadn't changed that much, and our state of dress only garnered a few stares. There were a few people dressed like us, but mainly they wore cotton trousers and long shirts, all in different colours, from black to rainbow.

A clock that was situated on a large, ornate building struck 8 am and the streets came alive, causing us to tighten our grips on each other.

'Look over there,' I said, pointing out a telephone booth-type thing with tourist information displayed on it. And so, much like salmon swimming the wrong way up a stream, Dana steered us to our goal. Some of the swear words that came our way weren't those that we had heard or used before. But that's what happens when people are trying to get to work and two idiots are getting in their way. Yay, us.

Tucking ourselves away into the booth, Dana pressed the screen bringing up a suitable cross-branding company, YAHOOGLE.

'What shall I ask for first?' she asked as I nestled in behind her.

'Gold buyers or pawn brokers?' I suggested and watched her tapping away. The technology was quick as lightning, which was surprising as it was primarily for public usage. The results showed those shops that were open and their distances from the booth. 'Shall we go then?' I asked and wrapped my arms around her.

Dana shook head, which was leaning against my chest. 'No, wait outside and let me do some quick searches.' Then she turned to look directly at me. 'You know I'm quicker at this than you. Plus, it's woman stuff, anyway.' That alone made me beat a retreat to wait outside.

Just like any city, people walked with their cell phones or other devices stuck in front of their faces. What surprised me was that they wore earpieces, which emitted a translucent screen in front of their faces. It truly was amazing. My mind kicked in, telling me that I shouldn't even attempt to purchase one. Life isn't fair.

'C'mon, Bri, let's get going,' Dana said, stepping out of the booth. 'Any longer, we might have to work out how the three seashells work, and if I'm honest I don't want to even try,' and I was pulled back into the tide of people.

Once again, arm in arm we made it to our destination. It was a pawn shop from yesteryear. Yes, it was glass and metal, like the other shops, but everything else was old school. The two front doors automatically opened for us, allowing us into the musty-smelling shop. There were things from the late 1800s onwards, even technology from our time, which gave us hope that they would buy the camera we had brought along.

'Good day, sir and madam, what can I do for you today?' a balding, thin man in his late 60s asked from behind the counter.

Dana smiled at him, took my hand and led me towards the man. 'Good morning, sir, I was wondering if you could help us?' she said, using an Oscar award-winning smile. 'We have just come back from living abroad, and we are in need of funds.'

'I will do what I can,' said the man. 'Where have you come from? You sound local,' he asked with a wry smile upon his wrinkled face.

'Yes,' I answered, 'we were born here, then went travelling and have never stopped. Until now, that is.' Then, with a nod from Dana, I handed her the leather pouch containing the small gold bars that I had bought with my ill-gotten gains. She passed it to the man, who unzipped it immediately.

'Six gold bars, fifty grams per bar,' he said, looking at the contents of the pouch.

The kindly old man's demeanor disappeared. In its place was a wily old shop owner, who nodded and muttered away as he weighed every bar and typed the results into the display that emerged from his earpiece.

'Three hundred grams of gold, four thousand adjusted dollars per fifty grams, so in total it will be twenty-four thousand dollars. Do you accept my offer?' he asked.

Dana then placed the camera onto the counter, and the man quickly examined it.

'Good condition, with working memory card. Very nice,' he once again muttered to himself. 'Thirty thousand total, take it or leave it,' he announced quickly and grabbed the camera and gold like the deal was already done.

My wife looked at me and I nodded back, not that I knew how much things cost here anyway.

'That will do nicely,' she replied to the man. 'We'll take that on a Government Bond card, please.' We watched as the man picked up a plastic-type card with a flag on it.

'The interest is awful on this, you do know that, right?' the old man asked as he pushed the card into some kind of reader and started to press buttons on the facial display. 'I can do you two Appsung headsets for only four thousand each?'

'No thank you, sir,' Dana replied. 'We are only here briefly to see some friends and then we are off again.'

I saw the man's eyes flick to me. He frowned. 'Don't speak much, do you, sir?'

Once again, I shrugged. 'Whenever I do, I get myself in trouble, so better to stay silent,' I explained.

The shopkeeper passed the card to Dana and asked her to sign a tablet on his counter. With that, we were out of there.

'Wow, you did well,' I said once we were out on the street. 'What the hell is that card?'

Dana linked arms and pulled me along. 'We have to hurry before they realise that signature is a false name.' She then explained that she had used names from a cartoon. We carried on our journey. The sidewalks had calmed down a bit now. 'All money transactions are done by fingerprint,' she added. 'So, the only way we can buy anything in this timeline is by using this government-backed card. The shopkeeper has put thirty thousand dollars on it, but the feds takes five per cent straight away. Thieving bastards. Then another per cent per transaction.'

'Shit, no wonder he said it's crap,' I replied as she dragged me to God only knew where. 'What now, honey?'

'To the Medic Centre,' she replied. 'It's a five-minute walk from here,' and we sped up as the last thing we needed was cops showing up. That alone would no doubt cause the FBI to prioritise their search for me. We arrived at the building, which had a frosted glass front. 'Now, let me do the talking, it will come better from me,' Dana instructed.

I saw her smiling face change to a sad, almost tearful, one as we walked through the automatic doors, making our way into the shop. The interior was completely white; it truly looked like they'd had a paint explosion in there. Everything looked so hygienic, too, making us feel dirty. Even the shop assistants wore white coats and masks. I followed my wife's lead again and we headed to the section marked 'Family Planning'. A small woman, who only just topped five feet, came up to us and bowed.

'Good day, my name is Kiri. How may I be of assistance today?' the Asian girl asked politely.

Dana cuddled into me. 'We have tried so long to have a family, my friend suggested one of your products could help us,' she sobbed and turned into my chest. 'If you can't help us, I don't know what we'll do.'

Kiri pulled a sympathetic face. 'Well, let's see, shall we? May I ask if the doctor has mentioned where the problem lies?' she asked.

My wife dipped her head a bit lower. 'My fertility is a bit low. My friend says that Uetarium Max worked for her,' she said, totally losing me. Clearly, she had been looking up more than Google maps on the net.

'Hmmm, that is an immensely powerful and expensive treatment,' said Kiri. 'We normally suggest other brands first of all.' My wife sobbed even louder, making heads turn and our helper fidget. Even I was becoming concerned at this emotional display.

'Please help us,' sobbed Dana again. 'We are going on a cruise for a month, and with all that fresh air it would be an ideal time for us to try again. We just need help,' she explained and then grasped the small woman's hand. 'Please...'

The woman bowed and walked behind a small counter and pressed her thumb against a reader. A refrigerator door opened and she took out a small box.

'One dose should be enough,' Kiri said and, closing the fridge door, began ringing the price up on the fancy till. 'The price is ten thousand dollars.'

'Please, can we have two?' begged Dana. 'My friend said it took her two attempts to have her little Timmy.' I saw the woman's defences come up. Then, as tears flowed down my wife's cheeks, Kiri's resolve crumbled to dust. I watched her take another box out and then sealed both boxes in what looked like a portable chiller.

'There you are, madam,' she said. 'That will be twenty thousand dollars, please.' Kiri frowned when she saw the payment card, knowing there were better ways to pay. However, she scanned the card on a tablet that lay on her counter, then handed Dana a stylus to sign with. 'Good luck to you. I'm sure it will work this time, and enjoy the cruise,' she concluded.

'Thank you, we will,' I said brightly and took my wife's hand. I picked up the bag and led Dana outside. Just as we did, the lights inside the shop flashed red, and we heard the little woman call for either us or someone else. 'Shit! Heads down and let's get moving!'

We didn't want to run and bring any attention our way, but some high-pitched sirens were getting louder and heading in our direction.

'Bri, press your button, quickly!' Dana said urgently as we cut through a side road.

'STOP, LAW ENFORCEMENT,' came an electronic voice from the main road. Looking up, we saw two men in what looked like a hover car.

'So cool,' I muttered and received a thump in my gut.

Dana gave me a pointed look and pulled me into a rundown alleyway. 'You can have a wet dream on the tech later,' she said. 'Let's get the fuck out of here!'

I dared a look behind us and saw nothing. However, what I feared were the cameras we couldn't see, and if we disappeared with a flash the FBI would be on our cases again.

The sirens were getting closer. Then I saw a door open. A worker in a brown jumpsuit walked out and away from us towards the rear of the building. The door stayed ajar.

'In there!' I instructed and we ran through the door into a small stock room. I pulled Dana with me into a dark corner.

'Well done, oh husband of mine. What now?' she snapped, and I could almost hear her eyes rolling at me.

'It was either this or be caught on the cameras, which will capture us disappearing. The feds will be on our asses again,' I returned fire.

'Law enforcement!' a voice boomed from behind the now closed door. 'Come out with your hands up. We can hear you!'

Dana huffed. 'Do you mind? We are having a domestic,' she shouted in return. 'How rude!' And, like ethereal fire hitting the earth, we disappeared, leaving pissed-off and embarrassed cops, as well as shop owners looking for the mysterious and fraudulent Mr and Mrs Elmer Fudd.

We landed, both relieved to be safely home. I looked at my wife and grinned.

'A hover car, can you believe it?' I said, in awe. Dana was almost bouncing on the spot as I gave her the chilled bag and picked up the abandoned recon truck. 'What is that, anyway? At ten thousand dollars a dose, that better be lightning in a bottle,' I commented. I then put the truck on charge again.

'You dofus,' she replied. 'Yes, it was a floating cop car that nearly caught us for fraud. As we aren't even registered in the country, they most probably thought we were illegal immigrants!' She laughed and looked at the bag. 'And yes, it is lightning. A bit like Red Bull for your reproductive system. Gives everything a boost. The web said even the lowest of fertility counts can get a woman pregnant, so cross your fingers.'

I was aghast. This would give Adam and Tabby a good chance of having a family. 'How shall I get it to them? If they tell my brother, questions will be asked. And if Agent Marcus is right, they will be knocking down our door soon enough, anyway.'

'Shut it all down, Brian,' replied Dana. 'I'll put this in the refrigerator, then we can talk.' She gave me a quick kiss before running up the stairs, leaving me alone with my thoughts and worries. It wasn't long until the room was quiet and dark, so I headed upstairs to see two cups of tea steaming away.

'So, what's the plan?' I asked.

Dana took a sip of the strong but sweet beverage. 'The thing is, we don't know this bloke Marcus or his timeline. It's not straightforward. They could be behind in time, so they could be sitting outside right now. Or they could be months, or even years, ahead and it'll take them ages to get here.'

'What about the text messages from the agent, though?' I replied. 'I'm happy that he's warning us about any developments, but how does that work?' That stumped us. 'Could we be linked by time? A bit like the remotes. How do they bloody work?' I knew it had something to do with micro wormholes that stayed open as we tore through the fabric of time.

'You could be right there,' Dana said, 'hence why you felt close to Molly, and now close to this Marcus. All because he joined you on the same timeline. You were both out of your own times and forced together.' She clasped her head in her hands. 'Where's that Hawkins fella? He may have been in a wheelchair, but his amazing intelligence... He knew his shit!'

'He's dead,' I offered and received the look of death back.

'What was the last text you had from Marcus?'

I stood up, walked to the sideboard and picked up the burner phone. It took a while to start up, as it wasn't a great one. 'There was one last week,' replied. 'Marcus said they had found us, but the judges weren't happy and wouldn't sign the warrants. So that gave me some hope.'

Dana stood up and paced around, mumbling as she did so. 'Text him back, ask him for an update. Also ask what the date is where he is,' she said and then waved at me to hurry, so I did.

We had just started dinner when we received a reply.

'wtf, warrants on hold, crazy but 06/20/2020, why????'

'Bugger,' Dana said sadly, as Marcus's text confirmed today's date. 'Thought we were going to have a real weird time distortion shit going on, but a girl can dream,' and then she looked out of the window. 'When shall we give the drug to Adam and Tabatha?'

I leant back, making my bones and the chair creak. 'My brother normally feels guilty about our troubles on national holidays, and Independence Day was always a big do when we were kids,' I replied. 'So, he will probably send Adam over here to check on me. I could leave him the book about the time machine for them both to read, and then pop back to see them a few days after that?'

Dana frowned. 'Why the charade, though? Why not just tell them outright?'

'Tabby is an engineer,' I explained. 'She won't believe us, unless she reads my accounts. But if she sees further evidence, like the photos on the walls of the basement, it might just sway her.' Dana nodded slightly. 'Adam is like me.'

'Poor boy,' she joked.

That made me huff. 'But he'll want to believe straight off the bat.'

Dana started to dish up the dinner. 'Okay, we have a plan,' she said. 'Let's get all our personal effects to the bunker and clear out totally. That way, they will see you have left with all your goods, and not just walked off into the woods in your boxers and a tin foil hat.'

'Hey, I made a hat for you too, you know,' I snapped at her crossly.

Dana rolled her eyes. 'I was twelve. It wasn't the most ideal gift to give a girl, you know,' she said mockingly.

I sighed. 'Fine. What are you going to say, though? "I have a gift for the future, *mwhahahaha!*"' I chuckled.

'Sounds about right,' she answered and handed me a plate of food.

'What about Karl?' I asked. 'We can't leave him here alone.' I gave my darling wife a winning smile.

Dana slammed her plate down. 'FUCK KARL!!'

Later that day, my cockerel-hating wife and I walked down the main street of Winsted carrying an icebox. She had just finished a business meeting at her practice, announcing to the team that she would be leaving, due to continuing ill health caused by her term of service with the military.

As a leaving gift, Dana made everybody who worked there a partner, so that they would work together and flourish – or go against each other and fail. She would remain as a partner in name only, no profits pending. There were smiles and tears from all of them. Even the parrot in reception, whose name was Freddie, seemed a little put out. But, in the end, they had all been handed the reins of their own financial destiny. Who can say that these days? I did my bit and went along, even though I felt uncomfortable doing such social things, but the woman I love was giving up something she'd built with her own hard work.

Then we continued our journey and we stood outside my nephew's house. God knows why, but it was painted yellow. Being 6th July and with the sun blazing, it truly was a sickly sight. And, on that day, I vowed never to have anything painted yellow.

'That's pretty,' Dana said before ringing the doorbell.

There were muffled voices deep in the house. Through the coloured, ornate glass window that covered the upper half of their front door, we saw what looked like Adam walking towards it. The door opened and his eyes shot wide open, while his mouth did an imitation of a guppy.

'Hey, Adam! You are looking well,' I said before my nephew had found any words, and then looked worriedly at my wife.

Dana shrugged. 'Well, it looks like all you Partridges deal with surprises the same way,' she chuckled, just as an auburn-haired woman pushed Adam out of the way.

'Yep, total mental shutdown,' Tabby commented and looked me up and down. 'Well, you are looking good, Doc,' she said. 'And I see you have finally found the female sex.' She smiled and shook Dana's hand. 'Hi, call me Tabby. Come on in,' she said welcomingly, turning to grab her husband's shirt and pulling him in with her. 'Coffee okay?' she asked.

'I'm Dana by the way, and yes, that will be fine, thank you,' my wife called out and followed them into a yellow kitchen. 'Nice colour,' she said, making her new friend smile, though my nephew and I died a little bit inside.

I pulled my nephew into a rare hug. 'How are you doing, Adam? Business okay?' I asked and stepped back to lean against a counter.

'Yeah, sure… well, could always be better,' he answered and offered us a chair each at the kitchen table. 'We heard that you had moved out of the farmhouse. Where are you living now?'

Dana took a cup of the proffered beverage. 'He's at mine now,' she replied. 'But soon we will be moving on,' she advised and smiled at the younger couple.

Tabatha smiled back. 'That's nice, old Doc needs some love in his life,' and she took a big breath and looked directly at her uncle-in-law. 'So, we read your book, and saw the pictures…' She took a sip of her drink. 'I have some questions?'

I thought this was going swimmingly. 'Sure, Tabby,' I said. 'Shoot.' I felt Dana's hand grasp mine.

'It truly is amazing, the pictures alone tell a story,' Adam stated happily, finally coming out of his coma. 'Have you accompanied Brian on any adventures, Dana?'

My wife laughed. 'Just one or two. My tastes run to events that are a bit more fun, that get your heart pumping a bit,' she said with a big smile on her face.

The kids were enthralled. 'Like what?' Tabby asked, wide-eyed.

'Oh, nothing much,' said Dana calmly. 'We saw Bonny and Clyde once.'

'Fuck! No way,' Adam spat.

Dana nodded. 'Hell, yeah! It was so cool.'

'Oh, yes, can't beat getting shot at by bank robbers,' I mocked and was shot down by my partner's steely eyed glare. 'But it was cool.'

'Tell them about Normandy, Brian,' Dana said, making the kids gasp. 'That's how we reconnected. I found him covered in blood, after being shot by a German soldier.'

I felt my cheeks flushing red as my family stared daggers at me. 'But we did do shots with Elvis,' I offered, trying to divert the conversation. 'Just that alone has got to be worth it!' I pulled out a USB drive. 'Have you got a laptop?' That caused the level-headed engineer to run off, giggling like a schoolgirl; she came back with a silver laptop. Within moments, we were showing them all the photos I had taken pre and post Dana.

While I talked to Adam about Dallas and Normandy, the girls opened a bottle of wine and chatted about our past and our future – well, some of it, anyway.

'WHAT!!' Tabby shouted and came back with Dana in tow, looking guilty. 'So, not only are you two *married...*' she said, looking at her husband, 'but you are bringing the fucking *FBI* to our door?'

'Ah yes, did I not mention that?' I chuckled nervously and heard Tabby's knuckles crack as her fist tightened. 'I had never planned on it, I promise.'

Adam stroked his wife's back. 'I know you didn't, Doc, but what do they want from you? They must have their reasons?' he asked, his wife nodding in agreement.

Dana and I swapped looks.

'Well,' I began, 'it seems they have a temporal department, and they found out I had changed something in history's timeline, and they were pissed,' I explained to the wide-eyed kids. 'But I have spoken to one of them, and he admits there is nothing they can do to me, or us.' They both sagged with relief.

Tabby jumped in. 'What's your plan, then? How are you going to get away?'

'We have a home under false names. I won't tell you where, for your protection more than mine,' I explained. They nodded in understanding. 'We have found that the time travel pods can be used for instantaneous travel between pods, and we wondered if you wanted the machine from the farmhouse? That way, after this FBI situation has all cooled down, you can come and visit, even bring your dad?'

'What about the feds? If they don't find anything, they won't stop looking for you will they?' Tabby asked.

Dana nodded. 'We have the original equipment in one of the sheds. You can have the upgraded kit, and we can swap them. So, when the farmhouse does get raided, they will get what they want.'

The young couple looked at each other.

'As nice as it sounds, we can't have the machine here,' said Adam. 'This house is too small, and the neighbours are way too nosey.' He thought for a moment. 'But I have a storage locker we can keep it in, for future use.'

I clapped my hands together. 'Perfect! We'll get the old kit into the farmhouse for you, then we shall use the machine in the basement to leave,' I explained and saw their faces drop. 'I know, but if we don't use the pods, it'll take too long to get to our new place, which raises the risk of being caught.'

'Also, you can have my Land Rover,' said Dana, to sweeten the deal. 'The pink slip is in the glove compartment already.'

Adam saw the smile on his wife's face and knew the British-built truck would never be his. 'Okay, we'll go over tomorrow and get it all moved for you,' he confirmed and smiled at his wife. 'After all, we are family.'

I leant across and took both of their hands. 'Talking about families, I know the trouble you have had in that respect…' I said and saw their faces sadden. 'We took a trip into the future, nothing much has changed though. I truly thought Trump would've invaded Mars by that time.' I lifted my hands to stop their questions.

'Brian told me about your heartbreak, and so we brought back two treatments, which give you two chances to have a family,' Dana said excitedly. She unzipped the freezer bag and pushed a box of the drugs to Tabatha.

'Uetarium Max? What does it do?' the redhead asked as she looked inside. 'A fertility treatment?'

We smiled at each other. 'It's lightning in a bottle,' I explained. 'It gives your body a boost. And, if you're lucky, it'll bring you a little one into your lives to love.' And that is when the tears started. It took a while for Adam to stop crying, while Tabby read the instructions.

'Oh yes, and this,' I said, and then I slid over an envelope.

Chapter Nineteen

The young Partridges stood in front of the family's farmhouse, just as they had done only a few days prior. This time, though, they had knowledge of all the information and secrets that the property held. Tabby had a set of new car keys and the pink slip for the second-hand Land Rover, with only the faintest whiff of farm animals around them.

'So, what's the plan then?' Adam asked and looked at his smiling wife's face. She only had eyes for her new car. He had his Uncle Brian's truck now. But it didn't matter how many positive thoughts he pushed into it the thing was a piece of shit.

Tabatha shook herself out of the daydream she was having about driving over fields in her new vehicle, and she turned to her husband. 'Right, jump in your new... ish truck,' she smirked at him. 'Go and pick up a U-Haul trailer which will fit those pods in. While you do that, I will start stripping the basement down.'

Her husband frowned. 'Should you be doing that, in your possible condition?' he asked with a loving look upon his face.

Mrs Partridge walked to her husband and cupped his cheek, making sure the hand she used was the one with the key in it so he could feel it against his skin. That way, he knew who the winner was at this particular moment in time.

'Darling, I love you to bits, you do know that, don't you?' she asked and saw him nod. 'We only spoke to Brian yesterday, and I only took the first tablet last night. Yes, we got drunk and freaky on the kitchen table, and it may be a miracle drug for us, but it won't work overnight.' She placed her lips on his. 'Now, don't be stupid. Piss off and get the trailer, okay?'

'Yes, dear,' he mumbled before slinking off, feeling very stupid.

With a chuckle, Tabby headed down into the bowels of the home, turning on lights as necessary. It still amazed her that time travel even existed; but what was at the forefront of her mind was the possibility of having a family. As if that wasn't life altering enough, Brian and Dana had given them an envelope which held the deeds to her husband's grandfather's property in the woods, and $250,000 of shares in Apple. Their lives had been flipped upside down in a matter of twenty-four hours.

Tabatha started to strip down all the cables and computers ready for transport. What was tickling her fancy was the proviso that they were to take the chickens with them. Well, they liked chickens. It was the strange smiles that Brian and Dana gave them that worried her. But hey, they were just chickens, right?

'Tabby, I'm back,' Adam shouted out and started to head downstairs to the basement. He saw the basement was in a mess, as everything had been stripped. 'Wow, you've been busy,' he said and laughed at his sweaty wife.

'Indeed,' she acknowledged. 'Now, come on, let's get this stuff upstairs. We still don't know when the feds will turn up, plus we have to give notice on our house,' and she threw a load of cables at him.

Adam tipped his invisible cap. 'Yes, ma'am,' he said and ran off to do his duty as a husband.

As the sun was starting to dip, they were both working together to move the travel pods upstairs. Their shouts echoed throughout the farmhouse.

'Turn it!' she screamed from the top end.

'I am!' he retorted angrily.

A very loud sigh escaped Tabatha's mouth, making sure he heard it. 'Not that way, dear. Turn it left!'

'Fuck's sake,' he muttered softly. 'I am!'

'Don't swear! Turn it to my left, your right,' she screamed back, and that continued for the next hour as they moved the two lightweight pods into the trailer. And that was all they could do that night, as they were both exhausted.

'Dad was chuffed that we bought Granddad's cabin. Surprised, but chuffed,' Adam said and passed the ice-cold Dr Pepper as they sat on the back of the trailer, watching the sun sink beyond the trees. 'Mum and Dad will pop over and help us pack up the things we don't need to live day to day, so we can start the move.'

Tabby rested her head on his shoulder. 'That's nice, shame we can't tell them that Brian really bought it for us,' she said and leant into her husband. 'I'll be glad when this whole FBI thing is over. It's scaring me.' She then locked eyes on a tall rooster, who had been staring at them for some time. 'When are we going to tell your dad about Brian?'

Adam sighed. 'I think I'll mention the feds during the move. Perhaps say that he got caught up in a business deal or something, then tell him the truth once the FBI have gone,' he said and felt his wife nod.

'Sounds like a plan,' she agreed, and took another sip of the bubbly drink. 'Let's get this shifted, I'm tired.'

It took them two more days to get the farmhouse set up as Brian had requested. The older time machine was back in the basement and running, so the feds would believe it was still being used. Within a month, they had moved into their new home, the time machine being hidden in a friend's lock-up garage. So now, they waited.

One evening, Jacob and Alison Partridge came over for dinner. While the women sorted out preparing the meal, Adam sat outside with his father drinking ice-cold beers and watching the birds swooping down catching bugs.

'Son, can I ask you something?' asked Jacob.

'Sure, Dad, you know me, I'm an open book,' Adam joked.

The older man put down his drink and turned towards his son. 'Are you in trouble? You can tell me if you are,' he said and placed his hand on Adam's shoulder.

'No,' Adam frowned. 'Why would you think that, Dad?'

His father sighed. 'The chief of police is an old high school buddy of mine, and he said that somebody from the FBI has been asking questions about our family. Gus hasn't told them much apart from who lives where… but, as you know, they don't ask questions for nothing, son.'

Adam rubbed his face with his palm. 'Yeah, it's not me, Dad. But…' He took another draught of his beer and sensed that his dad was on the edge of his seat. 'Uncle Brian called me, a few nights ago.' That caused his father to stand up.

'I bloody knew it! He's been nothing but trouble since the day he was born,' Jacob shouted. He had always tried to be kind to his brother, but there was just something off about him. 'And now he's got the FBI involved!'

'Calm down, Dad, it's not what you think,' Adam said trying to defuse the situation. 'He's not in trouble, they just want to speak with him about something.'

His father turned on him. 'And what is that, exactly?' he asked and prodded his son in the chest. 'He's never grown up, that's his problem. He lets everyone else carry him,' and he continued to mumble curses.

'Jacob Roy Partridge!' his wife called out as she and Tabby came from the kitchen onto the deck. 'Will you calm down!'

'No, that bloody Brian has gone and done it again,' Jacob spat and chucked his beer bottle into the line of trees.

His wife rolled her eyes. 'Listen, Brian has never been a criminal. It doesn't matter what you think, he hasn't caused any trouble in his whole life.' Alison looked up at her husband, whom she loved dearly. 'Tabby was just telling me that Brian gave them some shares and bought this home for them. It was all above board, mister.' It was her turn to prod someone.

'Then why is the FBI after him?' Jacob retorted.

Alison shrugged. 'If it was really that bad, the cops would be here now busting down our door,' she said. 'But they are not. They haven't even phoned us to ask where he is.' She saw her husband calm down slightly. 'I know you and Brian have your problems, just don't go adding to them before you find out the truth.'

Jacob expelled a blast of hot air from between his lips. 'And when will that be? A week, month, or a year?'

His wife placed a finger on his lips. 'We are family,' she said. 'And wherever Doc is, he is family too, including his wife.'

'What wife?' Jacob asked and proceeded to laugh himself silly as he was told about his brother's old schoolfriend.

***

Agents Martinez & Saunders
Boston Main Office

Like any other day, Agent Marcus Martinez walked around the office saying his hellos to everybody. Already months down the line, he had blended in very well with his fellow agents. His family had moved to a farmhouse some fifty minutes' commute from the city, and things were all good.

Unfortunately, his partner had had some issues integrating. Avery had tried to follow his partner's lead, but he was never much of a team player. His background was always computer based and, after having clashed with the Tactical Unit at his last posting, the animosity between himself and this city's Tac team seemed to be going the same way. Marcus had tried to bridge the gap, but in time he would come to realise that not all broken things can be mended.

Marcus walked into the office that he shared with Avery with an iced coffee. Although it was a warm day outside, he appreciated the air-conditioned office building.

'Morning, Avery, how are things?' he said in his typical jaunty tone, placing the cool beverage on a coaster for his friend, whose head was stuck in his dual screen displays. 'You alive there, buddy?' he asked, before taking his seat on the other side of the office. He spun around on his swivel desk chair to look out of the window to watch the comings and goings from surrounding offices.

'Why are they dragging their feet on these warrants? It's been weeks now,' Avery grumbled and looked up in despair, before seeing the drink beside him. 'Thanks, Marc,' he said, closing his eyes as he drank the rich drink.

'It's a tricky thing to get,' Marcus replied, though deep down he was happy. 'If we get drawn into court, it will never hold up. We are looking to confiscate items that aren't illegal. The only hope is, if we ever get a warrant, the man's family doesn't stand in our way.'

The blond again ran his fingers through his hair and groaned in frustration. He had pursued these warrants since the day he'd found out where Brian Partridge lived, but that was when it all had stopped. Even Director Walker had backed away from him, giving the pair till Christmas to wrap it up before being put back onto normal agent duties.

'It's just frustrating. He's there, just waiting to be picked up,' Avery continued incredulously, gesturing at the screen.

Marcus smiled at his friend. 'Like I said, we can't touch him,' he replied honestly. At the beginning, they had planned to drag Brian in, but as time went on the Director had to admit he just wanted the man's equipment off the street. 'All we can do is sit him down and tell him to stop, and then confiscate his machine. As you know, I have explained to him the reasons why he needs to stop, and if the reports are right, he has stopped.'

Avery was incensed. He felt like everybody was working against him. His girlfriend and now fiancé, Samantha Ivanov, had moved with him to Boston, become firm friends with Loretta Martinez, and told him to get over any grievance he held over Marcus and move on. He had listened, they were partners after all, but he couldn't understand why Marcus did not share his anger at the antics of this Brian fella.

'I know,' he replied, 'but the Director drove me so hard once we got here, now he won't even answer my calls. It pisses me off.' Avery bounced his forehead off his desk in frustration, but gently enough so as not to knock over the drink that his friend and co-worker had bought him.

Marcus stood up and closed their office door, then pulled a spare chair over and sat beside his colleague. 'Listen, not every case is a home run. We did our mission and survived. Now it's time to move on,' he explained and pointed at the list of files on the screen. 'I can't even count how many cases in my lifetime ended with nothing being resolved. It's part of law enforcement life.' He saw despair written all over the young agent's face.

Saunders nodded, realising that this case was taking over his life, and that his friend and partner was right. Maybe he should just take some time off, relax and wait to rejoin the agent pool so that they could be assigned new cases.

'You're right,' he agreed. 'Do you think your friend in the Behavioural Analysis Unit could get us some interesting work with them?' he asked, knowing his partner had links countrywide.

Marcus laughed out loud. 'Fancy rubbing shoulders with serial killers, do you?' he joked and pushed away his chair. He walked back to his own desk and settled down to go through the jokes that the Tactical team usually emailed him daily.

'Seems interesting, and I guess Walker will be okay with it, as we will still be together,' Avery said.

'Yep, I'll give the man a call in the New Year when we are clear. That okay, Ave?' Silence. Marcus looked over his single monitor and his partner's dual ones and saw him staring, wide-eyed, at one of the screens. 'Avery, you okay my friend?'

Avery looked up, his mouth hanging open. 'We got it,' he uttered.

'What, Ave? What have we got?' asked Marcus.

'The warrant for the farm,' replied Avery. He had a queer smile on his face. 'We can search and confiscate all technology that we deem dangerous.' He stood up suddenly. 'Right!' He took his jacket off his chair and slipped it over his shoulders, then straightened his tie. 'I'm going to tell Sammy,' and, with excitement vibrating through him, he turned to the door.

Marcus gave a whistle, making his partner turn around. 'What do you want me to do? How can I help?'

'Oh yeah… errrrm, right,' said Avery. He returned quickly to his PC and began typing something. 'Right, I've sent you the link for the warrant. Contact Tactical and see when we can raid the farm. Obviously, it's just a search and seize. Then, while they clear the house…' He stilled as he gave it some more thought. 'They can take the target for a chat, while we have a friendly talk with his family. If we shake the tree, we might find something on him.'

Marcus smiled and gave his colleague a thumbs up. 'Will do, boss,' he said and watched Avery run out of the room as giddy as a schoolgirl on prom night. Then he got to work sending emails to relevant people. He considered that, unfortunately, this case wasn't high on the priority list for any of the departments, so it would be a hard sell.

It was a full hour before Avery came back. There was a hint of lipstick on his lips.

'Clearly, Sammy was happy for you,' Marcus said, tapping on his lip, then pointed at the now blushing man. 'She okay up there in Cybercrimes?'

Avery sat down, wiping the incriminating colour from his lips. 'Yeah, she's knocking them into shape alright. They aren't happy about it, but that's what she was brought in for.' He then sighed and visibly relaxed. 'Okay, tell me the bad news.'

Marcus gave his partner a sad smile. 'Not good, my friend. They can't help us this month, so it will be next month, the earliest being 22nd August, what with training and other jobs. Plus, it's a long way to go for an inconsequential raid.' He waited for the explosion. It never came.

'Well, it's not ideal, but it will have to do. Tell them thank you from me, anyway,' Avery said and typed away. 'It's not like we could use the local SWAT, anyway. They all know each other in those towns, so they would know we were coming from the first phone call.'

Marcus smiled at the maturity his friend was showing. 'Good plan,' he said. 'Let's make sure we document the raid properly, just in case we can bring it forward.' He picked up his cell phone and sent off a quick text. 'Should make the locals jump a bit,' he added and smiled, making the blond man laugh.

22nd October
Briefing room, FBI Boston

Avery Saunders' stomach was rolling as he looked upon the men and women of Tactical team Bravo, including the man mountain called the Opener. The chief of Tactical – Jameson, an ex-Marine – was also there, eyeing him with a calm professional look. The others just whispered and smirked at the young agent.

Marcus stepped up. 'Alright, shut up and listen to the man, will you? It's been a long drive.' The room immediately fell silent. 'And remember, I'm Rogue One, got that?' he added, making everyone in the room laugh.

'Nobody has such a stupid name,' Avery groaned, shaking his head. 'I told you fifty times, Tactical is Oscar One. We are control.' Marcus did a comical pout, making the women in the group go 'Awww!'

Jameson coughed. 'What's the timings? How many people are we expecting? Are they armed?' He barked out the questions, making the room go quiet again.

'At two o'clock, we will move into position at the farmhouse,' advised Avery. 'According to sources, there is only one occupant, unarmed.' He hoped the police chief had been telling the truth. 'But remember, it's farming country, so there may be a shotgun at least.' He saw his partner frown at the added information. 'I will serve the warrant, while you secure the perimeter.'

Marcus stepped forward. 'We shall cuff the target and hand him over to you to transport back here for an interview.

Meanwhile, you search and confiscate any technology. That's why we will have a large truck accompanying us.'

The ex-Marine nodded. 'Okay. Is he dangerous? And does he have any prior convictions?'

Marcus shook his head. 'The only thing he has been seen with was a taser, but by all accounts, he is not dangerous and has no history of any crimes. We just need to talk to him, and to clear the house out, okay?' They all nodded. 'And if you are good, I will buy you all a Happy Meal on the way home,' he added, and the room erupted in cheers.

Avery looked at his watch and nodded. 'Okay, let's saddle up,' he called out over the laughing and chattering. They stilled and all smiled at him. Then, as one, they all mouthed what he had just said and began laughing.

Marcus shook his head. 'You heard the man. Fuck off and get moving!' he said and pointed at Jameson. 'Control your team, or there will be no toys.'

The six-foot-plus ex-Marine put his hands up. 'Hey now, no need to be mean,' he said and smiled then locked eyes on Avery. 'You heard him. Saddle up, yeeehaaaw!' That was mirrored by every team member as they filed out of the room, making the two agents feel very small in comparison to the size of the men and women of the Tac team.

The young agent slumped into his chair. 'They hate me, don't they?' he said miserably.

'Hate is a strong word, my friend,' Marcus said and slapped his partner on the back. 'Let's go before they fill your car up with peanuts… again.'

Avery put his face in his hands. 'Fuck…' as he realised that his car was parked next to the Tac team's truck. Eventually, they took a car from the carpool, while Sammy got Avery's car towed away to be cleaned.

There was a nervous silence in the car as they travelled. Avery knew this had to end one way or another. He was obsessed with the target and wanted Brian to pay for forcing him into situations that made him take a life. But, what was worse, in the young man's eyes, was being forced to Boston and away from the sun.

As the miles clicked by, Avery seemed to get angrier to the point that he was grinding his teeth and gripping the steering wheel so hard it creaked.

'Avery, my friend,' Marcus said in his usual calm tones, 'you need to relax. You're going to have a stroke at this rate.'

Saunders nodded in agreement, but his body shape resisted the change. 'It's just been so long, but now we are finally going to nail him, and make him pay,' he said, pushing his foot harder on the accelerator, making the car go that little bit quicker.

'Oscar One to control,' came the baritone voice of Jameson as it filtered over the radio waves.

Marcus picked up the radio and clicked the button. 'Jameson, I am your father,' he said in a perfect take of the original Dark Lord, the one and only Vader. This caused the airways to be taken over by some very hurtful critics. 'Fine, what do you want, Oscar One?'

'Tell your boy this isn't a race. He doesn't want a ticket while on the way to a bust. Doesn't look good on his file,' the voice boomed, making Avery go red and slow down slightly. 'Well done, control, Oscar One out.' However, before the call cut out, they heard laughter in the background, which made the young agent look angrier than before.

They lapsed into silence again for the rest of the trip.

'There's the turning. Get the boys ready,' Avery said and listened to his partner relay the messages, receiving mocking calls of 'Yeehaaaw!' back from Tactical. As they moved into position, there appeared to be only a beaten-up old truck in front of the weather-worn home. 'Ready, Marc?' Avery asked.

'Yep, let's get this done,' Marcus answered. He stepped out of the car and donned his bulletproof vest, readjusted his sidearm, then placed his mic on his lapel. 'Okay, kids, position one.'

The black-uniformed Tactical squad piled out of their two blacked-out RVs. They had also brought a rented box van to help take the equipment back to headquarters.

'Yes, Dad,' they all echoed over the radio as they moved around the property.

The partners readied themselves to enter the building.

'If things go south, remember the training I gave you,' Marcus said to Avery calmly. 'Grab cover and, if the target has a weapon and lifts it, shoot centre mass, never the head, okay? That's just for TV.' He received a nod from his partner, who looked far too wound up for his own good.

Marcus knew this was always a dangerous part of any operation, walking towards a closed door with only a piece of paper in their hands. He was sure Partridge would not be armed – if, indeed, he was even here. The fact that Marcus had warned the man meant that this should go easily, but he had to play the part. The two agents walked up the steps, where Avery banged on the front door with the bottom of his fist.

'FBI, open the door, Partridge,' he shouted, only waiting about thirty seconds before banging it again. 'We have a warrant!' he shouted again and unholstered his side arm.

'Ave, put that back,' Marcus said, receiving a death glare from his friend. 'We have the big boys here for a reason. Now, back up and put that thing away.'

The blond man shoved his gun back into the holster and walked back to their car. 'Oscar One, breach the farmhouse,' he snapped over the radio.

'Roger control,' Jameson answered. 'Let's go, people. Take your positions.'

The two agents watched the well-trained unit swarm around the house like ants over a picnic. The door was forced open thanks to the 6-foot 6 frame of the Opener, who used a small metal battering ram to devastating effect. The rest of the unit all swarmed past the big man.

'Hallway clear.'

'Room one… clear.'

'Kitchen… clear.'

'Bedroom one… clear.'

'Bedroom two… clear.'

'Room two… clear.'

'Breaching the basement…'

'Stairway… clear.'

'Breaching basement door…'

'Basement… clear.'

Then they heard Jameson's voice boom over the air. 'Rogue One, house is clear… nobody home, over!'

'FUCK!!' screamed Avery and kicked at the earth, bringing smirks from a couple of the black-clad team who were guarding the perimeter.

Marcus sighed and walked over to his partner and pulled him out of earshot of the rest of the team.

'Calm the fuck down, you're a professional!' he snapped with a steely eyed glare. 'Now, sit in the fucking car and cool down, man.'

'No, I'm good,' Avery stated. He tried to pry the Mexican's hands off him, but found the grip unbreakable. 'Let go!'

'Not a chance. Cool down,' Marcus ordered and opened the driver's side door. 'If you go in there, the boys will wind you up and you will blow.' He watched his partner sag.

'Good, now find out the directions to his brother's place, then his nephew's home. Maybe they know where he is.'

Avery nodded and got into the car. 'Sure, good plan,' he said coldly as the older man turned away. 'Thanks, Marcus,' he called out, making his partner turn and smile.

'No worries, my man,' said Marcus.

He headed into the farmhouse and down into the basement. He took in the sight of two old tin baths covered in wire, plus an old computer with white casing, turning yellow with age.

'What the fuck is he doing here?' Marcus laughed, along with the black-clad men and women, even though he knew exactly what it was.

A tall, athletic woman put her arm across his shoulders. 'Looks like something from *The Fly* with Jeff Goldblum,' she laughed. 'Where's Blondie? Throwing his toys about still?'

'Ah, c'mon now,' said Marcus. 'He's just disappointed. We've all been there.' He shrugged the woman's arm off and walked away from her. 'Okay, pack all this shit up and get back to headquarters. And another thing…' The team all turn towards him. 'Try and be more friendly to Avery. He's a good agent.' He dodged a book that was thrown his way by another man in black. 'No Happy Meal, people,' he added and stomped away with a chorus of catcalls following him up the stairs.

He slowly began to explore the house. It looked like it had been totally cleaned out. Marcus couldn't believe that the man he met on the night of Molly Brown's death would be this anal about cleanliness. *Were there other people involved?* he wondered.

'A girlfriend, maybe?' he muttered to himself. He shrugged off the thought and headed back outside, only to see Avery out of the car and waving him over.

'Marc, I've got the addresses! Come on,' he shouted and sat back in the driver's seat. The engine fired into life.

Chapter Twenty

Avery's mood was low and he still wanted answers – no, not wanted… needed. With Marcus beside him in the passenger seat, he pulled up in front of a large, plush-looking cabin in the woods.

'Doesn't anyone live in houses around here?' he exclaimed, then took a moment to look at the place. 'So that's the brother.'

Marcus stared at the view in front of them, then flicked through the file. 'Yep, that's him, my friend,' he confirmed as they observed a man sitting on the porch outside the cabin. The man sat at a large wooden table, working on something that they couldn't see. 'Smiles on. He looks like a tough one.'

They stepped from the car and saw the front door of the cabin open. A woman, whom they recognised as the man's wife, came out and stood by her husband, placing a small hand on his shoulder. She whispered something in his ear, making him nod. He looked at the approaching men.

'What can I do for you boys?' he asked.

The agents walked towards them. 'Good day, sir. Are you Jacob and Alison Partridge?' Avery asked, drawing closer to them.

'Yep,' Jacob answered. He stared at the two men. 'Manners dictate that you introduce yourselves, especially on my land!' he snapped.

'My apologises,' said Marcus smiling amiably. 'I am Special Agent Marcus Martinez, and this is Special Agent Avery Saunders. We're from the FBI.' They were both now able to see that Jacob was cleaning a rifle on the table in front of him. That made them stop in their tracks.

Alison giggled. 'Twitchy little things, aren't they?' she asked her husband with a southern drawl, which the agents knew was not authentic. 'Everybody has guns around here,' she said. 'Nothing to worry about, unless you start waving your little ones around.'

Avery was pissed. 'We are the FBI... ma'am?'

'Watch your tone with my wife, boy,' Jacob said firmly. 'She's just messing with you,' and he slapped his wife on the rump. 'Now, state your business,' he ordered.

Marcus stepped forward. 'We are looking for your brother, Brian Partridge. Have you seen him?' he asked, leaning his arm on the railing that surrounded the edge of the stoop.

'Not for a while, now,' Jacob replied. 'He comes and goes as he wishes.'

Alison sat beside her husband and smiled at the agents. 'He's a free spirit, our Brian. What has he done to bring the mighty FBI to our doors?' She giggled again. 'He wouldn't harm a fly.'

Avery huffed in anger. 'We heard that you and your brother don't get on, Mr Partridge,' he queried.

'That's between me and my brother, sonny,' Jacob snapped. 'We may not get on at times, but he's still our family. So, answer my wife's question.'

Marcus held up his hands to calm down the rising ire. 'We just need to talk to Brian, that's all. He's not in any trouble.' He shot his partner a look.

'So, you break down my parents' farmhouse door and empty their property,' Jacob said and looked from one agent to the other. 'Just for a chat?'

'Bullshit,' Alison snapped.

Jacob rolled his eyes. 'Ali, why don't you go inside? I will deal with these gentlemen,' he said, kissing her on the cheek. His wife stood up and walked back indoors, looking at the men with a steely glint in her eye. 'Sorry about that,' said Jacob. 'She cares for Brian a lot, as we all do.' He then began putting his hunting rifle back together. 'So, what's this all about?'

Avery walked closer. 'It's top secret, and it's only by luck that your brother won't be charged and convicted,' he said coldly. 'Now, have you seen him?'

Jacob slammed the bolt home into his rifle, making the agents' eyes shoot towards it. 'Like I said, no,' he replied and started to finger a shiny bullet. 'And if he knows you are here, which I'm sure he does, I won't see him for a while.' He picked up a rag and wiped over the gun as he held it in his right hand. 'Good day, gentleman. Have a nice journey back to Boston.' He stood up and made his way into the cabin, closing the door with a slam behind him.

'Shit,' Avery said and stormed off to the car. The two agents knew they were being watched, and that anyone living nearby were being informed of their presence.

A while later, their Chevy Impala pulled into a long, gravel driveway that led towards a largish cabin surrounded on three sides by woods. Marcus unwound the window, taking in the scene, and then shut off the engine.

He looked out towards the cabin, then around the front gate, which was wide open. Finally, he looked up to a tree on which was attached a top-of-the-line security camera.

'Well, they know we are here,' Marcus said, and he pointed up into the tree, making his partner lean across.

'Damn it,' Avery said and went back to his notes. 'So, this was Brian Partridge's parents' retirement home before they died. It was sold on, then the family purchased it back at over the market price, and with cash.' He flipped a page over. 'Now his nephew and his wife live here – Adam, aged thirty-four, Tabatha a year older.' He then put the file away.

Marcus turned the key in the ignition. 'So, this is it,' he said, 'the last lead.' Brian's brother and sister in-law had known nothing, or weren't willing to say, and they were not close, anyway. 'Okay, let's get this done. Loretta is cooking on the grill tonight. Samantha said you'll be coming?'

Avery smiled. He loved his partner's family; his twin girls were a menace, but he loved them like they were his own. 'As ever, sounds fun,' he said.

They proceeded down the track and watched as the front door was opened.

'And here's Adam. At least he's not armed,' Avery said dryly. Marcus nodded in agreement as he parked the car. 'Good afternoon, Mr Partridge. Agents Saunders and Martinez.' The two agents got out of the car and flashed their credentials.

'Welcome to my home, agents. You know my name already…' Adam said and shrugged. 'Want a coffee? Or are we waiting for SWAT to arrive, after smashing up my family's old home?' He turned and walked off.

The two agents followed. 'We did have a warrant, Mr Partridge,' Marcus explained, as they followed him through his tidy home.

'Please, call me Adam,' he said. 'And to whom did you serve said warrant? Nobody has lived there since my uncle wandered off.' He walked through to the kitchen and grabbed three mugs and the coffee pot. 'Only decaf, I'm afraid,' he advised and waved the two agents to the wooden table against the wall. 'Help yourself to cream and sugar.'

They sat quietly as they prepared their hot drinks to their individual tastes.

'Well, Adam, please call us Marc and Avery,' Marcus said and took a sip of his now creamy coffee. 'We are looking for your Uncle Brian. We thought he was at the farm?'

'That's what we thought, too,' replied Adam. 'But when my wife and I popped around on the 4th of July we found the place empty.' He smirked. 'Oh, apart from one of his crazy toys he had made.'

The agents looked at each other. 'And what toy would this be?' Avery asked, as he held his mug, waiting for the coffee to cool.

'We were busy, and he never invited us over,' replied Adam, 'but then my dad became worried and asked me to pop over and make sure he was okay. When we did go over there, he was gone, all bar his greenhouse and the time machine.' Although Adam had been keeping a straight face as he spoke, he suddenly burst into laughter at the surprised expressions on the agents' faces,

'So, you didn't see or know what he was doing up there, at your family's farm?' Marcus asked.

Adam shook his head. 'No, like I said,' he replied. 'But he had always loved the idea of time travel, learning about it in books and films. It seemed that he made one himself, using an old computer and two metal bathtubs!' He laughed even harder. 'Come on, it's hardly Silicon Valley down there, is it?' He calmed down and fell quiet for a moment. He had a sad look on his face. 'I think living in that place brought back too many bad memories, and he broke and ran. I hope he's okay.'

The two agents shared a look and Avery closed the file, for good this time.

'I'm sure he's safe enough,' said Marcus. 'We have impounded the so-called time machine. Not sure why, but that's the orders we were given.'

'Why does the FBI want him, anyway? What has he done?' Adam asked.

This time, Avery jumped in. 'He was just a person of interest in a much larger investigation,' he advised. 'Brian isn't in any trouble; we would just like to talk to him about his links to an author called Lancaster.'

'That's his favourite author,' replied Adam. 'A bit out there for my liking, but Doc enjoyed his writings.' He chuckled. 'I don't think they ever met or talked, but then again his life is a mystery to his family, let alone anyone else.' He sighed and rubbed his eyes. 'But if I see him, I'll get him to contact you. Do you have a card?'

Marcus and Avery stood, leaving two white contact cards on the table and shook the owner's hand.

'Where is your wife? Her car was here?' Avery asked kindly, but the man frowned at him.

'She's locking up the chickens,' Adam replied. 'As you can expect when living this close to the forest, it means they are on the menu for many wild animals.' Just then, the back door opened, and his wife Tabatha came in, shuffling backwards.

'Well, fuck you too, Karl! Good luck tonight, you feral piece of shit!' she shouted and slammed the door, before turning to see the two suited men looking at her aghast. 'What are you two looking at? Never heard a woman shout at a rooster before?' she asked incredulously and stomped out.

Adam chuckled. 'Errr, Tabby has a complicated relationship with the rooster, but he does protect his hens well. Saw him fight off a coyote once. That was a sight to be seen.'

'HE'S A DICK!' shouted Tabatha from another room.

Marcus nodded. 'Well, thank you for the coffee, and please tell your uncle to get in touch if you hear from him,' he said and made his way out of the cabin, with Avery in tow. They remained silent until they got into their car.

'Well, I believe them, do you?' Marcus asked his partner.

Avery sighed. 'Yeah, but I wanted Partridge. Why should he get away clean?'

Marcus rubbed his eyes. 'There is nothing legally we can arrest him on. The most we can do is pull him in and sweat him,' he explained, firing the car's engine up again. 'Let's go back to the farmhouse and have a look about?'

The blond agent nodded, and they drove out of Adam Partridge's homestead.

'Okay, I just want five minutes with the bastard, even if we can't charge him,' Avery said.

'We'll be lucky to see him again,' said Marcus. 'After this, we are shut down, so we'll check the farmhouse and then head home.' He glanced at the focused young agent. 'Loretta is cooking dinner for us all,' he added, looking with concern at his partner. Avery had to let this go and seeing the farmhouse may just do the trick.

Back at the cabin, Tabatha unconsciously rubbed her tummy, full of hope at what could soon be a developing pregnancy. 'Do you think they will be back?' she asked.

'I don't think so. They looked relieved,' Adam replied, and they walked back inside, closing the door behind them. 'Glad we moved Doc's machine into our root cellar,' he added, and they settled down on the plush sofa.

Tabby rested her head on his shoulder. 'We owe Doc and Dana so much,' she said happily.

Adam's cell phone pinged, announcing the arrival of a text message. He picked his phone up and read the message. It was from a farmer friend who lived nearby:

'The federal SWAT team have left the farm.'

Adam picked up the two FBI agents' cards and crumpled them up.

'Right, we better go and tell your dad about Brian and Dana,' Tabatha said and smirked at her husband's groan.

Adam rubbed his hand over the stubble that adorned his chin. 'Dad is going to have a fit when we tell him about Doc and his adventures,' he said and placed a kiss upon the auburn-haired beauty that was his wife.

'Just not about your grandparents,' she replied. 'It would break them, knowing what he tried to prevent.' Adam nodded in agreement.

Just then, Adam's phone rang. It was his father. 'Hey, Dad!'

'Hey, son,' said Jacob. 'We had the bloody feds here asking about your uncle.'

'Yeah, they came here, too, but they have gone now,' Adam replied.

'So, are you finally going to tell me the truth about what that crazy brother of mine has gotten himself mixed up in?' Jacob bellowed down the line.

Adam could hear his mother chiding his dad in the background. She always had a soft spot for Brian. 'Pops, can Tabby and I come over?'

There was a muffled conversation, then his father replied. 'Yeah, sure. I'll fire up the grill. Then we can have a long talk about Doc!'

'Well, that will make for a fun evening,' Adam said. There was silence.

'Shit, what has he done, son?' said Jacob.

'Ermmm, best we tell you face to face,' replied Adam. 'But I can tell you one thing.'

Silence again. 'What's that?' said Jacob.

Adam smiled to himself. 'His dream came true, and you won't believe it!' He smiled and felt his loving wife's lips on his cheek.

'Shit! Well, see you soon, son,' Jacob said, hanging up.

Adam looked at his wife and gave her a long, soft kiss. 'Right, get the photo album, we are about to blow the old duffers' minds,' he said. He gave his darling wife a squeeze in a place that would hopefully soon be full of milk for their first child. 'Honk honk… ow!'

'Saucy! Now, come on, time is a-wasting,' Tabby said with a naughty grin after swatting his hand away playfully.

***

Avery turned, once again, onto the dusty, bumpy farm track that those in the farming community call a road. All this did was fuel his disappointment and anger at the same time. The house soon came into view; such a simple home, but it was the hidden secrets inside and the man that had once resided in it that made this place the bane of his life.

As a result of this man's actions, Avery had been forced to move away from the sun-loving beach girls and his home and, instead, was thrown into a dangerous mission. What made it worse was that he couldn't tell anyone. He couldn't forgive the fact that he'd had to take lives during this mission. Yes, they were German combat soldiers who were trying to kill them; but, if it wasn't for that prick, he wouldn't have been in that situation, or having those dark dreams as a result. The only plus point was Samantha and the fact that they were solidifying their relationship, even though he did miss all those bikini-clad girls.

'C'mon, Ave, let's get this done,' Marcus said. 'Park up behind the barn over there, just in case someone turns up,' he instructed and smiled as his partner took his advice.

They parked up, climbed out of the car and walked up to the door with less nerves than earlier that day. Marcus pulled out his switchblade and flicked the blade out, cutting through the FBI stickers that adorned the door. He looked over his shoulder.

'Ready, buddy?'

'Yep,' Avery said coldly and stepped into what had once been the Partridges' family home. His eyes took in the sight. 'Bastards!' He kicked an opened jar of peanut butter, left behind by the black-clad shits. 'It's been totally cleaned out,' he said and looked at his partner, who was trying to hide a smirk.

Marcus nodded and waved towards the open basement door. 'That way to his lair, mwhahahaha!' he laughed demonically, trying to add some humour into the situation. It didn't work, as the other man stomped past like a petulant child. 'Well, I thought it was funny,' he said to himself and he heard the metal door at the bottom of the stairs being kicked open. With a sigh and a quick check of his watch, he followed the noise.

Saunders looked around. There was nothing to see, except tables and the odd piece of wire strewn about after the Tac team's less than delicate touch.

'So, this is where he did it?' he mumbled and took in the huge power cable that stuck out from the wall. 'How did he keep it a secret that he was up to no good?' He gestured at the cable. 'That is professionally done. You would have thought the installer would ask what it was for?'

'Money makes people forget many things, my friend,' Marcus replied and stopped as a creak came from upstairs.

He held up his hand to silence his partner and slipped out his service weapon, his actions quickly mirrored by Avery.

Footfalls echoed throughout the property.

'Look at this bloody mess,' a voice came, one that Marcus recognised. His eyes widened and he looked at his partner.

'It's him!' he mouthed and placed his finger to his lips.

'FREEZE, PARTRIDGE! FBI!' Avery shouted and shot past his stunned partner. He took the basement stairs two at a time, making the wooden steps scream in torture, especially after the day they had had with the heavy-footed Tactical team. The agent held his gun high, going against all his training, allowing his anger to control his actions. He burst into the light and saw a tallish man running away.

'FBI... HALT!' Avery shouted and continued the chase. Luckily, the man ahead was wearing work boots, which were not the best for running on the farm track.

Marcus made it out of the farmhouse, panting slightly. Ahead, he saw the running forms of Avery and what looked like Brian Partridge, wearing typical farm gear. With a shake of his head, he gave chase.

Avery fired into the air. 'FREEZE!' he screamed, making the target stop stock still, ducking down with his hands on top of his head. 'About fucking time, Partridge! Stand up and keep your hands where they are,' Avery ordered, levelling his weapon at the man's chest. 'What is it with you farmers and their overly large plaid shirts?' he asked angrily, and then tried to regain his breath and composure.

Brian looked at the young man, and the gun. 'They are comfy, son,' he replied and smiled. 'What is it that you want? You have already broken into my family's house, made a mess and upset the neighbours.'

'We are the FBI,' said Avery. 'If you had been here you would've seen the warrant.' He paused for a moment and took a good look at this evasive man. He seemed harmless enough, but he still had to pay.

That made Brian bark out a laugh. 'Oh, yes, that always ends well for the person in their own home. I've seen the news and I felt that I would be safer far away from here.' He pointed at Avery's unwavering gun. 'And rightly so!'

'We are the fucking federal government. My word is the law here,' Avery snarled, holding onto the gun even harder. 'You nearly got me killed with your escapades in time.' His pulse was racing. 'What do you think you are, a fucking Time Travelling Tourist?'

Brian wasn't sure why, but he shrugged in response. Strangely, it was a name he had considered when he started his adventure.

'Well, I'm sorry about that,' he replied, 'but wasn't it just mind-blowing? All the things you could see. Yeah, I am sorry that I fucked up, but that won't happen again.' He then looked at Marcus. 'Hey, Agent Martinez, can you calm your partner down please?'

That made Averys gun twitch, knowing how friendly his partner had become with the target. 'I'm the agent in charge, not your friend here,' Avery said, his temper rising as he spoke. 'In France, I was nearly killed. Not only that, I had to kill a human being just so we could survive!'

'C'mon, my friend, let's just cool it,' Marcus begged calmly. 'Just three guys talking, right?'

'FUCK THAT!' Avery shouted. 'He's a criminal, and we're taking him in to be charged.'

Once again, Brian's brain chemistry decided to mess with him. 'On what charges? For doing a stupid thing in the past?' he asked, throwing his hands up in the air. 'Look, I'm sorry you went through all that, I didn't mean to drag you into it. Yes, I messed up. Marcus told me and I'm sorry.' He took a deep breath, placing his hands on his hips. 'But you just need to get over it. I was shot, and I got over it.'

Avery blinked slowly. 'Just get over it? The nightmares and fear of dying and never being found? And you say just get over it?' His gun twitched again.

'Calm down, my friend,' Marcus said, trying to get closer to Avery.

The young agent's eyes squinted. 'Shut up!' he snapped, focusing his attention back onto Brian. 'So, just get over it?'

Brian chuckled. 'Yeah, it was an experience, wasn't it?'

Time stopped and Brian felt like somebody had punched him in the chest, sending him to the dusty ground. The gunshot echoed across the field. Then came another punch and, finally, blackness.

'FUCK!! What did you do?' Marcus screamed as he watched his young partner gun down an innocent unarmed man. He lunged forward and snatched away the smoking gun. 'Why did you do that? Shit!' Marcus raced to Brian Partridge's side as blood bubbled from the man's lips. He pressed his fingers to Brian's neck, then lowered his head. 'He's gone!'

Avery looked upon the scourge of his nightmares, at the blood splattered over the man's chest. Then he felt himself pulled around and away from Partridge's corpse.

'I had to, it'll make the nightmares stop,' he muttered like a shell-shocked soldier.

'Fuck, man, killing isn't the answer,' shouted Marcus. 'You're just going to replace one nightmare with another.' He began to drag the young agent back to the car.

'Where are we going?' Avery asked, sounding like he was drugged. He looked over his shoulder at the prone, bloody man on the ground. Deep down, he wanted the man to sit up and dust himself off and flip him the bird for being an asshole. It was all getting confusing now as the adrenaline in his body was dissipating.

Marcus threw Avery into the passenger seat of the car. 'I'm taking you bloody home,' he answered. 'Then I'm coming back here to sort this shit out. Christ knows how,' he spat and handed the gun back to his partner. 'Make sure you clean that. I have extra rounds at home, so you won't have to answer any questions at the next weapons check.'

Avery looked at him. 'I'm sorry, Marc. I didn't mean for it to go this far!'

The Mexican looked down at his partner. 'Sorry doesn't really cut it, my friend,' he replied and slammed the door on the sobbing man. He then gave Brian's still body one last look before climbing into the driver's seat and peeling away in a cloud of dust.

***

'OWWWW!' I screamed out after I heard the agents car drive away. There was fake blood everywhere. As I stood up shakily, I pressed the return home button and rubbed my chest underneath the bulletproof vest. 'That bloody hurt,' I muttered and then I disappeared in a flash of light.

Dana stood in the Missile Silo, which was our new home, with tears in her eyes. So many things could have gone wrong. She ran towards me and flung herself around me and kissed me furiously, smearing the blood from the bitten capsule I had hidden in my cheek.

'I was so worried,' she sobbed into my bloody chest.

I patted her on the back. 'It went perfectly. Hurt like hell, though.' She then stepped back and ripped open my shirt, which was coved in small, multiple blood packs. It's amazing what you can buy on the internet.

She counted the two bullets that were stuck against the Kevlar vest. 'He really didn't like you, did he?' she said and raised a quizzical eyebrow.

I smiled weakly, feeling for the man. 'Nope, but Marcus did his job well. The words I used to wind Avery up, even the training the man had been given, made his plan work precisely.' And we kissed again.

Dana looked up at me. 'So, it's over then? They won't be hunting us anymore?'

'Nope, that's it, Dana,' I replied. 'So, now we can get my family over and show them the place and get ready for the upcoming birth of Tabatha's child,' I added with warmth in my heart. 'Unless I fuck up again on one of our trips.' I smiled, before wincing as Dana prodded a finger into my chest.

'Dumbass,' she spat while shaking her head, then we fell into each other's arms again.

It was over. And yet, still the beginning, as now we knew the rules of being a Time Traveller.

The End...?

Made in the USA
Columbia, SC
19 October 2023

24652693R00228